THE GOOD COP

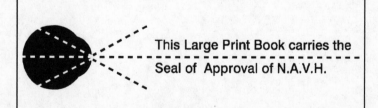

This Large Print Book carries the
Seal of Approval of N.A.V.H.

THE GOOD COP

BRAD PARKS

THORNDIKE PRESS
A part of Gale, Cengage Learning

GALE
CENGAGE Learning®

Detroit • New York • San Francisco • New Haven, Conn • Waterville, Maine • London

LIBRARY OF CONGRESS CATALOGING-IN-PUBLICATION DATA

Parks, Brad, 1974–
    The good cop / by Brad Parks.
      pages ; cm. — (Thorndike Press large print mystery)
    ISBN-13: 978-1-4104-5941-1 (hardcover)
    ISBN-10: 1-4104-5941-1 (hardcover)
    1. Ross, Carter (Fictitious character)—Fiction. 2. Reporters and reporting—Fiction. 3. Murder—Investigation—Fiction. 4. Police—Crimes against—Fiction. 5. Newark (N.J.)—Fiction. 6. Large type books. I. Title.
PS3616.A7553G66 2013b
813'.6—dc23   2013007706

Published in 2013 by arrangement with St. Martin's Press, LLC.

Printed in the United States of America
1 2 3 4 5 6 7 17 16 15 14 13

To my wonderful parents, who deprived me of the tormented childhood every novelist supposedly needs, instead showering me with endless love, affection, and encouragement that continues to nourish me to this day.

If my books aren't dark and twisted enough, it's totally their fault.

The exchange started with nothing more sinister than an ad on Craigslist.

It was a posting created by an outfit that called itself Red Dot Enterprises and placed in the jobs section of the Hampton Roads Craigslist, under the heading of security. The link said, simply, "Security Guard Wanted." The following came one click later:

Competitive pay for limited duration work.
No experience necessary.
No HS diploma or GED needed.
Must be able to pass criminal background check.
Must have own vehicle.
Current State of Virginia concealed carry permit required.

To John Bristow, it sounded like a good deal. He was an ex-marine who had kept his nose clean and an avid hunter who had gotten a carry permit shortly after mustering out of the service years earlier.

Most of all, he had child support, a landlord who was getting tired of partial payments, and a car that was being held together by rust and duct tape. He needed a job. Any job would do. He had been laid off during the depths of the Great Recession four years earlier and none of the employment he had found since that time had come close to replacing his previous income. The tips at T.G.I. Friday's just weren't that good.

So he answered the ad from Red Dot Enterprises, clicking on the "Reply to" link supplied. He wrote a note, saying he met all the qualifications. He heard back quickly.

Soon, there was an exchange of phone calls, always from blocked numbers. Bristow could guess it was something shady. He talked to a guy who even *sounded* shady on the phone, a black guy from up north who asked a lot of questions but gave few answers.

Bristow learned it was more of a onetime assignment than a steady job. But the money was good. And easy. The guy on the phone seemed mostly concerned about Bristow's discretion, and kept reminding him he couldn't discuss the work he would do — not with his wife, his girlfriend, his priest, or his rabbi. No one.

Bristow asked right away: Was Red Dot Enterprises involved in drugs? Because he wasn't interested in doing anything with drugs. He wasn't some junkie, and he sure as hell wasn't going to work for some scumbag dealer.

No, he was told. No drugs.

So what was it? When the guy finally got around to saying it, Bristow was relieved. It wasn't drugs. Or trafficking in whores or illegals or any of the other possibilities Bristow had been pondering.

It was just guns. They wanted him to buy some guns. They were going to pay him for the guns, pay him generously for his time, and then leave him alone. It was one day's work — less than that, actually. Yet it would pay him better than a month of working nights at Friday's.

Was he helping to arm an insurrection against the federal government? Procure firearms for ex-cons who couldn't buy their own? Enable some massive shooting spree? Bristow didn't particularly care.

Whatever someone did with those guns, that wasn't on him.

CHAPTER 1

Among the many reasons I enjoy being a newspaper reporter — not the least of which are the freedom, the fun, and the constitutionally protected right to announce when people are acting like idiots — one of the small-but-important pleasures is what I'm doing each morning at eight thirty-eight.

At 8:38 A.M., I imagine most gainfully employed, industrious members of our society are already enjoined in the struggle that is their daily grind. They have attended to their grooming needs, squeezed themselves into their workaday uniforms, rushed through a meal that puts the "fast" in "breakfast," and made the necessary concessions to their caffeine addictions.

At 8:38 A.M., they are inhaling the carbon-tinged exhaust fumes from the car in front of them on the Garden State Parkway; or they are recovering from the latest skirmish in the ongoing Battle of No, You *Cannot*

Wear That to School; or they are checking their e-mails, looking at their schedules, and generally girding themselves for all that is to come.

Me?

At 8:38 A.M., I do solemnly swear that I, Carter Ross, am asleep.

In my profession, this is not necessarily a sign of sloth. Editors typically have established hours, but reporters adapt their schedules to the demands of their beat. Courthouse reporters are at the whim of their trial; education reporters learn to make calls during the school day; sports reporters, the vampires of the journalism world, primarily work at night. As an investigative reporter, I don't have a beat per se. No one expects to see me in the office at any particular time of the day, and certainly not at 8:38 A.M., when most self-respecting American newsrooms are devoid of all but the barest minimum of personnel. Anywhere from ten to eleven is considered a more fashionable arrival time. So I pretty much get up when I feel like it. I have a need to set an alarm maybe five times a year.

I often make up for it on the other end because while my day may come in like a lamb, it often goes out like a lion, with sources and editors and deadline all screaming at me simultaneously. My employer, the *Newark Eagle-Examiner* — New Jersey's largest and most tenacious disseminator of responsibly vetted information — always gets its pound of flesh out of me.

Nevertheless, if I do happen to wake up when there is an unsightly number (like an eight or, God forbid, a seven) leading the digital clock by my bedside, I take pride in rolling over and snoozing until I see a more proper number (like a nine or a ten). The main characters in my life — be it my colleagues, my friends, or Deadline, the cat who reliably joins me in my morning slumber — know this about me.

So it came as something of a surprise when I became aware that my landline, the number almost no one used anymore, was ringing one sunless Monday morning in March at exactly 8:38 A.M.

"Hello?" I said, sounding a bit guttural.

"Carter, it's Katie Mossman."

Katie was one of the editors on what was formally called the Nonstop News Desk, which had been created a few years back to feed the insatiable content beast that is our Web site. Informally, we reporters called it the All-Slop News Desk — "the Slop" for short — because that's about what we shoveled into it.

"What's up, Katie?"

"We got a dead Newark cop," she replied, and I immediately sat up in bed and grabbed a notepad.

For as much as law enforcement and media sometimes find themselves at odds, we in the Fourth Estate recognize that those who are sworn to uphold the law not only perform a vital function for public safety but represent all of us in doing it. An attack on one of their number is an attack on everyone. Police officers who die in the line of duty are heroes and are treated as such. In other words, dead cops equal big news.

"Okay. What do you need from me?"

"I don't know. I don't think we have a game plan yet. I just called Tina to tell her about it and she said I should call you and, quote, 'Get his sorry ass out of bed.' "

As the assistant managing editor for local news, Tina Thompson was my boss. She and I also had a fairly complex, on-and-off relationship (currently: off). In both roles, she was not especially shy about expressing her needs.

"You can tell her it's out," I said. "What's this cop's name?"

"From what we're hearing, it's Darius Kipps. K-I-P-P-S. Detective Sergeant Darius Kipps."

14

The name meant nothing to me. While I wasn't strictly a cops reporter, I had a decent number of contacts in the Newark Police Department. Still, there were more than a thousand cops on the force and I knew only a fraction of them.

"What happened to him?"

"We don't know that yet, either. The Newark PD hasn't announced any of this. We're just getting this from sources. We haven't even put it online yet because we don't have it confirmed."

"So how do we know this mystery cop is dead?"

"One of the photogs was listening to the scanner this morning and said there was a lot of chatter about something going down at the Fourth Precinct. We figured it out from there."

I knew the Fourth Precinct well. It was in the Central Ward, in the heart of a Newark neighborhood that had been making news, not all of it good, for a long time.

"Got it. What does Tina want from me?"

"Plans are still being formed. At this point, she just wants everyone in here. It's one of those all-hands-on-deck things."

That, of course, was the reaction of most editors to a big story. Gather up your reporters — they sometimes referred to us as "resources" so we wouldn't be confused with human beings — and then figure out what to do with us later. It usually just meant we'd be bumping into one another all day long.

But, in truth, the only thing worse than doing all that bumping was being left out of it. I told Katie her message had been delivered, then hung up. There would be no dawdling in bed on this day. Anyone with reporter's blood flowing in his veins — and I fancied myself as having a lot of it — wanted in on a story like this.

As a thirty-two-year-old bachelor with no significant encumbrances, I can be showered, dressed, and ready to ramble in fifteen minutes. Twelve if I really push it.

I streamline this process in several ways. One, there is nothing complicated about my hair. It's brown and short — never more than four weeks away from being cut — and I part it on the side, the same way I've been doing it since I was old enough to hold a brush.

Two, my morning routine involves a bare minimum of lotionry and potionry. I've been told the modern male ought to concern himself with hair product, moisturizer, cologne and/or body spray, and perhaps a half-dozen other products from the health and beauty aisle, all carefully applied and then painstakingly primped. Me, I wear deodorant (primarily out of consideration to my fellow man).

Three, my wardrobe is, quite deliberately, the most boring thing you've ever seen. I have two possible colors of pleated slacks (charcoal and khaki), two colors of shirt (white and blue) and three colors of necktie (red, yellow, or blue). And if you notice, any of the twelve resulting color combinations match just fine. So I can pretty much dive into my closet and grab blindly for anything that's clean, knowing I can't miss.

The end result of all this is not particularly inspiring — I make a Land's End catalogue look avant-garde by comparison — but it works for me. You have to know what flavor of ice cream you are in this world, and I am vanilla.

On this day, my closet dive yielded the racy blend of khaki pants, a white shirt, and a blue tie. I tossed a bit of kibble in a bowl for Deadline — not that he would be awake to eat it for another few hours — then opened my laptop.

I had no intention of going into the office to be one of Tina Thompson's "resources," which would just involve sitting around a conference table until someone told me to do what any good reporter should have been doing all along. Sometimes editors just get in the way like that.

So I got to work. After about five minutes of accessing a few of the databases on which a reporter makes his living, I learned the late Darius Kipps had been with the Newark Police Department for twelve years and three months. He was thirty-seven years old, having celebrated his birthday on the first of March. He was making $93,140 a year, which is not unusual in a state with the nation's highest paid police officers. He had a variety of addresses associated with him — some in Newark, some in Irvington — but seemed to have settled in East Orange.

Sure enough, when I checked the East Orange property tax records, I found a dwelling owned by Noemi and Darius Kipps on Rutledge Avenue.

And that, I had already decided as I closed the lid on my laptop, was where I needed to be.

This was something of a calculated gamble on my part. Without knowing how Darius Kipps met his untimely end, there was no telling what would figure prominently in our story. But, sadly, I could proffer up a reasonable guess. He was a detective, which

18

is usually a pretty safe place for a cop. Unless, of course, you're undercover. Then you're just as exposed to danger as anyone else who tries to make a life on the streets. If not more so. All it takes is some punk deciding you looked at him the wrong way and, not knowing you're a cop, pulling the trigger.

Or maybe something else had befallen Detective Sergeant Kipps. Point is, we had cops reporters who were in a better position to figure it out, leaving me to work other angles. And in a story like this, it was safe to assume that the grieving widow, Noemi Kipps, would be one of those angles.

That meant every minute counted. This was not necessarily out of any concern for the paper's production schedule. It was all about the competition or, more accurately, the lack of it.

A Newark police officer killed in the line of duty would inevitably attract the attention of every television and radio station in the Greater New York area, which only happens to be the biggest media market in the country. All of them would know a grieving widow was a big part of the story, too. And since they have access to the same databases I did, they, too, would soon be heading in the direction of Rutledge Avenue in East

19

Orange.

The cumulative effect of all those reporters would be something like cattle in a field. Put one cow in a small pasture, and what you have is a nice, green plot of earth. She can roam freely, nibbling grass as she feels like it, and generally has a pretty good time of things. Put a whole bunch of cows in that same field, and what you have in fairly short order is a big, stinky, muddy mess. And none of the cows feel like they're getting much of a meal.

So the trick is to be that first cow, then find a way to lock the gate so the rest of the herd can't get in.

Bidding Deadline farewell — he would miss me, but only due to the absence of body heat — I went out into the gray morning, hopped in my car, and began the short drive from my home in Bloomfield to the Kipps household in East Orange.

Along the way, I called Tina. There was a time when Tina and I had a fairly simple understanding: she simply wanted my seed. After two decades of using her beauty and cunning to run roughshod over the male species, cycling through its representatives in a series of relationships that lasted anywhere from one night to one month, she had reached a point where she realized her baby-making years were running short.

She was far too practical and goal-oriented to engage in the imprecise business of courtship, so she mostly judged men on their potential to pass certain desirable characteristics onto her offspring. She was looking for a partner with blue eyes and broad shoulders (check). She wanted him to be at least six feet tall (I'm six foot one). And she was looking for a certain kindly, easygoing disposition (howdy, friend). Hence, she decided I was the ideal sperm donor — and that rather than making the swap in a laboratory, we might as well do it as nature intended.

She made it clear it was a no-strings-attached proposition, that I could taste the fruit without buying the orchard, as it were. The only problem was, I sort of wanted the orchard. So we had reached an impasse in our relationship: namely, I wanted one and she didn't.

Then she got promoted and became my editor, which imposed further impediments to the possibility of our getting together. So we sort of decided to cool it. I say "sort of" because nothing felt very cool when we wound up together after work, especially after a drink or two.

Then, in an unexpected development, I

got tired of all that will-they-or-won't-they stuff and started dating Kira O'Brien, a new librarian in the newspaper's research department. Actually, I'm not sure you could call what we did "dating." But that was another story.

Point is, things had been a little strained between Tina and me. She answered her cell phone with a testy: "What do you want?"

"I'm heading to East Orange."

"What's in East Orange?"

"The widow Kipps, from what I've been able to learn," I said.

"Who told you to go after the widow Kipps?"

"No one. But I live about five minutes from her. I can make it there and try to get her talking before every television station in New York has a hairpiece and a microphone camped on her front lawn."

Tina didn't respond for a second or two. I'm sure she was trying to find some reason my plan was a bad one — because that's sort of the way things had been going between us lately — but there were really no nits to pick.

"Fine," she said. "Don't screw it up."

Knocking on the door of a woman who has just lost her husband — and then having the nerve to ask her all about it — is certainly not one of the cheerier parts of my chosen profession. Done poorly, it can leave you feeling like some exploitative, soul-sucking parasite who feasts on the misery of others. Some reporters flatly loathe the task, even citing it as a reason for leaving the business.

But, strange as it sounds, it might be one of the things I find most satisfying. It's not that I enjoy other people's suffering or that I find the whole business any less discomfiting than anyone else.

It's that I see it as an opportunity to do some real good, in my small way. One of the fundamental things I believe as a writer is that words have the power to move people. They can make us feel angry or hateful or sad, sure. But they can also uplift us. They can provide hope. They can even comfort a grieving family.

And that's what I went into a situation like this trying to do. I believed I could wade into the agony of the Kipps family, and by writing a sympathetic story about Darius — something that captured the best of the man, his service to others and the sacrifice he made — I could make things a little better. Maybe not right away, when everything was still so fresh. But maybe someday it could be something his widow could look at and read with a smile on her face.

With this in mind, I made the turn onto Rutledge Avenue, a street lined with mature trees and cracked sidewalks. East Orange could be a rough town, having long ago been overtaken by the same urban malaise that blighted much of Newark. But this was one of the more livable areas. The definition of "livable" was, of course, that the dope fiends, dealers, and delinquents tended to stay at least a few blocks away.

I slowed as I reached the Kippses' residence, an aging two-story brick duplex with a flower bed full of dead leaves that had accumulated over the winter. There were no window treatments on the second floor, which gave the house an unoccupied look. Except, of course there were lights on. So obviously someone was home. I parallel parked, noting — with relief — the lack of vans with television logos on them. At least for now, it looked like I would have the place to myself.

Walking up a short concrete pathway toward the house, then up the brick steps onto a small front porch, I felt the usual excitement. You never really knew what you were going to get when you knocked on one of these doors. I could be welcomed into

24

the home with open arms, tossed into the street on my ass, or anything in between.

So I knocked, then held my breath.

The door was answered by a medium-height, slender African American woman with dark smudges under her eyes. She was wearing sweatpants and a T-shirt, with her hair pulled back in a ponytail. Her feet were bare. She looked like she hadn't slept that night. Or the previous night. Or, for that matter, the previous month.

"Can I help you?" she asked.

"Hi, I'm sorry to trouble you. I know this is a difficult time," I said as apologetically as possible. "I'm a reporter with the *Eagle-Examiner.* I'm here to write a tribute to Darius."

The word "tribute" was deliberate, of course. If I said I was there merely to write a "story," there would still have been some doubt as to my intentions. I wanted to make it clear I was coming in peace.

"Oh," she said, like this surprised her.

"I'm Carter Ross. Are you Mrs. Kipps?"

"Yes. I'm Noemi" — she pronounced it no-*em*-mee — "but call me Mimi. Everyone else does."

"I'm very sorry for your loss," I said.

"Thank you," she said, opening the door a little wider.

And, just like that, I was in. I walked into a living room filled with older women, most of them substantially larger than Mimi, all of them staring at me, all of them black.

I always get a kick out of white people who complain that blacks are "obsessed" with race and talk about it too much. If those white people could, just once, walk into a room like this, where suddenly they were the Other Race, they'd understand the "obsession" just a little better. Because you know what? We can all say we're color-blind, and we can claim that race doesn't matter in an America that has elected a black president.

But that's foolishness. Race matters. It mattered at my prep school, where in a student body of five hundred there were maybe fifteen black kids, thirteen of whom had been brought there to play football or basketball. It mattered at my alma mater, Amherst College, where we were all supposedly enlightened multiculturalists, yet we still fell back into the easy comfort of our groups, black, brown, white, and yellow. It matters in my workplace, where editors have been known to pair reporter and assignment based on skin color, simply because you just couldn't send a white reporter to write Story X, or you really had to send a Hispanic reporter to do Story Y. And until some distant time many centuries from now when there is a truly American race — when we've all interbred enough that the races are no longer distinct — it will continue to matter everywhere else in our society, too.

So I was the white guy in the room. And not just any white guy. I'm a purebred WASP, straight off the not-so-hardscrabble streets of Millburn by way of tennis camp. My quick read told me Mimi didn't have a problem with white guys. She had bought the "tribute" line. But these other black women were still undecided. They were eyeing me with a mix of curiosity and hostility, their protective instincts fully engaged.

"This is the man from the newspaper," she announced. "He's here to write about Darius."

"I just want to be able to write about what kind of person he was," I interjected, "tell some nice stories about him."

Mimi proceeded to introduce me to the six women in the room, a series of aunties and cousins whose names I didn't quite register. I'd get them later. I didn't even have my notebook out to write them down. For now, it was more important to smile pleasantly, make good eye contact, and

27

shake a hand if it was offered to me.

Then she led me around to the corner, where there was a crib, one of those portable Pack 'N Play things. Inside, a shriveled-looking baby slept soundly.

"This is Jaquille," she said. "Darius's son. He's five months."

That explained the raccoon eyes Mimi was sporting. I thought she looked like she hadn't slept for a month. She probably hadn't, with this little guy in her life.

And I do mean little. Since I hadn't entered the reproductive portion of my life — Tina's entreaties having been unsuccessful — I didn't know from babies. But this one looked awfully small.

"He was born two months premature," Mimi said, reading my mind. "He weighed three pounds, four ounces. He was in the hospital the first two months, because of some stuff with his lungs. But he's fine, now. He's up to nine pounds."

"He's beautiful," I said, which was a flat-out lie. Like most newborns, Jaquille looked like a spindly legged alien with a human diaper attached to him. But saying that didn't seem like it would ingratiate me to Jaquille's mother.

"Darius was so proud of him. We have a daughter who's seven, and he loves her like any dad loves his little girl. But he always wanted a boy. He said a man's gotta have a son. So we tried and tried. Darius only had one testicle."

Now *there* was a piece of information that likely wouldn't be making it into the next day's paper.

"And we were wondering if maybe that had something to do with it," Mimi continued. "We had him tested, and his count was pretty low."

Yet another piece.

"But we kept trying and praying. I had just about given up, but then God heard our prayers and gave us a son. I always thought of him as my miracle baby."

Mimi stared at Jaquille, while I furtively studied Mimi out of the corner of my eye. She had this calm about her that was almost eerie. A woman who loses her husband and is suddenly left to raise two children, one of them an infant, by herself? She ought to be oozing tears, snot, and despondence.

Instead, she was gazing down at her baby beatifically, like the Virgin Mary in a Renaissance frieze. She must have still been in shock, the tragedy so new her mind couldn't yet process it.

One of the aunties, the one sitting in the corner, picked up the dialogue where Mimi left off: "You should have seen Darius with that boy. He visited him in the hospital every morning after his shift ended. He would just go in there and talk and talk and talk. He'd say, 'You gonna be a Eagles fan, just like your daddy. And you gonna root for the Sixers, just like your daddy. And we gonna watch baseball together. And I'm gonna teach you to catch a ball and throw a ball. And you're gonna be real smart. And you're gonna go to college. And your daddy is going to be so proud of you.' "

Mimi chimed in: "Darius said our boy came out small, but he was going to love him so much he couldn't help but get big. He was just going to fill that little boy up with his love."

I looked down at Jaquille, the erstwhile miracle, and tried to swallow the cantaloupe that was suddenly growing in my throat. Right then, I knew what my story was going to be. It would be written as a letter to Jaquille, to be read on the day he graduated from college. And it would tell him all about the father he never got a chance to know.

Over the next few hours — as a succession of relatives, friends, and neighbors wandered to the house to offer their respects — I learned about who that man was.

Darius Kipps was born in Camden and grew up in nearby Pennsauken. Both places were in South Jersey, which explained why he rooted for all those Philadelphia teams. His father had been a cop, too, putting in twenty-five years with the Camden PD and retiring with a trunk full of commendations, which told me a little something about the tree from which Darius had fallen. Camden has long ranked in the top ten as the toughest American city in which to be a cop.

As a teenager, Darius was a bit of a prankster but also a natural leader, so he became the ringmaster of a group of quasi-misfits, who liked to party a little too much. It didn't sound like they were bad kids, by any stretch. But it was subtly explained to me there may have been a mailbox or two that succumbed to Darius's idea of a good time. I also heard an account of how he organized a group of fourteen guys to lift a principal's car and move it back to the Dumpsters behind school. The distraught man ended up reporting it stolen before someone finally let him in on the gag.

After Darius graduated high school, he tried a variety of jobs, none of which really fit him. And finally he went to school and got an associate's degree in criminal justice: police work was in his blood, after all. He took the police exam and posted a high score, such that he had a number of job offers — well-qualified black candidates were always in demand from departments looking to improve their diversity. His family urged him to accept an offer from one of the cozy, suburban police departments, where he wouldn't have to dodge the same dangers as his father.

But Darius wanted to be where the action was. He wanted to be where he felt he could do the most good. He chose Newark.

Smart and hardworking, with those natural leadership skills, he rose quickly through the ranks, never going long without moving up. After a few years on patrol, with his potential obvious to all, he earned his detective's shield. A few years after that, he aced his sergeant's exam and got that promotion, too. Lieutenant couldn't have been far away.

He was the kind of cop who kept the scanner on at home and listened to it as background noise — the way some people keep the television on — just so he knew what his fellow officers were up to. And if he heard something that sounded like trouble and was close? He stored his gun and his shield by the door so he could grab them quickly on the way out. He had once nabbed a carjacker that way. It was the kind of commitment to the job that had earned him commendation after commendation, just like his old man.

But he didn't just look out for other cops. I heard another story about a witness he worked with during one of his cases. The kid had been shot up pretty badly and was in the hospital for a while. Darius kept visiting the kid, finding different ways to cheer him up, and kept doing it even after the case was closed. Last anyone had heard, the kid had recovered and Darius had helped him get a part-time job with Newark Parks and Recreation.

Meanwhile, it seemed the former prankster matured into a level-headed, responsible young man. Around the time he started working as a cop, he met Mimi, fell for her, and fell hard. They had been introduced through a friend of a friend. She had heard of his reputation as a hard-partying boozer, and being a teetotaler herself, she told him she couldn't date someone who used alcohol. He quit cold turkey. They were married within a year.

"He said we were soul mates, so there was no point in waiting," Mimi said.

A few years into the marriage, they had their daughter, Jasey. They bought the duplex in East Orange because Darius felt a family ought to have a house to call home. He took to fatherhood quickly, doting on his daughter.

"He'd kill me if I told you this," said the corner auntie, "but he let that little girl paint his fingernails and toenails. He'd be running around before work, looking for the nail polish remover, trying to get that stuff off. Sometimes he ran out of time. I'm sure the guys down at the station just *loved* that."

It sounded like Jaquille's birth had cut into father-daughter time quite a bit. But once things settled down, he had talked of surprising Jasey with a family trip to Disney World as a present from her new baby brother. He had also been talking about moving his growing brood to a single-family house, maybe in a town with a better school system.

"He was all for the kids," Mimi told me. "He was always saying, 'It ain't about us no more.' "

All in all, he seemed like a heck of a guy. I'm sure some of the stories were being embellished for my benefit, but I didn't mind. Telling lies about the recently deceased is a long-standing tradition in our — and many other — cultures, and I wasn't about to take too hard a look at them. As a reporter, I've learned to make a distinction between lies that could hurt someone and those that won't. If I ended up making a slain police officer smell a bit rosier in death than he had in real life, it was hard to see who would be injured by that.

Throughout my interviewing, the phone in my pocket buzzed intermittently — no doubt Tina calling, looking for an update — but I wasn't about to answer it. I was getting great material out of these people, and I didn't want to break the spell.

The only mildly surprising thing is that none of the people knocking on the front door of the Kipps house were fellow members of the media. I would have thought for sure the rest of the horde would have learned about the dead cop and descended, locustlike, on the widow Kipps. It was hard to keep the lid on a story like this.

But there was no one. So as noontime came and went, I kept adding more good stuff in my notebook until, having filled it, I announced it was getting time for me to go. Mimi gave me her cell number, which I stored in my phone with a promise to keep in touch.

The last thing Mimi showed me was a picture of Darius with his kids at his birthday party a week earlier. There was a conical paper hat perched crookedly atop his bald head and secured with a thin white elastic band. His smile seemed to take up the entire photo. He was a burly guy, and the children practically disappeared in his arms — his infant son cradled tenderly in one, his daughter tucked in the other. They were arms that held and loved, arms that offered comfort and protection, the arms of a man who considered himself a father and a guardian.

"You can keep that if you want," Mimi said, handing me a printout, which I slipped in the back of my notebook. "I made a bunch of copies this morning. That's really how I want people to remember him. I can't believe he only had a week to live in that picture."

It gave me the opening to finally pose the uncomfortable question, the one I nevertheless had to ask: "What has the Newark Police Department told you about your husband's death?"

"They didn't tell me anything," Mimi said.

"What do you mean?"

"The chaplain came out last night and told me Darius wasn't coming home, that he had died, and that's all I've heard so far. I don't know the details yet. I'm not sure if I even want to know. My husband was in law enforcement. I . . . we all, all of us wives, we talk about this and we prepare for it. We hope it never comes, of course, but we have to prepare. However he died, it doesn't change who he was in life. And that's what I want to think about."

When I got back out on the street, my phone told me I had missed five calls, all of them from Tina. She had left no voice messages, just a text: "No story. Come back in."

"The *hell* there's no story," I said out loud to my phone. In what parallel universe was she living? I had a notebook crammed with material that begged to differ.

In a huff, I called her but got voice mail on both her work and cell numbers. Which was just as well. Some arguments were better had in person.

My car was, unsurprisingly, still sitting where I parked it. For some people, this is not a given. Newark and its surrounding environs are somewhat notorious for car thefts, having raised some of the nation's leading automobile pilferers for several generations now. But that is one of the only things I *don't* have to worry about when it comes to my ride, a six-year-old Chevy Malibu. Anyone who cared enough about cars to steal one would be embarrassed to be seen in mine.

I picked it up used when it was merely a three-year-old Chevy Malibu and it has since handled all the punishment I have given it, and then some. I'd love to brag how many miles it has on it, but the truth is, I'm not sure. The odometer has been stuck at 111,431 for a while now. I would worry about how that's going to affect the resale value, except I don't think the junk-yard I'm eventually going to push it into will much care.

Nevertheless, the Malibu faithfully delivered me to the *Eagle-Examiner* newsroom, into which I stormed, still spoiling for a fight. I didn't even bother stopping at my desk. I went straight to Tina's office, where I found her sitting in her usual loveliness.

Tina is thirty-nine, but she's got the body of a twenty-year-old. Make that: a twenty-year-old Olympian. She's long and lean, spends her prework time jogging and her postwork time doing yoga. In between, she sits around the office wearing short skirts that make me glad I'm straight. She has curly brown hair, which on this day she had clenched in one of those claw thingies. It had the effect of showing off her neck and shoulders, which also made me happy for my heterosexuality.

Still, this was one time I hadn't come into the office for the view.

"What do you mean there's no story?" I said, bursting in without knocking. "I just spent close to four hours recording the life and times of Darius Kipps in my notebook, and it's good stuff."

"Suicide," she said, without looking up from her computer screen.

"Huh?"

"It was a suicide," she said, this time at least lifting her eyes.

"What do you mean, suicide?"

"I mean suicide. It's a fancy word we use for people who kill themselves."

"No, I . . ." My voice trailed off. "Damn. This guy just didn't seem like the type. Not even a little."

"Well, the cops still haven't announced it yet. They've shut down all information, put a muzzle on the PIO, the whole thing — which is as good a sign as anything it's probably a suicide. They haven't even confirmed one of their officers died. But one of Hays's sources gave it to us off the record."

Hays was Buster Hays, our most senior reporter and a certified pain-in-the-ass. But he also had sources that reached from the FBI all the way down to the Cub Scouts. If one of his moles told us something, it was

39

usually pretty reliable. Buster never had to rely on the Public Information Officers for his stuff. If anything, the PIOs asked *him* what was going on.

"Apparently the guy went into the shower stall at the Fourth Precinct and blew his head off," Tina continued. "He even turned the water on before he pulled the trigger so there wouldn't be as much to clean up. Thoughtful guy."

"Wow. His family doesn't have a clue yet. When I left, I told them I'd be writing a big, beautiful tribute to the dead father and husband."

"Yeah, well, you know how Brodie feels about suicide, so . . ."

I knew, all right. Harold Brodie, the paper's executive editor for something like thirty years, had been there long enough that his pet peeves had solidified into hardened rules. And one of the rules at the *Eagle-Examiner* is that we never wrote in any depth about suicides. Brodie felt giving the subject extensive ink would "glorify" it. If Darius Kipps had been killed in the line of duty, it would have been worth several days of front-page stories in Harold Brodie's newspaper. Dying by his own hand, Kipps would get no more than a brief obituary buried inside the county news section.

Still, it just wasn't adding up. Sure, I had gotten a somewhat slanted view of Darius Kipps, one provided by loving friends and family. But he didn't seem like a man awash in inner torment. He had a wife he was nuts about, a job he enjoyed, a daughter he doted on, and a brand-new baby — the son he always wanted. What guy like that decides his brain matter would look better splattered all over a shower stall?

I was turning it over so vigorously I made a crucial mistake because I said the following out loud: "Hey, would you mind if I spent a little time nipping at this thing? I know we'd have to keep it off the books, for Brodie's sake, but this just doesn't feel right."

The mistake, of course, is that I should have just gone ahead and done it without telling Tina. Holding back information from one's editor is one of the privileges of being a reporter. In some ways, it is as necessary to good journalism as steno pads. It allows you to travel a road for a few days on what could be a loser without anyone in charge being the wiser that their precious resources — there's that word again — were being squandered.

Often the road dead-ends. But every once in a while it leads to a major score, which

41

you only got because you were willing to waste a little time on it. Except now I had deprived myself of the opportunity.

"Why doesn't it feel right?" she asked. "Because his mom told you how happy he was as a little boy playing with his G.I. Joe?"

"Come on, Tina, it —"

"No, you come on. I know you spent the morning with his family, but we're going to have to write that off. You've got that public housing story to finish."

"And I will. I'm mostly just waiting for documents anyway. I could keep juggling that while I plug at this for a few days."

Tina shook her head. "Brodie is really hot for that project. I told him we might have copy by the end of next week and —"

"Then I'll get you copy by the end of next week. I can do both without —"

"No, you can't. I can see it in your eyes. You're going to spend all your time chasing this fairy tale while —"

"It's not a fairy tale! Look, I know Brodie's thing about suicide. But I'm saying this is one of the times when we should ignore it. Can't you just trust me that I've been around long enough to have decent instincts?"

"Was I talking too quickly for you before? Let me slow it down for you: nnnooo," she said, sounding like an annoyed cow. "You have important work to be doing on a real story. I'm not going to have you wasting time on a nonstory."

"A nonstory, huh? You're really so certain — based on all you know about Darius Kipps — that this might not be something?"

"Monkeys will fly out of my ass first," she said. "As a matter of fact, I'm so certain I don't want you spending another second on that, I want copy on the housing project story by the end of *this* week so I can read it over the weekend. So you might as well get out of here. You've got work to do."

"Fine . . . fine! I'm going to have lunch now! And you can't stop me!" I said defiantly as I stood up.

But Tina was already ignoring me.

I scooted out of the building and walked down the street toward my favorite pizzeria, a place where I often went to sort messy mental laundry. I'm not sure if it was the two steaming slices or the cold Coke Zero, but somehow it always helped me gain perspective on things. Plus, Pizza Therapy is a lot cheaper than counseling.

Except this time I couldn't stop myself from thinking about Darius Kipps. Eventually, I began flipping through my notebook to look for something I might have missed — and to imagine what might be missing. Did happy-go-lucky Darius have a quiet, brooding side no one talked about? Was all that drinking he did in his early twenties self-medication of some kind? Was there some hurt in his childhood no one wanted to tell me about?

Midway through my flipping, I bumped into that photo of Darius at his birthday party. I sat there, studying it for a good three minutes, looking at his wall-to-wall smile, a smile with seemingly no reason to end.

A reporter comes to understand that *H. sapiens* is a highly unpredictable creature; that our large, cunning brains make us capable of a greater range of behavior than any other animal on the planet; and that the ability to hide our emotions, from others and even ourselves, is one of our defining traits. How many times had a neighbor told me that so-and-so "never let on" or "she seemed so upbeat" or "he must have just snapped."

It happened all the time. But had it really happened to Darius Kipps?

Finally, just to sate my curiosity, I grabbed my phone and called Newark Police Department Detective Rodney Pritchard. When I met him, Pritch — as everyone called him

— had been in homicide. He had recently switched to the Gang Task Force, though since gangs were responsible for most of the homicides in the city, I'm not sure there was much difference. We had done a couple of stories together, including several that made him look pretty good. We had developed a relationship where he knew he could whisper sweet somethings in my ear without having to worry about it coming back to him.

He answered his phone on the second ring, saying, "Hey, if it ain't Woodward N. Bernstein!"

Pritch was under the belief that the famous *Washington Post* reporting duo of Bob Woodward and Carl Bernstein was actually one person. I never bothered correcting him.

"Not too bad, not too bad," I said. "Though I did just come from Darius Kipps's house."

"Oh, you heard about that, huh?"

"Yeah. We're getting word he offed himself in a shower stall at the Fourth?"

"Yeah, man, that's the word. It's sad. Dude just had a baby and everything."

"You knew him?"

"Yeah. Before I came downtown, I was in the Fourth with him. I was already detective when he was hired on patrol, so I only knew him a little. He made detective not long before I went downtown, so we never worked a case together or anything. But, yeah, I knew him."

"What'd you think of him?"

"Good dude. Real good dude. He was one of those cops who was all about the law, you know?"

"What do you mean?"

"There are guys in the department who look at the law like it's an impediment. You know, like, 'We'd really be able to clean up this city if it weren't for the damn Fourth Amendment.' But Kipps, he wasn't like that. He understood the job was about upholding the law, even when the law didn't make sense. You know what I'm saying?"

"Maybe," I said. "Give me an example."

"Like, say a scumbag you put away got off on some technicality or got himself some slick defense attorney who was able to get armed robbery down to PTI" — pretrial intervention — "or something like that? Some guys get really pissed, go on and on about how the system is effed up. Not Kipps. He took that stuff in stride. He understood that the law was there to protect everyone — even criminals sometimes. He wanted to bust 'em as bad as anyone. But

46

he wanted to do it the right way. He treated everyone with respect. It's like, if you were going to play good cop, bad cop with a suspect, Kipps was always going to be the good cop. You know what I mean?"

"The good cop," I repeated. "Okay, I hear you. So what do you make of this, then?"

"What do you mean?"

I had been fidgeting with my empty Coke Zero bottle, the label of which was now completely removed. I took a deep breath and said: "I don't know, Pritch. It just strikes me as a little off. I didn't know the guy like you did. But I just spent the morning talking to his family and he didn't seem like the type to do something like this. There's the new baby. He was talking about buying a new house. Heck, he was going to be taking his kids to Disney World. Those are pretty optimistic things, you know? Is there something here I'm missing? Something his family didn't know or wouldn't tell me? I'm not writing it. This is just my own personal curiosity at this point."

"I know what you're saying. But I'll tell you what, this job" — he pushed out a large gust of air — "it chews you up. Being a cop, you see some stuff, man, especially in this city. Some guys, they can put a good face on it for years. They laugh it off and seem

47

to be good family men, but inside it's eating at them the whole time, you know? Some guys start drinking or they let it ruin their marriage. But other guys? It just gets to be too much. Then one day they go off and swallow their gun."

"You think what's what happened here?"

I continued folding and refolding the Coke Zero label as I waited for Pritch to answer.

"Well, probably, yeah," he said at last. "I don't know nothing. And I don't want to go giving Woodward N. Bernstein a big scoop. But . . ."

"But what?"

"Well, the Fourth is . . . like I said, I came up in the Fourth, so I know it pretty well. And it's tight. Especially the black officers, no offense," he said, as if I would somehow be offended I had been left out. "The brothers of the Fourth stick together."

"So?"

"So I'm just hearing some weird stuff, is all. Stuff I never thought I'd hear coming from the Fourth. I went over there this morning, just to pay a visit to some of the guys I still know over there, see how they were doing with it, and . . ."

"What?"

"You ain't writing this, right?"

"No. My paper doesn't write suicides. It's kind of a policy."

"Okay. Well. Shoot, man, I shouldn't even be talking about this. But they were saying Kipps might have been dirty."

"Dirty? Dirty how?"

"I don't know. But word is out he recently had contact with Internal Affairs. And a cop who's spending time with IA, man, that doesn't always look good."

"Yeah, I guess not. Did anyone say specifically what it might have been? There's all different kinds of dirty."

"No. No one said. And I didn't ask," Pritch said. "The truth is, I don't even want to know. The man is dead. Leave it at that."

"Of course, of course," I said as another call started ringing through on my phone. I took a glance at the screen.

It was Mimi Kipps.

"Pritch, I gotta run. Darius Kipps's widow is calling on the other line."

"Oh, geez," he said. "Well, remember: I didn't tell you nothing and you don't know nothing, especially not about Kipps being dirty. That's the last thing that woman needs to hear. She's going to have it hard enough."

As I clicked from one call to the other, I realized there was no good way to handle this.

I couldn't exactly continue the charade that I was going to be writing a glowing thousand-word paean to the life and times of Sergeant Kipps when I knew there were going to be about three paragraphs in the next day's paper. At the same time, if the Newark Police Department hadn't informed Mimi Kipps about the nature of or circumstances surrounding her husband's death, I sure wasn't going to tell her.

But I was spared at least part of that quandary when Mimi started off our conversation with: "He didn't kill himself."

"Mimi?" I said, just to make sure it was her.

"Yes, this is Mimi Kipps, and I want you to know: my husband did *not* kill himself. I don't want you writing it that way. I don't want anyone talking about him that way. I don't care what the Newark Police Department or anyone else has to say about it. There is *no way* he did what they're saying he did."

The preternaturally calm Mimi Kipps I had met earlier this morning was gone. This version was spitting sharp stuff.

"I know my husband," she continued. "And I know how he felt about suicide. You know what he called people who killed themselves? Cowards. Every time he responded to a suicide call — and he would catch them from time to time — he would always say the same thing: 'That's the coward's way out.' Especially when it was a man with a family. He'd said, 'That man had no *right* to do that to himself and leave those kids behind without a daddy.' "

I had already left the pizzeria by this point. The Green Street headquarters of the Newark Police Department was right around the corner, but I wasn't walking in that direction. I was going toward the *Eagle-Examiner* parking garage. I could tell Mimi and I needed to chat in person.

"Mimi, I —"

"Do you know why that chaplain didn't give me any of the details earlier this morning?" she interrupted. "Because the higher-ups down at Green Street were debating how to word the press release. *A stupid press release.* They didn't want to use the word 'suicide' because they thought it would make the department look bad. So they settled on 'self-inflicted gunshot wound.' As if nobody knows that it means the same thing. They were just out here, showing me a copy of it before they sent it out. Can you *believe* that? All they care about is how they're going to look to the media. I threw them out of the house. It's bull. It's bull.

51

No matter what they call it. There's just no way. And I don't want you writing it."

"Mimi, I'm coming out to see you right now," I said. "Can you just sit tight? I'll be there in fifteen minutes."

"I'll see you," she said and ended the call.

I reached my car and tried to put my head in order as I drove back toward East Orange. On the one hand, there was what Pritch told me about Internal Affairs. Was Darius Kipps dirty? He had been talking about buying a new house, taking his kids to Disney. A guy making ninety grand a year might be able to swing those kinds of outlays on his own, depending on his other expenses. Or it might have been a sign he was supplementing his income in some less-than-legitimate fashion. And once he got caught, the decorated cop — who was the son of a decorated cop — couldn't handle the shame. So he arranged himself a hasty exit.

On the other hand, I had my gut — and Mimi Kipps's loud, insistent voice — saying that suicide didn't fit. You didn't spend hours at the hospital telling your infant son how he was going to root for the Eagles someday if you didn't plan to stick around and do it with him, right? And there was also what I had learned about Kipps being an all-about-the-law police officer. Cops like that didn't go bad, did they?

The bottom line was . . . well, there was no bottom line. I had no real idea what happened. And perhaps I should have let it drop — I had a big story about a public housing project to hand to Tina by the end of the week, after all — but part of being a reporter means never turning off your natural curiosity. There was nothing wrong with spending an afternoon indulging it a little bit.

I arrived at Rutledge Avenue to find it looking much the same as it had when I left it a few hours earlier. There were still no news vans, which now made sense — a suicide wasn't good material for them, either. I walked around a group of friends and family on the sidewalk, some of whom were smoking cigarettes, nodding at them as I passed.

Mimi answered the door, but there was a different vibe to her, a certain set of the jaw, a certain look in her eye. Earlier in the morning, I thought she had been in shock. Now I was begin to recognize she was simply made of tougher material than most. This woman was going to keep holding it together as long as she needed to. She was a single mom now, after all. And if there's one thing working in the hood has taught me, it was to never underestimate a single mom.

"Thanks for coming," she said, opening the door so I could enter. "You have good timing. There's someone you really need to talk to."

I looked around the living room, which was empty.

"Follow me," she said, walking toward the back of the duplex.

She led me down a narrow hallway into a brightly lit kitchen with cheerful yellow cabinets and white linoleum floors. In the middle of the room, there was a small folding table with three matching plastic chairs. A thirty-something man sat on the far side. He had short-cropped hair that was just beginning to go gray. He wore jeans and a tight-fitting sweater that made it clear he was proud of the time he spent in the gym. A half-finished cup of coffee sat in front of him. Next to him was another half-finished cup and a chair that had been pushed out. He and the widow Kipps had obviously been sharing a beverage.

"This is Mike, Darius's partner," Mimi said, walking around behind him and draping a hand on his shoulder for a second. "Mike, this is the reporter I was telling you about."

We nodded at each other.

"I'm going to take a shower before the

baby wakes up," she said, then looked at Mike. "Tell him what you told me."

She backed out of the room, leaving me alone with a man who, I got the distinct feeling, didn't like guys who carried notepads for a living.

Although we serve vital functions in our respective ways, cops and reporters are oftentimes the oil and water of a democratic society. We just don't mix all that well.

The antagonism arises from a variety of fundamental conflicts — the short version: they like to keep things secret and we don't. While our differences could be overcome, it always took some effort. And I could tell in this guy's case, it would take more effort than most.

My instant read was that he fancied himself a tough guy and he would only respect other tough guys. This was a bit of a problem for me seeing as, under most circumstances, I'm about as tough as sunwarmed gummy bears.

But I could pretend otherwise. So, without saying a word — because tough guys are taciturn — I pulled out a plastic folding chair and sat across from him. I narrowed my eyes and reclined slightly because tough guys squint a lot and don't care about impressing anyone with good posture. And then I sat there. Just sat there. Because I was tough. Very tough.

It took all my energy to do this, of course. My natural tendency toward glibness made me want to fill long silences like this one. But I focused and kept my lips pressed together.

Finally, after an eternity of pretending to be tough — and I'm talking a good forty-five seconds here — he said, "You want some coffee?"

I didn't. Not even a little. I hate coffee. I don't like the flavor of it when it hits my tongue, and then — as if to reassure me of my first impression — it floods my mouth with this bitter, acidic aftertaste. I'd rather drink a stranger's toothpaste scum. So I said, "Coffee. Sure."

Because I'm *that* tough.

"How you want it?"

"Black," I said, because I knew that's how tough guys were supposed to take their coffee.

Mike got up from his seat and poured from a clear pot of dark brown liquid into a Halloween mug, complete with black cats and witches. It was not exactly a tough guy mug. But I accepted it and tried not to wince as I took a tough guy–sized swallow.

Then I set the mug down and continued our modified staring contest, which seemed to involve not actually looking at each other.

"Mike Fusco," he said eventually.

Feeling like I won some important victory, I replied, "Carter Ross."

He looked aside, as if he had nothing more to say. So I figured I'd let him win a round, adding, "Sorry about your partner."

"Yeah, it's rough," he allowed.

I paused, so as not to make our conversation feel rushed, then asked, "How did you find out?"

He shifted in his seat. From somewhere upstairs, I heard the shower turn on.

"I'm only talking to you because of Mimi," he said. "My name doesn't go anywhere near your story. We clear?"

"Sure. We can be off-the-record. To be honest, I'm not sure I'm going to be writing anything. We don't write about suicides."

I stopped there, curious if he would object to the word. But he didn't bite.

"So how'd you find out?" I said again.

"Well, I heard the gunshot like everyone else. I was at the precinct when it happened."

"Oh. Sorry."

Fusco shrugged. Nothing more, nothing less. Just a shrug. But it was a shrug that told me he knew more than he was letting on. For whatever reason, cops don't like to be the first one to tell reporters anything. But once we already know something, they don't mind expanding on our understanding — if only because it galls them so much when we get things wrong.

So I tried to make it clear that I already knew some stuff, in hopes he would help me learn more.

"We're hearing he went into a shower stall and turned on the water before he pulled the trigger," I said.

Fusco didn't respond. I was going to have to draw him out a bit.

"I spoke to a cop I know earlier this afternoon," I said. "He told me the talk around the Fourth is that Kipps was dirty."

Before I could react, Fusco leaped up, slamming his chair to the floor, then lunged across the table at me. He grabbed me by the shirt and tie, to make sure he had my attention, then unleashed a series of expletives — most of which involved fornication, defecation, or my mother. The diatribe finished with, ". . . so don't you ever say crap like that again!"

Because I was a tough guy, I had willed myself not to flinch. I just let him slowly release his grip on my shirt. He sat back down on his own side of the table.

"It was only a question," I said quietly.

"Yeah, well, it's crap, okay? Kipps was clean. Totally clean. Anyone who says otherwise doesn't know jack. You put that in the newspaper and you'll be printing a lie."

"Noted," I said. "Were you with him at any point last night?"

He glared at me a little more, his nostrils flaring, his over-developed chest rising and falling before he finally answered. "Mimi called us partners, but that's not exactly true. The precinct doesn't really have assigned partners. It's more, there are certain guys who often get the same shift — Kipps and I were mostly four to midnight — and sometimes you end up working with them on bigger cases."

"Were you guys currently working on anything together?"

Fusco shook his head. "I saw him when our shift started. I had a backlog of reports to write, so I stayed at the precinct. He went out. I didn't know where he was going. I never saw him again. The next thing it was maybe eleven or so, I hear that gunshot and . . ."

"Did you go down there to take a look?"

Fusco's head shook again.

"You know what he had been working

on?" I asked.

"Run-of-the-mill stuff. Nothing big."

He accompanied this revelation with another shrug.

"So what's this thing Mimi said you should tell me?" I asked.

My answer, at first, was only a stare. There was some kind of battle going on between his ears. I could tell he wished Mimi had kept her mouth shut. Finally, he coughed into his hand, turned his head, and said, "Kipps was drunk."

"What do you mean?"

"Some of the patrol guys said they found him passed out by the station with an empty bourbon bottle and puke all over his clothes. They dragged him back inside and tossed him in the shower to help him sober up. I guess they put him in with his clothes on because he was such a mess. So he must have still had his gun on him. The next thing they knew, *blam*."

Fusco pantomimed a gun to the head, in case I didn't know what "blam" meant.

"You told Mimi that?"

"I did. The higher-ups weren't going to tell her and I felt she had a right to know."

"And she's taking *that* as evidence her husband didn't kill himself?" I asked, wondering if Fusco was going to jump

60

across the table at me again.

But he just gave me another unreadable shrug. "Kipps didn't drink," he said.

"Yeah, but if you had decided to kill yourself, why not go out and get good and plastered one last time?"

"That's what I said. But Mimi . . ."

"What?"

"She said he hated bourbon. She said back in the day he drank vodka, or tequila, or maybe rum. But never bourbon. I guess he had a bad experience with it when he was young. She said he couldn't even stand the smell."

"That make sense to you?"

"I knew Kipps for ten years and I never saw him touch anything. So I wouldn't know."

It was hardly what I would call conclusive evidence. And Mimi Kipps would not be the first widow to use anything to convince herself — and others — that her husband's death wasn't a suicide.

But it was one more thing that didn't quite fit.

"Okay, so you're a detective," I said. "Was this a suicide?"

He didn't answer.

"You're investigating this, aren't you?" I said.

Again, no answer. But he also didn't contradict it.

"When Mimi gets out of the shower, tell her I had to run," he said, standing up.

I took out a business card, held it out for him, and said, "Maybe I'm investigating this, too. Let's keep in touch."

He didn't respond directly to my suggestion. But on his way out, he took my card.

In the state of Virginia, buying a gun is only slightly more complicated than buying a lawn mower. Buying a whole lot of guns is only marginally more difficult than that.

A state resident who is not banned by the federal government from gun ownership can purchase one weapon every thirty days. A state resident with a concealed carry permit — available from the county courthouse to anyone who has completed a gun safety class — can buy as many guns as he wants, no questions asked.

So, as a heretofore law-abiding citizen, John Bristow didn't need to make any extraordinary preparations or seek any special permission. On the day of the exchange — which came less than a week after he first made Craigslist contact — he just followed the instructions that had been given to him by his new employer. He drove to a Hilton just off Interstate 64 and left his dented Dodge Stratus in the parking lot, unlocked. Then he walked away, as per his directive. He killed the next hour at a Chick-fil-A.

When he returned, an associate of Red Dot Enterprises had placed $8,000 in cash in his glove box. The deal was that he got to keep the difference between the cash and whatever he spent for twenty guns, new in box.

He had wondered, briefly, what would stop him from just disappearing with the money. These guys didn't know him, after all. And what they wanted him to do was clearly illegal, so they wouldn't be able to report the crime to the police. But he had barely formed the thought when he was told he would be watched. It was strongly suggested he not deviate from the plan. He didn't ask for an explanation. He got the point.

Armed with the cash, he drove around the corner to Bass Pro Shop, a cavernous monument to outdoor play. He parked in the sprawling lot, wedging his Stratus in between a pair of large pickup trucks. He walked past a trio of glistening new boats, through a front entrance adorned with antlers, fishing nets, other rustic paraphernalia, and a sign that announced, WELCOME, FISHERMEN, HUNTERS, AND OTHER LIARS.

He was a liar, all right. Just a different kind than the store had in mind. He went to the gun section, bellied up to a glass-encased counter and said, "I need twenty guns."

The clerk behind the counter — who was balding, bespectacled, and sweating — did not hesitate.

"You got your carry permit?" he asked.

"Yep."

"Okay. What you want?"

Bristow hadn't given it any thought and didn't actually care. He started making selections based exclusively on price and availability, and within minutes he had cleaned out the Bass Pro Shop's stock of several smaller models, mostly .22s by Beretta, Browning, and Ruger, with a few .38s thrown in. Whatever was cheapest.

"You need bullets, too?" the clerk asked at one point, and Bristow nearly said yes.

If they were his guns, he'd need bullets. But no one had said a thing about bullets. Just guns. So he said, "Nah."

Then they began the approval process. Bristow presented his Virginia state driver's license, with its sky blue background and official state seal; his concealed carry permit; and a recent utility bill, which confirmed his state residency.

Luckily, the state of Virginia didn't particularly care the bill was past due.

Sliding over to a computer behind the

counter, the clerk entered Bristow's information — name, address, date of birth — onto a form that was sent electronically to state police headquarters, where trained personnel performed the necessary background check. Bristow had no felonies. He was clean.

And since there is no waiting period in Virginia, Bristow was soon at the register, paying for this small arsenal of weapons no differently than if it was a pile of personal flotation devices from the boating section. His total, which included sales tax, came to $6,228.95, which he paid in cash, under the watchful eye of the manager.

The entire transaction was perfectly legal, done in exacting accordance with all local, state, and federal laws. It took just twenty-eight minutes from start to finish.

Then he drove back to the Hilton, parked his car, and walked away. This time, flush with new money, he went across the street to a Wok'n Roll. When he returned, the guns were gone — heisted by Red Dot Enterprises.

That afternoon, Bristow walked into the Hampton City Sheriff's Office and reported the guns stolen. The paperwork took a while — they had to fill out a separate form for each gun. But Bristow didn't care. He didn't have anything else to do, and besides, he could now get reimbursed by his insurance company, adding significantly to his score.

He didn't know where the guns went. He didn't particularly care. He had bills to pay.

CHAPTER 2

It felt a little intrusive, sitting in Mimi Kipps's kitchen while she was upstairs showering, and I was contemplating whether I should take my leave when I heard the water shut off. Then, from the living room, baby Jaquille began making a noise that may or may not have been crying. It mostly sounded like a wind-up toy on the fritz.

"Would someone mind holding the baby for a second?" Mimi hollered from upstairs. "He's just hungry. I'll be down in a second to feed him."

In a house that had seemed so filled with relatives, I was sure someone more appropriate than the friendly local newspaper reporter would materialize and take care of this duty. My maternal instincts rank slightly ahead of wolf spiders — inasmuch as I know better than to eat my own young — though I'm not sure I had much to offer beyond that. So I sat still and waited for the noise coming from the Pack 'N Play to quiet. It was my version of the "not it" finger to the nose.

But I soon realized I was the only one in the house. And Jaquille's frustration was mounting. I went into the living room and looked down at him as he squalled.

"Uh . . . what . . . what exactly do I do?" I hollered upstairs.

"Just pick him up," I heard Mimi say.

And how do I do that? I wanted to say. Did the kid come with a handle on him or something? Among the many skills I had managed to pick up in the newsroom over the years, this was not one of them. We often talked about babysitting the interns, but our interns usually knew enough to keep their weeping more private.

Still, Jaquille's distress was only increasing, so I did what any good reporter does in an uncertain situation: I summoned all the confidence I had and faked it. Like a seasoned wet nurse, I reached down and grabbed him with two hands, then cradled him to my body. He was small enough that I'm sure I could have one-handed him. But since I cared enough to catch a softball with two hands, it seemed the least I could do for this little guy.

"Okay, pal, it's okay," I said in what I

hoped was a reassuring voice.

Jaquille was unconvinced. My faking hadn't fooled him. He screamed even louder, and even though his eyes were closed, he was thrashing his head around, his mouth searching for . . . something. But what?

Oh. Right. A nipple.

"Sorry, friend," I said. "I got two of those, but neither is going to do you much good."

Jaquille screamed some more and I became aware of my desire to do something, anything to make him stop. So I stuck my finger in his mouth. He immediately clamped down on it. Hard. Like he intended to suck the nail clean off my finger.

But at least he was quiet, contentedly taking these long pulls on my finger like it was going to get him somewhere. I kept worrying he would figure out nothing worthwhile was going to come of it, but he seemed unbothered. He was just looking up at me with those big, glassy, grateful eyes, like I was the only important thing in his tiny little universe. I was starting to understand how it is parents first fall in love with their kids. Another human being — even a shriveled, alien-looking one — gazes at you like that, and it makes you feel like you'll do anything for them.

"Don't worry, little guy," I cooed. "I got your back."

Jaquille sucked a few more times, his eyes never leaving my face.

"Oh, look at you, you're a natural," Mimi said as she descended the stairs.

"Yeah, don't let that get out."

"Here you go," she said, taking the baby from me. "How's my little man?"

As soon as I pried my finger from his mouth, Jaquille renewed his protest. I was going to take that as a perfectly good excuse to announce my departure, then the doorbell rang.

"I'm sorry, can you answer that?" she asked. "If this baby doesn't eat, no one around here is going to be able to think."

Since when had I become the nanny *and* the butler? As Mimi disappeared with the baby into the kitchen, I opened the door.

The man standing there was huge, dark-skinned, and cologne-doused. He had on a gray pinstripe suit that, at a quick glance, looked like it was silk and custom-tailored. He wore a hangdog look on his drooping face, gold-wire-framed glasses, and a fedora, which he doffed as he entered. He looked familiar, though I couldn't say why.

"Good day to you, sir," he said in a deep, bass voice, walking in like I had already invited him. "Is Noemi here?"

He took care to pronounce Mimi's full name, doing it so deliberately it sounded more like "No Emmy" — like it was something with which Susan Lucci would have once been familiar. As soon as he was done, I heard her call from the kitchen, "Pastor Al! Come in, come in!"

The man shuffled in and I backed up to give him room. He was at least five inches taller than me, and if I could guess from the size of the body filling his suit, he needed one of those scales that went beyond three hundred pounds. He was dabbing sweat with a handkerchief, even though it wasn't that hot.

"Have a seat, Pastor Al. I'm just heating a bottle for the baby," Mimi said.

Finally, my brain clicked in and I realized who Pastor Al was and why he looked familiar. He was one of Newark's celebrity ministers, a man well represented in the three Bs of local outdoor advertising — billboards, buses, and benches. His church, Redeemer Love Christian, was a nondenominational house of God that used the slogan "Let Jesus Redeem You" and always featured "The Reverend Doctor Alvin Le-Rioux, an Anointed Man of God" in its advertisements.

We had written a story about the church not long ago. It had something like eight thousand members, many of whom had been talked into tithing by the anointed man of God. The story raised the question of where that money all went — other than the three Bs and the chauffeured SUV that the good Reverend Doctor was known to ride around the city in — but never fully answered it. Unlike other nonprofits, churches are exempt from laws requiring them to expose their finances to public inspection.

Suffice it to say, the piece probably wasn't Pastor Al's favorite reading material. I had heard talk that after our story ran, he gave a sermon calling our newspaper an agent of Satan — or something similarly unflattering. I can't say that kind of talk made me want to like him any more than he liked me. Still, he was a man of some standing in the community, and I was going to treat him with all due respect.

"Reverend LeRioux, I'm Carter Ross with the *Eagle-Examiner,*" I said, extending a hand. He shook it, though I could tell he didn't want to. I could also tell I was going to smell like his cologne for the rest of the day, no matter how many times I washed myself.

"I'll be out in a second," Mimi called.

Pastor Al hobbled in arthritic fashion over to one of the couches, where he landed heavily. He stared straight ahead, dabbed his forehead, and seemed to be making a point of not talking to me. The baby was still caterwauling, then abruptly quieted — the bottle, at long last, had been delivered.

Mimi came into the room a moment later with a happily suckling Jaquille cradled in one arm.

"Pastor Al!" she said.

"Noemi, my child," he said, without getting up.

"It's so good of you to come."

"I came as soon as I heard."

I thought, at that point, he would offer a prayer, read some Scripture, or do something appropriately nonsecular. Instead, he gestured at me.

"Noemi, I was hoping we could share some words in confidence," he said. "I am troubled by the presence of a reporter here."

And I am troubled by ministers who wear two-thousand-dollar silk suits. But at least I'm polite enough to keep it to myself.

He continued: "I know the media enjoys publicizing tragedy for its own purposes. But these are private moments to be shared by family and loved ones."

74

Mimi looked over at me, obviously torn. I had earned her trust, and I could tell she liked me. But, at the same time, Pastor Al trumped Reporter Carter in her world.

I saved her the trouble of having to kick me out.

"Actually, I was just leaving," I said. "I'll call you later."

Pastor Al was still mopping his forehead as I left.

Relieved to be no longer serving as a human pacifier, I returned to my car, having already decided on my next course of action. With apologies to Mike Fusco, I had to figure out if Darius Kipps had been a straight-up cop.

If he wasn't, it meant he probably did kill himself, in which case I was just wasting my time. It's not that crooked cops don't make for great copy — they do — it was Brodie's suicide policy. There would just be no getting around it. Besides, I'd never get anything on-the-record. No one was going to piss on a dead cop's grave, even if he *was* bent.

Then again, if Darius Kipps wasn't dirty, it opened the possibility the suicide wasn't what it seemed, in which case I had a load of dynamite on my hands. Either way, I wasn't going to find my answer in the phone book or on the Internet. I was going to find it on the streets.

I started driving through the heart of the hood, down a series of avenues I have come to know as well as any place I've ever lived. During my years at the *Eagle-Examiner,* the milieu had become familiar, even comfortable: the vacant lots and abandoned buildings, the aging Victorians and ancient storefronts, the new construction and glistening chain stores. It's the hodge-podge that is present-day Newark, a city forever striving to renew itself, with mixed results.

I love it when some visiting journalist parachutes into town for three days to write the Definitive Newark Story. Because the fact is, if they're looking to write "Newark: City on the Rise," they'll find that. And if they're looking to write "Newark: Still the Same Hellhole Despite What the Mayor Keeps Telling People," they'll find that, too. To me, the city is like its own kind of Rorschach test. What you choose to see — whether you want to be optimistic or pessimistic in your view — says as much about you as it does about the place.

My destination was the Clinton Hill section of Newark and my man, Reginald "Tee" Jamison. The nickname came from the thriving T-shirt shop he ran — no one, other than perhaps his wife, called him by his real name. I had written a story about him a few years back, and we had since become unlikely friends. I say "unlikely" only in a statistical sense, inasmuch as there are roughly two hundred million white people living in America, and Tee is friends with only two of them.

Still, I was glad to be one of the two. Despite the superficial differences between us — he has more hair in two of his dread-locks than I have on my entire head, not to mention more muscle in one of his pectorals than I have in my entire body — we were kindred spirits in more ways than not, and we enjoyed deciphering our respective worlds for each other.

Plus, he grew up in Newark, shuffling between a variety of foster care placements in all parts of the city, so he has a network of contacts that would make any reporter envious. If Darius Kipps was dirty, Tee might or might not know it. But he sure would know someone who knew.

I arrived at his store to find a half-dozen knuckleheads hanging around his front door. They were generally good kids — if you could ignore the pot smell that clings to their clothing — though their presence

77

on Tee's sidewalk led people to make certain assumptions about what was going on inside. Tee, who was a legitimate business-man, finally got fed up one day and posted a sign in his front window, NO, WE DO NOT SELL WEED HERE.

As I got out of my car, six heads im-mediately swung my way — well-dressed Caucasian men tend to have this effect on Clinton Avenue in Newark — but then they saw it was me. I'm a frequent enough visi-tor to Tee's store that they know I'm not there to arrest them, harass them, or other-wise disrupt their mojo. With their alarm level back down, they returned to what ap-peared to be a dice game. And not Dun-geons & Dragons.

I hit the buzzer by Tee's front door and waited for the lock to release. When I walked in, Tee was designing a T-shirt for a pair of customers, who were seated in front of his desk.

"Uh-oh, it's the IRS!" he hollered from behind his desk.

"Sir, this is a random audit," I said, play-ing along. "I'm going to have to ask for your last five years of returns, including all as-sociated receipts."

"Receipts? What's that? You know a

brother like me can't read. My massa won't let me."

"Well then, I'm afraid we're going to have to throw you in jail with all the other darkies. Now excuse me for a second, I have to plant some drugs on you."

"C'mon now, don't make me go all Rodney King on your pasty ass."

I think the customers knew we were kidding because we were both smiling broadly. But they looked like nice folks, and I could tell we were making them feel uncomfortable. So I pulled out of the act and said, "You want me to come back later?"

"No, no, I'm just finishing. Gimme a second."

Tee took another five minutes wrapping up with his customers, while I perused some of his inventory, including the ever-popular shirt that showed a stick figure lying on the ground under the words, WHY DON'T YOU GO PRACTICE FALLING DOWN?

I was admiring another one — a top-ten list of "Yo Mama's So Ugly" jokes — when Tee came over and shook my hand.

"So what's going on?" Tee asked. "You working on something?"

I told him what I knew about Darius Kipps, finishing with, "So, basically, I need to figure out if he's crooked."

"Oh, that's easy," Tee said. "They all crooked."

I had repeatedly tried to convince Tee of my belief that, in fact, the vast majority of policemen are not corrupt — in the same way the vast majority of newspaper reporters don't make up stories. But it only takes a few reprobates to skew the reputation of the rest of them. Newark, for example, had roughly 1,200 police officers last time I checked. If even 99 percent of them were law-abiding, that still meant there were a dozen cops rampaging around the city, wreaking havoc.

Alas, it seems like Tee had experience with all twelve of them.

"C'mon, I'm serious," I said. "I've got a picture of him. You think your friends outside are hard-core enough to know if Kipps was involved in something he shouldn't be?"

"Them? Nah. They just playin', you know what I mean?"

I did. In Newark, there were pretend gangs and then there were serious gangs, and it was important to know the difference. Kids like Tee's knuckleheads might call themselves a gang. They might adopt some of the gestures, mannerisms, and clothing of a gang. They might even say they were Bloods or Crips. But, in reality, they were a gang in roughly the same sense as the Little Rascals. They hung together for camaraderie and mutual protection. They were basically harmless.

"Besides," Tee pointed out, "you said this guy is Fourth Precinct, right? Those kids never get out of the South Ward. The Fourth is up in Central."

"Oh, yeah, good point. You know anyone up that way who might be able to help me?"

Tee got a far-off look.

"What?" I asked.

"Well, I know these dudes up there. Trust me, if your cop was dirty, they'd know. They got that neighborhood wired. Hell, I think they got the whole city wired."

"Okay. I'm not going to have to get stoned again, am I?"

Tee had once set me up with sources who felt the only way to ensure I was not a member of a law enforcement agency was for me to smoke pot with them. It was an experience that proved two things to them: one, I'm not a cop; and two, my tolerance for marijuana is not especially impressive.

"No, no, nothing like that this time," he assured me. "But let me ask you something: You need a new pair of boots by any chance?"

"Huh?"

"Just say yes."

"Yes?"

"Okay, let me make a call."

Fifteen minutes later, I was out the door with an address scribbled on a piece of paper and instructions to stop at an ATM machine to pick up a hundred dollars in cash. I was also instructed not to get too attached to said money.

The address was on Irvine Turner Boulevard, which was one of Newark's most notorious drug corridors for one reason: it offered a straight shot to Route 78, an east-west interstate that led rather quickly to some of the state's nicest bedroom communities. All the suburbanites who came to Newark to get their drugs — and make no mistake, that was a big part of the clientele — knew they couldn't get lost if they just stayed on Irvine Turner.

I relied on my GPS to guide me to the address Tee had written for me, which turned out to be around the corner from the Fourth Precinct headquarters. It was a cream-colored, two-story, warehouselike building that encompassed a good chunk of the block. The only apparent tenant, and it occupied perhaps one-tenth of the building, was a bodega that had a door onto the street. It had dark windows — behind bars, of course — made of one-way glass, the kind that would allow someone inside to see out, but not the other way around.

Where was Tee taking me, anyhow? I pushed through the bodega's door to the sound of little bells chiming — a few had been tied to the door. The store was empty except for a turban-wearing cashier sitting in a bulletproof box.

I approached the man, who I guessed was Sikh, and said, "Tee sent me."

He tilted his head and peered at me like I was speaking a soon-to-be-extinct Javanese dialect.

"I'm the guy Tee sent," I said.

More peering.

"Is this one-sixty Irvine Turner Boulevard?" I asked.

"One-sixty A," the guy said in a thick Indian accent. "You want one-sixty, you go around the corner."

"Around . . . which corner?"

The guy pointed out the door and vaguely to the left, so that's the direction I took. I reached the end of the building without seeing anything obvious, just a narrow alleyway. It was far cleaner than most Newark alleys — spotless, actually — which *really* got me suspicious. I hoped Tee remembered that I had a cat who depended on me as his sole means of support.

I turned and, midway down the alley, found a meshed steel door, the kind that served as a superstrength screen for another door inside it. I pulled on the screen, but it was bolted solid. A security camera, attached to the side of the building about fifteen feet up, looked down on me.

There was no knocking on a door like this. But I also couldn't see any other way in. I studied the door frame, the door itself, and saw nothing obvious. Was I supposed to stand there until someone saw me on the camera?

Then I found it, just to the left of the frame: a small, recessed doorbell button, practically camouflaged because it had been painted the same cream color as the concrete around it.

I pressed the button and waited. Nothing happened. I pressed again. Still nothing. I was beginning to think it was broken — and there was no way into this hulk of a building — when I pressed the button a third time.

Then I heard a metallic voice: "Keep your shirt on, keep your shirt on. What are you, dying or something?"

The voice sounded . . . Jewish? Were there still Jews left in Newark? I thought they all left a half-century ago. I couldn't even tell where the sound was coming from. My head swiveled in every direction.

"Over here, over here," the voice said.

This time I was able to place it as coming from the camera, which had a small speaker.

"Oh, hi," I said, feeling weird because, to anyone who walked by, it looked like I was talking to a wall.

"You just gonna stand there all day, looking like a putz? What do you want?"

"I'm . . . I'm the guy Tee sent."

More faintly, like he didn't know I could still hear him, the voice asked, "What did he say?" Then another guy — who also sounded like an older Jewish man — replied, "He said he was the guy Tee sent. The boots. The boots."

"Oh, yeah," the voice said, returning to its previous volume. "You here about the boots?"

"That's right."

"Why didn't you say so? You think I'm a mind reader or something? Hang on, hang on."

I waited another moment, until the door was opened by a granite block of a black man who, I assumed, was not the owner of

85

the voice I heard on the speaker. I followed him down an unadorned, windowless hallway until we reached another door, where he punched in a numeric code.

The door opened, and suddenly I felt like I was in a chaotic, mismatched Macy's. It was a large, open space filled with merchandise, loosely organized by category: luggage to the immediate left, cookery and housewares straight on, hardware beyond that, clothing and footwear to the right, electronics in the back left. The only thing missing was the perfume section.

"What . . . what *is* all this?" I asked, but my granite-block guide was not a talker.

I heard a pleasant dinging sound and turned to see two men appearing out of a freight elevator. The first had on yellow-tinted glasses, a dark yellow shirt with the top three buttons undone, light yellow slacks, and white slip-on shoes that reminded me of something a nurse would have worn forty years ago. His saggy skin was deeply tanned, even though it was March. His jewelry — a necklace, multiple bracelets, and rings on several digits, including both pinkies — was all yellow gold. His hair, what little of it there was, had been dyed blond and was gelled back. He looked like a wrinkled human banana and walked like the only rooster in a hen house.

The second man was slump-shouldered and appropriately pale for the season. He wore light gray pants and a blue cardigan sweater over a white oxford shirt, which was buttoned all the way to the top. He had no jewelry. His hair was its natural gray. He walked like a man who had lost every bet he ever placed.

The man in yellow said, "I'm Bernie. Everyone calls me Uncle Bernie. This is my brother Gene. Which one of us do you think is older?"

Both guys were at least seventy, though it was hard to tell beyond that. Either one of them could have been 138 for all I knew. If he had asked me who was older, him or Methuselah, I still wouldn't have been able to answer.

"I have . . . I have no idea," I said.

"Come on, guess."

"He's older," I said, pointing at Gene, if only because I could tell that was what Uncle Bernie wanted to hear.

"See? That's what everyone thinks, Gene! You look like a *shlamazel*. You're not gonna get any tail at the bar dressing like that."

I suspected both of these guys were a bit beyond their bar-cruising years — unless you were talking about the salad bar at an assisted living facility — but I at least appreciated his spirit.

"Anyhow, I know you didn't come here to admire my good looks," he said. "C'mon. Let's go."

Uncle Bernie led me through some racks of clothing toward a footwear section that would challenge a Nine West.

"You sure you don't need some pots and pans?" Uncle Bernie asked me on the way back. "I just got some new All-Clad. That's top of the line, All-Clad. The best. The *best.*"

"No thanks."

"What about a TV? Samsung. Sony. Those Japs make a good TV now. Fella like you, I bet you like sports, right? Me? I like the ponies. I go to the track. I place a bet. I take a little nap in the sun. It's very relaxing. But you young guys? You all like the football and the basketball. Need a good TV for that, am I right? How about a new high-def?"

"That's okay."

"Boots," Gene reminded Bernie. "He came for the boots, remember?"

"Yeah, yeah, I know. I'm just talking here. What, you think I'm some kind of *goyishe kop*?"

"That's Yiddish for 'stupid,' " Gene translated.

"Okay, here we are," Bernie said as we arrived at a series of wire racks, filled from top to bottom with shoe boxes. "What size are you? Ten? Eleven? You're so tall, I bet you're eleven."

"Yeah, eleven works," I said.

"Okay, okay, where are we . . . boots, boots," Bernie said, pawing through some boxes. "Here we go. Timberlands. Excellent company, Timberland. They make a fine product and they stand behind it a hundred percent, a thousand percent. Now these? These are the top of the line."

He pulled out a pair of work boots and continued: "These are from their premium collection. Steel toe. Waterproof. Eight-inch upper — that's two inches more than their usual. You wear these boots, people say, 'Hey, look at that *feinshmecker!* ' "

"That's Yiddish for someone who has good taste," Gene interjected.

"Now, you get these boots retail for one fifty, one sixty, even on sale. You? You're a friend of Tee's — as far as I'm concerned, you're *mishpokhe.* I give 'em to you for a hundred even. We good?"

I was so stunned by everything I was seeing — much less by what a *mishpokhe* was

— I had to slow down and make sense out of it. "I'm sorry, Uncle Bernie, I just have to know, what is all this? Where did this come from?"

"What do you mean, where did this come from? You think I'm back here tanning leather all day? It came from the manufacturer."

"No, I'm just asking . . . I'm sorry, are you guys some kind of fence or something?"

Bernie recoiled, looking genuinely offended. "Fence? Fence! *A broch!* My mother would rise from the grave and cuff me behind the ear if I stole so much as a lump of sugar! A fence! Shame on you."

"So how did you guys . . . get all this stuff?"

"Warranties," Bernie said. "It's all about the warranties."

"Huh?"

"We're a warrantied product reseller," Gene explained.

"What's . . . what's that?"

"Well, take those boots you got there. Timberland," Uncle Bernie said. "Now, Timberland is a popular boot around here. And these young black guys, they all want their boots to be crisp and new, all the time. The moment a boot gets a speck of dirt on it? Feh! They're done with it."

"But these look brand-new . . ."

"I'm not finished. Am I finished? Geez, this guy. It's like he's sitting on *shpilkes*."

"That means that you're impatient," Gene said.

"Anyhow," Bernie plowed forward, "Timberland, they guarantee their product for life. For life, you hear me! So we have people all over, people who know us, people who know what we're looking for. And they recover these kind of things for us — for a small fee, naturally. So say we get a pair of slightly used boots. We send them back to Timberland and, whammo, new boots."

"They just . . . send you boots?"

"Well, there's work involved. You have to write a letter — the letter is important, make 'em know you're serious. And then sometimes we might have to, what's the best way to put it, massage 'em a little. This is an art we're talking about here."

"Timberland guarantees its product against material or manufacturing defect," Gene said. "So we —"

"Tut, tut," Bernie interrupted. "What are you, making a *megillah*? He gets the point. Geez, Gene, someone asks you what time it is, you build 'em a clock."

"So all this stuff," I said, making a sweeping gesture with my arm. "The pots, the pans, the power tools. All of it is —"

"Straight from the manufacturer, never been used, good as new," Bernie said. "Same as you get in the store. But for the right customer, Uncle Bernie gives you a discount."

"But can you . . . do that?" I asked. "Is it legal?"

"Legal?" Bernie spat. "Was it legal what the Pharaoh did to my people? Was Auschwitz legal? Don't talk to me about legal!"

"But don't these companies, I don't know, protect against this somehow? You must have twenty pairs of Timberlands there. Doesn't Timberland eventually figure out it's shipping all these new boots to the same place?"

Bernie just smiled and said, "We in the tribe have a saying for that: *'Mensch tracht, Gott lacht.'* "

"Man plans, God laughs," Gene said.

I felt like laughing, too. Newark: there are a million scams in the naked city.

"So, I'm not here to dance with you, I'm here to sell stuff," Bernie said. "You want the boots or not?"

"Yeah, I'll take the boots. But I need a quick favor," I said, extracting the picture of Darius Kipps from my pocket. "My guy Tee tells me you know all the cops around here."

"The cops, the pawnbrokers, the shop-keepers, the *machers,* the *kurves,* the *bub-bas,*" Bernie assured me. "We know every-one. In this line of work, someone farts, you gotta be able to smell it, kid."

"Okay. Well, I'm trying to figure out if this one detective is dirty or not."

"Dirty? What, you mean is he on the take?"

"Yeah, something like that. I just want to know if he's involved in anything he shouldn't be involved in."

"Time was, they were all on the take," Bernie said, chuckling. "You remember that, Gene? They paid those poor *shmendricks* a hundred fifty bucks a week and then they wondered why they were all in the mob's pocket."

"Tell him about Addonizio," Gene said.

"Addonizio! Remember him? He was a real Moyshe Kapoyer. He was the mayor. He used to be a congressman, but you know what he said? He said 'You can't make any money as a congressman, but as mayor of Newark you can make a million bucks.' "

"Said it right into a wire," Gene added. "To the FBI."

"Ah, but that was the old days," Bernie continued. "Now? Not so much. The pay. The benefits. It's all too good. These guys don't want to risk their pensions. A few of them get involved in some funny business here and there, but nothing like it used to be. Let me have a look at this fella."

I handed Bernie the photo, which he held out at arm's length for perhaps a half a second.

"Him? Oh, he's all right. He's fine."

"Are you sure? You want to look —"

"Sure? Yeah I'm sure! Listen to this guy, thinking I don't know what I'm talking about. I got stains in my shorts older than you, kid. You gonna tell me my business? I say this guy's okay, he's okay."

"Gotcha. Thanks for taking a look."

"No problem. Now, hey, you need a briefcase by any chance?"

Somehow, I made it out of Gene and Bernie's Warranty Emporium without acquiring any more merchandise, though not for lack of effort on Bernie's part.

I tossed the Timberlands in my backseat, wondering when I'd ever have a chance to use them — I'm not exactly a steel-toe kind of guy — then turned my gaze to the Fourth Precinct headquarters, a hulking, fortress-like edifice whose windows had all been bricked over. The building had a famous — or, rather, notorious — history as the place where the Newark riots began in 1967.

Most folks thought the riots began when some cops beat up a cab driver (named John Smith, of all things) and then dragged his broken body back to the Fourth Precinct, resulting in the rumor the cabbie had been killed — and prompting a spasm of violence and looting from the outraged citizenry. That's true, but it's only part of the story. The city actually calmed down the night of Smith's arrest, to the point where the local National Guard Armory, which had been put on alert, was told to stand down. Violence didn't flare up again until the next night, when a protest outside the Fourth Precinct got out of hand, leading to four days of sustained unrest.

Either way, the Fourth played a central role in a cataclysm that left twenty-six people dead and caused ten million dollars in physical damage, to say nothing of what it did to Newark's reputation. On the fortieth anniversary of the riots, a group of citizens and community leaders led an effort to have a small plaque mounted on the front of the building to commemorate what happened there. Otherwise, the Fourth Precinct was more or less the same place it had been in 1967. There had been talk about tearing it down, but no one had quite gotten around to it.

Now here it was, harboring secrets once again, playing an oblique role in another tragedy — even if I couldn't quite measure the angle.

Lacking any kind of real plan, I locked my car and wandered in the direction of the precinct. I wanted to get a read on the place, imprint an image of it in my brain. I kept my eyes fixed on it as I walked up the sidewalk, then stood there for a while, like if I stared at it long enough its walls would start spilling what they knew.

I was still rooted there when a voice interrupted me.

"Can I help you?"

It was a patrol cop in uniform, taking a smoke break by the side of the building. I'm not sure how I missed him — he had to be at least six foot eight, with the arms of a seven footer — but somehow he startled me a little.

"I was just . . . I heard a cop killed himself in there last night, and I guess I wanted to have a look. Is that a problem?"

"No law against looking," he said, taking a drag on his cigarette.

I did my best to study the guy out of the corner of my eye while I pretended to examine the building some more. Maybe I had watched a few too many bad eighties movies, but he was tall, black, and wearing a policeman's hat that made him appear even taller, and I couldn't help but be reminded of Hightower from *Police Academy.*

So. How to handle him? If I told him I was a reporter, the guy's mouth would cinch up tighter than Uncle Scrooge's change purse. But there's a rule about identifying yourself to sources: you only have to do it if you planned to quote them. And since there's no way a beat cop would ever be cleared by his superiors to be quoted on something like this, I wasn't exactly risking anything by posing as a nosy bystander.

"Did you know him?" I asked.

"We all did."

"What happened?"

"Seems like you already know," Hightower said, stubbing out his cigarette on the wall of the building, then dropping the butt.

"Was he a good guy?"

"You must be a reporter."

Busted. Another rule: you don't necessarily have to identify yourself, but if you're asked whether you are in fact a reporter, you can't go lying about it.

"Yeah, how'd you know?"

"White guy in this neighborhood? If it's

97

nighttime, you're here to buy drugs. If it's daytime, you're either a reporter or a social worker. Social workers don't wear ties."

I nodded my head. "You got me," I said.

I figured those would be among the last words Hightower and I ever exchanged. But, to my surprise, he pulled a pack of cigarettes out of his pocket and lit another one. He was going to get as much nicotine in as he could while he was still on break. And that suited my purposes fine.

"So I'm hearing a bunch of patrol guys found him drunk on bourbon, covered in puke," I said. "They tossed him in the shower to sober him up. And then he did himself in in the shower."

"You hearing all that, huh?"

"We got sources."

"What else you hear?"

I paused, not sure how much further to push things. Mike Fusco damn near strangled me when I asked him about Kipps being corrupt. But at least I had a little bit of a size advantage on Fusco. Hightower? If he wanted to, he could fold me in quarters and stuff me in his pocket.

Still, nothing ventured, nothing gained. So I took a deep breath and said: "There's talk that Detective Kipps might have gotten himself tangled up in something inappropriate, that he might have gotten caught, and that maybe that's why he pulled the trigger. But then I've had other people telling me he was legit. So I guess I'm trying to figure out which it was."

I braced myself, and Hightower's face twitched a little. But all he did was take a drag on his cigarette. "What do you care?" he asked.

"Well, the way my bosses think, a crooked cop who shoots himself is probably getting what he deserves, and therefore we don't have much of a story," I ventured. "Then again, maybe the cop is straight. Maybe he didn't even kill himself in the first place, in which case there's a lot more going on than we might realize. You follow me?"

I had set him up to tell me all kinds of wonderful things about Darius Kipps. And mindful of what Pritch said about black officers in the Fourth being tight with each other, I figured that's what I was going to hear.

But he flicked his cigarette on the ground and exhaled a long line of smoke. Without any expression, he said, "Sounds to me like you don't got a story."

"What makes you say that?"

But he didn't reply, just brushed past me and up the front steps, disappearing into that long-infamous building.

It was starting to feel like I needed a score-card just to keep track of who was in the "Darius Dirty" column and who belonged in "Darius Clean." Pritch and Officer High-tower seemed to be in the former, while Mike Fusco and Uncle Bernie were in the latter. Me? I was right in the middle, in a third column that might as well have been labeled "Carter Clueless."

I was trudging back to my car when my phone chirped with a text message. It was from Tommy Hernandez, our city hall beat writer and a coconspirator in what had turned out to be some of my finer capers. Tommy and I did our best to look out for each other in the newsroom. So I took it seriously when his text read: "TT on war-path. Watch ur back."

TT was, of course, Tina Thompson. And I didn't know what he was talking about until moments later, when my phone rang. It was coming from a number with a 315 area code, which I knew was Syracuse, N.Y. Over the years, we had enough interns from Syracuse University's Newhouse School of Public Communications to know those three digits cold.

"Carter Ross."

"Hey, Carter, it's Geoff Ginsburg."

Geoff was another Syracuse intern. In the modern newsroom — which has more demand for work than money to pay for it — interns have two of the things editors prize most: enthusiasm and affordability. Like some invasive species, interns started in relatively small numbers, but with no natural prey — beyond their own inability to survive on the near-poverty-level wages we pay them — they have been allowed to proliferate to the point where I think the interns now outnumber the full-time staff members.

Talent-wise, they were a mixed lot, though Geoff was better than most. He was a smart kid, an excellent writer, and a keen reporter. Because of his surname, some wiseacre on the copy desk had taken to calling him Ruth Bader. That turned rather quickly into Ruthie, the name that stuck. Mind you, unlike the Supreme Court justice, our Ruthie looked like he was about thirteen years old. He had an enthusiastic demeanor that made you wonder if he was getting his Journalism Merit Badge and a round, boyish face that I'm fairly certain didn't require regular shaving.

That youthful appearance made his obvious crush on Tina Thompson all the more funny. It was unclear whether the crush was professional or personal. Ruthie struck me as the kind of kid who might go for an older chick, especially a hot one like Tina; but he also struck me as a total suck-up, so it could go either way. All I knew is he spent an awful lot of time hanging around her office, following her on trips across the newsroom, yapping around her heels like the lap dog he wanted to be.

"Hey, uh, Geoff," I said, barely resisting the urge to call him Ruthie. You never knew whether the interns were aware of the clever nicknames we had awarded them. "What's up?"

I started my engine, just to get the heat going. It had been a mild day for March, but it was starting to get chillier now that the sun was going down.

"Well, I remembered you were working on that project about public housing," he said. "I happen to be really interested in public housing, so I was seeing if you wouldn't mind me tagging along."

I felt my eyebrow arching. It was highly unlikely he "remembered" anything. The only people who would know about that project were the editors who had access to the master work-in-progress spreadsheet that tracked all reporters' activities. Plus, no one is really interested in public housing. Not even the people who live there.

Tina had obviously dispatched her little puppy dog to spy on me. The only question was whether he knew he was a spy or if he was just an unwitting pawn. One way to find out.

"Geoff, did Tina tell you to call me?"

"N-no," he said, faltering slightly. "I'm just . . . really interest . . . interested in public housing and . . . the issues that go along with them."

Okay. I could play that game. I felt a wicked smile spread across my face. *Ruthie,* I thought, *meet my wild goose. Have fun chasing it.*

"Well, in that case, you have great timing," I said. "I could really use your help with something."

"Awesome!"

"You got a notepad out? You should be writing this down."

"Absolutely."

"Good. Okay, first I need you to get some food coloring."

"Food coloring. Will do."

"Wait, it's not that easy. It has to be organic food coloring. Gluten-free, of course. Vegan, if possible. If you get the regular stuff, the hydrocarbons just mess up everything. You might have to go to one of those all-natural food stores, and they don't have any of those in Newark. Millburn or Montclair might have one. Be persistent. It's important."

"O-okay," he said.

"Then you need to get some pregnancy tests."

"Pregnancy tests?"

"I'll explain it in a second. Just write it down. Get some pregnancy tests. At least a dozen of them — we'll need more, but that should get us started. Get First Response or EPT. Don't mess with the store brands. We need reliability here. Pretend your girlfriend missed her period and you really have to know."

"All right. What next?"

"Well, there's a group of Newark Housing Authority town houses on Eighteenth Avenue that are brand-new, just occupied," I said, giving him a range of addresses. "We're hearing reports that the contractor in charge of the project never connected the toilets to the main sewer line. You know what it looks like when you try to flush a toilet that doesn't drain to the sewer?"

"I would imagine it's pretty gross."

"Yeah, but not at first. There's a lot of pipe to go through before you get to the sewer, so it doesn't back up right away. It might take a month before that happens. There's only one way to test."

"Okay, how's that?"

"That's where the food coloring comes in. I want you to knock on every door on the block and tell the residents you need to test their toilet. Put a few drops of food coloring in the toilet. Then ask them to flush it for you. It's important the residents flush it. It makes them feel involved in the process, you know?"

"Right. Sure."

"Then you have to dip into the toilet and take a water sample. That's where the pregnancy test comes in. Not many people know this, but if you use regular toilet water on a pregnancy test, it will come back positive every time. *Every time.* I'll explain the science to you someday. It has to do with amino acids and naturally occurring lipids and, well, it gets pretty involved."

"Okay," he said. I could tell the kid's head was spinning. It should have been: I was talking total gibberish. But there was no way this twenty-two-year-old Boy Scout was going to know enough to call me on it.

"Anyhow, there's only one way that a pregnancy test will come back negative, and that's if there are traces of organic, gluten-free food coloring in the water. You follow me? And if there's organic, gluten-free food coloring, what does that mean?"

"Uh . . ." he said. Yep, I had definitely lost him.

"It means the pipes are backing up. So, again: if the pregnancy test on the toilet water comes back negative, some of the food coloring has bounced back at you. That means the pipe hasn't been connected to the sewer and we have a scandal on our hands, because you can bet the contractor charged the Newark Housing Authority for pipes that connected to the sewer."

"Oh, yeah. Yeah, you're right."

I grinned. Having spun him around on a verbal baseball bat, it was now time to push him in a random direction and watch him fall down.

"Now, if the toilet is backed up, I'm going to need a full social history on each of the family members," I said. "I want to know everything about them — where they came from, how they got here, what brand of toothpaste their grandfather used. I want everything. It should take a minimum of two hours, possibly four hours to get all the information you need. I want to be able to really tell these people's stories. Then, once you're done with the first house, you have to move onto the second. We need to get the whole street."

"Okay, got it," he said. "Are you going to meet me out there?"

"No. I've got other stuff to do. I figured this is simple enough for an intern to handle."

"Umm . . . uhh . . ." he said, because I knew his instructions from Tina were probably to follow me and report back to her. I also knew that the block in question had twenty-six new units on it. If he was diligent — and worked nights and weekends — he ought to be done in about three weeks.

Then I went in for the kill: "Now, whatever you do, don't tell Tina. She'll get really, *really* excited that you're doing this and she might not be able to contain herself. She might force us to rush this into the newspaper, and we don't want to rush it. We want all our ducks in a row on this one."

"R-right," he said.

"Okay. I want a progress update tomorrow afternoon," I said before I hung up. "I expect to hear from you in twenty-four hours."

Maybe then I'd let the kid off the hook. Maybe.

With Ruthie out of my way, I turned my at-

tention back to the Kipps conundrum —
and my knotted scorecard. I needed some
kind of tiebreaker, some unimpeachable
source that could give me a definitive
thumbs-up, thumbs-down.

The answer, I suspected, lay with the
Newark Police Internal Affairs. But that was
a safe I wouldn't be able to crack by myself.
The kind of officers who gravitated to
Internal Affairs are not your normal cops.
To want to join the police takes a certain
adherence to order and structure. To want
to police the police requires an altogether
different level of regimentation. It's not the
kind of makeup that makes one prone to
blabbing with reporters.

Still, I knew there was one person who
might have the keys to that particular
kingdom. And, unfortunately, that man was
our veteran cops reporter, Buster Hays.

I say "unfortunately" because Buster — in
addition to being cantankerous, curmudgeonly, and condescending — delighted in
lording this sort of thing over me. He came
to the *Eagle-Examiner* by way of da Bronx,
and he fancied himself the last common
man in a newsroom overrun with elites who
are overeducated and out of touch. And, in
that respect, he believed I was the personifi-
cation of everything that had gone wrong

with the newspaper

And yet? Though I'm sure we would never admit it, we shared a certain commonality of purpose and values, inasmuch as we both believed in getting the story right. So he seldom could resist helping me. Buster had a network of moles, informants, and gadflies — contained in four bulging Rolodexes that he steadfastly refused to computerize — that could shame the director of the CIA. He had developed them carefully, and through a reporting career that spanned parts of five decades, he had never burned a source. And you better believe his sources knew that.

His Rolodex was a kind of treasure that he had shared with me, albeit judiciously, throughout the years. And in the hopes he would again show his grudging generosity, I sat in my still-running car and dialed his desk.

"Hays."

"Buster, it's Carter."

"Whaddayuwant, Ivy?" I heard in response.

In Buster's world, Amherst was an Ivy League school. I had stopped trying to convince him otherwise.

"I'm working on a story about Darius Kipps —"

"The cop who swallowed a bullet? They finally put out a press release about that. I already shoveled something into the Slop. You're wasting your time. I don't think the dead tree is going to want more than six inches."

The dead tree is what even dinosaurs like Buster had taken to calling the physical newspaper.

"Yeah, I know, I'm just indulging my curiosity a little bit. I spent some time with the family this morning and learned some stuff that made Kipps seem like he wasn't the type to go killing himself. But then I also got a guy who says Kipps might have been tangled up with IA."

"I got a guy who said the same thing," Buster said, because, of course, I could never be allowed to have sources who knew stuff his sources hadn't already told him. "What about it?"

"Well, you got anyone in IA who might tell us what the deal was?"

"What's it matter at this point?"

"I don't know. I just feel like we're not getting anything close to the full story."

"Well, Ivy, maybe they never taught you this at your fancy college, but you know the I in IA stands for 'internal,' right? That means it's stuff they don't want to get out."

"So, what, you saying you don't have anyone?" I asked, because there was no better way to goad Buster into action than to challenge the depth or breadth of his law enforcement contacts.

"I'm not saying that. I'm saying it's going to take a little finesse, is all. I might have to call in a favor or two."

"Well, I'd appreciate it if —"

"So that means *you* have to do *me* a favor."

"Uh, okay, shoot," I said, fairly certain this was somehow going to involve picking up dry cleaning or mowing a lawn.

Instead, Buster said: "You're doing my Good Neighbors."

Good Neighbors was the name of a feature that ran six days a week in our community news section. As its name suggested, it was a puff piece about someone who had done a kindly deed, whether it was volunteering, rescuing a cat from a tree, or selling hair to Locks of Love. It was a lovely thing for the readers and for the person featured, I'm sure. But from a journalistic standpoint, it was about as useful as bunions.

Back before the economic tsunami that washed away all trace of newspapering as we once knew it, we had enough resources — okay, it's a handy word sometimes —

111

that we could farm out Good Neighbors to our network of stringers, mostly housewives who delighted in doing stories that made everyone feel warm and fuzzy. Then the stringer budget was unceremoniously eliminated. As a result, every reporter at the paper had been put on a rotation that required them to produce one Good Neighbors piece every six months or so. In terms of things I liked to do with my time, it ranked ahead of oral surgery but behind trips to the DMV.

"Oh, what the . . ." I moaned. "Are you serious?"

"As a heart attack."

"Jesus, Buster, I'm busy. I got this Kipps thing and a big thing about public housing that Tina wants by the end of the week. I don't have time to —"

"You want IA? You give me Good Neighbors."

"You . . . you wouldn't."

"Oh, I would. I am."

"Couldn't I just pick up your dry cleaning?"

"My clothes are wash-and-wear."

"Mow your lawn?"

"I live in a condo."

I thought about making some kind of argument about how, as colleagues working

112

for the same noble cause, we ought to help each other without expectation of reward. But I didn't need to be treated to the sound of Buster cackling in my ear.

"Couldn't you just . . . I don't know, do me a solid?"

"I'm gonna teach the Ivy boy a foreign language. Quid pro quo. It's Latin for 'quit your whining.' We got a deal or not?"

Not seeing any other way out, I just sighed and said, "Deal."

"It's due Wednesday morning," Buster said. "Don't make me wait."

The sun was getting low in the sky by this point, which meant it was high time to get off the streets. Like Officer Hightower said, the only white people who came into this part of Newark after dark were there to buy drugs. For someone of my pallor, sitting alone in a car on Irvine Turner Boulevard was an invitation to dealers to approach the window with that innocent-but-loaded question, "You looking?"

And I wasn't. So I went back to the newsroom, which was nearing that familiar peak in its daily intensity level. For as much as things had changed in the world of news-papering — with the de-emphasis of the dead tree product and the movement to put more online faster than ever before — some things were the same as they had been a generation ago. Six o'clock is still a busy time. Nonbreaking stories are due, and reporters who have otherwise been procrastinating all day finally get serious about their tasks.

I knew, with a Good Neighbors now on my plate, I should probably join them. But having mentally tabled that until the morning, I sauntered back to the library — or the "Info Palace" as the librarians liked to call it — where I knew I could find Kira O'Brien, my newly discovered romantic interest.

Kira was twenty-eight, a fairly recent graduate of Rutgers' Master of Library Studies program. In some ways, she's textbook librarian, at least at work. She dresses like a Young Republican, keeps mostly to herself, and has a bookish air about her — all of which belies the fact that the moment she leaves the office, she's basically insane.

Our relationship began at a house party being hosted by a mutual friend from the newspaper. It was late and we were somewhere between a little and a lot drunk. She was dressed like she had come from either a comic book convention or a sci-fi/fantasy convention. (I get them all confused, I just know each seems to involve women in skimpy clothing being leered at by nerds.) I went over to her to make some kind of clever comment about her hair, which had been dyed blue and purple.

We ended up having a lovely chat. And I noticed, to my surprise, she had a tongue piercing, which she never wore at the office. So — and this was, clearly, the booze talking — I asked her if she had anything else pierced. She hauled me into a bedroom and showed me. Before very long, the demonstration became rather aerobic in nature.

And that, more or less, was the basis of our relationship so far. We went places (often with her in costume). We got drunk with her friends (because hers were more interesting than mine). And then we did our aerobics (oftentimes in unconventional and/or public places). It was an arrangement that had allowed me to cross a number of items off my bucket list, some of which — like getting intimate with Princess Leia in an elevator — I didn't even know were on there in the first place.

It was unclear if she was going to be a girl I could take home to Mother, or if we would even last that long. But she was feisty and fun, and we had dynamite chemistry. I have come to recognize that, between my sensible car, bland wardrobe, boring hairstyle, and the other totally uninteresting aspects of my life, I need a little crazy to balance things out. And that's what Kira has been for me lately. My quota of crazy.

"Hey, what's going on?" I said.

She looked up at me and smiled. Kira is small, dark-haired, and dangerously cute — dangerous because she knows just how cute she is. She has blue eyes that manage to be sweet and mischievous at the same time. Plus, what man can resist the naughty librarian?

"Hey," she said, "want to go to a party in a bit?"

"A party . . . tonight? It's a Monday."

"What, you not allowed to go out on school nights?" she taunted.

"No, I just . . . okay. A party. On a Monday."

She cast her eyes left and right, tilted toward me, and whispered, "It's an absinthe party."

"What's an absinthe party?" I whispered back.

"I don't know, actually," she said, still hushed. "And I don't know why we're whispering about it." She returned to regular volume: "I guess it's just a party where we all sit around and drink absinthe."

"Hasn't absinthe been shown to cause mental illness?"

"I don't know. Hopefully, yes."

"Uh, okay, sounds like a blast."

"I'm done here at nine," she said. "We can go over together. Now go away. I have work to do."

Following orders, I walked back to my corner of the newsroom, passing the All-Slop News Desk along the way. It was actually a collection of desks, of course, with a half-dozen small televisions coming down from the ceiling in the middle. The monitors are equipped to show both Internet and television, allowing us to monitor our competition across a variety of media simultaneously.

This time I was surprised to see one of the televisions contained an image of the Reverend Doctor Alvin LeRioux, all three-hundred-plus sweat-mopping pounds of him.

But it wasn't one of his commercials. It looked like he was just beginning . . . a press conference? He was standing on the steps of Redeemer Love Christian Church in front of a bank of microphones. All the local television channels had obviously been invited. The agent-of-Satan local newspaper had not been.

"Oh, what the hell is *he* doing?" I asked no one in particular.

A few of the reporters chained to the All-Slop looked up at me, then reburied their heads in their laptops. We were getting the feed from the local twenty-four-hour news station, which always cut into press conferences on the early side, so it hadn't quite started yet. But it was clearly about to. The camera was tight on Pastor Al, who was gesturing for someone to join him at the podium. Then the camera panned out slightly to capture Mimi Kipps, dressed in her finest suit, with her chin held defiantly high, coming to her minister's side.

"Now what the hell is *she* doing?" I asked, but again no one paid attention to me.

I grabbed the appropriate remote control and turned up the volume just as the festivities began.

"Thank you for coming," Pastor Al boomed in his best basso profundo. "I have gathered you here to discuss the death of one of our community heroes, Detective Darius Kipps of the Newark Police Department."

Wait, what happened to "private moments" and sharing words in confidence and not publicizing tragedy? I guess all that went out the window when the good Reverend Doctor realized he could get himself some face time out of this. He had timed the press conference perfectly to be able to get sound bites on all the six o'clock news programs — and I'm sure they would be recycling it at ten and eleven as well.

"The Newark Police Department has put out a press release, indicating the death of Detective Darius Kipps was due to a self-inflicted gunshot wound," the pastor said, then he brought down the hammer:

"The proud family of Detective Kipps disputes this finding. We are calling on the Essex County Prosecutor's Office and the Essex County Medical Examiner's Office to recognize its conflict of interest and step aside in this matter. We would like the attorney general of the State of New Jersey to perform an independent investigation into the cause of death."

In the State of New Jersey, buying a gun can be a tedious process. Buying a whole lot of guns is not legally possible.

It was this basic fact that helped Red Dot Enterprises to thrive.

New Jersey is one of just six states that does not have a version of the Second Amendment — guaranteeing the right to bear arms — in its state constitution. It has outright bans on any weapon that chambers more than fifteen bullets, and either restrictions or bans on a variety of other weapons, including semiautomatic guns.

Then there's the paperwork. Would-be gun buyers must first acquire a Firearms Purchaser Identification Card from their local police department. The application fee is only five dollars, but it requires fingerprinting, which costs an additional sixty. Processing of the form takes a minimum of thirty days, though it can sometimes take longer, depending on how rushed the municipality feels. And not many of them feel rushed.

Felons are, of course, denied, as per federal law. But New Jersey codicils restrict gun ownership further. Anyone who has committed a crime that could have required them to spend six months or more in jail — whether or not they actually served the time — are banned from buying a gun. So are people convicted of crimes involving domestic violence. Other grounds for denial include treatment for mental illness, juvenile delinquency, alcoholism, narcotics addiction, or physical defects. Police chiefs or their surrogates are expected to conduct an interview and check references, and are given broad authority to reject applications.

But that's only the first step. Holders of a valid Firearms Purchaser Identification Card must then obtain a separate Permit to Purchase a Handgun for each individual gun they wish to buy. That requires filling out another form with the local police — with another minimum thirty-day wait and another thorough background check — and can again require fingerprinting, though the police chief has the discretion to waive that requirement if fingerprints already exist on file and valid identification is presented.

Once a person has obtained both permits,

the latter of which is only good for ninety days, they may then purchase a single handgun from a licensed dealer. If they can find one. The onerous nature of the state's gun laws pushed many dealers out of business decades ago. In most of the state's cities — including Newark and Camden, its most violent municipalities — there are no retail outlets that sell guns.

The result of all this regulation means that, each year, at least three out of every four guns used to commit a crime in New Jersey come from outside the state. And those are just the guns that are traceable. According to the Bureau of Alcohol, Tobacco, Firearms and Explosives, the origin of roughly half the guns recovered by law enforcement in New Jersey cannot be determined. The record-keeping is either incomplete or nonexistent; or the guns' serial numbers have been obliterated. It is widely assumed these guns come from states whose laws allow guns to be acquired more easily.

Indeed, New Jersey's laws — enacted in response to the epidemic of gun violence that has plagued its cities for decades — have had the unintended consequence of proving that old NRA bumper sticker: *when you outlaw guns, only outlaws will have guns.*

If anything, Red Dot Enterprises hoped New

Jersey's gun control laws would get tougher. It would mean even less competition.

CHAPTER 3

The anointed man of God prattled on for a while about Jesus, Lady Justice, heroism, and other topics on which he felt he could speak with some authority. There were a lot of pretty words and some fine elocution, though anyone listening carefully would have heard that he wasn't offering any real information. To distill it to one sentence: the family of Darius Kipps didn't know much, just that they weren't buying the official version they were being sold.

Midway through the sermon, I saw Tina Thompson leave her roost and scurry three doors down to the corner office, where Harold Brodie presided. I wanted to alert her to what was happening, but she was heading in the wrong direction and I didn't want to miss anything on the off chance the good reverend said something useful.

He didn't, of course. But once he got himself wound down, he invited Mrs. Kipps to the podium. Next to him, she looked small, and she was partially obscured by the microphones, which had been set at the right height for a six-foot-six minister, not his five-foot-five parishioner. She was gripping a folded piece of paper, from which she read:

"Darius Kipps was a proud father, a caring husband, and a dedicated police officer. Under no circumstance would he take his own life. We are calling for this investigation in the hopes that the truth will come out."

She stepped away from the podium, with nothing more to say. And, of course, the TV people didn't need anything else: properly edited, she had just given them the perfect ten-second sound bite. She even punched the words "the truth" to give it the necessary bit of drama.

Shortly after she finished, the all-news station cut back to the studio, so I never got to see if there was anything more to the performance. Then again, I doubted that any of the questions and answers that followed — if there even were any — would have elucidated much. The Kipps family was making a big, public stink. That was the only takeaway that mattered.

I was still holding the remote control in my hand, figuring out what to do about any of this, when Tina emerged from Brodie's office and walked straight for me.

"Brodie just saw that press conference and he's decided we need to go after this, guns blazing," she said. "I guess he feels like he owes it to this minister guy after the rough ride we gave him a little while back. You got enough stuff to put together something by maybe eight, eight thirty? Lead with the family calling for the investigation, get the AG's office comment, then pad it out with all that touchy-feely stuff about him and the G.I. Joe dolls."

I couldn't help myself. I made a display of walking around her, bending down and pointed toward her behind.

"Oh, hey, look at that!" I exclaimed.

"What?" she said, trying to look back at what I was doing.

"I think there are some monkeys flying out of your ass."

She stuck her hands on her hips and looked in another direction.

"I just don't know if I want to *waste* my time on a *nonstory* like this," I said.

As she sighed, I continued: "I have copy due on something else by the end of the week, and the editor, let me tell you, she won't accept any excuses for it not being done because she's *never* wrong."

I stopped for a moment just to make sure, you know, we were still having fun with this. And I think we were.

Or maybe it was just that I was having enough fun for two because she finally said, "Are you finished?"

"Let me think about it," I said, paused for five seconds, then added, "Yes, I think I am."

"Great. Then please get to work. Brodie has a massive, throbbing woodie for this" — it was *Eagle-Examiner* tradition that Brodie's interest in stories was often described in penis metaphors — "and he's even talking about splashing it out front. He's going to stick around to make sure it's something he likes. So don't dawdle."

"Ja, mein Führer," I said.

I returned to my desk, glancing up at the clock on the way: 5:48. After hours.

Fortunately, the AG's spokesman was a former *Eagle-Examiner* reporter. This was one of the few benefits of all the buyouts, layoffs, and other staff reductions that had ravaged our numbers through the years: many of the high-level public relations people in the state were former colleagues, having switched from covering the news to slanting it. Ben Hilfiker had left us a few years ago after a long and distinguished stint

127

doing stories about the attorney general's office and the state police, so I had his cell phone number programmed in mine.

"Uh-oh," he said, "the state's largest newspaper is calling. It must be very, very important."

"Yeah, yeah. I know a lazy government bureaucrat like yourself probably left the office two hours ago, but you think you can give me a comment on something?"

"I wish I left two hours ago. I'm still here. I tell you, I can't speak for the rest of Trenton, but there are still a lot of lights on in this place right now."

I told him to save the spin for someone else, then enlightened him about the LeRioux-Kipps press conference — which, as I suspected, he hadn't seen. He grumbled a few unmentionable words about how this better not screw up his date with a Devils game and a beer, then said, "Okay, let me check with my boss. I'm guessing you'll need this for first edition?"

"Yep, Brodie wants copy by eight. That going to be a problem?"

With any other flak, I would have said seven thirty. That was the downside of dealing with a Ben Hilfiker: he knew our deadlines.

"No, that should be okay. He's out of

pocket right now, but I think he's having dinner with Mrs. Attorney General later on. As long as I get him before his second martini, I should have something for you."

I thanked him and got to work. I would be surprised if the AG wouldn't at least pay lipservice to looking into it. The attorney general of the State of New Jersey is not an elected official. He serves at the pleasure of the governor. That might seem to make the position less political, but, if anything, it was more. An elected AG at least knew he had four years to do his job before he faced the voters. An appointed one could get bounced at any time.

And in this case, I knew that Pastor Al — whose eight thousand worshippers included a lot of old ladies who voted as religiously as they attended church — had stumped for the governor the last election. The AG would know that, too. Mimi Kipps had chosen her friends wisely.

Then again, politics cut all ways. The mayor of Newark was a Democrat, like the governor. And if Newark's police director put in a phone call to the mayor, who put in a phone call to the governor? Well, it could complicate matters.

I left a blank spot in the story for the AG's comment, then put in a perfunctory call to the Newark Police Department. Unsurprisingly, the spokesman on duty told me the department was standing by its statement that "Evidence gathered at the scene supports a preliminary determination that Detective Sergeant Darius Kipps died of a self-inflicted gunshot wound."

The next two hours fled by as they often do when you suddenly find yourself writing a thousand words on deadline. I was nearing the end when Hilfiker called back.

"Hey, got anything for me?" I asked.

"Yeah, you ready?"

"Go."

He read: "The attorney general's office is aware of the request for an independent investigation into the circumstances surrounding the death of Detective Darius Kipps. We hope to make a determination within the next twenty-four to forty-eight hours as to whether such an investigation would be appropriate."

I waited for the rest of it, but there was nothing more coming. "So in other words he's waiting to see which way the wind is blowing?"

"More like how hard it's blowing. But you get the idea."

"I was hoping for something a little more

definitive. You sure that's the best you can do?"

"I got him midway through his second martini," Hilfiker said. "You're lucky I got anything at all."

It took another half hour to finish the story, and Tina was doing what I call "the semi-hover" all the while. Basically, she didn't want to make it seem like she was cruising over my shoulder. But she also seemed to be walking in my part of the newsroom more than she normally might.

I hit the Send button at 8:28, gave Tina a thumbs-up, then stretched my legs, doing a brief stroll just to get my circulation back. I was starving but stayed away from the break room. The thought of foraging dinner from the vending machines was too depressing. There had been too many vended meals in my past. Maybe I could convince Kira to grab a bite before we started sucking down absinthe. No reason she wouldn't — the girl weighed ninety-eight pounds but ate like she had a tapeworm.

When I returned to my desk, I placed a call to Mimi Kipps, just to get the back-story on how Mr. Privacy, Pastor Al, talked her into a press conference. Her phone went straight to voice mail and I didn't leave a message. My morning had given me enough quotes from Mimi and besides, if Brodie was as amorous toward this story as Tina suggested, there would be more time to talk to Mrs. Kipps in the coming days. Sometimes you have to avoid wearing out a source.

Mostly because I had time to kill, I started halfheartedly working some digital databases for more background on Darius Kipps — as if finding out he was a registered Democrat was going to make a large difference in my understanding of the man. I still had my head buried in my laptop screen twenty minutes later when Tina approached.

"Hey, nice job," she said. "Brodie glanced at it on his way out and said it was fine. But you mind sticking around in case the desk has any issues?"

"Yeah, actually I do mind. Can't they just call me?"

"What, you have a hot date or something?"

I shrugged. This is where my relationship with Tina was altogether too complicated — moral of story: never get involved with a woman who might end up being your boss — and I thought about keeping my mouth shut. Then again, having started work at the ungodly hour of 8:38, I felt the *Eagle-Examiner* had gotten enough of my time for one day.

"Yeah, maybe I do," I said.

"Oh, what, with that mousy little thing in the library? What's her name, anyway? Minnie? Maisy?"

Tina knew Kira's name, of course. She was obviously trying to get a rise out of me, and I wasn't going to take the bait. Don't engage, don't engage, don't engage . . .

"You get her to go out with you by offering a wedge of cheese or something?" Tina asked. "You know, peanut butter works better. Or, wait, you're using those little glue traps, aren't you? Very humane of you."

I kept my jaw clenched. She kept prodding: "Just to warn you, some Irish women don't age well. I'm sure she looks fine now, but by the time she's forty, she'll have more wrinkles than a linen suit."

Don't engage, don't engage, don't engage . . .

"What do you see in her, anyway?" Tina asked.

Unable to hold myself in check any longer, I fired back, "I see someone who doesn't try to screw with my head all the time and is actually interested in a normal, steady relationship. I see someone who doesn't have a million ridiculous issues about commitment. I see someone who isn't afraid to fall in love just because she may have failed at it in the past."

Tina had been smiling — albeit maliciously — when she was making her mouse jokes. But now the smile had been replaced by this hard mask.

"Great," she snarled. "Normal. Committed. Have fun with that, big guy. Does she make you turn the lights out during sex? Keep her eyes closed the whole time?"

I was going for blood now: "Actually, we mostly do it in public places. She likes it when people watch. She says it makes the orgasms better. Wanna bring your pom-poms sometime? Cheer us on?"

"If you're involved? I think I'd rather watch bowling on TV. More action."

I inhaled to respond — something about how the pins probably stood a better chance of getting knocked up than her — then stopped myself. I just couldn't believe the venom that was coming out of my mouth. Why was I trying to hurt her? For whatever might have happened between Tina and I — and it had been too stunted and strained to ever really find out what it was — we were still friends, or something, at one point. We had cared about each other, or at least I thought we did.

Now here we were, going after each other

like we were on opposite sides of the table in a divorce lawyer's office, trying to singe each other's skin with our words.

She was standing there, braced, like she was waiting for the next salvo. Instead, I said, "Tina, what the hell? Can't we at least be civil to each other?"

"Relax. I'm just busting your chops. Don't take it so seriously. There's no need to get all girly on me."

"Ah, so you're not at all upset that I started dating Kira? Because, you know, the way you've been acting around me lately I would beg to differ."

"What are you talking about?" she said, the mask still in place. "Because I asked you to stay late tonight rather than . . . whatever you were going to do?"

"Tina, we barely talk anymore . . ."

"You think I really care that much what you do after work? Don't flatter yourself. Look, you're a damn good reporter — my best, if you have to know. That's the only thing that matters to me. Whatever chick you're bouncing on your balls is none of my business."

"You're . . . you're really going to play that game?"

"It's no game, stud," she said. "Anyhow, since you're not sticking around, I have to.

Someone has to make sure the desk doesn't massacre this thing. Have a nice night. Just keep your cell on, okay?"

She walked away without bothering to hear my answer.

I was in such a foul mood about Tina, I forgot all about dinner — which would prove to be something of a mistake — and instead talked Kira into leaving five minutes early. It was either that or lure her into making out in Tina's office. And I figured that would just make things worse.

We got in my Malibu and started driving toward an address just off University Avenue. I half expected she might have changed into after-work garb — Kira seemed to celebrate Halloween roughly a hundred times a year — but she was still in the dark pink sweater set she had worn to work.

"So tell me about this party we're going to," I said as I maneuvered out of the parking garage.

"Well, it's hosted by this guy named Powell."

"Powell? Is that his first name or his last name?"

"Actually, his name is Paul," Kira said. "But he prefers people pronounce it Powell.

Like he's foreign. He's really from Mahwah. I guess he thinks it gives him mystique."

"Ah, mystique."

"Yeah, he's a bit of a character."

"You don't say."

"Wait until you meet him," she said, lightly tracing the bones of my right hand with her fingers. "He is getting a Ph.D. in what he calls 'Death Studies.' "

"I didn't realize Rutgers-Newark offered courses in Death Studies."

"They didn't until Powell came along. I'm not sure how he talked them into it. He's basically just making it up as he goes along. He takes courses from the School of Criminal Justice, the Law School, even the Nursing School."

"The *nursing* school has a course on death?"

"Oh, I have no idea. I met him because he was taking a library sciences class at the New Brunswick campus. I think maybe he just likes being a student."

"I'm sure his parents love that," I said.

"I think they have enough money that it doesn't really matter."

"Mmm," I said, and left it at that. A guy with my background couldn't exactly make a wisecrack about the Lucky Sperm Club simply because I didn't have a trust fund waiting for me.

We drove until I pulled up in front of a five- or six-story industrial-looking building badly in need of a paint job. A hundred years ago it might have been some kind of flourishing factory. But now it was dark and appeared to be abandoned.

"What is this place?" I asked.

"Oh, it's the coolest thing. It's this loft. I think the lower floors are still being renovated by someone who is going to turn it into condos or something. But they started with the top floor and that's where Powell lives."

An artist's loft. In Newark. Could trendy, overpriced boutiques be far behind?

We rode a creaky elevator up to the top floor, which, sure enough, looked like it had been transplanted from Greenwich Village, with high ceilings, hardwood floors, and exposed brick. There were no lights on, just votive candles set in the broad windowsills. Most of the furnishings — what little I could detect in the dark — were milk crates that had been creatively stacked together. I detected a few life-forms sprawled on pillows and blankets on the floor. It was all very bohemian.

"Welcome," I heard someone say. It was

the voice of a man trying to sound like Vincent Price but failing.

"Hi, Powell!" Kira chirped out.

A young man with perfectly mussed dark brown hair and black eyeliner approached and kissed Kira on the cheek. He was about my height but scrawny and ghostly pale, perhaps with the aid of foundation makeup. He wore skinny black jeans and a tight black T-shirt and also had a variety of piercings on his face and ears. His neck and arms were festooned with tattoos, not that I could discern the significance of any of them. He reached out to shake my hand, and I saw he was wearing black nail polish. It was a look that used to be called goth. Now maybe it's called emo. My parent's generation would have just called him a freak.

But I'm open-minded enough to give anyone a try. And, hey, freaks are fun.

"I'm Powell," he said.

"Powell, this is Carter, he works at the paper with me," Kira said.

I couldn't help myself: "Powell. What an unusual name. Spell it for me."

Kira stuck an elbow in my side as he said, "P-A-U-L."

"Isn't that . . . Paul?" I asked innocently.

"Yes, but it's pronounced Powell."

"How exotic," I said. And I knew —

because I was a few years older than him and dressed like one of those squares who didn't understand his music — he couldn't tell that I was messing with him.

"Come in," he said. "Can I offer you something to drink? We have beer and wine or, if you're not afraid, we also have what the French would call *la fée verte* — the green fairy."

If I'm not afraid? I thought. I felt like telling skinny jeans boy that I trafficked in a part of Newark that was far more frightening than anything doled out by some hundred-and-forty-five-pound guy who wore eyeliner. But that might get our relationship off to a bad start. So I just said: "Sure. I'll try some of your poison."

"Kira?"

"Of course!" she said.

Paul/Powell led us over to a stack of milk crates that was serving as a bar. From one of the crates, he extracted a bottle of mint green liquid that was either absinthe or mouthwash. From another crate, he removed two glasses, each of which had a bubblelike bulge toward the bottom, which he filled with the liquid. Then he produced a flat utensil that reminded me of a pie cutter — albeit with holes in it — a jar with cubes of sugar, a lighter, and a bottle of

Dasani water.

He did this all with great flair — Paul/Powell was clearly one for the dramatic — then, in that Vincent Price voice, announced, "You might want to stand back."

He positioned the pie cutter over one of the glasses, placed a sugar cube on top of it, then sparked the lighter. The sugar must have been treated with something because it caught fire, much to the delight of Kira, who started clapping. He let it burn for a moment or two, then dumped it into the glass — which also went aflame.

He quickly doused the flame with a shot of Dasani water, then handed it to Kira. "Ladies first," he said, before performing the same magic trick on my drink.

As he handed me the concoction, he said, "You know, legend has it this is what van Gogh was drinking when he cut off his ear."

"I'll try to stay away from sharp objects," I said, accepting it. *"Prost."*

I downed a large gulp. It tasted kind of like burnt licorice. But all things considered, it went down pretty smoothly. So did the second one. Kira and I had joined the party, which included maybe ten other people arrayed on pillows. All of them were younger than me, much more casually dressed, and talked to me like I was their father. In truth,

it didn't bother me because without anything in my stomach, the alcohol in the
absinthe had temporarily muddied most of
the synapses in my brain.

Sometime during the third drink, I decided that Paul/Powell — for as ridiculous
as he looked, talked, and acted — was actually a pretty good guy, full of useful information. He told me, for example, that of all
the currently accepted methods of state-
sponsored execution, the firing squad was
actually considered the most humane.
("They're dead before they hit the ground,"
he said cheerily.)

I wound up telling him about Darius
Kipps and how I had my suspicion whether
he had really killed himself. At the end of it,
he said, "Well, you want to go have a look?"

"A look at what?"

"At this dude."

"What the hell are you talking about?"

"I have a key," he said.

"To what?"

"To the Essex County Medical Examiner's
Office."

As the party died down and the other guests
went home, Paul/Powell explained how this
had come to be. His "Death Studies" Ph.D.
was, technically, in the School of Arts and

Sciences, but it was multidisciplinary, looking at death through a variety of lenses, from social to financial to spiritual to literary. As such, it involved a lot of external study and cooperative learning experiences — including an internship at the Essex County Medical Examiner's Office.

"It's a perfect place to study the physical manifestation of the expiratory process at its end stage," he informed me.

"You mean, it's a good place to see dead people?" I translated.

"Exactly!" he said, gleefully.

Apparently, Paul/Powell liked hanging out with stiffs so much that he didn't get enough of it during the day. So he sometimes snuck in late at night to spend time with them. He called it research. I called it creepy. Then again, I wasn't the guy with "D" "E" "A" "T" and "H" tattooed onto the fingers of my left hand.

He wasn't supposed to have a key, of course — they don't just hand those out to interns. He explained that he and a janitor had made a swap: a copy of a key in exchange for some embalming fluid he had swiped from a funeral home. Believe me, this is *not* something I've experienced personally, but apparently when you dip a marijuana cigarette in embalming fluid, it gives it certain psychotic effects.

It also means you're smoking chemicals that are only put in dead people for a very good reason. But, hey, to each his own.

So Paul/Powell had a key to the Essex County Medical Examiner's Office. It was all very shady and nefarious, and I'm sure had I been remotely sober, I could have come out with dozens of very good reasons why a responsible reporter for the state's largest newspaper should not take advantage of it.

Except, of course, I had a head full of absinthe; and I had wild-child Kira goading me on, because to her it seemed like a fine adventure; and, well, to be honest, it was actually Paul/Powell who sealed the deal when he taunted, "Yeah, man, we can go see him. Unless you're, you know, afraid of corpses at night."

So, really, I had no choice. We waited to shove off until midnight, when the place would be empty. According to Paul/Powell, the midnight to 8:00 A.M. security detail — which he, naturally, referred to as "the graveyard shift" — had been axed in some recent budget cuts. In theory, the Essex County Police were supposed to have added the office to their patrol. But Paul/Powell said he had never seen them.

I drove — yet another stupid decision, but by that point I was actually the least drunk of the three of us. We were laughing the whole way, though for the life of me I can't remember about what. Though I do seem to recall Kira making an off-hand comment about how she always wanted to have sex in a morgue, and I had to resist the urge to drive faster.

I managed to get us in one piece to the Essex County Medical Examiner's Office, a brick building at the corner of Norfolk Street and South Orange Avenue.

Paul/Powell instructed me to park in the employee lot, which I balked at. Then he explained that's how he always did it, and I suppose illegal parking was chump change compared with the variety of crimes I was about to commit.

I felt incredibly conspicuous as we spilled out of the Malibu: three stumbling, giggling white kids in a Newark parking lot late at night. We went around to an unlit back door, where Paul/Powell seemed to know what he was doing. He slipped his key in the door in a practiced manner and turned it easily.

"I think if you tried the front one, the alarm would go off," our tour guide explained. "This one isn't wired, for whatever

145

reason."

With Paul/Powell in the lead, we went through a series of antiseptic corridors and then down some stairs until we reached the morgue, which was, appropriately enough, in the basement. He went through the door into a room that felt colder than the others. When he flipped on a light, I saw the bank of large, stainless steel drawers on the far side. They must have been refrigerated. Did each of them have a body inside? Or was there still room at the inn? I didn't see any neon "No Vacancy" signs.

There were three stations in the middle — did you call them examining tables? chopping blocks? what? — all of which were, of course, empty at this time of day. But I could imagine that in a county like Essex — home to roughly a million people, at least a few of whom died each day under circumstances that required an autopsy — they could get fairly busy.

Paul/Powell had stopped at a clipboard that was hanging from the wall by a chain and he was flipping pages.

"You said his name was Kipps, right?"

"Yeah," I said, still trying to take everything in.

Kira had hooked her arm in mine and was pressed against me, perhaps to get warm, perhaps because this whole thing was starting to get more than a little spooky. Maybe it was the cold or the brightness of the lights — or, you know, all the dead people — but I was definitely feeling much more sober than I had been just moments earlier. No one was giggling or talking about sex anymore.

Paul/Powell let the clipboard drop and walked calmly over to one of the drawers. Kira and I shuffled after him, both of us acting like we were trying not to touch anything. I've heard dead bodies are, in some ways, much more hygienic than live ones — it's not like they can sneeze on you. But still, I didn't feel like going around licking stuff.

"You ready?" Paul/Powell asked, his "D-E-A-T-H" fingers on one of the handles.

I nodded.

"Okay," he said. "Here goes."

A photographer buddy of mine who did a lot of work in war zones once gave me some valuable advice when it came to the dead: look at their bodies all you want; just don't look at the faces. The bodies you can forget. The faces, he said, stay with you forever.

So I tried to keep my eyes fixed on the drawer as the long tray containing Darius

Kipps slid toward me. Only when it was fully extended did I let myself glance at him, and even then I looked only at his chest. It had a long, slightly uneven scar running up the middle of it. He had obviously already been autopsied, and whoever stapled him back together hadn't been tremendously concerned about aesthetics.

Paul/Powell must have noticed me averting my gaze because he began lecturing.

"Death is very natural, you know," he intoned, again going Vincent Price on us. "In some ways, it's the most natural thing that can happen to an animal. Yet there remains an irrational fear of death. You can touch him if you want. I really believe the dead like to be touched."

Out of the corner of my eye, I saw he was running his hand along the corpse's jawbone. I wouldn't have stroked Darius Kipps's cheek when it was part of a warm, pliant human being. Why the hell would I want to do it now that it was cold and stiff?

"The transformation to death — I call it the change from lucidity to morbidity — is one of the better understood biological processes, something that has been a subject of fascination for humankind throughout recorded history," Paul/Powell continued. "Still, with fascination has always come fear.

148

A study by Wickstrom and Zhuang out of Berkeley found that —"

It was Kira, who had been silent ever since we entered the building, who interrupted: "Powell, would you shut the hell up?"

"Fine, fine," he said, returning to his normal voice. "Geez, I'm just talking."

"I know," she said. "But you're freaking me out. This is weird enough. Stop it."

I guess Kira was starting to come to her senses, too. And I was relieved she did. Paul/ Powell was freaking me out, too. Plus, I wanted to get us back on track.

"So why don't you tell me what you see here?" I said. "I really don't know how much I want to look. This death thing is your business."

"Yeah, although this particular part of the death industry isn't really my area of expertise," he said. "The people who do these autopsies are full-on MDs. They spend years studying this stuff. I just come to observe. They only called it an internship because my dad is a pretty big donor to the Democratic Party and, of course, the Democrats rule Essex County. So he, uh, you know, made a phone call . . ."

Ah, yes, politics in New Jersey — the money always comes attached with strings.

"Just do your best," I instructed.

"Well, okay, you saw somebody already cut this guy open, right?"

"Yeah."

"So that means they've already removed his internal organs. That's part of the autopsy. They weigh all the organs and then study them to see if they had anything to do with the death. In this guy's case, the cause of death was pretty obvious, right? But you learn all kinds of interesting things. I observed this one autopsy the other day where the guy died of cirrhosis, but he also had a major blockage in one of the arteries leading to the heart. Basically, if he hadn't drunk himself to death, he would have —"

"Powell!" Kira interrupted again.

"Sorry, sorry. I'm just into this stuff, you know?"

"Let's just try to stay focused," I said.

"Well, okay. He, uh . . . I'm not sure the perfect phraseology, but the back of his head is a big, bloody mess. You need me to get graphic?"

"No, that's okay," I said. "It's an exit wound. I get the point."

So Kipps had, in fact, been shot in the head. The only question now was whether it was self-inflicted. But how would I know? I guess if he fired the gun himself, there would be gunshot residue. But was that visible?

"Do you see any powder burns on his hands?" I asked.

"Nope," he said.

Then again, the story — and no one had contradicted it — was that Kipps was found in a shower stall, with the water running. That might have washed off any powder. I was beginning to run out of ideas when Paul/Powell piped up.

"Well, this is sort of interesting," he said.

"What?"

"There are ligature marks on both of his wrists," he said. "Don't worry. You can take a look. It won't kill you."

Paul/Powell held up the arm on the far side of Kipps's body, and sure enough, the wrist had dark marks on it that were vivid even against his coffee-brown skin. The wrist on my side had similar wounds.

"These look like rope burns to me," Paul/Powell said. "It's almost like someone tied him to a post or a chair or something. It's obviously premortal. That's always a big distinction with these guys — pre- versus postmortal — because sometimes a body can get roughed up, especially if someone found it in a Dumpster or something. But these definitely happened while your guy was still alive. There was some bleeding and clotting on the parts that got rubbed really raw."

"Yeah, I see that."

"They're fresh, though. This is just a guess, but this looks like something that happened shortly before death. Within six hours, for sure."

Paul/Powell was on the move, heading down to the end of the tray. There was a sheet around the body's lower half — someone thought the dead cop should have some modesty — but Paul/Powell was lifting it out of the way and studying Kipps's feet.

"That's what I thought," he said. "Check out the ankles. He was tied to a chair for a while. And he didn't like it much."

I went down and inspected. There were bruises just above the ankle bone that looked like they could have come from a rope. These didn't break the skin. Maybe Kipps had been wearing pants or socks that cushioned the abrasiveness of the rope.

Whatever it was, something very strange had obviously happened to Darius Kipps in the hours before death, and it was now officially beyond making sense to me. As a reporter, I'm always telling stories. And I could tell a story where the detective, hav-

152

ing decided to permanently lower his body temperature, got plastered on bourbon and then blew his head off. I had a harder time telling a version of the story where he also spent some time tied to a chair, struggling against his bonds so hard they made him bleed.

It introduced another actor — or, rather, several of them — into the equation. There had to be one person to do the tying and at least one other person to convince Kipps not to move while the tying was being done, presumably by aiming a weapon at him.

And in any reasonable person's mind, it had to throw the Newark Police Department's press release about a self-inflicted gunshot wound into doubt. Serious doubt.

What's more, it opened up another gaping, open question in my mind: If Darius Kipps didn't kill himself, who did? And why?

I could tell Paul/Powell was of a mind to linger for a while, maybe visit with some of his other perished pals, but I have very strict rules about how many human remains I want to disturb in a day, and one is my limit.

Plus, Kira — now most assuredly out of the mood for love — was off in a corner by herself, taking occasional glances at a big biohazard container like maybe she wanted to make a deposit. I didn't know if she was squeamish around the dead or around the 120-proof spirits we had just been imbibing. Either way, it was time to start bringing the illegal portion of my day to a close.

"You see anything else interesting?" I asked.

Paul/Powell spent a little more time looking under the sheet (better him than me), then went back up to inspect the head wound some more (*definitely* better him than me), before finally announcing, "That's all I got for you."

"Would you have any way of knowing whether this guy was drunk when he was killed?"

"Well, they'll test for that as part of the tox screen."

"No, I mean right now."

Paul/Powell rested his hand on Kipps's shoulder — no, it hadn't gotten any less creepy — and pondered this for a moment. "Well, maybe if we compressed his chest and forced some air out of him, you could smell his breath."

"Ah, that's okay. I'll pass. It would be reported in the autopsy, right? The booze. The marks on the wrists and ankles. That would all be in there?"

"Yeah, definitely. Any kind of wound or scar, premortal, postmortal, it's all in there. And of course the toxicology reports would be there, too."

I knew that, of course. I was already thinking about ways to get what I had just learned on the record and in the newspaper. In this case, merely having observed it wasn't good enough — it would raise the question of how the reporter had been in a position to see it. Journalism Ethics 101: you can't commit a crime to get information.

The autopsy report was no good to me, either. Autopsies were not automatically public record. You could get them unsealed, but that involved making an argument to a judge that there was a compelling public need to view the information — a need that outweighed an individual family's right to privacy. And you could bet Essex County, the Newark Police Department, and probably even the Fraternal Order of Police would have lawyers fighting like mad to keep it sealed. It would take forever, cost a fortune, and we might not even win in the end.

No, I had to find another way.

I looked at Paul/Powell, who was drumming his "D-E-A-T-H" hand on the metal tray.

"Your phone have a camera by any chance?"

"Yeah, of course."

"Mind doing me a favor and taking a picture of his wrists and ankles and then texting them to me?"

"They'll take pictures as part of the autopsy. They'll be better quality than my cell phone."

"Yeah, but the nosy reporter won't be able to access them," I said.

"Ohhhh," he said, grinning.

As he set about his task, I congratulated myself on my small stroke of genius. My phone had a camera, too, but again that would have bumped into the problem of how I had gotten to the body in the first place. But that wasn't an issue if Paul/Powell, a sort-of employee of the county, sent me the photos as a kind of whistleblower. With Brodie's blessing, I could use them to anchor an explosive story about a police cover-up, with my angry family — and publicity-hungry minister — providing me all the needed outrage.

He sent the pictures one at a time, which meant the first was buzzing into my phone even as he was still taking the subsequent ones. They weren't great quality, but they didn't need to be. It's not like we were going to run photos of a dead cop's wrists in a family newspaper. We just needed to have them for verification.

Much to Paul/Powell's dismay and Kira's relief, I announced it was time to close up this little shop of horrors and head on home. We followed the same path out as we had going in, making a quick — and, hopefully, unobserved — dash across the parking lot toward the Malibu.

We rode back in silence, each of us with his own thoughts, and by the time I dropped off Paul/Powell at his loft/lair, Kira had fallen asleep in the front seat. Waking her and making her drive — still somewhat tipsy — back to Jersey City, where she lived, was out of the question. Then again, driving her there myself didn't seem like much of an option, either.

So I made the executive decision to take her back to my tidy two-bedroom home in scenic Bloomfield. If you've seen *The Sopranos,* then you've seen a certain depiction of Bloomfield — or at least what is represented as being Bloomfield — on your television screen. And there are certainly parts of town that are like that: a little urban, a little gritty, very Italian.

But there are also nice, leafy little neighborhoods, and my house — nestled in one of those neighborhoods — was a welcome sight when I pulled into the driveway. Kira didn't move when I turned off the car, so I went around to her side, unbuckled her belt, and lifted up all ninety-eight pounds of her. Having a girlfriend who is roughly half my weight has its advantages, especially when my beer muscles, courtesy of the absinthe, hadn't quite worn off.

She began stirring as I brought her into the house, smiling and pulling herself closer to me, enough that I could tell she at least knew where she was and who she was with. I brought her upstairs to my room and lowered her gently on top of my bed. Deadline, who was in his usual spot — sprawled in the precise, geometric middle of my comforter — hopped down and meowed indignantly at being disturbed, finishing his protest by walking out of the room.

I was enough of a gentleman that I was going to leave Kira there and spend the night on the couch when she murmured, "Aren't you going to help me get out of my clothes?"

I decided that would be gentlemanly, too.

The next morning, the Kipps story was

stripped across the top of A1. We didn't have a picture of the press conference — because we hadn't been invited — so the only photo that ran was a canned headshot of Reverend Alvin LeRioux on an inside page. But that did little to diminish the impact of the story. We had gone big with it, which — along with the television news treatment of it the night before — would mean all the radio stations would continue to stoke it this morning.

Which meant, because media tended to feed on itself, Brodie would be hungry for a follow-up. And while ordinarily that might cause me some angst as I worked through my Frosted Flakes, Tony the Tiger and I were feeling pretty relaxed. If all went well, I had all the follow-up I needed stored on my cell phone.

Kira had woken up with me and was walking around my kitchen in one of my T-shirts — and nothing else — which soon led to a demonstration of the sturdiness of my couch. But, eventually, the fun and games had to end. I showered, did my blind closet grab, and came out with charcoal pants/blue shirt/yellow tie. See? Works every time.

After making sure Deadline had enough food to sustain a rigorous day of napping, I drove us to the office. Kira, who didn't have to be at work until one o'clock, had plenty of time to head home and replenish herself for the day, maybe even take a nap.

But there was no rest for the wicked reporter. If the day was to end successfully — with me as the heroic journalist who had just delivered the big scoop — a number of things had to go my way. The first, and perhaps most important, was convincing the higher powers to let me use my (slightly ill-gotten) photos.

It is perhaps assumed, thanks to some of the less scrupulous practitioners out there, that newspapers simply run anything they can get their hands on. That is far from the case. Readers would be stunned if they knew the stuff we had that never made it into print — bombshells that we leave un-exploded simply because we don't think it's responsible to detonate them. We're especially cautious when it comes to unnamed sources. Anytime I use one, I need to have it okayed by multiple editors. And they're cautious when it comes to giving that permission. Anyone who'd like to under-stand why can Google "Janet Cooke Wash-ington Post."

As such, I knew having these pictures and being able to base a story on them were two separate issues. Paul/Powell hadn't been savvy enough — or sober enough — to tell me not to use his name. But I knew the kid would get fired faster than a bullet if I put his name in the paper. Hence, I needed clearance to use him unnamed.

I went straight upstairs to the newsroom, got the pictures off my cell phone, blew them up the best I could and made print-outs. Satisfied they would do the job, I took them into Tina Thompson's office. I tapped on the frame to her door but hadn't yet settled my butt into one of the two chairs in front of her desk when I was greeted with: "Uh-oh, Mickey and Minnie got busy last night!"

I thought about telling her we had actually gotten busy this morning, too, but instead took the high road: "I do not feel it necessary to dignify these spurious accusations with a response."

"You don't need to. I saw Minnie driving out of the parking garage wearing yesterday's clothes, singing, 'It's a small world after all.'"

"Funny, last night she was singing the *Hallelujah Chorus*," I said. "But I didn't come to talk music with you. Check these out."

I slid the photos at her. She spread them out, flinched when she saw the subject matter, then drew in for a closer look.

"What . . . what are these exactly?"

"Those are postmortem photos of Darius Kipps's arms and legs, taken late last night in the Essex County Medical Examiner's Office. I know the quality isn't superior, but let me help you out: they're rope burns. Someone tied Detective Kipps to a chair shortly before he made his exit from this world."

"Tied him to a chair? Holy crap. Do the police know about this?"

"I don't know how they couldn't know. Presumably, they saw the same dead Darius Kipps that I did."

"But if that's the case, how could they say he —" Tina began, then it dawned on her. "Holy crap."

"Yeah, that about sums things up."

"And if Kipps didn't kill himself, then —"

"Who did?" I completed her sentence. "I really don't have a clue. I figured I'd get this story in the paper before I worried about the rest of it."

"Do we . . . how did you . . . hang on, I'm calling Brodie," she said, picking up her phone and tapping four numbers. She waited for what sounded like two rings, then said: "Hey, it's Tina. Carter Ross has something you're going to want to see," she began, then told him about the photos. She finished with, "We'll be right down."

"I'll save you having to repeat yourself in explaining how you got this stuff," she said, and before I could slow her down, she was already out from behind her desk and on the way to see our executive editor.

Harold Brodie had inhabited the corner office in our newsroom so long there weren't many people around, besides perhaps Buster Hays, who remembered otherwise. He was a legend in the state of New Jersey and in the newspaper industry generally, a much-beloved patriarch.

In some ways, it was hard to take Brodie too seriously. He was now somewhere beyond seventy and he had this pleasant, grandfatherly manner about him, like he was going to offer you the maraschino cherry from his manhattan any moment. His high-pitched voice had gone raspy, as tends to happen to men of that age, and his wispy gray eyebrows were long enough to need braiding. A small man to begin with, he was now entering into the advanced stages of geriatric shrivel, such that I expected him to disappear altogether one of these years.

Still, for all that, something about Brodie scared the crap out of me. Hays had told me stories about him as a young editor that made my toes curl. And I had enough of my own experiences with his non-mellow side to know that he had the capacity to turn himself into a windshield — and me into a bug — at any time.

In truth, I had hoped that I could tell Tina the real story and then let *her* figure out what to tell Brodie. It wasn't so much we wanted to lie to the old man. It's just sometimes things needed to be, well, sanitized. Wasn't that what direct-line editors were supposed to do for you?

But there would be no time to disinfect anything now. He was going to get the whole, dirty, absinthe-swilling truth.

Brodie was playing classical music, as was often the case, but turned it down when we entered. Tina didn't even bother sitting down before handing him the photos. As we settled into the chairs in front of him, Brodie took his time studying the pictures, shuffling back and forth between them.

"So," he said, in his old man falsetto. "How did we come into possession of these?"

Brodie had directed the question at Tina, not even looking at me. Brodie is big into chain of command, to the point you'd think he had a military background. On most matters, he preferred talking to the editors who reported to him, not the lowly reporters. It wasn't unusual for Brodie to discuss things with his editor as if the reporter wasn't even in the room. I think that's part of the reason Brodie scared me: I almost never talked to the man.

"I actually haven't heard the story myself yet," Tina said, turning to me.

Brodie followed her gaze. Showtime. I cleared my throat and said, "They were sent to me by an intern in the Essex County Medical Examiner's Office."

"Not for attribution, I assume?"

"Correct," I said.

"And what is this person's name?"

Another thing reporters owed to the legacy of Janet Cooke: editors insisted on knowing the identity of the unnamed source. They were then bound by the same ethics as reporters not to reveal it. Of course, I didn't even *know* my source's last name. I'm sure Kira did. But it was too late to ask her. So I just said, "Paul Powell."

Whatever. We could sort it out later.

"And what do we think motivated Mr. Powell in sending this to us?" Brodie asked.

A lot of alcohol, I almost said. But that wasn't the answer he was looking for. Brodie just wanted to know whether Paul/Powell had some kind of axe to grind, which was always something we had to take into account when using unnamed sources.

"Well, he's a student, so I don't think he has any ulterior motive," I said. "He struck me as a kid who's just trying to do the right thing."

And besides, he had drunk enough absinthe to stone a horse.

"How do you know him?"

"Met him at a party last night. We got to talking. One thing led to another. He's a little bit of an odd duck — if you met him and saw his tattoos, you'd understand — but all these kids have tattoos these days. There's nothing he said or did that made me concerned about him. I think he was acting in good conscience."

"I see," Brodie said, his eyes again scanning the photos. "And how do we know for sure this is Darius Kipps?"

Here goes: "Because I saw it with my own eyes. I was with Paul late last night when he took these pictures."

Brodie raised his scraggly eyebrows but kept his mouth closed. It was Tina who blurted out, "You were *what?!?*"

"I was with him," I repeated.

"Carter, you can't go breaking into the Essex County Medical Examiner's Office!"

166

Tina moaned. "Jesus, why are you wasting our time with this? You know we can't use these. You better hope . . ."

"Hold on, hold on," I said. "We didn't break in. Paul is an employee. He told me he had a key and offered to take me in for a little show and tell. Look, I know it's a little shady, but we're not teaching Sunday School here. We're putting out a newspaper."

I decided to skip the backstory of how he had acquired the key. Tina and Brodie didn't need to be bogged down in such petty details. The fact is, while we were strictly concerned that our staff members didn't break the law in their reporting of a story, we were somewhat less concerned about that where our sources were involved.

"Okay, okay, I know," Tina said defensively. "I'm just trying to make sure our ass is covered here."

"There's no need to mention in print that I was there, obviously," I said. "We can just say the photos came from a county employee who didn't want to be named for fear of reprisal and that the photos have been independently verified as being authentic. All of which is true."

Brodie was watching us go back and forth without comment. He often let his underlings slug it out before he decided what to make of something. We were expected to make a good show of it. But, in this case, we were done.

"A tour of the morgue late at night, huh?" Brodie said, chuckling.

The old man leaned back, tented his fingers, and closed his eyes, his signal that he was ready to render a decision. In our shop, this was a celebrated pose known as the Brodie Think. Often imitated by staff members, though never perfectly duplicated, it made him look something like a praying mantis — albeit a praying mantis in need of a face-lift and eyebrow tweezing. He could go into this state for a minute or more, to the point when you could wonder if he had drifted off. It was unsettling, even when you knew to expect it.

This one seemed particularly lengthy, and at one point his breathing got so slow and steady I thought maybe he really *had* fallen asleep. But there was nothing to do except wait it out and hope for the best.

The fact was, I needed a win here. There were few things more agonizing for a reporter than knowing something — especially something as incendiary as this — and not being able to put it in the newspaper. And in this case it wasn't just my big scoop and

168

my interests as an ambitious reporter being served. It was a lot bigger than that.

It was Mimi Kipps's husband being thought of not as a suicidal coward but as a murder victim. It was a killer — or killers — being brought to justice. It was his children getting to know the truth about their father someday. It was the Newark Police Department's credibility, to say nothing of the Essex County Medical Examiner's Office. Maybe it would all come out eventually, if the Attorney General's Office did decide to conduct an independent investigation, but there was a chance it would bow to political pressure and take a pass. There was a lot on the line here.

Finally, the old man opened his eyes, untented his fingers, and said, "Okay. Let's go for it."

According to the U.S. Department of Transportation's Federal Highway Administration, the road that begins at Route 1 in Miami and terminates 1,952 miles later at the Houlton/Woodstock Border Crossing in northern Maine is called Interstate 95.

In law enforcement circles, it's got another nickname: the Iron Pipeline. It earns the moniker each year by being the most heavily used gun-running road in America, serving as the quickest conduit from states with lax gun control laws to states with strict ones.

As such, the associates of Red Dot Enterprises — who took turns making the drive south to pick up the latest shipment — knew the road well. Take the New Jersey Turnpike south, through the merge around Exit 8 that always backed up on weekends. Go over the Delaware Memorial Bridge, through that congested stretch of Delaware. There was usually a brief break from traffic through the northeastern part of Maryland, but that ended outside Baltimore. Then it was the Harbor Tunnel, the Capital Beltway, and the hellish run south of the Springfield mixing bowl, which could back up at anytime — not enough road for way too many cars.

Then, after traveling over the Occuquan River, through Prince William County and past Quantico, it was onto what the rest of the state referred to as "the real Virginia." It's no accident that you don't reach the Virginia Welcome Center until you've been in the state for more than forty miles. Whoever built it there knew what they were doing.

The Virginia Welcome Center was, at minimum, how far south the associates of Red Dot Enterprises went.

Then the mission became: find the straw buyer. They always set up the rendezvous ahead of time, having found the buyer on Craigslist and given him the usual instructions. But nothing ever felt routine about it. They rotated which area they used, so they were never going to the same place twice. And it was always a bit of a trick finding the buyer's car in a busy parking lot, even when they knew the make and model.

Next came the wait for the buyer to do his end, which was usually a nice excuse to grab a meal and relax, albeit not for long. Then it was time to swipe the guns and begin the trip back north.

The drive back was what really took forever, especially the way they did it. They kept it exactly five miles above the speed limit, so even when traffic was moving, they still weren't making great time. They didn't dare use E-ZPass. Each tollbooth cost ten minutes or more — and if there is anything more frustrating than waiting around just to pay some highway authority money, it hasn't been invented yet. They took frequent breaks and drank a lot of caffeine lest they nod off or get into an accident while distracted.

The whole goal was not to be noticed in any way, which — on one of the busiest roads in America — wasn't terribly hard. You just had to be smart about it: drive a bland car, something solid and domestic, without tinted windows or a tricked-out exhaust; wear the kind of clothes that can be bought at an outlet mall, something like Old Navy or Van Heusen; act like every other road-weary traveler at the rest stops; and make sure the trunk stays shut.

There are people who say I-95 is one of the most boring roads in America, and they're right. But for Red Dot Enterprises, boring was good.

A boring trip was a successful one.

CHAPTER 4

I've never been pregnant — just not my thing — but I've entered the phase of life where enough of my friends have borne fruit to know how they agonize over how they'll handle the Big News. Oh, eventually they'll do the mass Facebook blast. But there are some people who need to know first, and there's a certain order in which they must be informed: her parents, his parents, the best girlfriend, and so on. The hope is that no one high on the list slips up and tells someone who's lower on the list, like Aunt Kathy, who then blabs it to everyone else and ruins the precious surprise.

Being a reporter with a big scoop can feel like being pregnant. Eventually, you're going to tell everyone; in truth, you're *dying* to tell everyone. Still, you need to be careful about how you dole out your information. You have to play fair with the various parties involved and give them time to properly digest your surprise. But you also have to be discreet lest some other media outlet gets wind of it and blows your big scoop. And until you do the equivalent of the big Facebook blast — in our case, putting it online and in the newspaper — you're constantly worried about that damn Aunt Kathy.

So I had to move cautiously, do things in the right order, and hope for the best.

My first phone call was to Hakeem Rogers, the Newark Police Department's public disinformation officer. Or at least that's what I called him. I have no doubt what he called me was much worse. We were friendly on rare occasions — basically, the occasions when I wrote something he felt reflected well on his department — but otherwise we're a bit like a small dog and a big raccoon. We fight constantly, scratching, clawing, and squalling the whole time, though no one ever seems to win.

I dialed the number and was just starting to talk to one of his underlings when I heard Rogers shout, "Is that that" — unrepeatable word, one suggesting an incestuous relationship — "Ross? Put that" — another something unrepeatable, this time suggesting homosexuality — "on my line."

My call was transferred straight into: "You

got a lot of nerve calling me after what I read in the paper this morning. I've got every media outlet in New York on my ass because of that crap."

I stifled the urge to reply, *Why, Detective, since when did you learn to read?* Instead I said: "Crap?"

"Some blowhard minister grandstands for the cameras — talking out his big, black ass the whole time — and you guys run with it like it's real news. Since when did one person making totally unverified statements become something you print? I used to have respect for you, but you guys have totally gone in the toilet."

This was, perhaps, the fundamental reason Detective Rogers and I didn't get along: we each had pronounced opinions about how the other handled his professional responsibilities. Rogers thought it was my job to make the Newark Police Department look good to the outside world. I thought it was his job to provide information, not pass judgment on what we did with it.

"Newark Police: blowhard minister talks out his black ass," I said. "Can I use that as a headline? That was on the record, right?"

"Stop being a dick for once. You know damn well it's not."

"Well, I got news for you, Detective, that

blowhard minister might actually be right."

"What the hell you talking about?"

I relished what I had to say next: "The *Eagle-Examiner* has acquired autopsy photos of Darius Kipps that indicate he was tied to a chair shortly before his death —"

"You *what*?" he tried to interrupt.

"— and I'd like to know how that information fits into the Newark Police Department's finding that Detective Kipps died of a self-inflicted gunshot wound," I finished.

For the next five minutes, he peppered me with questions about how I got these photos, what they showed, and what we intended to do with them. For as much as I didn't like Rogers — and for as much as we might be at cross-purposes on a story like this — I still had to give him and his bosses every opportunity to comment intelligently on this news, perhaps even to contradict it, before we published it. Playing fair can be a real pain that way.

When I finished, Rogers stayed quiet. I thought I heard him grip the phone tighter. He had been around long enough to know a reporter had just lobbed him a stink bomb — and that he better be careful with it.

"Well, I'd like to remind you that 'self-inflicted gunshot wound' was a *preliminary* finding," he said. "I'll have to call you back."

176

Then he hung up. He didn't even lob one last swear word or insult at me, so I knew I had him reeling. And that was fun.

But the fun didn't stop there. My next call was to Ben Hilfiker, the AG's spokesman. I went to his cell phone first, which he answered by saying, "Come on, it hasn't even been twenty-four hours yet. Isn't there a law that says you're not allowed to start bugging me until after lunch?"

"Actually, I've got something new to bug you with. So I think that resets the clock," I said, then filled him in on the photos.

"Wow, Carter. Look at you, all grown up, with the big excloo," he said, shortening the word "exclusive," as journalists sometimes did.

"You think this is going to make your boss take a swing at this?"

"I don't know. It still depends on how hard the wind is blowing," Hilfiker said. "Why don't you e-mail me those pics and I'll get back to you."

My final call was to the spokesman at the Essex County Prosecutor's Office, who was a nice guy — for a political hack. I went through the same rigmarole, asking to interview both the prosecutor and the medical examiner. At the end, I received the same response from him as I had from

Rogers: a somewhat worried, "Let me call you back."

I guess that's one way having a scoop is unlike being pregnant: not everyone is thrilled to hear your news.

The final person who needed to be advised of the latest — and be given ample chance to react — was Mimi Kipps. But since this fell into the category of Things You Don't Do Over the Phone, I knew it would require another visit to the Rutledge Avenue duplex.

I grabbed an umbrella, because a gray morning looked like it was going to turn into a rainy afternoon, and made my way across the street to the parking garage. About halfway there, on the sidewalk, I passed Buster Hays, who was wearing the usual menagerie of wrinkles and stains that he called a wardrobe. He topped it off with a trench coat. With all due respect to the long and honorable history of the trench-coated foreign correspondent, Buster might be the last reporter in the world who still wears one.

I can't pretend, walking along in my charcoal gray peacoat, that I was living at the zenith of fashion. I was probably closer to the nadir. But at least my coat was younger than the interns we had running around the office. I'm not sure I could say the same about Buster's.

"Hey, Ivy, you got my Good Neighbors done yet?" he asked.

Good Neighbors? Good grief. I had forgotten.

"Didn't you read the paper this morning? Things have kind of blown up with the Kipps thing. As a matter of fact, I was hoping you could do me a favor and —"

He immediately cut me off: "Forget it. No Good Neighbors, no IA."

"You know, I could go to Tina, tell her you're holding out on me, and she'll make you give it up."

It was a bluff — there *is* honor among thieves when it comes to ratting out fellow reporters to editors — and he knew it.

"Go ahead. Run off to your little girlfriend. By the time you get back, I'll have forgotten I ever knew anyone at Newark IA. I'll probably have forgotten I know you."

"Come on, Buster, can't you just give it to me?" I said, aware that I was now whining. "I'm working on a breaking story here. It led the paper today and it'll probably lead the paper tomorrow. Brodie's got a big ol' boner for this thing, and I need to —"

"And then come tomorrow morning when you still haven't done my Good Neighbors, what leverage do I got? I got Nuttin' Honey."

Only Buster would still be referencing a commercial for a cereal that had probably been out of production for twenty-five years. He was just standing there, not quite grinning at me, knowing he had me between a rock and a Good Neighbors. So I gave up.

"You're a bad man, Buster."

"I do what I need to do in order to survive in this cruel world," he said, strolling onward. As he rounded the corner toward the front entrance, he started whistling.

There was no way that in the midst of chasing a scoop of this magnitude, I was going to have time to dig up a story about how Mrs. Doreen Robertson of Bedminster had been so moved by the suffering of *the children* on her safari trip to Zanzibar that she had convinced her bridge club friends to give money to Tanzanian malaria relief.

But I knew someone who did.

After crossing the street, I surfed through my received calls until I reached a 315 number. As I walked through the garage toward my car, I dialed my new favorite intern, Geoff "Ruthie" Ginsburg.

"This is Geoff," he answered.

"Geoff!" I said, feigning as much enthusiasm as I could. "How you doing, pal? It's

Carter Ross!"

"Oh, hey! I'm so glad you called! You wouldn't believe it, but every single pregnancy test has come back negative."

"Every. Single. One?" I said, now trying for incredulity. Good thing I took a drama class at Amherst. True, I only took it to meet cute girls. But I paid attention. A little.

"Yeah, as a matter of fact, I need to go to the drugstore and get some more. I'm starting to run low on food coloring, too. You were right, that stuff wasn't easy to find. I went to three stores before I —"

"Yeah, yeah, Geoff, that's great, now I . . ." I tried to interrupt. But Ruthie had been hard at work and wanted to get full credit for it — the interns often act like they're still in school, still being graded, and don't want to settle for that B plus. So he kept yammering:

". . . found the exact stuff we needed — they have it in Bernardsville, by the way — but it comes in these small bottles. I've been squirting it in pretty liberally because I wanted to make sure the tests were accurate. I didn't want any false negatives. You were right about having people flush their own toilets, by the way. Some of them are a little hesitant about it. The first guy looked at me like I was out of my —"

181

"Geoff, this is really amazing and you've done great w—"

"— mind, but most of them have been really into it. This one lady even had me do it again just because she liked the flushing part so much. It cost me another pregnancy test, but I figured no one would mind too much. I'm going to be expensing all this —"

That was going to be a sight on an expense report: "24 First Response pregnancy tests . . . $375.58." I'm glad it was going on his, not mine.

"— stuff. And I figure the paper won't mind when they see the article we're going to get out of this. You should *hear* some of these people's stories. They've been on a waiting list ten, fifteen years to get into these town houses. And now to have them be defective? Can you just —"

"Yeah, Geoff, slow down, big guy. I got something you need to —"

"— imagine what that feels like? And then — this is maybe a sidebar — but I talked to some guys out on the street in front of the town houses and —"

"Geoff!" I said. "That's all great. And we'll —"

"But let me just tell you about what these corner boys told me. According to these

182

kids —"

"Okay, okay, take it easy, Geoff," I said. "I'm sure it's great, and later you can tell me all about the corner boys. But for right now, we have a bit of an emergency situation and I need your help."

"Oh!" he said eagerly. "What is it?"

"I need you to do a Good Neighbors feature."

There was a brief but deliberate silence, followed by: "That . . . that's an emergency?"

"I'll explain later. But for right now, I need that Good Neighbors and I need it quickly. This afternoon if possible. Tomorrow morning at the absolute latest. You know what they're looking for with a Good Neighbors?"

"Yeah," he said, sighing. "I spent the entire first month of my internship doing nothing else."

"Terrific! So you're pro. Give me a shout when you're done."

"O-okay," he said. "But I really want to tell you about these corner boys and —"

"Yeah, we'll talk later, okay? I gotta run."

I hung up before I could hear his dejected response. I really felt bad for the kid. But in the endless war that is putting out a daily newspaper, there are always going to be casualties. And I'm afraid Ruthie Ginsburg needed to be tallied among today's body count.

A light drizzle was falling as I pulled out of the parking garage. Right around the time I passed the seamless border between Newark and East Orange, it had turned into a steady rain. My windshield wipers could keep up, but the sky was so dark I'm not sure I could say the same for my headlights.

I spent the drive giving my brain its first real chance to grind on the big picture: the why, who, and what of a murder. Why would someone want Darius Kipps dead? Who would profit from it? What would they gain?

They were the kind of questions a good detective like Kipps had probably asked himself a thousand times on a hundred different cases. But for as much as I tried to spin a variety of theories, I had neither the information nor the imagination to make any kind of brilliant deductions. By the time I arrived at the Kipps residence, I was no closer to anything resembling an answer. So I focused on the small task at hand — getting a comment from Mimi Kipps for my story — and left the rest for later.

There were no family members milling outside the house on a day like this. I could see light pouring out of those curtainless second-floor windows, so I suspected someone was home. I parked on the opposite side of the street, folded my printouts and tucked them in an inside pocket of my peacoat, where they wouldn't get wet, then grabbed my umbrella, doing the awkward open-the-umbrella-while-getting-out-of-the-car move. As I walked up the front walkway with my head down, I could feel the chill and the damp trying to work their way in through my coat.

The porch had an awning so I shook out the umbrella, then dropped it to the side. I rang the doorbell and waited.

No one answered. I rang again. Was she in the shower again? Feeding the baby? Maybe I should have called first.

I pressed the bell again, impatient and cold, holding it for a second, listening hard to make sure it was working. And, yes, I could hear a chime. But no Mimi.

Still standing on her front stoop, I pulled out my phone and dialed her cell number. Maybe she was out at the grocery store and left the lights on. She answered on the first ring with, "Please go away."

"Mimi? It's Carter Ross."

"I know. And I know you're standing on my porch right now. But I have nothing to say to you."

"I . . . I'm confused. Did you not like the story today?"

"The story was fine, but I need you to leave."

"Can I . . . can I come back later?"

"No."

"Can we talk on the phone later?"

"No."

"Uh," I said, at an unusual loss for words. I had been rehearsing parts of my conversation with Mimi on the drive out, and this was not in any of the versions that had played out in my head. "Mimi, am I missing something here? Yesterday I spent a few hours at your home in the morning. Then I came back in the afternoon. You seemed very keen to have me working on this and now you're freezing me out? What gives?"

There was a pause. Then: "Pastor Al says I shouldn't talk to you."

Ah. The anointed man of God strikes again. "And why did he say that?"

"He . . . he says you're an agent of Satan."

I couldn't help it: I laughed. "Mimi, no offense, but that's absurd. Do I *look* like an agent of Satan? Do I *talk* like an agent of Satan?"

"Pastor Al says Satan comes in many forms and can be very persuasive."

"I grant you the prince of darkness is

probably a little too subtle to send someone here with horns and a forked tail showing," I said. "But, honestly, use your head. Use your heart. I was holding your baby yesterday. The little guy was sucking on my finger, for goodness' sake. You really think one of Satan's minions would go for that?"

In my time as a newspaper reporter, I had stood on a lot of front porches and tried to talk my way into a lot of houses. This, I was fairly certain, was the first time I had to convince someone I wasn't shilling for Mephistopheles.

"Maybe . . . maybe you're just trying to keep my guard down. I just don't think Pastor Al would —"

"Look, Mimi, maybe I'm Satan's soldier and maybe I'm not — it doesn't sound like anything I can say will convince you anyway — but right now I know one thing I am, and that's a reporter with a job to do. I came here because I have some photos of your husband you need to see before I write about them in the newspaper. Will you please let me in so you can look at them?"

I heard the deadbolt slide and there was Mimi Kipps, standing on the other side of the screen door, still holding her phone.

"What photos?" she said. I guess her curiosity — to say nothing of her desire to clear her dead husband's name — was stronger than her fear of whatever menace I posed as Beelzebub's buddy.

"They might be a little hard for you to look at," I admitted, slipping my phone in my pocket. "They're autopsy photos."

Her hand had traveled as far as the handle of the screen door, but it wasn't going any farther. Still, I was making progress.

"I still don't think I . . . Maybe, maybe I can have Mike look at them."

Mike as in Mike Fusco, Darius's sometime-partner. It sounded like a fine compromise to me.

"Okay. Can you call him? Have him come out here?"

"Just wait here," she said, closing the door.

I shoved my hands in my pocket. I was a little miffed at having to stay out on the porch like I was a Labrador who had been playing in puddles. But, at the same time, it was hard not to feel empathy for Mimi. The poor woman had to be reeling. She had lost her husband and didn't really understand how or why, but probably didn't have much time to think about it, mostly because she still had two kids to care for. She had her minister filling her head with superstitious nonsense, a pushy reporter trying to get her to comment on his story, untold numbers of relatives coming and going and yet — through it all — she was, in some very basic way, alone.

I looked down at the flower bed, where the dead leaves had gone slick and shiny in the rain. Somewhere underneath, there might have been a bulb yearning to push through, or a perennial with roots full of possibility, or a seed waiting to germinate. The leaves had been like a blanket through the long winter, providing needed insulation. But unless someone got in there and cleaned them out, whatever lay underneath would be smothered, lacking the air and sunlight it needed to thrive.

The dirt needed to be uncovered. There seemed to be a lot of that going on around here.

Three, maybe five minutes later, Mimi again appeared at her front door.

"Mike is on his way," she said. "Here. You look a little cold."

She opened the screen and handed me a mug of coffee. I expressed my gratitude because that's how my mother raised me. Mimi closed both doors, and as soon as I was sure she couldn't see me, I emptied the contents of the mug in the flower bed.

After roughly another ten minutes on the

porch, time I spent trying to fend off a case of the chills, Mike Fusco rolled up in what was clearly not a Newark Police Department vehicle. It was a shiny, black Ford F-150 with jacked-up suspension. Between that and all the muscles, I was beginning to think maybe he was overcompensating for something.

I watched him get out of his truck — actually "descend from his truck" might be more accurate — and walk with long but unhurried strides through the rain. He wasn't wearing a jacket, just a different color tight-fitting sweater from yesterday, and he didn't have a hat or umbrella. Yes, he was a tough guy. I tried to pretend like I hadn't been shivering.

When he reached the porch, he nodded at me, then slid by me. He opened the front door, announcing, "Hey, Mimi, it's me."

He did a quarter-turn in my direction and said, "Come on in."

I was barely inside the small entryway when Mimi appeared at the back of the living room, saw me, and said, "He can't come in."

"Why not?" Fusco asked.

Mimi immediately looked sheepish. But she still said, "Pastor Al says he's an agent of Satan."

"You gotta stop listening to that nut," Fusco said, scowling.

"He's not a nut, he's —"

"You still giving him money?" Fusco interrupted. "I thought you said you were going to stop."

Mimi looked down at her bare feet and started mumbling something. I couldn't figure out the dynamic between her and Fusco, who not only felt comfortable enough to walk into the house without knocking — and invite me in — but knew about her finances. Maybe this was a battle Darius had been fighting, trying to get his wife to stop donating to the too-slick pastor, and now Fusco was stepping in, providing backup for his fallen partner.

"Never mind. We'll talk about it later. Why don't you go up and shower. I'll keep an eye on the baby," Fusco said, nodding in the direction of Jaquille. The miracle baby was sleeping in the Pack 'N Play, wrapped in what appeared to be a baby straight-jacket.

"Okay," she said, disappearing upstairs. Fusco sat. I sat. And, like that, there we were again: eyeballing each other while Mimi Kipps showered. He broke the silence more quickly this time. "So you got some photos to show me?"

"Yeah," I said, reaching inside the pocket of my peacoat and pulling out my folded printouts. I handed them to Fusco, who went through them one by one. He brought two of them up to his face for closer inspection, then put them down.

"You sure this is Kipps?"

"Yeah."

"Jesus," he said.

"Yeah."

"And someone just leaked these to you?"

"Something like that."

"You sure they're not doctored or anything?"

"Positive. Saw it with my own eyes."

He nodded.

"My source said it looked like someone tied him to a chair," I added. "That how it looks to you?"

He grimaced. "Those photos are pretty blurry. Without really being able to look at them? I don't know. But, yeah, he was restrained somehow, with something. A rope? Some wire? Shoelaces? Believe it or not, a good forensics guy can tell the difference."

"Okay," I said. "But just to make sure I'm not jumping to conclusions. I mean . . . this isn't a suicide. Something weird happened, yes?"

"Yeah," he said, staring at the screen of the television, which was off. Then he added a more emphatic: "Yeah."

I let him sort through things for a few moments. He was no longer looking at the television but rather through it, at some distant spot that may as well have been a mile away.

"So what's the scene like at the precinct right now?" I said, just to snap him out of it. "How did that whole Pastor Al press conference play?"

"I wouldn't know."

"What do you mean?"

He turned his head toward me. "My captain basically told me to disappear for a few weeks, said I was going to be placed on administrative leave, said to call it a 'mental health break.' I said no way, I don't want that nut bird stuff in my file. You get something like that on your record, it can seriously screw up a promotion. So captain said, 'Call it what you want to. I won't put anything in your file. I just don't want to see you around here for a while.' "

It sounded like the cop version of that shirt at Tee's place, the one that said, why don't you go practice falling down?

He shook his head in disbelief, adding, "I even had to turn in my service weapon."

Mostly to keep Fusco talking, I said, "What do you make of that?"

He grasped the corner of his lip in his teeth. It was a very untough look. He might not have been aware he was doing it.

"You think the captain knew you were . . . looking into the Kipps thing?" I prompted.

"Who says I'm looking into the Kipps thing?"

I made a palms-up, you-think-I'm-stupid-or-something gesture. "I think there's a grieving widow upstairs who is convinced her husband didn't kill himself, and I'm betting she's asked you for help. And you don't strike me as the kind of guy who would turn down a request like that."

I thought for sure I had him now. *That's right, Mike Fusco. You're a big hero. Now tell the friendly newspaper reporter all about it . . .*

Most guys would grab that and run with it. But Fusco just sat there, looking at me with the same mile-off stare he had been giving the television.

"At risk of stating the obvious, your department is trying to throw a big old blanket over Darius Kipps's death," I said. "Unless I'm missing something, there's no way anyone with half a brain could look at the marks on that body and say, 'Oh, yeah, this man killed himself and was acting

194

alone.' Now, some people are saying Kipps was mixed up in something. Other people, like you, are telling me no way. All I know is, *something* is up. Someone killed Darius Kipps, for some reason I have yet to determine. Are you going to help me figure it out or not?"

"I don't —" he started, then stopped himself. "Look, I can't be talking to you. You know that, right? I shouldn't have talked to you before. My department has policies about that, and even on leave — or whatever they're calling it — I have to follow that. I'm only here as a favor to Mimi. I'll show her these pictures, and if she has something to say, she'll call you, okay?"

"So you're just going to —"

"She'll call you," he said more firmly.

I could tell I was shoving him too close to the edge. And furthermore, I realized trying to move him any more was going to be futile. Mike Fusco didn't *get* pushed around.

"Okay," I said. "But, look, why don't you just give me your number? That way, if I get anything else, I can call you and I don't have to bother Mimi directly? I don't want to upset her any more than she's already upset, you know?"

It was, I thought, a reasonable request.

And apparently Fusco thought so, too. I held out my pad and pen. He grabbed them, then wrote "Mike Fusco" with a phone number underneath.

For the time being, it seemed like the best I was going to get.

The rain had slackened but was still coming down hard enough to make the puddles dance as I went back outside. I grabbed my umbrella from where I had left it but didn't bother opening it. If Fusco didn't need one, neither did I.

Which just meant I was damp by the time I got back in my Malibu. What *is it* with these tough guys, anyway?

Feeling defeated, I considered consoling myself with an early lunch. A good, wholesome lunch. The kind that would be served on a real plate and, perhaps, even include vegetables and a side salad. Unfortunately, I was in a part of town where the food options were boundless — as long as you were looking for fried chicken. It's hard to eat healthy in the hood.

I was still considering what to do about this dilemma three minutes later when my phone rang. It was a 609 number, which likely meant state government.

"Carter Ross," I said.

"Hey, it's Hilfiker."

"That was fast. What's going on?"

"Well, we're about to have two conversations."

"Okay."

"The first is the one we're having on the record, that you can go ahead and print in that silly newspaper of yours," he said. "The second is the conversation I always wished people would have with me when I was a reporter, the one where I explain why the first conversation doesn't make much sense."

"Oh, this ought to be good," I said, pulling over to the side of Central Avenue and fishing my notebook out of my pocket.

"Right, so here goes with the first one. You ready?"

"Yeah."

"The attorney general's office has determined that there is no need for an independent investigation into the death of Darius Kipps. The attorney general has every confidence that the Newark Police Department and the Essex County Prosecutor's Office will conduct a thorough investigation and resolve this matter in a satisfactory fashion."

I scribbled furiously, writing in the self-taught shorthand I had developed over the years. Hilfiker helped by saying it slowly enough — "talking at notebook speed," is what we call it — so I could get it down verbatim. I waited until he was done and then said, "Really?"

"Really."

"You got a feather by any chance?"

"No, why?"

"Because you could knock me over with one right now," I said. "You guys are seriously taking a pass on this? You told your boss about the pictures, right?"

"I did. I even showed them to him."

"And he knows we're going to run with this?"

"Yeah, I guess so. I didn't say that explicitly. But he's not a dummy. I don't need to explain to him what mud-mucking journalists like you do for a living."

"So . . . okay, I guess let's have the second conversation now. Because, you're right, I'm totally perplexed."

"Okay, well, basically — we're off the record now — your pastor took the heat off."

"My *pastor*?"

"Yeah, whatshisname. The megachurch guy. LeRioux."

"Why would he . . . that doesn't make any sense."

"I don't know. Maybe he felt like he had gotten all the mileage he could out of this thing and decided he was done."

"So he gets his face time and he goes home?"

"Something like that," Hilfiker said.

"That's cold."

"Tell me about it. It's also pretty stupid, frankly."

"How so?"

"He's screwing himself out of a payday."

"I'm not following you."

Hilfiker sighed. "Haven't you learned to be a little more cynical by now? Think about it. I'm sure Detective Kipps has a life insurance policy — all cops do, especially Newark cops. Problem is, if his death is ruled a suicide, the policy is no good. That means the Widow Kipps is destitute. On the other hand, if she is suddenly flush with a half million bucks' worth of insurance company money . . ."

"Maybe she expresses her piety by giving ten percent of it to the anointed man of God, in loving memory of her dead husband," I completed.

"There you go."

"So why would he call off the dogs?"

"I don't know. I wasn't part of the phone call. And his honor the attorney general didn't say. But I'm guessing once he heard LeRioux was dropping it, he thought there was no reason for him to pick it up. You can bet no one in Essex County is going to be clamoring for him to step in."

"Okay, but let's leave the politics out of this for a second —"

"This is New Jersey," Hilfiker said. "You can *never* leave the politics out of it."

"I know, I know, but . . ." I began, struggling to put words to my thoughts. I watched a woman in a hijab hurry down the street, carrying two plastic grocery bags, bowing her head to keep her face out of the rain.

"Well, call me naïve, but I thought maybe your boss might just do the right thing here," I said.

"Who says he's not?"

"Come on, you saw those pictures."

"Yeah, but you're thinking like a reporter. This is a lawyer you're dealing with. He might have just decided that, legally, it was right to let the locals deal with it. Just because the attorney general is the top law enforcement agent in the state doesn't mean he has to get involved every time someone disputes a traffic ticket."

"This is hardly a traffic ticket . . ."

"You know what I'm saying. Sometimes the AG has to pick and choose, and maybe

200

he figures this one is best left where it is."

"In other words, the Newarkers made this mess, so let them clean it up."

"Well, that's another way to look at it. But yeah. And, remember, Newark makes the mess, but it's really Essex County that ought to be cleaning it up. That's how the food chain goes. Sure, it leads up to my guy eventually. But it hits the Essex County prosecutor first."

"Right, right," I said.

The hijab woman had rounded the corner, out of sight. I couldn't think of anything else to ask the attorney general's spokesman, so I didn't object when Hilfiker said: "Anyhow, I gotta run. Good luck with it."

"Thanks. For both conversations," I said, ending the call and putting my car into Drive at the same time. I pulled a quick U-turn and pointed myself back in the direction of Mimi's house.

I didn't know if she'd believe me — what with me being an agent of Satan and all — but she needed to know that her beloved Pastor Al, the man she trusted so implicitly, had simply been exploiting her to get free advertising on the evening news. And now, having used her, he was dropping her and going back to whatever it was he really preferred to be doing.

Like drop-kicking orphans.

Arriving back at the Kipps household, I got out of the car with my umbrella open this time. I didn't need any more of that tough guy stuff.

I was about to walk across the street when I happened to glance up at those naked second-story windows. I saw Mimi Kipps — or at least the top half of her — wearing one towel on her body and another on her head, having an animated conversation with someone. And being the naturally curious reporter that I am, I stopped to see who.

She wasn't looking at the person very often. She was mostly puttering around the room. Making a bed, maybe? On occasion, she would bend over, pick something up, and put it somewhere else, like she was cleaning up toys in a child's bedroom. She moved with the practiced efficiency of a mom who had done this before, but she also maintained her half of the dialogue the entire time. Her body language suggested she was angry, tense.

I kept watching — yeah, so I'm a voyeur, what's your point? — but still couldn't tell who was carrying the other side of the exchange. I moved up the street a little bit, to give myself a different angle. And there, standing with his arms crossed, was Mike Fusco. He was leaning against the wall with his head tilted to one side, giving no hint as to his emotional state.

And it struck me as, well, a little strange that Mimi would be talking with him while she wasn't dressed. I realize that as a starchy WASP, I tend to be a smidge prudish about such matters. But still. There are a scant number of women in my life who would feel comfortable talking to me while wearing a towel. Half of them I'm related to and the other half I've . . .

Slept with? Could Mimi and Fusco be . . .

No. I chased the thought from my mind. Or at least I was trying to. And then Mimi made a large, frustrated motion — an "I've had it" kind of gesture — and Fusco walked up behind her and started rubbing her shoulders.

She didn't fight it, just immediately let her body slump, giving in to the massage. Fusco worked on her for about a minute or so while Mimi stood there, giving me the chance to think that, well, maybe they were just really, *really* good friends. There was still some possibility this could be platonic, right? Mimi needed a human touch. Fusco wanted to give her some comfort, and he was probably the kind of guy who'd be better communicating with his actions than his words.

Besides, no woman who had given birth five months earlier — to say nothing of a woman who had just lost her husband — would be trolling for some kind of random hook-up. A guy might. Guys can pretty much turn off their brains and shut out those kinds of petty distractions when it comes to sex. But women are too practical about human relations for that sort of thing. So this was probably just . . .

I was still trying to work out that line of reasoning when Mimi Kipps blew it right away. She turned into Fusco, wrapped an arm around the back of his head, and pulled him close for a kiss. And it didn't look like it was their first. Their heads fell into a familiar rhythm. His hands went for her back and butt, and I wondered how much longer the towel was going to stay in place.

Before things shifted to something more suited for latenight cable, Mimi pushed Fusco out of sight — into a back bedroom, perhaps — leaving me to sort out the ramifications of it all.

Fusco and Mimi. Ramifying, as it were.

Yikes.

I'm sure Mimi wasn't the first widow to

take up with her husband's best friend, but wasn't this a bit . . . soon? Don't they usually wait a month or two — or, heck, at least until the deceased is in the ground — before they . . .

And then, finally, the lightbulb went on above my head: there was no need to wait because it had already been going on. This wasn't a new romance. This was an affair. I thought about the first time I saw Mimi with Fusco, how they had been sharing a cup of coffee with such intimacy, how she had draped her hand so casually on his shoulder.

Then I thought about that conversation they had earlier, where Fusco had essentially berated her for giving money to the pastor. I had dismissed it as Fusco taking up his buddy's battle, never thinking it was possibly his own battle. I had been watching a lover's spat.

Yeah, Mimi and Fusco had probably been doing this for a while, which meant . . .

I felt like I needed one of those feathers to knock me over again. Here I was, slamming my brain around, trying to imagine these big, complicated scenarios that led to the death of Darius Kipps. And all along, it had been one of the oldest and simplest of sins. Lust.

Mimi Kipps was just another adulterous wife. Mike Fusco was just another swinging dick. And they both wanted the third wheel out of the way.

I began imagining a new scenario, one that made the pieces fit: Darius learned his quasi-partner was having an affair with his wife, got blisteringly drunk for the first time in a decade, and, while still smashed, angrily confronted Fusco. And sure, Kipps was a big guy. But he was also borderline blacking out, so Fusco was able to subdue him easily.

Maybe that's when the chair tying came in. I could imagine Fusco tying up Kipps, just so they could talk without Kipps trying to throw punches. Maybe Fusco argued that he and Mimi were in love and that Kipps might as well face the fact that his marriage was over.

But Kipps refused, raved that he was going to get Mimi back no matter what, maybe even threatened to harm her. Whatever it was, it made Fusco realize he had to get rid of Kipps. So Fusco grabbed Kipps's gun, untied him, pushed him in the shower in the locker room, and, *blam,* game over.

The ballistics would match. And Fusco would have known the water from the shower would destroy or alter key evidence, like gunshot residue or blood spatter. And when other cops heard the gunshot and came to investigate, there's Fusco, just another cop in the bedlam. No one would have realized he was there all along.

Or heck, maybe it was even more sinister than that. Maybe this was a premeditated act, and Mimi and Fusco had come up with some kind of plan to get rid of Kipps and make it look like suicide. They tied him down, forced him to drink a bunch of booze, then went for the kill.

Either way, it worked. Sure, Mimi had been hell-bent on clearing her husband's name, trying to convince me and others he never would have committed suicide, even going so far as to have Fusco tell me about the inconsistency with the bourbon (which may have been invented). But all that — as Ben Hilfiker had so cynically pointed out — was just for insurance purposes.

The reaction of the Newark Police Department certainly made sense. The cops were just embarrassed that one of their own had killed himself and wanted the thing to be over with as soon as possible.

Even Pastor Al's actions were now a little more logical. He must have learned about the affair or guessed it was happening — Fusco and Mimi weren't being terribly discreet, if glomming in front of a window was any guide — and washed his hands of it, dropping his call for an independent investigation.

Or maybe he just decided to let a higher authority sort it out.

I could have stood there for another hour, cataloguing the implications of my new discovery. But a car rolled by slowly, its occupants — an elderly couple — peering at me curiously. I suddenly became aware I was just a weird white guy standing in the rain in a town where I didn't belong, staring at someone's house. I couldn't have been any more obvious with binoculars and a telescope.

I folded my umbrella, got back into my car, and skittered away before I attracted too much more attention. Or before my two lovebirds finished. Maybe I should have given Fusco more credit than that. But if he was still stuck in the backrub-as-foreplay method of seduction, he couldn't necessarily be ruled out as a member of the Minute Man Club.

Back on Central Avenue, I again considered my dining options — there's a Popeyes *and* a KFC, after all — but instead drove toward Redeemer Love Christian Church.

It was time to pay a visit to the anointed man of God and I knew, both from my travels and from a multitude of billboards, that I could find him and his spiritual healing on West Market Street in Newark.

My plan was, basically, to play both smart and dumb. I knew he had called the attorney general — though, since I had that from an off-the-record source, I needed to get him to admit it. That would be the smart part. The dumb part was to ask why he made that call and pretend like I didn't know the answer.

As I drove, I accessed our archives on my phone so I could quickly read over the story we had written about him and the church a few months back. The narrative started in early seventies Newark with Pastor Al, then a high school gym teacher, holding services in his basement. During a bleak time for still-riot-scarred Newark, a time when vacancy rates were soaring and "urban renewal" had become a grim joke, LeRioux was a charismatic preacher who offered hope. He took in wayward souls, gave them new birth through Jesus, and joined them with his flock.

Membership doubled every few years. Most tithed, and the money was constantly being plowed back into expanding facilities.

Before long, the gym teacher was preaching full time and moved into a storefront on Sussex Avenue, then a former bowling alley on Norfolk Street. A church-affiliated day care was opened. Then a senior living facility. Redeemer Love Christian could take care of you from cradle to grave.

As the congregation grew, so did Pastor Al's reputation and import. The story left as an open question when, exactly, LeRioux had found the time to get his doctorate or what institution had given it to him. But somewhere along the line he started calling himself Reverend Doctor. Maybe he just liked how it sounded.

Either way, the story made it sound as if Pastor Al had a mastery of political science, turning the perception that he could influence his parishioners' votes into leverage to get what he wanted, whether it was funding for his day care, tax breaks for church-owned housing projects, or contracts to wash police vehicles at a chain of car washes the church had opened around the city.

Sometime in the nineties, he convinced the city council to more or less donate a chunk of land on West Market Street, and that was where his congregation built its current home — a massive, modern mega-church, complete with offices, broadcast facilities for Sunday's services, and a theaterlike sanctuary with a large stage and seating for two thousand. The sanctuary was called LeRioux Chapel — named after Pastor Al's parents, of course, because he was far too modest to name it after himself.

But no one was fooled. The church was essentially a monument to the Reverend Doctor Alvin LeRioux.

The real nut of the story came from a splinter group who said they had been cast out of the flock for asking too many questions about church finances. According to them, Redeemer Love Christian had revenues of approximately $22 million a year from tithes and various ancillary industries. But no one would give them — or our reporter — any accounting of where the money went. I guess they had noticed Pastor Al's silk suits, too.

It reminded me of the old joke about the priest and the televangelist, talking about how they determined what percentage of the offering stayed with them and what percentage went to God's work. The priest said he drew a line in the middle of his office, then tossed all the money in the air. Whatever landed on the left went to him, to the right went to God. The televangelist said he had a slightly different method: he threw all the money in the air, and whatever God caught, He could keep.

So I more or less knew what I was getting myself into as I parked on the street — eschewing Redeemer Love's large, recently paved, fenced-in lot — and walked through the front door of the church offices. I passed a sign on a stanchion that read, PLEASE TURN OFF YOUR CELL PHONE WHILE IN GOD'S HOUSE, and I complied, just in case God was ready to hit me with His version of roaming charges. I was greeted by a receptionist, and when I told her I wanted to talk to Alvin LeRioux, she looked at me like I had just asked for an audience with the pope.

Nevertheless, I was ushered toward a set of double doors that had REV. DR. LERIOUX imprinted on a brass plate to the side. The doors led to a large office suite that contained several efficient, diligent female underlings, dressed in conservative suits that ran the color spectrum from black all the way to slate gray.

The one who appeared to be the alpha underling — she was wearing a wireless headset, like she was the operator standing by to take my order — was in her midthirties and, I must say, quite easy on the eyes. She was tall and elegant, with light-brown skin and the kind of cheekbones that were made for modeling. She fairly oozed cool professionalism, but I still couldn't help but wonder if Pastor Al was getting some of her on the side. If he was? Well, bravo for him.

She greeted me by saying, "How can I help you?"

"I'm here to see Reverend LeRioux."

"And may I ask who you are?"

"You may," I said, and left it at that. I hate it when people beat around the bush.

It tripped her up for just a second, enough to put a small crack in her Little Miss Unflappable façade. But she recovered quickly enough. "Well, then, who are you?"

"Carter Ross, agent of Satan," I said, smiling.

Another crack. She actually frowned.

"Sorry, that's just what your boss calls me behind my back. I'm really a reporter for the *Eagle-Examiner,* and I have to say the Satan thing has been way overblown. We were using him as a stringer for a while, but we canned him. He kept trying to convince everyone that Milton had misquoted him in *Paradise Lost* and we all got tired of hearing it."

This time she was determined not to miss a beat: "And may I say . . ." she paused to rephrase, "Why do you need to speak to the

213

reverend?"

I kept right on smiling. "I'm writing a story about Darius Kipps, the dead cop Pastor Al was very interested in last night but has apparently forgotten about today. He also forgot to invite us to the press conference, but it's okay — I won't hold it against him."

"Please have a seat," she said, pointing to a pair of easy chairs and a couch that surrounded a small coffee table in the corner.

Then she disappeared behind a door to her right. Probably to fetch security.

But it wasn't a security guard who soon came out to greet me. It was the reverend-perhaps-doctor himself. And if irritation correlates to perspiration, he was plenty aggravated. He was already mopping himself by the time he greeted me.

Still, he seemed determined to play nice. With what was intended to be a friendly smile, he looked down at me — being six-and-a-half feet tall, I suppose he looked down on most people — and gave me a cologne-doused handshake, guaranteeing me another day of smelling like eau de Al. He asked me if I needed anything to drink and I declined. Then he thanked the alpha underling, whose name was apparently

Desiree, and invited me into his personal chambers.

I followed him into a room with high ceilings and dimensions large enough to accommodate a decent game of Wiffle ball. He hobbled over behind his desk like a man ten years overdue for a knee replacement, and I tried not to pop an Achilles tendon every time my feet sank into his extra-plush carpeting. It was like DuPont had started making a brand called StainMaster Quick-Sand.

Pastor Al plopped himself in a chair, removed his gold-wire-framed glasses, and took another opportunity to mop his hang-dog face. As he did so, I pulled a pen and notebook out of my pocket. No need to make him think this was a social call.

He replaced his glasses, sighed, and in that voice-of-God bass asked, "So what can I do for you today, Mister Ross?"

So I was Mr. Ross now. It was an upgrade from Lucifer's cabana boy, or whatever he called me around Mimi.

Since he was showing courtesy, I did the same and kept my tone respectful, even while my words were sharp: "I'm working on a follow-up story about Darius Kipps, and to be honest I'm a little perplexed by your actions, Reverend. Last night you held

215

a press conference and announced that the Newark Police Department was telling a big, bad lie. Then you said the state attorney general ought to step in. But this morning you called the attorney general and told him thanks but no thanks. Can you explain that for me?"

Pastor Al actually squirmed in his seat. He did the face-wiping routine again. "You ask very challenging questions, young man," he said. "I can see why your editors would consider you a good reporter."

And I can see you're stalling me, Pastor Al, I thought. But, mindful I had to keep my inner wiseass on a leash, I just sat there with my notebook open and my mouth shut.

"Have you ever heard of the Parable of the Pharisee and the Publican?"

"You'll have to refresh my memory, Reverend. It's been a long time since Sunday school."

"This comes to us from the Gospel of Saint Luke. Now, the Pharisees were very pious men, and they were much admired for their righteousness. The Publicans were the tax collectors, and I think we all know, no one likes the tax collector" — he threw in a pause because I guess this is where his congregation would usually share a chuckle. "Now, as the parable is told to us by Luke, these men enter the temple to pray. The Pharisee stands up and prays to God about his own virtue, telling God that he fasts and tithes, thanking God that he is not like the lowly tax collector. The Publican, now, the Publican, he stands at a distance. He dares not raise his head to God. And when it is his time to pray, he beats his breast and humbly asks God to have mercy on him, for he is a *sinner.*"

Pastor Al paused to let his words have their impact. For all his flaws, he was a mesmerizing preacher.

"Now, who do you think Jesus tells us is justified in the eyes of the Lord? Who is more favored by the Father?"

"Uh," I said, because I felt like it was a trick question.

"The Publican!" he boomed. "The Publican is justified because he recognizes his unworthiness before God! Jesus teaches that 'everyone who exalts himself will be humbled, and he who humbles himself will be exalted.' So I am mindful of the Pharisee and the Publican as I admit to you I made a mistake in my handling of this matter."

"Mistake?" I said.

"Yes. I believe they call it looking before you leap."

What, I wanted to say, *because you didn't*

know your parishioner was two-timing with the deceased's best friend? But mindful of my plan to act somewhat dumb, I said, "How so?"

"I'm afraid I fell back on some of my old instincts. In my days as a young pastor, I felt there was only one way to accomplish a goal, and that was to pursue it with straight-forward tenacity and intensity — to make a lot of noise, in essence. It is only in my more senior years that I have come to realize there are many different ways to accomplish a goal, and sometimes they are quieter. The Lord hears a whispered prayer just as well as He hears one that is shouted."

And in my days as a young reporter, I might have fallen for a line of fiddle-faddle like that. But in my more senior years, I recognized the reverend was talking out his ass. And while in polite conversation we allow people to obfuscate like this all the time, I wasn't going to let Pastor Al get away with it here.

"I'm sorry, Reverend, but I don't have a doctorate in religion" — *and chances are neither do you, you fraud* — "so you're losing me a little bit. Let me keep it simple for a second: Did you call the attorney general this morning?"

I thought maybe Pastor Al wasn't going to

give in so easily — that I was going to have to wade through more than a few more miles of Confusion Creek to get to where I needed to go — but he just squirmed a little more and then, finally, said, "Yes, I did."

"And did you inform him you were dropping your call for an independent investigation into the death of Darius Kipps?"

"Yes, I did," he said, without squirming this time.

"And why did you do that?"

"I received information at the highest level that made me think differently about the matter."

It was the first semi-useful thing he said, and I was scribbling it in my notebook as I asked, "Did the attorney general give you that information?"

"No."

"Then who, at the highest level, did?"

"That is something I would rather not say," Pastor Al replied. "I have to respect certain confidences in this matter. But what I heard satisfied my . . . curiosity in this matter, enough that I considered it closed."

"So what did you hear?"

"I was asked not to divulge the details publicly, and I will honor that request."

"Okay. So you . . . you now trust in the conclusions reached by the Newark Police

Department?"

"I do."

"Because, you know, my paper has come across evidence that Detective Kipps's death may not have been a suicide."

I told him about the photos. He paid careful attention but asked no questions. When I was done, he said, "Well, that sounds like something to leave to the authorities. I'm sure they will handle that according to their policies and procedures."

"Right," I said, mostly just to stall so I could consider how to word my next question. It was time to start playing a little less dumb about the Mimi-Fusco affair. I doubted Pastor Al would get too explicit in his answer — it didn't seem like his style — but I wanted to know if he knew. Maybe he could whip a biblical passage on me, something fearsome from the Old Testament about torturing fornicators.

The question came out as: "Was there anything in Mimi's actions or in the actions of Detective Fusco that might have . . . influenced how you felt about this matter?"

"Detective Fusco?" LeRioux boomed. "What would Detective Fusco have to do with this?"

"Oh, you know him?"

"I do."

"Well, he just seems to have taken a lot of *interest* in Mimi," I said, hoping Pastor Al would catch my drift.

He didn't. "Are you saying Detective Fusco is continuing to investigate this matter on his own?"

Oh, he's investigating a lot more than that, I thought.

"I'm not sure what Detective Fusco is or isn't doing," I answered honestly. "But he sure seems to be providing Mimi with a great deal of . . . *comfort.*"

It was, I decided, my last gambit. If he didn't play into it this time, I was dropping it.

"Well, that is a very Christian thing of him to do," Pastor Al said. "I will have to make sure he is lauded for that in some way. Perhaps we can invite him to our Law Enforcement Recognition banquet next fall."

I looked at Pastor Al for any sign of falseness. But there was nothing on his drooping face except for loose jowls.

He didn't know about the affair. And I sure wasn't going to be the one to tell him. For the time being, I didn't want Mimi and Fusco knowing I was onto them. I couldn't take the chance of informing Pastor Al and having him turn it into an opportunity to lecture Mimi about the seventh commandment.

Why Pastor Al dropped his call for an independent investigation was once again a mystery to me. Maybe he really did learn something that made him buy into the official version. Or maybe what he learned was that someone "at the highest level" was making him an offer he couldn't refuse, just to shut him up.

Somewhere, I suspected, one of Pastor Al's car washes might have a fleet of Newark City street sweepers in it.

The myth of gun-running is that given the large numbers of illegal weapons found on city streets, the traffickers must be pushing product in huge quantities. The truth is that Red Dot Enterprises, like other criminal syndicates that dealt in guns, kept their quantities modest. A small number of guns was, quite simply, easier to hide.

So there was no huge cache of weapons, no warehouse stockpiled with firearms. Their entire inventory, stashed here and there, was contained in a few duffel bags.

That said, selling them was a nice, lucrative sideline — a great way to supplement other income.

The economics of gun-running are really no different than any other prohibited product. The prohibition itself helps drive up the perceived value of the item because it means the demand cannot be met through the ordinary mechanisms of legitimate commerce.

The prohibition also creates an imperfect marketplace for the item, wherein information — about everything from supply to price — can be easily obscured.

From there, Red Dot Enterprises relied on the simplest of all business principles: buy low, sell high.

The guns that Red Dot Enterprises offered to their clients, those brand-name .22s and .38s that were so easily tucked into waistbands, typically retailed for somewhere between $299 and $329. Sure, you could get guns for less — Hi Point made a 9 mm that went for roughly $150 — but Red Dot Enterprises didn't bother with those. The margins were too low.

Every once in a while, Red Dot Enterprises had a customer ask for something with a little more "stopping power," as gun people liked to call it. Those requests were honored on an as-needed basis. Requests for automatic weapons were rejected. They were just too hard to find. Besides, they tended to attract a little too much attention.

Mostly, Red Dot stuck with the low-caliber guns it could acquire easily. A typical shipment involved twenty guns for the standard $8,000 — or $400 apiece. The associates at Red Dot Enterprises had a rule that they didn't sell a new gun for less than $500, which guaranteed they'd made at least $2,000 per shipment. That more than compensated for the time and gas money.

But, in truth, the new guns were only part of where the money was. New guns were great for luring in customers. They were a kind of status symbol in the hood — every corner punk wanted to be the guy with the new gun — and they had a certain practical value, because the owner could be reasonably assured a gun that came in a new box would function properly when it was absolutely needed.

A big chunk of the money, though? That was in the used gun market. Old guns littered the hood like so much McDonald's trash, getting used and reused many times. Red Dot Enterprises had devised a variety of ways to acquire old guns while spending virtually no money to do it. As a result, every used gun Red Dot Enterprises sold was nearly 100 percent profit. And Red Dot had devised a way to get a far better price than most of the other gun runners, who might sell a used gun for as little as $50 or rent one out for even less.

So, essentially, Red Dot Enterprises had two types of customers. There were high-end buyers, who were looking for — and received — the high-end, new merchandise. And then there were the customers who came to Red

Dot Enterprises for a new gun, balked at the price tag, and happily settled for used merchandise. Either way, there was money to be made.

And for Red Dot Enterprises, the great thing about guns were: the more people have, the more other people feel they need one. It was a business model based on a fear that fed itself.

CHAPTER 5

With little more to be learned from Pastor Al — or at least little that didn't involve a sermon — I soon excused myself, thanking him for the interview. I went back out on the street and, having departed God's house, decided I could risk powering up my cell phone without incurring any unnecessary wrath.

My phone told me I had two missed calls and two messages waiting. From looking at the numbers, I knew it was my two spokesmen. Flaks love it when they get a reporter's voice mail. It allows them to dump their canned, one- or two-sentence statement and get away before you can ask difficult follow-up questions that require them to do more work. But at the same time, it allows them to ignore your return phone call because, hey, they called you back already! You got the statement! What are you griping about? Come on!

In this case, the flaks were doing a neat little do-si-do. Hakeem Rogers was in full duck-and-cover mode, saying he had no comment because the matter had been referred to the Essex County Prosecutor's Office.

The Essex County Prosecutor's Office spokesman, meanwhile, called to say that for the time being, he had nothing to add beyond what the Newark Police Department had already said; and that I couldn't interview the medical examiner, on the grounds that it was an ongoing case.

So, in other words, Newark was deferring to Essex County, which was deferring to Newark. It was overlapping governmental bureaucracy at its absolute finest. Each part could claim it was in the right, even while the whole was still very wrong. Meanwhile, someone was getting away with murder. And he was a cop, no less.

It was enough to make me, at the very least, hungry. And since I still wasn't keen for fried chicken, I went back to the office, parked, and sought some Pizza Therapy.

On my way toward the pizzeria, I saw Tommy Hernandez on the opposite side of the street and heading in the same direction. Tommy is twenty-four, second-generation Cuban American, and gay as the day is long. I'm not sure his family knows about the last part — Tommy still lives with his parents, and his bedroom at home might as well be a closet, because he's still in it — but the rest of the world doesn't have a very tough time figuring it out. Tommy is trim, neat, slightly below average height, well above average in looks, and, at all times, perfectly accessorized.

At least technically, Tommy is still an intern. His one-year assignment with us began well over a year ago and has developed into an interesting stalemate: the paper cannot afford to bump him up to full-time status, inasmuch as then he might actually start expecting raises, 401(k) matching, and other wild extravagances; at the same time, the paper couldn't let him go because he was one of our best natural reporters and he covered Newark City Hall, one of our most important beats.

So he had earned permanent, temporary status and, barring unforeseen changes — or Tommy coming to his senses and enrolling in business school — he might become the newspaper industry's first fifty-year-old intern someday. Selfishly, I hoped he stuck around. He's become one of my closest friends, not to mention a semiregular pizza partner.

Such being the case, I crossed the street and said, "Hey, what's a handsome young man like you doing for lunch?"

"You know, if you really are going to convert to my side, you're going to have to do something about those pants."

"What's wrong with my pants?"

"If I had to describe it in one word? Pleats. Pleats are what's wrong with your pants. Pleats are what's wrong with your entire world."

I grinned, just because that's Tommy: my own, personal episode of *Queer Eye for the Straight Guy.*

"So what have you been up to?" I asked.

"Nothing half as interesting as what you've been up to, apparently. You got any kind of follow-up working?"

As we continued to the pizzeria and ordered our slices, I told Tommy about my trip to the morgue, my time as a Peeping Tom, and all the various denials and contradictions I had heard along the way.

Tommy listened thoughtfully and, at the end, said, "So why do you think the cops don't want to take this thing on? Usually when it's one of their own getting killed, they go all out."

"Yeah, except when it's one of their own doing the killing," I cracked. "But I don't think that's it. My guess is they really think it's suicide, and they just want it to go away. You know how a lot of cop shops are when it comes to mental health issues. They deal with it like five-year-olds deal with cooties. I don't think the thing with Fusco and Mimi is in their sights because they're trying to keep the blinders on."

"Are you going to tell them about it?"

"I hadn't really thought about it yet. But . . . yeah, I guess I have to."

And I did. I'm a reporter, yes. But I'm also a citizen, which means I have the same civic duty to report information about a crime as anyone else. Depending on how things worked out, it could also result in my being taken off the story, for at least a half dozen reasons — not the least of which is I couldn't very well cover a trial in which I was also testifying. But I suppose that might be unavoidable. Such is the price of virtue.

"So is there anything a bored city hall reporter can do to get in on this?" Tommy asked.

I pondered it for a second, then said, "That depends. Are you still friendly with that secretary in the council clerk's office?"

The secretary was a middle-aged Latina who was sweet on Tommy and, apparently, didn't have much of a Gaydar. Tommy winked in her direction a lot and cooed at her in Spanish so the other secretaries couldn't understand what they were saying.

"Yeah, what do you need?"

"Keep an eye out for any new city contracts involving Redeemer Love Christian Church or Alvin LeRioux," I said. "It would sort of help complete a certain picture for me."

"Redeemer Love Christian. That's one of those churches that reads a lot of Leviticus — the whole man shall not lie with man thing, right?"

"I believe so, yes."

"Okay," Tommy said. "I'll get right on it."

Having revived myself through the miraculous combination of thin crust, tomato sauce, and mozzarella, I returned to the office, put my head down, and started doing some serious typing. It was two thirty, and since this story wasn't going to be winning any awards — news like this required an unadorned, just-the-facts-ma'am approach — I vowed to be done no later than four thirty, so that the story could be posted online by five.

Once upon a time, sitting on a scoop like this, I would have continued cautiously reporting for another few hours, maybe hectoring some more sources or trying to round it out by having an independent forensics expert comment on the pictures. That was back in the hoary days of the late nineties and early millennium, when a scoop was something you guarded jealously until it could be revealed, in its full glory, in the next day's paper.

At most, you would send a version of the story to the Associated Press around midnight — too late for the other papers to catch up but early enough so you could get credit for the scoop on the morning radio and television shows, which would be using that wonderful phrase "according to a story in the *Newark Eagle-Examiner.*"

The Internet has changed all that, of course, scrunching down the time of the news cycles to the point where it has obliterated the concept. When you have news, you post it. No one waits for the dead tree anymore.

I actually finished by four. I looked around for Tina, to tell her I was about to file, but she was nowhere to be seen. So I shipped the story over to the All-Slop and treated myself to a Coke Zero from the office vending machine.

Then I took the long way home, swinging by the Info Palace for a quick visit to see how Kira was recovering from any absinthe-related maladies she may have been suffering. I found her fully engaged by something on her computer screen. She was looking properly prim, dressed in a starched white blouse, with her dark hair up in a bun.

The room was empty except for her, so I said, "Tell me, are you going to do that randy librarian thing, where any second you're going to let your hair down and start roaring like a lioness and demanding I be your lion?"

"Huh?" she said, looking up from her screen.

"Never mind. You just . . . you have your hair up, and I was . . . entertaining certain librarian-related fantasies."

"Oh, that. That's just so I know where I've put my pen. Otherwise I lose it fifty times a day," she said, pulling a Bic ballpoint from the back of her head and letting her hair cascade around her shoulders. Sadly, there were no feline sounds involved.

"How's it going?" I asked. "Feeling okay?"

"Oh, I'm fine. I don't get hangovers."

"I thought hangovers were God's way of making sure the Irish didn't take over the world."

"No, that's whiskey," she said. "Hey, why does your editor keep coming in here and shooting me dirty looks?"

"Who, Tina?"

"Yeah, she's probably sneered at me three or four times today."

"I'm sure she's not sneering."

"Oh, she's sneering. You think I don't know what a sneer looks like? She keeps going like this," Kira said, then twisted her face into a countenance I thought could only be achieved by eating jalapeños.

"Oh, she does that to me all the time. That's just how she looks when she's thinking hard."

"No, these were definitely intentional, directed looks. Seriously, what's up her butt?"

"I'm sure it's nothing."

"I barely even know her."

"All the more reason why it's not about you."

"Well I . . ." and then she stopped, tilted her head and shot me a sly grin. "Wait, you guys didn't used to . . ."

"To what?"

"Shag?"

"Uh . . . not quite."

"But she *wanted* you to shag her."

"I suppose so, yes. Periodically. Or, rather, nonperiodically. It's a long story."

"Did you guys have a fling or something?"

235

To most in the newsroom, Tina Thompson's love life was an open book, and our former . . . whatever . . . was common knowledge among those who cared. But I guess that book somehow hadn't made it back to the library.

So Kira didn't know about me and Tina, and clearly it was in my best interests to tell her now rather than later. After enough years of singledom, one accumulates a certain number of former relationships — some might call it baggage — and I've always felt it best to deal with it in a forthright manner. It's not like I've got some big heavy, nine-piece luggage set. Mine is just your basic, middle-of-the-line Samsonite: a few high school girlfriends, a few from college, a few post-college, one live-in who didn't work out, and a smattering of random dates along the way. It's so unremarkable I always have to check the tags when it comes through at the airport to make sure it's even mine.

Still, this was the first potentially complicated moment of our young relationship. We had yet to define what we were — exclusive/not exclusive, going somewhere/ just playing around, et cetera — and I had to treat this with due care.

"Well, I guess Tina and I had some adult

situations, but we never —"

"What, you never made the move?"

"No, I made the move —"

"But you never sealed the deal? What's up with that?"

I explained, as best I could, how the combination of a ferociously ticking biological clock and an irrational fear of committed relationships had led to Tina's desire for my seed and my seed alone.

When I was done, Kira said, "Oh. That's kind of weird. But you said no?"

"I guess it's not my idea of how fatherhood should work."

"So, what, now she has voodoo dolls of you somewhere? You're not suddenly going to start grasping your side when she puts a pin in you?"

"No, but it sounds like you might want to watch out. She's practiced in witchcraft, you know."

"I'll be careful," she said, then, thankfully, changed subjects. "By the way, Powell called me a little while ago. He wants to talk to you."

"Why didn't he just call me directly? He's got my number — he sent me those text messages last night."

Kira gave her eyes a quick roll. "I don't know. He's a little flighty sometimes. He spends so much time thinking about the dead he has a little trouble focusing on the living."

"Yeah, I suppose I figured that."

"Anyway, he seemed really excited to tell you about something. So you might want to call him."

"Okay, I'll go do that," I said. "You want to grab dinner tonight or something?"

"Can't. My steampunk book group meets tonight."

"Oh. Can I come?"

"Well, we always do it in costume. I'm dressing as a proper Victorian widow who's really a zombie. My character lures men into marrying her and then eats their brains. You want to come dressed as one of my soon-to-be-dead husbands?"

"That's tempting, really, but maybe I'll pass. I haven't read the book, after all."

"Yeah, I guess you're right."

"Well, have fun," I said, giving her a quick kiss on the cheek, because I knew no one was looking, then departed.

Kira hollered after me, "Watch out for the aging voodoo sperm witch!"

I was perhaps two strides back out into the newsroom, and still chuckling about what Kira had just said, when I saw something that made me immediately remove the smirk from my face.

It was the aging voodoo sperm witch herself. She had her arms crossed and was demanding to know, "*What* did she just call me?"

"Huhwhawho?" I said, hoping perhaps she had been too far away to really hear it.

"Oh she did *not* just say that."

"Say, uh . . . say what?"

"Aging voodoo sperm witch?"

Ah, so apparently Tina was doing that pissed-off-chick thing, where they ask a question to which they already know the answer. There was only one response, of course, and that's to do that conflict-avoiding-guy thing, where we try to say anything to stem a total cataclysm.

"Oh, she wasn't . . . that's a . . . a movie we saw. Kira's into all that fantasy stuff, you know. Some of the titles are a little bizarre."

"For the hundred millionth time, Carter Ross, I know when you're lying," she said and began stalking away before I could have much say in the matter.

About three steps into her stalking, Tina turned like she was going to say something. Then she changed her mind and continued on her way. There was no sense in going after her — in the same way there's no sense in running your fingers under a working power saw — so I retreated to my desk.

I was at least semicurious as to what had Paul/Powell riled up, so I made him my first call. His phone cut straight to some indistinct-yet-ominous-sounding symphony music, which droned on for a good twenty seconds. There are few things more annoying than people who turn voice mail into an opportunity to foist their music on a defenseless listener.

Finally, his wannabe Vincent Price voice said, "You have reached Powell. Please leave a message in which you recognize that life is fleeting and death is forever."

I wasn't prepared to give up on reincarnation just yet, so I hung up.

This led to a few minutes of thumb-twiddling — more in the figurative sense, since literal thumb-twiddling gets exhausting if you try to do it for more than about thirty seconds — during which time I pondered my next step.

This was one of the other ways in which the Internet had changed the dynamics of the modern scoop. As soon as you posted something, it set the clock going: the competition would start scrambling to catch up with you, meaning you had to scoop your own scoop if you were going to stay in the lead.

In this case, I decided fairly quickly what my new scoop would be. A story that said the *Eagle-Examiner* had obtained autopsy photos contradicting police findings was good. But a story that said the police had recognized their egregious fault and renewed an investigation because of photos uncovered by the *Eagle-Examiner*? That was even better.

They just had to be given a reason to do it. And, of course, I happened to have witnessed that reason earlier in the day, when I saw the first few minutes of what could have been Mimi and Fusco's amateur porn video. As Tommy had made me recognize, I would need to tell the police about that sooner or later. Might as well make it sooner.

I briefly considered telling Tina what I was about to do. But I knew how that would go. I would inform Tina I felt ethically obligated to tell the police about something. Tina would ask Brodie, who would ask the lawyers, who would dither about it for three days — at $400 per dithering hour — and then eventually decide I was, in fact, ethically obligated to do it. It would then go back down the food chain, making everyone feel justified they had done their job. And all the while, I wouldn't be doing mine.

Not being in the mood for any of that, I dialed the number for my good friend Hakeem Rogers.

After a minute on hold and two minutes of insisting I really *did* need to speak directly with the Newark Police Department's esteemed public information officer — and, no, I couldn't just send him an e-mail — I was finally connected.

"Check your voice mail," he said as soon as he picked up the line. "Everything I have to say is already on there."

"I know, I know. And we're about to post your very informative words online. I'm calling about something else. I'd like to report information about a crime that may have been committed. I'd like to speak with the investigating officer on the Darius Kipps case."

Rogers took a second to swallow this before saying, "Really? You serious?"

"Yeah, I'm serious."

"You're not trying to backdoor yourself into an interview, are you? Because if I hear you were just —"

"No," I cut him off. "I have real, actual, credible information."

"What is it?"

"Ha, no way. I'm not doing this through intermediaries. I talk to the detective in charge of the investigation or I don't talk."

There was another pause on his end before he said, "What are you up to, Ross?"

"Just doing the right thing. Isn't this what you guys are encouraging responsible citizens to do in all those tips posters you plaster all over the place?"

"Yeah, but . . ." He let his voice trail off. "Okay. Let me make a call."

I went back to twiddling my thumbs (again, not really) and watched as my story went live on our Web site. This is horribly old-fashioned of me, I know, but a scoop online never feels quite the same as a scoop in the newspaper. The online scoop seems to disappear into the Internet ether — or, worse, into some message forum where five trolls who still live in their parents' basements make comments on it like "yeh hahaha that remind's me ov the time my cuzin got tyed up by his girl frend n the beeeyatch didnt let him go 4 like 3 dayz hahahahaha lol."

The newspaper scoop, meanwhile, has a certain immortality to it. Mashed pulp and indelible ink are used to note it, and it is entered into the permanent record, such that if anyone in future generations feels like checking in on this day in history, it will be there waiting for them. You just don't get that online.

Or maybe you do. I know they call them "PermaLinks." But still. I just don't see it. One of these days, our paper is going to make the inevitable switch to being online only, and I swear, that's the day I quit and go work for the *Amish Times.*

I was somewhere in the midst of that reverie — thinking of how I'd handle a story about one of those gruesome three horse-and-buggy tie-ups — when my phone rang.

"Carter Ross."

"Hey, it's Rogers. I called out to the Fourth. Captain Boswell out there wants to talk with you."

"The captain? Why is he dealing with it?"

"The better question is why is *she* dealing with it. It's Captain *Denise* Boswell."

"Really? How enlightened of you guys."

"Yeah, she's been out there about six months now. She's the first female officer we've had in charge of a precinct. I sent you a press release, but of course you guys didn't run squat about it, because that's positive news, and you guys aren't interested in positive news about the NPD."

I let him take his shot, then said, "Okay, now just to make it clear: I am *not* going out there to conduct an interview. I am going out there to offer information. But if she feels like making a statement after I'm done, I'm not exactly going to stop her."

"I already told her you'd probably try to weasel your way into an interview and that she shouldn't let you. But she's a captain. That's above my pay grade. If she feels like running her mouth, I can't stop her."

It was exactly what I wanted to hear. "I can live with that. When does she want to talk?"

"Right about now, from what it sounds like."

"Okay," I said. "I'm on my way."

Twilight was coming fast, what with the cloud cover, and it was a lights-on drive out to the Fourth. I thought about stopping by Uncle Bernie on my way — because, you know, I really *could* use some new All-Clad cookware — but decided I didn't have time for the bartering or the bantering. I let the Malibu roll to a stop across the street from the Fourth Precinct, in front of a group of relatively new town houses that had been erected in the footprint of what had once been a blighted public housing high-rise.

It hadn't been raining for several hours, but the front steps to the Fourth still had that wet, gritty feel and sounded like sand-paper as I trudged up them. I went inside and announced myself. Then I sat on a small bench that was designed for maximum discomfort and read the wanted posters. Some bad men stared back at me.

I was soon greeted by an old friend of mine: Officer Hightower. All six foot eight of him.

"You again?" he said. "Thought you didn't have no story."

"Yeah, I'm here to talk to —"

"I know. Come on."

I followed him up some stairs and through the precinct, which had the kind of cramped feeling that obsolete buildings often did. It was dimly lit, which accentuated the fact that everything in it was either yellowish beige or bluish gray, and there seemed to be stuff — just stuff — stacked everywhere. It was basically clean, on a superficial level, but there hadn't been cleaning products invented that could cut through all the grime accumulated from too many people toiling for too many hours across too many decades.

The door to the captain's office was open, and Hightower preceded me in. Captain Boswell was a stocky African American woman in her late thirties with a mop of curly black hair that appeared to be extensions. She was dressed in a blue uniform with a neatly knotted black tie and sat behind a large, cluttered desk. When she stood to greet me, she didn't get much taller. Her butt protruded in a manner that suggested it could accommodate a small shelf.

"Mr. Ross, thank you so much for coming," she said, smiling and extending a small hand, which soon gave me a firm handshake. I had expected the first female precinct captain in Newark Police Department history would be a real ballbuster — you'd have to be tough to make it in that environment, right? — but Captain Boswell had a warm, friendly, almost motherly manner about her.

"Thank you, Captain. Thanks for seeing me."

"Please have a seat."

I settled into a wooden chair in front of her desk. Hightower had assumed a position in the back corner of the room, almost like a bodyguard. I didn't realize I looked threatening enough to require such protection. The captain made no move to introduce him, or even acknowledge him, and seemed to pay about as much attention to him as she did to the furniture. She leaned back in her seat, quite comfortable in her little domain, and folded her hands across her round stomach.

"I just read your story about the photos," she said. "It was very interesting. You reporters do have your ways of getting things, don't you?"

"I guess we do, yes."

She waved it away, like it was of little consequence to her, and started looking around the room with a crinkle in her brow. "I have to apologize for the state of my office. I generally try to keep it a lot tidier than this. Things have just been a little crazy the last few days, as you might imagine. Detective Kipps is . . . was . . . a popular officer. This has been very hard on everyone here."

"Yes, I can imagine."

"I know this runs counter to what you might think, because police work these days has become so data-driven and numbers-oriented, but we also do old-fashioned community policing here. It gives you the best of both worlds. And to me, part of that is creating an atmosphere in the precinct that's like a family. I encourage my officers to support each other like brothers and sisters. So this has been like losing a family member for a lot of us."

"Uh-huh," I said. I was aware Hightower was nodding in agreement, in the back corner of the room.

"Well, enough about our troubles. I understand you have some information for us."

"That's right," I said. "And like Sergeant Rogers told you, I'm coming to you not as a newspaper reporter but as a citizen."

"Yes, I'm aware."

"It concerns Detective Fusco and Mrs. Kipps," I said.

"Detective Fusco? Mike Fusco?" she said, like it surprised her.

"Yes, as I'm sure you know, Detective Fusco was close with Detective Kipps and . . . his family. And . . . he was also close with Detective Kipps's wife, Mimi . . ."

I let my voice trail off for a second. I'm not sure why this was difficult for me to say. Maybe it was because Captain Boswell was so motherly. I felt like I was telling her one of her children was a naughty, naughty boy. At the same time, a mother needs to know certain things, so I continued:

"Yesterday, I was going to interview Mrs. Kipps when I saw her and Detective Fusco through a window. Mrs. Kipps was wearing only a towel, which I thought . . . a little odd. And then Detective Fusco began rubbing her shoulders, which I thought even odder. Then they started kissing, quite passionately. I didn't see any more than that, but it looked to me like they were having an affair."

"I see," she said. She was listening intently, but her face gave no indication as to her thoughts on what I had just shared.

"Anyhow, that — along with the photos and everything else I've been able to learn about Detective Kipps — made me wonder if there was more than a simple suicide here."

The captain was still silent, so I completed the thought: "It made me think this was some kind of love triangle gone wrong, and that Detective Kipps may have been killed because of it."

The more I talked, the deeper the crease in her forehead became. "Mmmm . . ." she said, like she was considering this.

"So . . . I thought perhaps the investigating officer would like to know about what I saw," I said, then I shut up because it was feeling like time for Captain Boswell to start contributing to the conversation.

"Well, at this point, we don't have an investigating officer," she said. "I had been of the understanding that there was nothing to investigate."

"Nothing?" I said. "But what about the

marks on Kipps's arms and legs?"

She took a long moment, then said, "To be honest — and this is off-the-record — I was unaware of those until your story broke. They would have been included in the autopsy report, of course. But even under the best circumstances, it takes the medical examiner several days, if not several weeks, to get us an autopsy report. So that hasn't become part of our investigation yet."

"But now that you know about them, you'll reopen your investigation, yes?" I asked.

A simple "yes" was all I needed to give me the follow-up I had been looking for, but she only allowed, "At this point, I can't say."

This, I must say, perplexed me. I had thought this conversation, while guarded, would be fairly cut and dry: I'd say what I know, and she'd act. I hadn't expected more uncertainty, unless . . .

"Does this . . . does this have something to do with an Internal Affairs investigation?" I asked. "We had heard something about that early on . . ."

She shook her head. "I can't talk about that. Anything involving IA is strictly confidential. That's department policy."

"So you guys are sticking with 'self-inflicted gunshot wound'?"

"For now, yes."

"But . . . how do you explain those marks on his ankles and wrists? Someone tied the man to a —"

She was again shaking her head. "I don't mean to be dodging your questions, Mr. Ross, and they're good questions. But I really can't say anything more."

"Are you saying he tied himself to a chair?"

From behind me, Hightower coughed. Captain Boswell didn't look at him or even seem to notice it, but the noise broke what little rhythm I had going.

"Is there anything else you have to tell me?" she asked.

"No, I guess not. You know my paper is still going to run with the story about the autopsy photos."

"And that's your right to do that," she said.

She smiled again. I got the feeling that while she took Kipps's death personally, none of the rest of the maneuvering associated with it was personal to her. It was the job.

I guess that's one way you get to be the first female precinct captain in Newark history: you learn to separate the two.

■ ■ ■ ■

We finished up with some polite but entirely uninformative small talk, and soon my long-limbed escort was leading me back through the dimly lit hallway and down the stairs. I figured he'd stop once we reached the main door, but he kept going as we went down the front steps.

"Might as well go the whole way," he said, seemingly reading my thoughts. "You get mugged and it messes up our CompStat numbers, and then the captain would get all pissed at me."

"Very thoughtful of you," I said.

When we got to the sidewalk, he pulled out a pack of cigarettes — likely his real motivation for going outside.

"That your ride?" he asked, nodding at my Malibu.

"Yeah, it's bitchin', ain't it? The ladies can't get enough of it." He let out a deep laugh, lit his cigarette, and took a draw. "Drive carefully," he said.

Smoke carefully, I thought. But instead I just said, "Thanks, Officer. Have a nice night."

On my short drive back to *Eagle-Examiner* headquarters, I pondered what very little new information I had gleaned from Captain Boswell. Really, the only semiuseful thing she said was when I asked her about Kipps and Internal Affairs. This is me reading into things, sure. But when someone says, "I can't talk about *that*," it suggests there is something to be discussed.

I returned to the office determined to lean on Buster Hays until he gave up what he had, especially now that I had the necessary inducement: while I was gone, Ruthie Ginsburg — God bless industrious interns everywhere — had e-mailed me a completed Good Neighbors. It was about Stephen Rosenberg of Livingston, who had planned, fund-raised, and created a picnic area in Riker Hill Art Park as his Eagle Scout project. It more than met the high standards we expected of our Good Neighbors pieces, which is to say it appeared to have letters, spaces, and punctuation in approximately the correct distribution.

At the end of the e-mail, Ruthie wrote, "When can we talk about the Eighteenth Avenue town houses? I got some great stuff for you about that and the neighborhood."

I actually felt a little badly all that "great stuff" was going to die in his notebook. But he would hardly be the first reporter to have that happen to him. Anyone who has been around this business for more than a minute has had to eat a story they thought was dynamite.

Looking over to the small armada of unassigned desks where we corralled the interns, I didn't see Ruthie. Perhaps, having tested enough toilet water and uncovered enough good deeds for one day, he had gone home. I rattled off a hasty thank-you e-mail, then printed out a copy of the story and took it over to the wrinkled dean of the newsroom himself.

"Okay, Buster, give it up," I said. "I got your Good Neighbors right here. I want IA."

Buster had been concentrating on his computer, looking at it with his usual contempt, like he wished it would turn back into a typewriter, his preferred drafting instrument. He turned and peered at me from over a pair of reading glasses.

"I'm on deadline, Ivy," he said. "You're going to have to wait until I'm filed. Contrary to what your parents have probably been telling you your whole life, the sun doesn't rise and set out of your ass."

"A deal is a deal."

"Yeah, yeah. Give me five minutes."

I rolled my eyes — not that he saw it — and retreated to my desk. I tried calling Paul/Powell and was again requested to consider my eternal and everlasting death. This time I left a quick message: "Powell, it's Carter Ross at the *Eagle-Examiner.* Kira said you were looking for me. Give me a call."

Returning to my desk, I saw I had a fresh e-mail. It was from "Thompson, Tina" and had the subject line, "???" which made me cringe as I clicked on it. What had I done wrong this time?

But it was just one line: "Want to have dinner with an aging voodoo sperm witch tonight?"

I considered this for a moment. Did I? Tina had been such a pill lately, I was actually looking forward to spending less time around her, not more. Then again, it's not like I had any pressing plans — watching college basketball with Deadline curled up against my leg didn't count — and maybe Chief Tina was finally making a peace offering. We could use a burying of the hatchet.

I looked over to Tina's office, which was dark. She hadn't been in there for at least ten minutes — we had those motion-sensing lights that shut off after so long. I fired back a quick, "Sure. Details?"

As I awaited a reply, I heard Buster bellow from a few desks over, "Okay, Ivy, I'm filed. Let's do this."

I grabbed the printout of Ginsburg's story and returned to Buster's desk.

"Let's see that Good Neighbors," he said.

I slid the story in his direction. He adjusted his granny glasses and took a quick gander at the top.

"You farming out your dirty work to interns now?"

I summoned my best impersonation of Buster's Bronx accent and repeated the words he had said to me earlier in the day: "I do what I need to do in order to survive in this cruel world."

The right corner of his mouth lifted — for Buster, that counted as a smile — and he said, "Good. You're learning."

He spent another five seconds scanning the copy, then proclaimed, "This'll do."

"Okay, so let's have it."

Buster removed the glasses, rubbed his face, then said, "At the time of his death, there was no IA investigation into Darius Kipps. Nothing. Zip. Zilch."

"Are you sure?"

"Yeah, I'm sure. My source is gold. IA is bound by an attorney general's directive to investigate all complaints, no matter where they come from. If there was a complaint about him, there'd be a file. And my source said there's no file. He did some checking with the other IA guys just to make sure. Kipps is clean, as far as they're concerned."

"Huh."

"Now," he said, grinning as much as Buster ever allowed, "ask me what else my guy told me."

"What else did your guy tell you?"

"It's going to cost you another Good Nei—"

I stopped him immediately: "Forget it, Buster. There's quid pro quo and then there's extortion. Don't cross the line."

"Okay, okay. Hang on," he said, opening up a notebook and flipping to a page filled with random pen marks that may have been an attempt to represent actual letters. "Okay, according to my source, Kipps called an IA guy. My source wouldn't say which IA guy, just that it was someone Kipps knew and trusted. The call came in late Saturday night so the guy wasn't around. Kipps left a message."

"What did the message say?"

"My guy said it was pretty vague. It didn't make any sense to him. Something about . . ." Buster was looking at his notes like he was struggling with them. "It was something about . . . seeing blotches on something . . . or . . . I don't know. Point is, Kipps wanted the guy to call him back."

"And did he?"

"Nope. By the time the IA guy got to the message, it was Monday morning. Kipps was already dead."

If nothing else, Buster's source helped illuminate the rumors floating around the NPD about Kipps and Internal Affairs. I'm sure as the news about Kipps was getting out, the IA officer — whoever he was — had been telling people something along the lines of, "Wow, Kipps just left a message for me over the weekend."

Once that got out into the wind, it could have blown in any direction — cops love gossiping as much as reporters, and gossip can always get twisted, advertently or otherwise. That's why my guy Pritch would have heard that Kipps had contact with IA, which could turn easily into "Kipps was dirty."

The more intriguing question was what he was calling to say. If it had to do with "blotches" — whatever that was — maybe Kipps had a health problem. Weren't blotches on the skin a symptom of HIV/ AIDS? That would certainly be something Kipps wouldn't want to get out. And maybe he would rather kill himself than let the world know he had contracted AIDS.

That would still leave the matter of those marks on his arms and wrists, but perhaps there was something I hadn't thought of or didn't know that explained those.

Or maybe Kipps was calling IA about misconduct by a fellow officer: Mike Fusco. There's probably nothing in the Newark Police Department handbook that expressly prohibits sleeping with another officer's wife. But it was possible Kipps had some kind of other dirt on Fusco he was suddenly willing to spill. If that was the case, and Fusco found out about it, it gave him yet another reason to put Kipps on the dead side.

Or maybe, I realized as I returned to my desk, I could just face facts that I was still speculating. A larger truth was out there, waiting for me. I just had to keep plugging away until I found it.

In the time I had been gone, Tina had sent me another e-mail. "My place. Eight," it said. "Bring a bottle of wine and your appetite."

That sounded promising — for a skinny girl, Tina knew how to cook — and it certainly beat the repast I had waiting for me in Bloomfield, which would have involved a hasty phone call to Panda Palace. I wrote back, "Sounds great. See you then."

I was clicking the Send button as my phone rang.

"Carter Ross."

"Carter, it's Powell," he said. I could hear street noises in the background.

"Hey, what's going on?"

"I saw you posted a story about those photos I took. Pretty awesome. But why didn't you run the pictures? Did they not come out well or something?"

"No, they came out fine. We just . . . they might be a little graphic for some of our readers."

"Would you have run them if that dude was still alive?"

"I don't know. Does it matter?"

"Well, yeah it matters. See, this goes to one of the central points of the Death Studies movement, and that is challenging the irrational fear of death in our culture. Until we change some of the basic assumptions about what it means to make the change from lucidity to morbidity, we will never —"

"Right, Powell," I said, because I didn't need to hear the lecture he was going to give when he became Professor Death. "Kira said you were hot to talk to me about something?"

"Yeah, I, uh . . . I was at the M.E.'s office

today — because my internship is Tuesday and Thursday afternoons, you know? And I overheard him talking to someone."

"Him? Who's him?"

"The medical examiner. And he was *pissed.* I couldn't tell about what at first. But I had never heard him that mad before. He was *fired up.* You could hear him *going off.* I thought he was going to have a conniption."

I realized I needed to indulge Paul/Powell's penchant for verbal meandering. So I said, "Okay. What was he mad about?"

"You couldn't even really tell, at first. And I couldn't, you know, just be seen hanging outside his office, eavesdropping. Technically, I'm supposed to be in the examining room, observing the autopsies, taking notes, you know? I have to be able to justify this internship to my adviser at the end of the term, and I can't —"

I lost my patience: "Right, got it. Let's get back to the mad medical examiner."

"Oh, right. Well, it was tough to tell what he was pissed about, but I heard him say 'Kipps.' That's the name of your dude, right?"

"Right."

"Yeah, well, I guess somehow they had found out about the photos. I don't know

262

how they knew you had them —"

"I called them and told them."

"You did?"

"It's sort of what reporters do, Powell."

"Oh," he said, as if he couldn't quite figure out why I would tip my hand like that. "Well, anyway, someone — like his boss or something — must have been asking him about the photos. And he kept saying stuff like, 'I have no idea' and 'Well, they didn't come from me,' and 'If I find out, I'll fire the bastard,' and all that."

I smiled. I love it when government agencies go on witch hunts to figure out where a leak is coming from. It expends a tremendous amount of energy and almost never catches the real witch. Half the time the person who ordered the investigation into the leak is actually the person behind it — but knows he has covered his tracks well enough to never be caught. The other half of the time the source is someone they'd never suspect, like the intern who got the key from the janitor. They'd be better off trying to find Santa Claus's workshop.

"So I had to walk away at that point because, you know, I'm supposed to be —"

"In the examining room, right." I cut him off.

"Yeah, but anyway, everyone in the office

was totally buzzing about it. It wasn't hard to hear him. I was talking to one of the secretaries about it, and you know what she said she heard him say?"

"What's that?"

"She said that he said, and I quote, 'What you're asking me to do is unethical.' "

"What was he being asked to do? Did she know?"

"No. That's just what she said he said."

"Hmm . . ."

"Anyhow, I thought you'd want to know," he said. "I gotta run. I volunteer at a funeral home on Tuesday nights. I'm doing it for credit, so I have to be on time."

"Have fun with that. Thanks for the call."

"Later."

So the medical examiner was being asked to do unethical things. And he was understandably upset about it.

I just hoped he was upset enough to unburden his worries to the *Eagle-Examiner.*

From a reporter's standpoint, public employees are wonderful creatures because they have no way of hiding from us. Within a few mere keystrokes, I can learn their full name, date of birth, and annual salary — time was, in the days before identity theft became so rampant, I could even get their

Social Security number. Maybe that all sounds a little invasive of their privacy, but the framers of the Constitution didn't *want* public officials to have privacy. They were deeply suspicious of anyone with authority and wanted citizens to have lots of tools with which to resist tyranny.

As such, I was able to learn in fairly short order that Essex County Medical Examiner Raul Ibanez was born on August 9, 1964, and was paid $177,716 a year to slice and dice dead folks and make pronouncements about them. A few keystrokes later and I was looking at a Google Maps overview of his home on Lenox Avenue in Westfield. It looked like a nice crib, though his trees needed some trimming.

I looked at the clock, which told me I had just enough time to ambush the medical examiner and still make it back to Tina's by eight — but only if I hustled. So I grabbed my peacoat and made like a man in a hurry.

The best way to explain Westfield, New Jersey, is that someone cracked open an upscale shopping mall above it, then sprinkled all the stores onto the streets below. As such, I could have given directions to Ibanez's place as I would give directions to a food court: take a left at the Victoria's Secret, pass the Williams-Sonoma, take another left after the Banana Republic.

After making the turn on a suitably genteel suburban street, I found Ibanez's nicely appointed home on the left side. It had a basketball hoop mounted on the garage, healthy shrubs lining a slate walkway, and a handsome red door with a brass knocker that I was soon putting to use.

A smallish man with a neat goatee and a thin semicircle of hair around his otherwise bald head soon answered. He was wearing suit pants and a button-down shirt — no scrubs for this doctor — but had ditched the jacket and tie. He had a wireless device clipped onto his belt.

"Dr. Ibanez, I'm sorry to trouble you at home, but I thought it would be better to see you here than at your office. My name is Carter Ross and I'm a reporter for the *Eagle-Examiner.* I'm the guy who posted that story with the autopsy photos today."

He exerted an effort at keeping himself impassive, though I got the sense hearing my name was like a small kick in the nuts. I was, after all, the guy who had ruined his day.

"What . . . what are you . . . I have no comment," he said quickly, with a slight accent, and I expected the statement would soon be followed by a whole lot of red door being slammed in my face.

But he kept the door open. This was encouraging. Maybe he didn't want to comment, but he did want to talk. I might be able to leverage what little information I had into a whole lot more — with help from a little semieducated bluffing.

"Dr. Ibanez, I can totally respect that. But I gotta tell you, you seem like a nice guy, and I don't want to have to end up writing a story about you needing to answer charges from the state ethics board, you know what I'm saying?"

I didn't know if the state even *had* an ethics board for medical examiners — much less what this guy was being asked to do that was unethical — but the words "ethics board" were like another shot to his bits. Since pretending to know more than I actually did seemed to be working, I continued:

"I just see how this is all coming together — I'm sure you've heard the AG's office has looked at this thing — and I hate to see you being railroaded on this."

That got him.

"Railroaded?" he said. "Oh, for the love of . . ."

"It's happened before. If this thing spills out all big and ugly, they might be looking for a scapegoat. Look at all the players here"

267

— right, whoever they were — "you think any of them are really going to fall on their swords? Really, who's going to fall on his sword? You'd be an easy target."

I was really winging it now, but Ibanez was too wrapped in his own drama to recognize it.

"Oh, damnit. Damnit! Are you . . . Who's saying that? Where are you getting that?"

"You know I can't tell you. Let's just put it this way: it's the same place I got the photos from. And it's someone who's in a position to know you're being asked to do something unethical."

That, of course, was true, in a manner of speaking. That Paul/Powell was in that "position" because he happened to be skulking outside Ibanez's office was immaterial. The doctor brought his hands to his forehead and massaged his temples. His cheeks were getting flushed. I went in for the kill.

"We're off the record here. So why don't you just tell me this thing from your perspective, beginning, middle, and end. And when I put this all in the newspaper, I'll try to make it look as good for you as I possibly can."

I thought I had him right where I wanted him: cornered, scared, a little off balance.

Total capitulation was just moments away.

But I guess I had cornered him a little too much because he came out fighting. What I heard next was, I imagined, the same version of Raul Ibanez that Paul/Powell had heard earlier in the day.

"You know what? You know what? You want to write something in your paper? You write *the facts*. I'm not . . . I . . . I give them the mechanism. I give them the cause. But the manner, that's . . . I'm not . . . I'm not a detective. I give them the science. That's my job."

He started jabbing his index finger at me: "*That's* my job. And I did my job. They're the ones not doing their job. You tell *that* to the damn state ethics board! You tell *that* to your damn sources! You tell them I'm going to get this all documented. They want to railroad me? Let 'em try. Let 'em try!"

There appeared to be a Mrs. Ibanez coming down the stairs to learn what all the yelling was about. But I never got a glimpse of more than her feet because the next thing I saw was what I suspected I might get all along: an up-close view of his red front door being slammed in my face.

My last official act of the evening was to slip my business card through Ibanez's mail slot, just in case he decided he needed to yell at someone in the middle of the night. Then, having done enough damage for the evening, I flipped the "off duty" light in my mind and started driving toward Tina's.

Except, of course, my brain kept trying to pick up passengers the whole way. Even as I did my requested wine shopping — a connoisseur, I always insist on a silly name or a pretty label — I thought of what I could read into Ibanez's performance.

The doctor was absolutely correct, of course: a medical examiner makes objective determinations as to the mechanism of death (in this case, a bullet traveling at high velocity) and the cause of death (that Darius Kipps didn't have much of a head left by the time the bullet departed his person). When it comes to mechanism and cause, a homicide and a suicide can be virtually identical. From a purely medical standpoint, those ligature marks on Darius Kipps's arms and legs were about as involved in his demise as a shaving nick.

No, those go more to the *manner* of death, which is what really counts, legally. The manner of death is a more subjective call on the medical examiner's part, and it relies on what he can learn from the body *and* what he's been told by investigators.

I didn't know what the investigators had

told Ibanez, of course. But in the face of what appeared to be foul play, someone had informed Ibanez no more investigation would be done, giving him little choice but to rule the manner of death a suicide. And he considered going along with that unethical.

Or at least that was my best guess. By the time I reached Hoboken, I hadn't come up with anything better.

The last available street parking spot in Hoboken was snatched up in late 1995. So rather than join the legion of people circling patiently for the next one, I parked in a garage. I was just getting out of the car when I got a text from Tina. "Hopping in shower. Let yourself in."

Tina's door code, 2229, was easy to remember, thanks to the handy, if slightly disturbing, pneumonic she had given me: it spelled the word "baby."

Tina's condo was a one-bedroom on the fourth floor with a view of Manhattan that made you feel like you owned the world. I took in the panorama for a second, then went over by the bathroom door, which was slightly ajar.

"Hey, it's me," I announced.

"Hey. Sorry. I'll be out in a second. My

jog lasted a little longer than I thought," she called over the hissing of the shower.

"No problem."

"Did you pick the wine based on the name?"

"No, I went with a cute label instead. It's got this little black dress on it and it's called, get this, 'Little Black Dress.' It's a pinot noir."

"Oh, that stuff is actually pretty good. Pour me a glass and I'll be out in a second."

After pouring us both glasses of wine — I drink wine when beer is unavailable — I went and spied what my dinner was going to be. I saw broiled salmon with dill sauce, snap peas with some kind of fancy onions on them, and asparagus sautéed in what smelled like lemon butter. A fish, two vegetables, and no starch. Such was the peril of accepting a dinner invitation from Tina, who mostly eschews red meat and treats carbohydrates like they're an aggravating relative she visits only on holidays.

I was sitting on the couch, taking in the view when Tina emerged and gave me a better one. She had pulled back her still-damp hair and was wearing a pair of men's boxers and a black camisole that nicely showed off her shoulders. She wasn't wearing a bra underneath, but I could hardly blame her. I wasn't wearing one either.

"Thanks for being patient," she said as she took a sip from her glass of wine, then moved into the kitchen to begin plating our meal. "I just needed that run *so* badly. I skipped yesterday, thanks to Darius Kipps, and if I had to skip today I would have felt like a giant slug."

My need for exercise goes into hibernation a little more easily, but I said, "Well, we wouldn't want that."

"I left the office early tonight, too. I had to sell my soul to do it — I'll be closing the paper Wednesday and Thursday thanks to this — but it was worth it. I just needed a break."

"Yeah, I bet," I said. The rationalization was as much for her sake as mine. Knowing Tina as I do — take a prototypical Type A, then add three parts of ambition and four parts of ceaseless drive — she was still feeling guilty about leaving early.

She inquired as to the state of my story, and I filled her in on the latest while she continued puttering around the kitchen. She was asking more as a friend than a boss — you can tell the difference because her questions don't have as fine a point on them when she's being my friend — and soon we were seated before the dinner she had prepared.

"This ought to be a switch for you," she said. "Everything you're about to eat is non-processed and a hundred percent organic."

"Yeah, but I'd like to remind you cavemen ate organic, unprocessed food, too. And they're dead."

She shook her head but smiled. "Sometimes I think *you're* the caveman."

"Cheers," I said. "To evolution or the lack thereof."

We clinked glasses and set to eating. When we're not fighting like crazed badgers, Tina and I really do get along quite well. And it was pleasant to finally have a cessation of hostilities. The salmon was dynamite. The wine wasn't bad, considering who picked it. And we fell into easy chatter.

We were finishing up our meal — and had made the rather easy decision that, yeah, it wouldn't kill us to open up another bottle of wine — when Tina finally got around to what was, as I figured, her agenda all along.

"You know, I've been a real bitch to you lately, and I want to apologize," she said as I refilled her glass.

"No, no, it's okay. We've all been stressed."

"It's more than that. I've been . . ."

"It's okay."

"No, let me just say this. I feel like I've been, I don't know, not myself. Like today, with Kira, she called me a voodoo sex witch, or whatever it was, and I was already scheming of ways to make her life hell — really, how *dare* she? I never did anything to her, right? And then I realized I had been inventing reasons to go back into the Info Palace all day just to give her dirty looks. I know she noticed. She must have thought I was a nut."

"She didn't mention anything about it," I said, and for once Tina failed to intercept the blatant lie I had just tossed up.

"And the thing is, I don't really even care that you two are seeing each other, or dating, or whatever it is you're doing —"

"It's sort of still undefined," I interjected.

"That's fine. It's none of my business and, besides, it's not — I mean, no offense — it's not something I'm even interested in doing, you know? I don't want a relationship with you. I don't want a relationship with *anyone.* And yet there I was, getting jealous and acting crazy because you guys are . . . whatever. I think sometimes my competitiveness gets the best of me. I need to win for the sake of winning, never mind that I don't even particularly want what I'm trying to get."

"It happens to all of us sometimes," I reassured her.

"Me more than most. Anyhow, please accept my apology. I'll try to be on my best behavior from here on out."

"No problem. Thanks for apologizing."

"You're an easy person to apologize to," she said.

We clinked glasses again. It soon turned out I was easy in other ways, too.

For the record, it really *wasn't* my fault. I try to own my mistakes in this life and know when I am to blame for things. I accept full responsibility when I am. But it wasn't me. Not this time.

First, it was the kitchen. Tina has this narrow, galley-style kitchen, as is often the case in crowded Hoboken, and there isn't room in it for two people. So as we did the dishes — with me manning the sink and her puttering around me — she kept brushing into me with that lithe body of hers or having to put a hand on my hip for balance as she scooted past. It was just slight, incidental contact, yes, but sometimes that sets a tone for the less incidental kind.

Next, it was the couch. Tina only has one that faces her television at the right angle. So when she suggested we watch a movie

— and, really, I needed at least a movie's worth of time before I was remotely in shape to drive home — there was no choice but for us to both sit on it lest one of us have a ruined viewing experience.

Finally, it was her calf. The movie was perhaps ten minutes old when she announced that it had been giving her troubles lately and was starting to stiffen up after her jog. She asked if I wouldn't mind rubbing it, and being the amiable sort of chap that I am, I acquiesced. Isn't that what good friends do?

The next thing I knew, I had both of Tina Thompson's long, lovely, bare legs stretched across my lap. I began rubbing her left calf, finding the kink in the muscle and slowly kneading it out. She let out a series of delighted sighs.

Then, because I was already in the neighborhood, I rubbed her right calf. After all, as any jogger knows, it feels good to have your legs rubbed after a run, whether you've strained a muscle or not. So she kept right on making those pleasant little noises.

Next thing I knew, Tina had scooched down closer to me so I could rub her quads. And I figured that was reasonable because they are, after all, the largest muscles in the legs, and they get sore from running, too. I worked around the knee, then moved up to the thick part of the thigh. Tina was really getting into the massage, having closed her eyes and flung her arms up over her head, such that her camisole was riding up a little, exposing part of her lean midriff.

At a certain point, she asked if I could rub her hip flexor as well because, she reported, that was also a little tender. And because apparently I wasn't quite hitting the sore spot with her boxers "getting in the way," she removed them, leaving her in a pair of rather insubstantial black panties.

I kept up the pretense of the massage for a little while longer as I worked on one hip, then the next. Then somehow I was rubbing her arms, then her shoulders. Then, well, of course she had to remove the camisole so I could really work on her back a bit without *that* "getting in the way."

So somehow, in this purely innocent fashion — through no fault of my own — I ended up with Tina more or less naked and writhing on the couch, moaning in pleasure. And it would hardly seem sporting of me to let her do all that writhing and moaning by herself, so I joined in.

Tina and I had gotten to this spot — or variations of it — a number of other times during our dalliances through the past few years. And usually one of us pulled back, knowing that taking the final step could change everything. Especially at the right time of the month.

And so I kept expecting she would announce a halt to this little romp. Only she was way too into it, perhaps because my hands were straying into areas where the massage therapist at the health club wouldn't go.

Then I kept expecting *I* would finally come to my senses. Except I was way into it, too, perhaps because she had tugged off all my clothes and started playing with some of my happier places.

Soon what started on the couch went to the floor, then to the bedroom, where very, very bedroom-type things started happening. This was, technically, our first time at this, but it didn't feel like a first-time thing. There was none of the awkwardness or the haltingness. No one was checking in to make sure anyone was okay — the answer was already obvious.

I let her cross the finish line first because I'm just that kind of guy, then followed her soon thereafter. We held each other for a while without discussing any of what had just transpired. And frankly, I didn't have the energy left to ponder what we had just done, how it would impact Kira and me — that relationship was still so undefined — or whether the Ross family tree had just added another branch. I just lay there and let my senses enjoy the smell, touch, and sight of Tina in her postcoital glory.

The next thing I knew there was a dim, morning light coming through the window and a phone was ringing somewhere. It sounded like a home phone, but it wasn't my home phone. Then I remembered that's because I wasn't in my home. Tina grabbed it and offered a "hello" that managed not to sound like she had just been ripped from sleep.

"Oh, hi, Katie," she said. There was only one Katie I knew of that would be calling at this hour, and it was Katie Mossman from the All-Slop.

"No, no, perfect timing. I'm just getting back from a run. What's up?" Tina continued. She was perched on the side of her bed, still naked, and had grabbed a pen and small pad. There was another one of those unsightly numbers — a six, of all horrible things — leading her digital clock.

She began scribbling as I listened to her half of the conversation, which consisted of a lot of "Uh-huh, uh-huh" and "No, I'll do that."

It ended with: "Okay, I'll be there in forty-five minutes or so. Thanks, Katie, bye."

Tina turned to me and said, "Well, so much for lying in bed this morning."

"What's going on?"

"Pretend like I'm calling you on the phone to tell you we got another dead Newark cop — another suicide, from what it looks like. He was found dead in his home. Apparently it's already all over the incident pagers this morning, so we better get moving."

"They know who it is?"

"Yeah," Tina said. "It's Mike Fusco."

Red Dot Enterprises didn't get into business to kill anyone.

It might supply would-be killers with guns. But it left the act to the customers. As the old saw goes: guns don't kill people, people kill people.

Really, for the associates of Red Dot Enterprises, it was more of a practical decision than a moral one. Most police departments didn't focus their efforts strictly on guns. They had gang units, drug units, or homicide units, but never gun units. When they bothered with weapons charges, it was always in connection with (or sometimes even in lieu of) other charges. The classic is the drug dealer who is wily enough to hide his stash but goes to jail for being caught with a gun. It was like getting Al Capone on tax evasion. Even though the cops are happy to get a dirtbag off the street, the gun isn't seen as the real crime. The police cared about guns, yes. But they didn't care that much.

Murder was an entirely different story. Murder was a messy business, one that attracted undue attention. Newspapers wrote stories about it. Voters paid attention to it. Most of all, police commanders in cities large and small cared about it. Deeply. Many of the same police commanders who would have to scramble to the Uniform Crime Report to find their gun arrests could tell you their homicide clearance rate off the top of their heads.

Especially when it involved a police officer. It was something the associates of Red Dot Enterprises couldn't believe they were even talking about when the subject first came up. They just wanted to keep their low profile, sell their guns, and make their money quietly. Not kill cops.

So there was more than a little debate about Detective Michael Fusco. There were those in the group who thought they didn't need to bother with Fusco. Sure, he had some investigative skills and could bring certain law enforcement resources to bear on them. But it's not like he was the world's greatest detective. He was a meathead who drove around in a big pickup truck and wore tight sweaters. He wasn't that much of a threat.

And yet, before long, even the doves in the group were going along with the hawks when it came to Fusco. The clinching factor was when it was learned, through reliable sources, that he had started a relationship with the Widow Kipps shortly after her husband's death. It was a sign Fusco was too close, and that he probably wouldn't give up. He had to go, plain and simple.

So they quickly set about planning it. Had Fusco been a civilian, they could have hired some help. Red Dot Enterprises certainly had enough contacts with dangerous men, thugs without conscience who would kill for next to nothing — a little free merchandise would have been all the payment required.

But a cop was a different matter entirely. This was a job they were going to have to do themselves.

CHAPTER 6

Since they were scattered around Tina's apartment, it took longer to find the various pieces of my clothing than it did to get into them. Around the time I finally discovered my pants — what were they doing out by the front entrance? — at least one of the problems of waking up in my boss's apartment was beginning to become apparent. If I was in my own place, I would have at least grabbed a quick shower. Tina was of the mind-set I didn't have time to brush my teeth.

I managed to win that battle, making use of a spare she had in her medicine cabinet. Otherwise, it was all go-go-go. On my way toward the door, Tina pressed a pear and an apple into my hand — the closest I was going to get to any fruit, forbidden or otherwise, on this morning — and shooed me out.

The address Tina gave me for Fusco's

place was in Belleville, a small but densely packed slice of New Jersey just north of Newark. It was just under twenty minutes away, and I knew I had to hurry. Still, I stopped for a Coke Zero. I had gotten four, maybe five hours of half-drunk slumber in someone else's bed and, while wearing yesterday's clothes, was being horsewhipped by my editor into frantic action. Such things are not meant to be borne without at least a little caffeine.

Plus, I needed to get my head working properly. It just couldn't seem to swallow the idea that Fusco was dead. The killer had become the killed. Was Mike Fusco's last act to give himself the ultimate punishment for the crimes he had committed? Or was this another staged suicide?

I had just gotten back on the road when I heard a news tease on the radio that ended ". . . and another police officer is dead in Newark, apparently by his own hand."

This elicited a rare but emphatic swear from my lips. There would be no head start for me this time. To return to my pasture metaphor, there were few things worse than being part of the herd. There was no way to avoid smelling like dung.

It came as no surprise that when I pulled onto the narrow street in Belleville where

Mike Fusco had lived, until very recently, three news vans were already there. Undoubtedly more were on the way. I parked outside one of the tidy little clapboard houses just in from the corner, then walked briskly toward Fusco's place — the one with the crime scene tape strung along the outer edge of the property — about midway down the block.

Outside the house next door, two of the three cameras present were trained on a hirsute middle-aged white man who was telling a story that involved a lot of arm-waving and hand gesturing. I wouldn't say the man was exactly ready for his fifteen minutes of fame — he had a three-day scruff and a torn New York Giants sweatshirt featuring Lawrence Taylor, which made it at least twenty years old. But I also wouldn't say he struck me as the kind of guy who was too bothered about appearances. The slippers on his feet were one hint. The parachute pants were the dead giveaway.

I let the TV cameras finish up with him, then moved in. In short order, I learned his name and that he was claiming to have been the one who made the initial call to the police. He said he worked "in the sanitation industry" — like there was somehow shame

in just saying he was a garbage man —
which meant he was up early and just about
to head out on his route. It was shortly after
four when he heard gunshots.

"Gunshots with an 's'?" I asked. "As in,
more than one?"

"Yeah. Two of them. It was a bang" — he
waited for approximately ten seconds, his
eyes wide and casting about the whole time,
like he was still performing for the cameras
— "and then a bang. Two shots."

"Two shots," I repeated. "What, did he
miss the first time?"

"Beats me. I'm just telling you what I
heard."

I nodded and started taking notes. Sad to
say, but if Mike Fusco lived in certain parts
of Newark, his body would still be lying
undiscovered right now. In a lot of neighborhoods, people long ago stopped bothering
to call the police when they heard gunfire.

"So what happened next?" I asked.

"Well, it was tough to tell where the first
shot was even coming from. But the second
shot, I knew it was coming from Fusco's
place. I was paying attention at that point,
you know? I didn't know if someone was
robbing the place or if it was some kind of
gang thing or what. I didn't think we had
any of that out here. But sometimes a

neighborhood can turn, you know? I mean, I heard some, you know, some blacks just moved in the next block over. I'm not racist, I'm just saying."

"Uh-huh," I said. Because it was better than saying: *"Actually, sir, that is the very definition of racism."*

"So, anyway, I went over to my window to have a look."

"Did you see anything?"

"Nope. Nada."

"And then you called the police?"

"Yeah, I figure that's what I pay all those property taxes for, right? Let the police do their job. And I gotta give them credit, they were here in, like, two minutes."

He continued: "So I went out and met them, told them the same thing I told the dispatcher. They asked me if I could hang out for a while, so I called into work — I got about a million sick days piled up anyway — and they went in. Ten minutes later one of them comes out and tells me what happened."

"And what was that?"

"Well, Fusco was lying in bed with his brains blown out, that's what. I guess he couldn't take it no more."

If there truly was anything Mike Fusco couldn't take no more — sorry, any longer

— the guy didn't know. And neither did anyone else on the block. Over the next two hours of hanging out and chatting with various neighbors, I heard a lot of the same thing about Fusco. He lived by himself, no kids, no pets, no hobbies that took him outside with any great frequency; he would offer a nodding hello to people but otherwise didn't say much; he drove a big truck with jacked-up suspension; he had big muscles; and he was a cop.

At a certain point, I became satisfied there was really nothing more the good people of Belleville could tell me. And I was starting to consider pulling up the tents and hitting the trail when my phone rang.

The caller was Mimi Kipps.

I stared at the phone for one ring, two rings, trying to give myself a chance to come up with some clever idea how to play this thing. By the third ring, I hadn't produced anything, but I answered anyway.

"Carter Ross."

"Carter, it's Mimi Kipps," she said in a husky voice.

"Hi, Mimi."

"Are you writing a story about Mike?"

"I am, yes."

"Can you . . . can you come over? I was

hoping I could . . . talk to you a little bit."

"About what?" I said.

There was no immediate response. I thought I heard some hard breathing, definitely some sniffling. When she finally spoke, it was through a voice box squeezed with emotion: "I think . . . maybe the people who killed Darius might have killed Mike because he was . . . I don't know."

"He was what?" I pressed.

"I just . . . I think I may have gotten him killed," she said. That was about as far as she made it before the sobs came. It was tough to tell what was coming out of her mouth. Words? Sentences? Random syllables? It was unintelligible.

I let her carry on like that for a little while. She was trying to compose herself, unsuccessfully. Finally, I said, "Mimi, I'll be there in about fifteen minutes, okay?"

She blurted out something that might have been "thank you" and I hung up.

Say this much, she had addled my easily aroused curiosity. I wondered if she was warming up to make some kind of confession. She "may" have gotten him killed? What, exactly, did that mean?

I'm not saying I was ready to believe the worst about Mimi Kipps, but neither did I think she was just the pitiable, grieving widow. In a world where there are seldom coincidences, the two men she was sleeping with had both ended up taking bullets to the head. It was getting hard to imagine a scenario where she wasn't involved in that somehow.

As I merged on the Garden State Parkway for the short trip down to East Orange, I called Tina just to check in and let her know I was on the move. I told her about how, other than the fact that there were two shots fired — which would require some explanation — I had gotten a whole lot of nothing from the neighborhood.

She informed me I had missed a similar amount of nothing in the office. The Belleville Police had promised some kind of statement in "a few hours," though they had started making that pledge a few hours ago. The Newark Police were in total shutdown mode — Hakeem Rogers's office was letting all calls go through to voice mail and no e-mails had been answered.

Even Buster Hays's normally inexhaustible Rolodex was, so far, getting shut out. Not that I had lost faith in him. It was not quite ten o'clock, still early in the news-gathering day.

"So, anything else I need to know?" Tina asked, and I could tell she was in a hurry to get off the phone.

"No, I guess not . . . except . . . well, we never got a chance to, uh, talk about what happened last night."

"What, the sex?"

"Yeah."

"Oh, it was fine. Better than fine. I'm sorry, I'm just distracted. It was great."

"Well, thanks, but I wasn't looking for a grade on my report card. I meant . . . are you, I don't know, okay with everything?"

"Oh, honey," she said with a chuckle, "I'm not in high school anymore. You're not exactly my first. Daddy isn't coming after you with a shotgun."

"I just . . . After all this time, I didn't expect . . . I didn't go over there thinking anything like that would —"

"I swear, you're more of a girl than I am sometimes," she interrupted. "Look, we're grown-ups. We had sex. It happens. Not to me a lot lately, but it does happen."

I slid through a toll plaza going perhaps a little too fast, still not feeling I was getting my point across. "But did you, I don't know, did you mean for it to happen? Was it the wine? Was it an accident?"

"What do you mean? Like did I just accidentally get naked and stumble onto your cock? No, I'd say that was pretty intentional."

"You know what I'm talking about."

Tina gave an exasperated sigh, then blurted out, "Look, you were a booty call, okay?"

"I was?"

"Yeah. I just wanted to have sex last night, and it was either you or a random bar hookup. I didn't feel like going out. So it was you. My God, what did you think that was about? I was barely wearing any clothing to start with, and then I began taking it all off. I would have been offended if you *hadn't* had sex with me."

"Oh. Right," I said, and the conversation took a moment to lag as I thought of how to form my next question in a way that wouldn't make me sound like an insensitive lout.

"What, you feel cheap now?" she said.

"No, I . . . No, that's cool. What guy doesn't want to be a booty call?"

"Great. I'll talk to . . ."

"Wait, just . . . we weren't . . . we didn't exactly use protection. Was this . . . are we . . . am I going to be attending Lamaze classes soon?"

"First of all, don't be an idiot, no one uses Lamaze anymore. All it does is make the woman hyperventilate and deprive the baby of oxygen. Haven't you read *any* childbirth books? Second, I'm on the pill. So you have nothing to worry about."

"The pill? Since when?"

"Since . . . I don't know, a couple months now."

"But what happened to . . . all your plans? Last I knew, you had everything from a car seat to a Bumbo Baby in your closet."

"Yeah, I regifted the car seat and gave the Bumbo Baby to Goodwill."

"But . . . why?"

"I just decided I'm just not cut out for that," she said. "Lately, I feel like I can barely keep my own stuff together. Somehow adding another life-form into the mix didn't seem too smart, especially if it was a life-form that was going to be totally dependent on me for its physical and emotional development."

"Oh," I said, because sometimes I like to offer my friends and loved ones brilliant insights like that.

"Anyhow, I have to go," she said. "I'll talk to you later."

"Okay, bye," I said to an already empty phone line.

The Malibu had made enough trips to Rutledge Avenue in the past three days that I wondered if it was going to steer itself there. Still, I kept my hands on the wheel — just in case — and arrived a few minutes later.

I hastily ditched my car a few doors down, the only place I could find a spot, and walked briskly toward the front porch, where I was confronted by Mimi's doorbell button. I pushed it and waited. At least I knew she'd answer this time.

As I looked down at her leaf-insulated flower bed, I pressed the button again, growing frustrated. She had invited me there all of fifteen minutes earlier. What happened? She slipped into narcoleptic slumber?

"You've *got* to be kidding me," I muttered.

I backed away from the porch and stepped down onto the sidewalk to have a look at the house. There were no lights on and no one making out in the second-floor windows, either. I whipped out my phone and dialed Mimi — maybe she had just taken the baby for a walk? — but didn't get an answer.

Walking back up on the porch, I decided to knock this time. I did knuckles first, then switched to the butt of my palm, which is louder and, besides, it hurts less. But that got about as much attention from inside the house as the doorbell did.

"Mimi?" I eventually yelled at the door. "Mimi, it's Carter. Are you there?"

A woman from the other side of the duplex appeared on her front porch, which was no more than ten feet away from the Kippses' entrance.

"She ain't here," the woman said.

"But she just called me," I said, as if this woman, upon hearing the injustice of this fact, could somehow change it.

"Well, she left."

"How long ago?"

"You just missed her. Two minutes ago, maybe?"

"Was she alone?"

"No, she was with a man."

A man? Another one? I wondered if this guy knew what the life expectancy was for men who hung around Mimi Kipps. "What did the man look like?" I asked.

The woman shifted on her heels and appraised me with suspicion, giving me the kind of look you give someone who is suddenly asking too many questions and might actually be a stalker. So I added, "I'm a reporter with the *Eagle-Examiner.* I was supposed to be meeting her here for an interview."

"Oh, well I think it was her preacher. It looked like they were in a hurry."

Her preacher? What was he doing back here? I thought he was finally out of the picture. "Was he a big guy?" I asked, holding my hand above my head to indicate a man of some stature. "About yay high? Probably wearing a suit? Glasses?"

"Yeah, that's him."

The woman was leaning her weight back toward the door, giving me a "can I go now?" look. So I said, "Thanks for your help. Sorry for the noise."

She disappeared inside, and I buried my hands in my jacket, hunched my shoulders, and began walking back down the sidewalk, feeling annoyed. I had told Mimi I'd be there in fifteen minutes. It had taken me maybe twenty. Where had she rushed off to with Pastor Al in such a supposed hurry? An emergency prayer meeting?

True, I was only coming to her house because I thought she was going to confess to murder. But still. Rude is rude.

I was still stewing about this when I saw a silver Mercedes cruising with quiet majesty down the street toward me. It was one of the larger kind, an E-class maybe, and it had tinted glass and tricked-out chrome wheels. I'm not sure what made me even give it a second glance — other than that its list price was probably about forty grand higher than any other car on the street. But I was still looking at it when its rear driver's side window rolled down maybe six inches.

That, in itself, was curious. It was forty-five degrees outside, not windows-down weather. So I kept staring.

The next thing I saw was a gloved hand protruding from the window, holding a black, metallic object of some sort. It took me a long nanosecond to parse what I was seeing. Was it a length of pipe? It wasn't registering.

The car had slowed to perhaps fifteen or twenty miles an hour as it came close to pulling even with me. I couldn't see the driver through the front window or any of the passengers through the tinting. I was considering the vehicle with unguarded curiosity when, suddenly, I figured out what that black thing emerging from the backseat was.

That's not a pipe, you idiot, my brain shouted, *that's a gun. And it's aimed at you. Dive, idiot. Dive!*

I was still in the process of making myself horizontal when a clap sounded in front of me and wood splintered behind me. The gun wasn't silenced. It was the opposite of silenced. It was deafening. More bullets followed the first in a ceaseless and terrifying procession.

My dive had put me halfway between the sidewalk and the unkempt flower bed, in the middle of the small strip of grass that made up the Kippses' front lawn. I was utterly exposed, and I was certain to experience the flesh-tearing agony of a bullet ripping into my body any moment. Perhaps, if I had any wherewithal whatsoever, I should have crawled closer to the cars parked along the street. But damn if I could shove myself *closer* to that Mercedes. I could barely move at all.

I tried to go flat, pancake flat — hell, *tortilla* flat — as the rounds kept coming. It wasn't an automatic weapon, just the incessant fire of someone who was pulling the trigger as fast as his pointer finger could manage. I couldn't even count how many times I heard that awful thunderclap of exploding gas and propelled lead. All I knew was it was more than five and less than twenty million. How much less? That I couldn't say.

And it kept coming. I heard glass shattering behind me, parked cars being hit in front of me, and bullets ricocheting all around me. At some point, I covered my head with my hands — like that would

300

somehow be good defense — and buried my face in the ground. I wondered if the last thing I would ever see in this world was cold, dead grass.

Then it ended. The quiet was, in its own way, as loud as the noise had been moments earlier. There was no squeaking of tires, no wailing of car alarms, no shrieking of wounded humanity.

Just silence.

The first thing I forced myself to do was crawl toward the curb and the parked cars. I wanted metal at my back and something to dive under should the need arise. I probably looked ridiculous, going on all fours across the sidewalk, but it would be a little while before I felt like having the precious contents of my skull more than about two feet off the ground.

Eventually, I reached a rusting Toyota Celica, against which I stayed huddled for a minute or so, trying to resist the involuntary shaking that was overtaking my body. Still dazed, I looked back at Mimi's house, which was pockmarked with bullet holes like a modern-day Alamo. Several of the windows had been shot out. The siding was going to need a serious patch job.

Finally, I stood up on gone-wobbly legs.

The Mercedes had disappeared. For now. Was it coming back? I didn't have much experience with drive-by shootings — watching *Boyz in the Hood* twenty years ago just doesn't count — but I sure as hell wasn't going to stick around to find out.

I ran, or maybe just stumbled, to my car, fumbling nervously with my keys until I got the door open. I dove in, turned the engine over, and started driving. For the next few blocks, I have to admit I was rather generous with the accelerator, rather stingy with the brakes.

My first thought, once my heart rate returned to something like normal and my breathing was back under my own control, was that I ought to call the police. Shooting at someone, that's illegal, isn't it? I didn't have a book called *Being Target Practice for Dummies* handy, but I was reasonably certain the law frowned on citizens discharging firearms in the direction of other citizens.

Right. Definitely. Once I put sufficient distance between myself and all those spent shell casings on Rutledge Avenue, I dialed the number for the East Orange Police Department.

A female voice answered: "East Orange Police, Officer Heyward speaking, may I help you?"

"Yes, I'm . . . I'm calling to report a shooting," I said in a voice that sounded too faltering to be my own, almost like I was going through puberty again.

"What is your address?"

"Well . . . I . . . I live in . . . in Bloomfield, actually . . . but the shooting happened on Rutledge Avenue."

"We're already responding to a report about shots fired on Rutledge," she said. "Do you require officer assistance?"

"No . . . it's . . . it's over now. I was just on Rutledge Avenue when these guys started shooting at me."

"Were you hit, sir? Do you require medical assistance?"

"No, I . . . I guess I just thought it was the sort of thing you guys liked to know about for, I don't know, statistical purposes. I was shot at, you know?"

"Can you identify the person who was shooting at you, sir?"

"I didn't really get a look at him. It was just these guys in a Mercedes and suddenly one of them started shooting at me" — I had said that already, hadn't I? — "and, well, it was just a lot of bullets and . . ."

I could tell she was thinking, *Yeah, and what do you want me to do about it?* Instead, she said, "Are you still at the scene, sir?"

"No, I . . . I took off. I just . . . I wanted to get out of there."

"I understand, sir. If you'd like, you can come into the station and file a report."

A report? This wasn't my briefcase being stolen out of the back of my car. These were killers who just happened to have bad aim. She wanted me to file a report?

I was building up some good, indignant outrage when I started thinking about this thing from the cop's perspective. She was getting a phone call from a guy who was informing her of a shooting about which she already knew. And he couldn't tell her much of anything new or useful. I realized that if our roles were reversed, I'd blow me off, too.

"Yeah, thanks. Maybe I'll . . . maybe I'll do that," I said, and then hung up.

I became aware I had just run a red light — the honking of the person I nearly T-boned alerted me to this — and I finally pulled over. Like most guys, I'm a bad multi-tasker under even the best of circumstances. Thinking and driving were two things that weren't going to be able to coexist for me at this moment, and right now I needed to think more than I needed to drive.

It is one thing to be shot at. It's quite

another thing to not know who's doing it or why.

Everything happened so fast. I needed to slow down the scene. Maybe it would tell me something I didn't know.

The first thing I saw was a silver Mercedes sedan with tinted windows. Immediate, knee-jerk reaction: it was driven by a drug dealer, a fairly high-level one — because the kids standing out on the corner selling dime bags for seven dollars couldn't afford a ride like that. And it was obviously a drug dealer who didn't particularly care about being too clichéd in his vehicle choices.

But why would a drug dealer — or a drug-dealing gang, if it was one of those — want to shoot me? I wasn't in the drug game. Guys who are don't usually bother with civilians. And how would they have even known I was there? It's not like I posted my itinerary online.

I thought back to my scene. The next thing that appeared was the gun. I am not any kind of firearms expert — I don't know my calibers from my millimeters — but it was not a large gun. Then it started firing.

If it was supposed to be a hit, it was incredibly sloppy (as evidenced by the fact that I was still around to critique it). Maybe they were just trying to scare me off. The stubbornly high murder rate that persisted in urban areas — most of which related to the drug trade — suggested that when a professional wanted you dead, chances are you ended up dead.

Unless these weren't pros. What if they were amateurs who happened to drive a nice car?

I tried to think back on the sequence of events that had led me there. I had gotten a call from Mimi Kipps asking me to come see her. I responded to the call, only to learn she had left in a hurry minutes before I arrived, escorted by the anointed man of God. Then someone was shooting at me.

Oh. Right. The weepy woman calls. The gallant, dumb man answers — never knowing he's walking into a trap. *That's* how the shooters knew I was going to be there. Mimi Kipps told them.

In the immortal words of former Washington, D.C., Mayor Marion Barry: bitch set me up.

Having this knowledge, proving this knowledge, and then figuring out what to do with it were all distinctly different issues, of course. And I was stuck on the middle part. Could I prove that this was anything more than a bad coincidence? I knew better, of course, but there was nothing to definitively say the gangbangers weren't just shooting up the duplex next door.

Another question: Was her pastor in on it? Since he showed up minutes before the shooting started to whisk Mimi away, it would suggest he was. Then again, was it possible Mimi was playing him like she was playing me? Maybe she called him all weepy, too, knowing he would come running just like I did?

Yet another question: Why would Mimi need me dead? How was I threat to her? Sure, I might be the only person who was really onto her. But how did she know that? I thought about my conversation with Pastor Al, where I had hinted about the affair but never directly stated it. Had he known what I was trying to get at and alerted Mimi?

But if that was the case, and Pastor Al was complicit in Mimi and Fusco's conspiracy to kill Darius Kipps, then why would he have called for an independent investigation — and then dropped it? For that matter, if Mimi and Fusco had teamed up to kill Darius to get him out of the way — so their affair could blossom — then why was Fusco now dead?

Nothing made sense at all, unless . . . were

Pastor Al and Mimi somehow romantically involved?

Now, that was just gross. He was old enough to be her father, and he hadn't aged particularly well — he looked like he could be her grandfather. Merely the thought of them bumping uglies was revolting. Then again, could I rule it out? Not really.

Was it even possible — and, oh, this was *really* sordid — that Pastor Al was Jaquille's real father? I thought all the way back to my first interview with Mimi, when she had told me about how much trouble she had getting pregnant, thanks to her one-testicled husband and his low sperm count. Had Jaquille's conception been a bit less miraculous than originally advertised?

Short of getting Pastor Al to submit to a paternity test, I wasn't sure how I would ever substantiate this theory. But it was a possibility I couldn't rule out: that the call for an investigation had been a smoke-screen, and that all these dead police officers were really just Pastor Al's way of clearing away competitors for Mimi's affections.

For all I knew, Mimi really was innocent — relatively — in everything. Maybe Pastor Al had called her, told her to invite me over, and then cleared her out of harm's way just in time for me to get shot at.

These and other thoughts were doing laps around my cranium when I received a text message from Tina: "NPD presser @ 11. Command center. Can u make it?"

Could I make it? Yeah. Did I want to? Negative. I was starting to think the representatives of the Newark Police Department were the last people to know what was going on, so spending time with them seemed rather pointless. Given what I had just been through, shouldn't I get special dispensation from having to attend pointless press conferences?

Then again, Tina didn't know I had spent part of my morning ducking bullets. And maybe she didn't need to know. For whatever her current feelings for me were — was going from potential baby daddy to booty call a promotion or a demotion? — she had shown the tendency to be plenty protective of me. If I told her about my little drive-by incident, she'd pull me into the office and not let me leave until I was eligible for Medicare.

And while I still aspired to reach a ripe and gummy old age, I didn't feel like remaining at large was necessarily going to jeopardize it. As long as I didn't agree to meet Mimi Kipps in any dark alleys, I would be okay. I just had to be a little more wary.

I texted Tina back, "On my way," then shifted into gear, trying to pay a little more attention to traffic signals this time. The Newark Police Command Center was on University Avenue, not to be confused with its headquarters on Green Street. I guess whenever the Green Street facility had been built — by either the Holy Roman Empire or Alexander the Great, judging by how antiquated it was — no one worried about satellite hookups. The Command Center was, therefore, a little better suited to press events.

Arriving all of two minutes before it started, I was ushered to the conference room where they held these kinds of functions. The chairs in the middle of the room were filled with a variety of reporters. Along the back wall was a row of cameras on tripods, including some that belonged to cameramen I had seen earlier in the day on Fusco's street. They were now going to have everything they needed — sound bites from the scene *and* from the police — in plenty of time for their noon broadcasts.

Hakeem Rogers was up front, fussing with something, but he still found time to shoot me a scowl when he spied me standing along the side wall. I nodded at him, but I was mostly distracted by who was — or, in this case, was not — alongside Rogers.

Typically, these press conferences consisted of Rogers introducing the police director, who, as an appointee of the mayor, wanted to be putting in a good word with the voters of Newark. The director usually appeared in front of a wall of blue-clad men, officers who were somehow involved in the law enforcement triumph the director was there to announce. The officers didn't say much — they were just there for decoration — but they sure gave the director a good background for the cameras.

This time the director was nowhere around. Nor was there a wall of blue. Indeed, there was only one officer alongside Rogers: Captain Denise Boswell. She was in full dress uniform, right up to her hat, which she was nervously fussing with as she waited for the show to begin.

The other oddity about this was that I didn't know what she planned to say. Generally at these kinds of gatherings, you had some inkling of what would be announced — a break on a case, a big drug bust, a fugitive from justice apprehended.

This time it was a total mystery. And as Rogers approached the podium, I found myself leaning forward, just a little bit curious.

■ ■ ■ ■

Rogers opened the proceedings by introducing himself, thanking everyone for coming, and taking an unveiled swipe at me.

"There has been a great deal of speculation about the death of Detective Sergeant Darius Kipps, specifically in print," Rogers said. "While ordinarily we prefer to let our investigation run its course before we make any major public statements, the Newark Police Department has determined that, in light of the death of Detective Michael Fusco and some apparent connections between the two investigations, it was time to put an end to the speculation."

He looked up and rewarded me with another scowl. "Toward that end, I would like to introduce Captain Denise Boswell. After a long and decorated career with the Newark Police Department, Captain Boswell was placed in command of the Fourth Precinct late last year, becoming the first female officer in Newark history to attain that level. Since she was the commanding officer to both Sergeant Kipps and Detective Fusco, we felt it was appropriate for her to make this difficult announcement. Captain Boswell?"

The room was quiet as Boswell approached the microphone. She had a sheet of white paper that had been folded into quarters, and the rustling as she unfolded it was amplified by the conference room's sound system. Captain Boswell was not a tall woman, far shorter than the men who usually appeared at these things, and the variety of microphones that had been strapped to the podium — representing various local radio, television, and Internet outlets — had not been adjusted properly. She was practically lost behind them.

Her voice, however, was not. It was strong and confident as she began reading from her sheet of paper.

"This has been a tragic week in the City of Newark, with the loss of two of our finest officers, Darius Kipps and Michael Fusco. It has been particularly hard for those of us in the Fourth Precinct who had the privilege of working alongside these officers as they attended to their duties. And I would ask that we all keep the families of these officers in our prayers during this difficult time."

She paused for a quick moment of solemnity, then pushed onward:

"As many of you are aware, the department announced a preliminary determination that Detective Sergeant Darius Kipps

313

died of a self-inflicted gunshot wound. That will not be our final determination in this matter. And on behalf of the Newark Police Department, I would like to publicly apologize to the family of Darius Kipps for this error."

My internal Surprise-o-meter was registering one of its highest possible readings. As a rule, police departments didn't admit to botching *anything,* much less an investigation into the death of one of their own officers. Then Boswell pushed the Surprise-o-meter clear off the charts.

"Early this morning," she said slowly, deliberately, "I received a call from Detective Fusco's cell phone. During this call, he confessed to killing Detective Sergeant Kipps over a personal dispute and then to altering certain aspects of the crime scene to make it appear to be a suicide."

She paused again, and some of the reporters actually squirmed in their seats. Professional decorum demanded that they not react in a demonstrable manner. But I knew that if this had been a movie they were watching at home, half of them would have been yelling at their television screens, "Whoa!"

Boswell continued her statement: "Detective Fusco informed me he could not live with himself as a result of this act but that he wanted to set the record straight. He then terminated the phone call. As we now know, it appears that placing that phone call was his last act before he turned his service weapon on himself and ended his own life."

As soon as I heard the term "service weapon," I felt a prickle from the base of my spine all the way up to my neck. In my head, I could hear the voice of tough guy Mike Fusco telling me about how he had been placed on administrative leave and lamenting, *I even had to turn in my service weapon.*

When had he told me that? Yesterday, when I came by with those photos of Kipps. Had he somehow gotten the gun back during the eighteen hours or so between when I last saw him and when he supposedly pulled its trigger? Did he have another department-issued gun that had simply been confused for his service weapon?

I didn't know. But it was another inconsistency. That and the two shots that had been fired. I still didn't know of any cop — or anyone who knew which end of a gun fired — who could miss his own head from six inches away.

Meanwhile, Captain Boswell was finishing up, "I'm sure many of you will have questions about how such a tragedy could have occurred and about whether it could have been prevented. We in the Newark Police Department are asking ourselves the same questions today. Unfortunately, we may not have many answers, as so much of this seemed to involve issues known only to these two officers."

Boswell lifted her head for the first time, refolded her note, then stepped aside so Hakeem Rogers could take her place in front of the microphones.

"We will now take a limited number of questions," he said. "Please wait for me to call on you."

I immediately raised my hand in the air, but Rogers motioned to one of the television guys, who asked, "Captain Boswell, can you describe the nature of this personal dispute between these two officers?"

Boswell didn't make a move toward the microphone. Instead, Rogers handled it: "That's not something we're going to be able to discuss. It was a personal dispute of a personal nature."

A personal dispute of a personal nature. Well, *that* sure cleared things up. A reporter from one of the New York tabloids — who would probably be getting on the front page if he was able to discover this was the result of a sordid love triangle — got the next question. "Can you say how the crime scene was altered? Does this have something to do with the rope burns that were found on Officer Kipps?"

Good question from the Murdoch minion. I was expecting another dirty look from Rogers, but he was too busy conferring with Boswell. Eventually, he came back with "We don't want to get into specifics. We'll just say that as an officer who was well trained in our investigative techniques, he was able to use his insider knowledge to mislead us."

There were several more queries from the press, none of which elicited anything in the way of new information. I had continued trying to get in my question about Fusco's service weapon — as in, why did a suspended officer have one? — but Rogers had been ignoring me. I usually didn't ask questions during these sorts of events. I tried to get the cops on the side, after the cameras stopped rolling, when they might be more likely to loosen up. But in this case I knew I wouldn't get another chance. You only got that on-the-side time when the cops had something to brag about.

But even when there were no more hands being raised except mine, even when some of the other reporters were looking at me in the expectation I'd be called on, Rogers didn't so much as glance in my direction. It was my punishment, obviously.

In some ways it was just as well. I doubted I was going to get a straight answer.

From the way everyone was packing up after the press conference — hastily, without much lingering or second thought — I could tell the assemblage of notebook holders and microphone monkeys were satisfied by what they had heard. Cop A personally kills Cop B over personal dispute of personal nature, becomes personally overwhelmed with guilt, turns gun on own person, end of personhood.

It was obvious the police director wanted this embarrassing story to become yesterday's news as quickly as possible, so he offered up Captain Boswell, the most sympathetic emissary he could find, and had her tie up the whole sloppy mess with one neat little bow.

But I just wasn't accepting the package. There were too many inconsistencies, too many things that didn't fit into the narrative.

Did Fusco *really* call her moments before committing a two-bullet suicide? Maybe. Had Fusco somehow repossessed his own gun? Maybe. Had Fusco acted alone in killing Kipps and then been able to fool the entire Newark Police Department? Maybe.

There were just too many maybes. And, all the while, the roles of Mimi Kipps and Alvin LeRioux — who was up to his sanctimonious jowls in this somehow — were left undefined.

It was all still out there for me to discover, but in the meantime, I had a story to write. Regardless of whether I fully believed what the Newark Police were saying, I still had a duty to report it. And, at the very least, I could lend some understanding to the dispute between the officers. How I would word it might be a bit thorny. The truth — "A reporter spied Detective Fusco and Mrs. Kipps in the smoldering beginnings of what was undoubtedly going to become scorching, unbridled, hot-hearted passion" — would probably make it past the editors on the All-Slop, who didn't bother to read stuff before posting it online, judging from the typos they let through. It might even get me a contract to write romance novels. But I would still probably need to find a better way to word it.

After making the short drive back to the office, I had barely settled into my desk when I was accosted by Ruthie Ginsburg, the twenty-two-going-on-thirteen intern. He was looking typically chipper and fresh-faced, and for a moment I wanted to turn him over to some of the more curmudgeonly members of the copy desk for a wedgie and a chocolate swirly, just to put him in his place a little. I'm not exactly sure when, during the decade or so I had been hanging around this place, I had switched over to the side of the grizzled veterans. But with my unshaven jaw and bloodshot eyes, I certainly fit the part.

"Hey, I've been looking for you! I got some great stuff, it's really going to blow your mind," he chirped.

"Sounds swell, Jimmy. We'll be sure to get it in tomorrow's *Daily Planet.*"

"Huh?" he said, adding a head tilt. The Superman reference was lost on him. I was beginning to realize why these interns made me feel so old.

"Never mind. Why don't you step into my office?"

He looked around, confused.

"It's an expression," I said and pointed to an empty chair across from my desk. "Take a seat."

Jimmy — uh, sorry, Ruthie . . . uh, I mean, Geoff — gleefully took his place and opened up his notebook.

"Okay, first, let's just get something out of the way," he said. "Pregnancy tests don't come back positive in toilet water. I spent two hours last night on Google researching it. I even tested my own toilet. It came back negative."

He looked at me earnestly and I thought about trying to convince him it was just *Newark* toilet water — you know, something in the aquifer that supplied the city's drinking water. But it was time to let him off the hook.

"Yeah, you got me," I said.

"Why would you do that to me?"

"Look, Ruthie . . . first of all, you know everyone is calling you Ruthie, right?" I asked.

He gave me a dejected look and said, "Yeah."

"Don't worry about it. Around here, nicknaming is a form of flattery. Anyhow, I know I might have misled you a little bit, and I'm sorry. But I'm also not sorry. You were obviously spying for Tina, and I didn't want her to know what I was up to."

"It was kind of a douche move."

"You're right. And, okay, really I am sorry. But . . . look, I don't want to sound like I'm lecturing, especially when I'm the one in the wrong, but you've got to understand

321

that editors are . . . well, they have their usefulness at times. Then there are times when it's best they not know everything. So I might have just needed you to spin your wheels for a little while."

"And the Good Neighbors piece? Was that more wheel-spinning?"

"No, that was actually a big favor. And I appreciate it."

"Okay, so maybe now you owe *me* a favor?" he asked.

He said it tentatively, like a good little intern should. But he had played me rather nicely. I was beginning to appreciate that Ruthie Ginsburg just might have the chops to make it in this business.

"Maybe I do," I said. "What did you have in mind?"

"It's what I was trying to tell you about before. It came from an interview I did with these kids who were hanging out on the corner by the town houses. Have you ever heard of red dot guns?"

"Uh, no."

"Well, from what these corner boys were telling me, they're all the rage in the hood. All the skels are using them."

I laughed — albeit internally — at Ruthie using the word "skels." He had been watching too many cop shows.

"So, what, Red Dot Guns is the hot new gun manufacturer? Like Magnum or Colt or something?" I asked.

"No, it's an actual red dot that's been branded into the butt of the gun handle. One of the kids showed it to me and that's all it is, just a red dot. But they say everyone wants their gun to have one."

"I still don't get it. What's so special about this red dot?"

"I don't know," Ruthie admitted. "Maybe it's just one of those weird ghetto fashion things? I'll ask the next time I see them. We'll obviously have to do some more reporting . . ."

"Whoa, whoa, whoa," making a "T" with my hands, the internationally accepted gesture to call for a timeout. "What do you mean 'we'?"

"That's the favor. I want you to work with me. I think this could be a really cool story and a great clip for me to have. But you know how things go around here. I'm the intern. They want me to do Good Neighbors, write about car accidents, and leave the heavy lifting to guys like you. But if you and I were to do it together . . ."

I grinned.

"Well played, young Ginsburg, well played," I said. "I got a few other things on my plate right now. But as soon as I come up for air, we can work on it. It sounds like a fascinating glimpse into thug culture."

"Okay. Great."

Thinking our conversation was over, I began moving my mouse to knock the screen saver off my computer. But Ruthie was still sitting there, looking at me expectantly.

"One more thing," he said.

"Yeeeessss?"

"I still have, like, half a dozen pregnancy tests in my car. I got them on sale and they can't be returned. Do you know what I should do with them?"

I couldn't help myself. "Yeah," I said. "Give them to Tina."

It took an hour to transcribe the tripe I got from the press conference and then mold it into something that would clear the very low hurdle of the All-Slop's quality standards.

By the time I was done, I had concluded that my first order of business needed to be a visit to Dr. Raul Ibanez, the one man who might be able to enlighten me about my unanswered press conference question. I hoped he would be more talkative than he was the last time I had seen him. Alas, I was out of clever ideas as to how to make that happen.

So, lacking a better plan, I decided to go with a direct assault. I fortified myself with a stop at a local convenience store on my way — and, really, what's *wrong* with having two MoonPies for lunch? — and was soon parked on the street outside the Essex County Medical Examiner's Office. I was going in the front door this time.

I'm often astounded by what you can get away with when you're a well-dressed white man who moves fast and acts like he knows what he's doing. As I got out of my car, I reminded myself I had faked my way into tougher places than this. So my plan, quite simply, was to keep walking toward Ibanez's office until someone stopped me.

Hence, I didn't pay attention to the security guard at the front desk, and he returned the favor. Then I passed a pair of people in lab coats who didn't give me a second glance, either. I took a guess that Ibanez's office would be on the top floor, but I eschewed the elevator — the passengers would have too long to study me — and instead took the emergency stairs, charging up them without hesitation.

And that, conveniently enough, is where I bumped into Dr. Ibanez, standing on the

325

third-floor landing, talking on his cell phone. He wasn't looking at me any more carefully than anyone else, and I practically had to plow into him to get him to stop.

"Hi, Doctor, nice to see you again," I said.

The reaction I received assured me Raul Ibanez's startle reflex was in perfect working order. He even jumped back a little.

"I have to go," he said into the phone, then stammered, "Did you . . . how did you get in here?"

"With my legs. No one stopped me."

"I told you last night I can't comment."

"Things have changed since last night."

"I still can't . . . it's . . . it's improper for you to even be here."

"Doc, just give me a second," I said. "I'm sorry to ambush you like this, but I really don't have a choice. If I try to go through proper channels, I'll get blown off."

"Well, that's not my problem. You're still going to have to —"

I cut him off: "Captain Boswell said at a press conference just now that Fusco killed himself with his service weapon. He didn't *have* his service weapon, okay?"

"What are —"

"The day before he was killed, Mike Fusco told me he had been placed on administrative leave. His captain made it

326

out like it was some kind of mental health thing. Maybe she just wanted him out of the way so she could investigate him for Kipps's murder. I don't know.

"Point is, when he was placed on leave, he was forced to hand in his gun. He told me that, explicitly. So I guess I just want to know: Are you absolutely sure that was his service weapon?"

Ibanez studied me for a moment, and I watched as his posture made the subtle shift from defensive to accepting. Finally he said, "The better question is: Are you absolutely sure he was the one who fired it?"

"What do you mean?"

"Look, it's probably good you found me here. This just happens to be where the cell phone reception is best. If you had made it all the way up to my office, I would have had to throw you out. There's a damn leak in this place somewhere, and I sure as hell don't want anyone thinking it's me. So I can't —"

"No one will ever know we spoke," I assured him. "Just like no one has figured out — or will figure out — who my last leak was."

"Okay." He stopped for another few seconds, then again said, "Okay. I'm only telling you this because the NPD is trying to jam stuff down my throat, just like they did with the Kipps case. They want me to shut the hell up and rule the manner of death suicide — even after I told them what I'm about to tell you. And I just can't go for that this time. So I need you to take this and made a big stink with it."

"I'll do my best," I promised.

"Okay, to answer your question, it is his gun. We matched the serial numbers and everything. We haven't test-fired it yet, but I'm sure it'll match the slugs recovered at the scene, just like I'm sure there won't be any other prints on it besides his. Whoever did this was being pretty careful. Really careful, in a lot of ways. But not careful enough."

"What do you mean?"

"Well, let's start with the obvious. The decedent had powder burns around the entrance wound, so we know the gun was fired from close proximity. The gun was discovered on the floor next to him, but that's not unusual — the gun is actually only found in the victim's hand in about one out of every four suicides. So this was set up to look like a suicide."

"But you're saying it's not?"

"That's right. A lot of things happen when a gun goes off. There's gunshot residue.

There are what we call cylinder gap effects from where exploding gas escapes the gun. The recoil of the gun can leave marks on the hand that, in a suicide, don't go away like they do in a living person. The recoil can also cause injury to the hand, particularly in the webbing. You follow me?"

"So far, yeah."

"Okay, in this case, did the decedent fire a gun? Yes, it would appear he did. The grip of the gun was clearly imprinted on his palm, as we would expect. There was also gunshot residue on the hand — I'll get back to that in a second. But I'd bet my house that gun didn't go off in his hand until he was already dead. The blood was wrong."

"What do you mean?"

"If you bring a gun up under your chin and fire the trigger at close range," he said, miming the act with his own hand, "there is going to be blood — kind of like a fine mist — that spatters back onto your hand. How much blood will change based on the caliber of the gun and the tip of bullet used. But my spatter analyst is telling me there's no blood on Fusco's hand. None."

"And no blood means —"

"Wait, there's more. We got this body early, and I made it our number one priority, so I've had people working it all morning. Okay, so no blood. Also, like I said, there's a problem with the gunshot residue. This is a little more art than science sometimes, but this one was pretty clear. In a suicide you expect to see a certain pattern under the microscope from the swabs you take of the gun hand, particularly on the back of the hand. But in this case, there was a big area on the back of the hand where there was almost no residue at all. And you know what that, along with no blood, tells you?"

"Not . . . not really."

Ibanez, who was relating all this with the joy of a scientist who has made a discovery, finished: "It tells you there's only one possible scenario, or at least only one I can come up with. The perp had watched enough *CSI* to know there needed to be gunshot residue on Fusco's hand. So first the perp killed Fusco, then he put the murder weapon in Fusco's hand, wrapped his hand around Fusco's, then fired the gun a second time."

Which explains why Lawrence Taylor's biggest fan heard two gunshots.

"You'd testify to that scenario in a court of law?" I asked.

"Sure would. And I'm sure the defense attorney would try to shred me," he said,

330

cracking a smile. "But the science is clear. Mike Fusco didn't kill himself."

They weren't supposed to miss.

For the guys in the silver Mercedes, that had been a mistake. A rookie mistake, yes, but a mistake all the same. They weren't trying to scare the newspaper reporter. They weren't trying to shoot up the house behind him or the cars in front of him or any of the other numerous targets they hit. They certainly weren't trying to merely scare him, either.

They had been hired to kill him. Their employer, Red Dot Enterprises, had been quite explicit: if they killed Carter Ross, they'd all be given brand-new guns. But they would only get paid if Ross was dead.

And they missed. Even when they had been tipped off as to exactly where Ross was going to be, they flat-out missed. Fifteen times.

It turns out drive-by shootings are not as easy as the movies make them look. Start with the "drive-by" part: it supposes the car is moving. And without the proper training, shooting someone from a moving vehicle is not easy. Most people have a hard time figuring out how much to lead a wide receiver in a game of touch football, and that's just for a person running perhaps ten miles an hour. Trying to make the same kind of calculations in a car going thirty for a bullet that will travel faster than the speed of sound is that much trickier.

That was the first degree of difficulty. The second was that they couldn't risk being identified. Kill some no-good punk drug dealer and most folks in Newark get a quick case of myopia. They figure he had it coming. Kill a newspaper reporter and someone is going to come up with twenty-twenty vision. So the Mercedes guys couldn't afford to have the window rolled down more than just a crack, which made aiming a matter of guesswork.

The third degree of difficulty was the gun itself. In truth, they didn't even know what kind of gun it was. Guns weren't their thing. That was the Red Dot Enterprise guys' specialty. All the guys in the silver Mercedes knew was that their piece was a bitty little thing, with a snub-nosed barrel — a Saturday Night Special, as the media so derisively referred to that kind of firearm. Even under the best of circumstances, it wasn't particularly accurate.

Take all those factors and add their general ineptitude with this sort of thing, and it wasn't hard to understand why they had missed so badly. It would have been something approaching a miracle if they had actually killed him — a hundred to one shot, especially with that popgun.

They knew before they even rounded the corner, as that fifteenth shot was still echoing, that they hadn't killed him. They hoped the Red Dot Enterprise guys maybe wouldn't find out, but of course they did; Red Dot seemed to know exactly where this Ross guy was at all times, so it knew quickly that Ross was on the move again.

The Mercedes guys worried that perhaps the Red Dot wouldn't give them a second chance, that they had blown their one and only opportunity to get those free guns. But their contact at Red Dot had been very understanding.

His only request was that they not botch it the second time.

CHAPTER 7

Having shared his big theory, Raul Ibanez got in a hurry to have me depart. I guess he was worried someone else might step into the stairwell in the endless search for good cell reception. We agreed that if I had any more questions, I would call his secretary and identify myself as Robert Upshur. (An obscure reference to the first and middle names of the greatest reporter in journalism history, but I digress.)

That left me to stumble out back onto the street, into an afternoon that was trying to get sunny without much luck. Not to get all literary, but it was an appropriate metaphor for how my brain was working on this story.

If Fusco didn't kill himself — and I believed Ibanez's science more than I believed anything else I heard so far — then someone else did. Brilliant deduction, I know, but I *did* graduate in the top 10 percent of my high school class. Was it the same person who killed Darius Kipps? Or did Fusco kill Kipps and then someone else kill Fusco for revenge? I couldn't say.

At the very least, I had enough new information that when I presented it to Public Disinformation Officer Hakeem Rogers for comment, it was going to make him feel like he was passing a kidney stone. Because, really, I could only imagine two scenarios here, neither of them particularly flattering for Rogers's employer: One, Newark's finest were allowing themselves to be snowed by cunning bad guys — possibly a minister, of all people — who were killing cops and getting away with it simply because the police chief didn't want to look bad in the media; or, two, Newark's finest were lying.

I couldn't imagine why they would want to lie about something like this — other than that they're cops, so lying to reporters comes rather naturally. But I had a fairly simple test to determine which scenario was true.

It hinged on the phone call Fusco allegedly made to Captain Boswell. If that call actually existed, then Fusco was acting under duress — calling because the cunning bad guys put a gun to his head. If that call didn't exist, I was going to ask our editorial cartoonist to draw a caricature of Captain Boswell with a nose like Pinocchio.

Luckily, I had a way of finding out which it was — providing Fusco was a Verizon Wireless customer and the bosses at that fine company hadn't yet gotten wise that fearless *Eagle-Examiner* reporter Tommy Hernandez was dating one of their customer service representatives.

I called Tommy to find out.

"It's *so* good to hear from you," he answered.

"And why is that?"

"Because I wanted to ask: When I saw you in the newsroom earlier, were you, in fact, wearing the same horrifically boring shirt, tie, and pleated pants combination you were wearing yesterday?"

"I was."

"You know my eyes were still hurting from the last time I had to see it. Couldn't you have given me a rest?"

"Guess not."

"So, okay, he was wearing the same clothes . . . his eyes looked like a raccoon's . . . he had a certain rumpled look . . . did someone have a big night last night?"

"Something like that," I said. Tommy was a notorious gossip — the TMZ of the newsroom — and didn't need to know I had spent the night at Tina's place. He'd have the paparazzi hounding me for weeks.

"Oh, you don't need to play coy with me. Everyone knows you're shacking up with Kira the cute library chick."

"Yep, you got me."

"What about Tina?"

"What about her?" I asked, perhaps a little too quickly.

"I thought you guys were going to make me Carter Jr.'s special uncle. Or, even better, his fairy godfather."

"I think that's on hold for the time being."

"So you can sow your oats?" Tommy said, clucking his tongue at me. "You're such a mhore."

"What's a mhore?"

"A man-whore."

He giggled, then apparently decided I had received a sufficient amount of abuse for one phone call, because he switched subjects.

"Hey, I visited my girl in the council clerk's office this morning," he said. "She told me there's been nothing new put in for Reverend Alvin LeRioux, Redeemer Love Christian Church, or any of its various affiliates. So if your pastor is getting something for his cooperation, it isn't coming from the Newark city fathers."

"What if it was just expanding or extending an existing contract?" I asked.

"If it meant more money was being spent, it would still have to be approved by the city council. That's Government 101. The council controls the purse strings."

"Okay. Thanks for checking," I said. "Mind if I press you for one more favor."

"Sure."

"Your current love interest still work for Verizon Wireless?"

"Yeah."

I found Mike Fusco's phone number in my notebook and recited it to Tommy. "Ask him if there were any outgoing calls made by that number around four o'clock this morning."

"Sure. Want me to do it right now?"

"Wouldn't hurt."

"I'm going to put the phone down and call on the landline. Hang on."

I leaned my elbow against the car door and rested my head on my hand as Tommy called "Stephen" and bantered a little bit before getting around to the purpose of his call. I listened as he asked a few follow-up questions, then made some way-too-precious kissing noises before getting off the phone.

"Sorry you had to hear that," he said. "I know it offends your hetero sensibilities."

"Yeah, why do you queers have to rub it in everyone's face all the time?" I teased back. "I mean, next you're going to want to hold hands in public or, God forbid, sully the sacred institution of marriage."

"Yeah. Can you imagine the horror?"

"Anyhow, what did Stephen say?"

"Your subscriber made a phone call at four-oh-four this morning to here," he said, reading a number with a 973 area code, which I copied. "It lasted a grand, whopping total of two minutes."

"Two minutes, huh? Do you think you could confess to murdering your best friend and then announce your intention to kill yourself in two minutes?"

Tommy thought about it for a moment and said, "Sure. Not everyone is as wordy as you."

Especially not when they're a taciturn tough guy with a gun pointed at his head. I thanked Tommy for his assistance and promised his next fruity, umbrella-topped girl drink would be on me.

Just to make sure the call was for real, I dialed the number he had given me. It rang four times and then went to a voice mail for Captain Denise Boswell.

So Fusco really did talk to her. And it was his last worldly act. As I pulled out of my parking spot and began traveling back down South Orange Avenue toward the office, I conjured this image of Fusco in his final moments. He was bewildered, scared, and fuming, being made to call his captain and confess to a crime he never committed. And then, maybe while he was still trying to figure out how he might save himself, the gun pointed at his head went off.

I was so distracted by that thought, I nearly missed another image — and not one that existed only in my imagination. This was a real image, in my rearview mirror.

It was of a silver Mercedes. And it was closing in fast.

Daytime running lights save lives. I can now testify to that because it was the Mercedes' daytime running lights that first caught the corner of my eye in that mirror. Otherwise, I never would have seen it coming, and that very likely might have cost me the privilege of continued respiration.

As it was, I had perhaps two seconds to make sense of what I was seeing, and four seconds of useful reaction time. I was puttering along, doing thirty miles per hour in the right lane of an avenue that had two lanes heading in my direction. The Mercedes was coming up behind me in the left lane doing at least sixty.

I had, as best I could figure, two choices: try to stop in the hopes that the Mercedes would overshoot me; or hit the gas and lose them in a chase.

My six-year-old Chevy Malibu couldn't outrun a well-tuned moped, much less an E-class Mercedes with a magnificently engineered eight-cylinder engine. But I knew if I stopped, I might as well just strip off my shirt and scrawl "shoot me here" on my chest. Besides, for all my outward refinement and education, I'm still a Jersey guy. Aggressive driving is a state birthright. So I straightened my right leg to the point of hyperextension and pressed the accelerator down into the floorboards.

The Malibu's engine hesitated for an instant — its protest to the more-than-111,431 miles it had been forced to carry me and other travelers throughout its life — then finally caught with a roar reminiscent of a gas-powered golf cart climbing a steep hill. In my peripheral vision, I could see the speedometer begin a determined journey up the dial.

The Mercedes was still gaining on me, albeit more slowly as I blasted through the intersection of Norfolk Street — if "blasted" is, in fact, a verb that can be used in conjunction with a used Malibu. South Orange Avenue squeezed down to one lane at that point, which meant I had a momentary reprieve from being overtaken, assuming my friends in the Mercedes weren't going to want to tussle with oncoming traffic.

But I was knowledgeable enough about the roads of Newark — probably more familiar with them than any town I ever lived in — to recognize I had a problem coming up. South Orange Avenue would soon funnel into Springfield Avenue, then cross Martin Luther King Boulevard, then feed down into Market Street. And there was no possible way, here in the middle of the day, I was going to get through all of that without having to stop for a traffic light, a pedestrian, or a slow-moving city bus.

And stopping, as previously mentioned, was not a real savory menu option.

Without touching the brake, I pulled my wheel hard to the right at the next intersection. The Malibu's tires, which I had replaced relatively recently — I had, right? — made a horrible squealing sound, and for a moment I wondered if they were going to slip right off their rims and leave me running steel-on-asphalt. But they held and I was soon hurtling down Prince Street, a narrow two-lane road and one of the better car chase venues in downtown Newark, if only because there wouldn't be as much stuff on it to hit.

I hoped my one fancy maneuver would be enough to lose my chasers, but the Mercedes easily made the turn with me and was closing in on my rear bumper. The driver was not being particularly subtle about his intentions. Then again, why did he need to be? He didn't exactly need to rely on artifice or subterfuge. He had the vehicle with the better engine, the better handling, the better suspension. Me? I was probably better at Scrabble, but that was about it.

He made a move to pass me on the left, which I countered by drifting to the middle, leaving no room to pass on either side. Knowing he couldn't get by me, I laid off the accelerator a little but was still getting along quite quickly.

In this manner we sped down Prince Street, with the town houses of University Heights on my left just a blur, toward the first of two traffic lights. The second one, I knew, I wouldn't have to worry about. It was just Court Street, a road that wouldn't have much traffic on it. But the first? The first was a concern — the aforementioned

Springfield Avenue, one of the most heavily traveled arteries in New Jersey's largest city.

As I closed to within about a hundred yards, I could see the light facing me was still red, while the light for Springfield was still green. There was no chance it would be able to cycle through from yellow to red in time. I thought about slowing down a little. I couldn't just bomb right through, kamikaze-style, could I?

Then, with about fifty yards to go, I heard a popping sound from behind me, then another, and I knew damn well it wasn't the Mercedes backfiring. I was being shot at, again. And that sort of solved the dilemma of whether to slow down. My quandary, instead, became how to elude whatever was in the intersection as I barreled through it. I glanced left and saw the way was clear. I wasn't so lucky with the right. A red sedan of some sort, a Pontiac maybe, was approaching. If I maintained my current speed, I judged my front bumper would impale its side panel at roughly a ninety degree angle, and that wasn't going to be good for either of us, especially the driver of the Pontiac.

Then again, if I jammed on the brakes, there was a good chance the Mercedes — now mere feet off my back bumper — was going to rear-end me. And that didn't seem like it would end well, either.

I was left with one option, and that was to ask for more from the Malibu than it was perhaps able to give me. Using every muscle in my right leg to generate as much force as I could, I hammered the accelerator. Then I laid on the horn with my right palm, hoping it might alert the red car's driver to the fact that I was coming, traffic signals be damned.

Then I held my breath and tensed my body for the collision.

I careened through the intersection like that, with the expected impact never coming. The red car responded to my blaring horn with an angry bleep of its own, but its antilock brakes were doing the job, bringing the Pontiac to a noisy but safe stop.

The next block was a short one, and I could already see the light was green. I was in the clear for a little while, except for the minor annoyance that there were some hostile young men behind me. I finally allowed myself a glance at my pursuers in the rearview mirror. On the passenger side of the car, I saw an arm stuck out of the front window holding a handgun. The muzzle flashed twice more, and I heard the shots, though the noise was surprisingly distant, almost like a BB gun.

I couldn't tell where the shooter was aiming or where the bullets were going. I was fairly certain they weren't hitting my car — I would have felt that, right? — and I knew for sure they weren't hitting me. This, I was rapidly discovering, was the way to go when being shot at: pick assailants with lousy aim.

Still, there's this thing about bullets. They're cheap, disposable hunks of metal, and therefore no one thinks twice about expending a lot of them when the situation arises. And I was betting it would take only one landing in the right/wrong spot to make this whole little jaunt a lot less fun. I needed some kind of plan beyond hoping the jarring of Newark's potholes would keep the shooter unsteady.

Prince Street made a quick jog to the left as it passed through Kinney Street. I followed the road, riding the brakes slightly as we sped through a residential area. The Mercedes kept attempting to overtake me on the left. And I continued blocking him. The Malibu may not be good for many things, but getting in people's way is one of them. It has got a nice, wide rear end — the J. Lo of the car world.

Another shot echoed harmlessly behind

me, and I was beginning to feel like I must have had some kind of force field behind me or guardian angel on my shoulder. Then the force field disintegrated, and the guardian angel flew off as two more shots rang out and definitely hit . . . something.

All I knew for sure is that I was starting to lose control of my car. One bullet felt like it had hit somewhere in the vicinity of my trunk, which shouldn't have been debilitating to anything other than perhaps the golf clubs I had stored in there. Then I quickly began to figure out where the second one hit: my right rear tire.

The entire car listed back and to the right. Even with power steering, staying straight was suddenly a battle. The only thing that was saving me was that the Malibu was front-wheel drive, and the front wheels seemed unaffected.

The light at Muhammad Ali Avenue was blessedly green. Still, a pivotal decision time was coming. There had been a lot of construction in recent years, so I wasn't entirely certain about this, but many through streets in Newark now dead-ended, and I was fairly sure Prince Street was one of them.

Partly because of that, and partly because it was the direction my car seemed to want to go, I made as hard a right onto Muhammad Ali as I dared, veering out into the oncoming lane just slightly.

The Mercedes dropped back slightly and made the turn smoothly. I could guess having all four tires intact probably helped in that regard. Then it began closing in on me anew.

And this time, maybe because my flapping right tire didn't give me much choice, I allowed it. It was beginning to dawn on me that letting the Mercedes slowly shred my car from behind was a losing proposition. The Malibu was the only weapon I had, and I needed to find a way to use it while it was still running. Unless I could make this a demolition derby — not a carnival shooting gallery — I would be facing the prospect of a prolonged underground slumber.

Knowing the shooter was on the right side of the car, at least for the time being, I fought the wheel to stay in the left lane, giving the Mercedes plenty of room to overtake me on the right. As soon as its front bumper was even with my back bumper, I hit my brakes.

It was all happening at about fifty or sixty miles an hour on an urban street, so it all felt very fast. But as soon as my passenger side door was even with the thugs' driver side, I went back to the accelerator, veered out slightly to my left — to give myself a little room to build some momentum — then brought whatever tonnage the Malibu had slamming into the Mercedes.

The cars hit with a jolt and a thump that sounded more like plastic-on-plastic than metal-on-metal. Without being able to see through the tinted windows, I couldn't say this for sure, but I felt like I caught the bastards by surprise. The collision sapped us of some of our speed, though we were still traveling fairly fast, with our cars acting like they were caught on each other.

The intersection for Irvine Turner Boulevard was quickly approaching, and I saw that, on our current course, I was going to be steering the Mercedes straight into a utility pole. It was going to be a head-on collision. A nasty one.

The driver of the Mercedes obviously saw it, too, because at the last minute he peeled right, bouncing over a low curb onto the sidewalk and then through a small, empty parking lot. Then, to my surprise, he continued the right turn, hopped down on Irvine Turner Boulevard, and kept going, actually speeding up, like he was eager to get away.

I pounded my brakes and screeched through a (thankfully empty) intersection, barely missing a fire hydrant on the other side — at the price of plowing over a pedestrian crossing sign.

Still, that had to be significantly better than plowing over a pedestrian.

My Malibu finally came to rest in the side yard of some garden-style apartments. I sat in it for a moment and did some deep, grateful breathing, then got out to assess the damage to my car. It wasn't as bad as I thought it would be. The small crease in the front bumper could be hammered out. The glass in the passenger side mirror was gone, but at least the housing was intact. The scrapes along the right side of the car were superficial, and I wasn't exactly worried too much about cosmetics at this point. The right rear tire was a floppy mess. I couldn't see any damage from where the other bullet had hit.

Before long, a lanky teenager wearing a too-long white T-shirt, riding a too-small bicycle cruised up behind me.

"You aight?" he asked in a languid voice. He seemed unimpressed by what he had just witnessed, as if car chases rolled through his neighborhood every Wednesday afternoon right around two o'clock.

"Yeah, thanks."

"They dropped they gun."

"They . . . they did?"

"Yeah, it's back there," he said, jerking his head behind him.

"Show me," I said.

He wheeled his bike around, and I followed him as he crossed the intersection and pedaled back up the sidewalk. Sure enough, there was a handgun lying on its side against the curb, right around the spot where I had sideswiped the Mercedes. That explained why it sped off the way it did: the occupants were no longer armed.

I squatted next to the gun and studied it, not wanting to touch it in case there were usable fingerprints on it. Using the sum total of my knowledge about handguns, I could tell this one was black, plastic, and nasty.

Out of curiosity — and because I wasn't exactly going to pick it up and check out its action — I shifted myself to get a good view of the underside of the gun. Sure enough, there was a tiny red dot emblazoned on the butt of the handle. It was so small I'm sure I wouldn't have noticed it unless I had been looking for it specifically.

"There's a red dot on this gun," I said to my bike-riding friend. "You ever heard of red dot guns?"

He smiled at me like he knew something but said, "I ain't into nothing like that."

Yes, I'm sure a teenaged kid who was puttering around on his bike during school hours wouldn't know anything about a criminal enterprise. Oh well. At least I was getting shot at by the very latest in thug chic.

My buddy rode off, leaving me alone to ponder what had just transpired. Obviously, I had been attacked by the same punks who had given me the drive-by treatment outside of Mimi's place — I didn't need to match license plates and VIN numbers to recognize that Mercedes. But how had they found me this time? It's not like I rang up Mimi and tipped her off I was going to see the medical examiner. Heck, I hadn't even told Tina.

Had they been following me? They obviously knew where I was. But then, if they had really tailed me from the newsroom all the way to the medical examiner's office and watched me park and walk inside, wouldn't they have just waited for me there and put a slug behind my right ear as soon as I departed the building?

So was it just dumb luck? Were they driving around, doing their gang thing, when one of them happened to recognize my car? No, that didn't work. Because when they shot at me the last time, I wasn't in — or near — the Malibu. They wouldn't have known it was my car, and besides, it's not like an aging Chevy Malibu is a rare, priceless vehicle scarcely seen on the streets of Newark.

I hadn't made much headway on the subject when I saw a Newark Police patrol unit roll to a stop near the corner. They had either gotten a report about shots being fired and had come to investigate, or they were going to give me a ticket for abandoning my derelict car on someone's lawn.

I walked back to my Malibu just as the two officers emerged from the squad car.

"Man, I could have used you guys about five minutes ago," I said.

The driver, an older black guy with a bull-like build, a shaved head, and "B. Jones" on his nameplate, looked at me like he was thoroughly uninterested as to when or how I could have used or not used him. This set the tone for what followed, when I explained to Baldy — that's what the "B" stood for, right? — who I was, what had happened, and how I was truly the victim in this whole scenario.

I went through my story at least three times, and he remained circumspect throughout. Finally, I took them over to the gun, which he picked up bare-handed and walked over to his patrol car, dumping it in the front seat.

"Isn't that . . . evidence or something?" I asked. "Aren't you going to check it for prints?"

Baldy glowered at me and said, "This isn't television, sir. We never get usable prints off of guns like this."

"Oh," I said. "But did you see the red dot on the bottom of it?"

"Huh?"

"There's a red dot on it, and . . . I didn't know if it was something you guys were tracking. I'm told guns with red dots on them are all the rage. I was going to be writing a story about it, and . . ."

He was fixing me with this I-don't-give-a-crap stare, so I shut up. He seemed mostly concerned about getting me and my car — and him and his car — out of this area just as soon as was possible, so he could return to . . . whatever it was he did with his time. Presumably not conditioning his hair.

He asked where I wanted my car to be towed, which seemed like a real leap of faith, inasmuch as I'm not sure the thing was worth fixing. But I gave him a name and number for Mickey the mechanic, the guy who owned the garage across the street from the *Eagle-Examiner* offices, whom I entrusted with keeping the Malibu in its pristine condition.

Next, I called Tommy, swore him to the usual secrecy, then told him briefly about how my automobile had been incapacitated and that I therefore needed his services as a chauffeur. He responded with a crack about how it would have been better if a bullet had caught me in the ass, thus ridding the world of one more pair of my pleated pants. But he also promised to come pick me up.

The cop eventually gave me a card, which identified him as Bryson M. Jones — personally, I liked "Baldy" better — of the Newark Police Department's Fourth Precinct. There was a report number on the back that he said I could use when making a claim with my insurance company. I had already given him all my contact information, and he halfheartedly assured me someone would be in touch if they needed anything more from me.

"Are there going to be any criminal charges against the guys who, you know, tried to shoot me?" I asked.

"Yeah, just as soon as we find 'em," Baldy replied, heavy on the sarcasm. "You know where they are?"

"No, I suppose not."

"Yeah," he snorted in reply. "Me neither."

■ ■ ■ ■

As I waited for Tommy to arrive, I began
focusing on the matter of my immediate
survival. Somehow, outwardly, I was main-
taining a placid façade. Inwardly, I was
more like one of those big-eyed purse dogs
that gets scared by its own chew toys. I
needed to figure out who was shooting at
me and hopefully figure out why — and
how to avoid any future encounters.

Somehow, I didn't think Baldy Jones was
going to be much help, so I decided to tap
a different part of the Newark Police Department and call my buddy Pritch. He was
in the gang unit, after all. Chances were
good — if my assailants were, in fact, affili-
ated in some manner — he might be familiar
with them.

"Hey, Woodward N. Bernstein!" he
crowed. "I might have to pretend I don't
know you, with all the stuff you been stirring up lately. You a bad man."

"You've been hanging out with Hakeem
Rogers again, haven't you?"

"That ass hat? Naw. I'm just talking about
what I'm reading in the paper. You been
lighting fires, my friend."

"It's what I do," I said. "You got a second

to help me put out a fire by any chance?"

"Yeah, I'm just walking to get some lunch downtown. You want to join? I'll let you pay."

The *Eagle-Examiner* had paid for a number of Pritch's lunches, and he was worth every one of them. "Love to," I said. "But my transportation has just been shot up by some guys I'm thinking might be acquaintances of yours."

"No kidding. Who?"

"Well, I'm not exactly sure. That's why I'm placing this call to the pride of the Newark Police Gang Unit. You know of a crew that rolls around the city in a silver Mercedes E-class with tinted windows?"

I absentmindedly toed the pedestrian crossing sign that was still sticking out from underneath my car like it was the Wicked Witch of the West's legs.

"Yeah, that sounds like BMF," Pritch said.

"And BMF is . . . ?"

"Black Mafia Family. I actually should say it's a group of knuckleheads *pretending* to be Black Mafia Family. The original BMF was out of Michigan, Detroit or Flint, I think. They got hooked up with some Mexicans that were supplying them with product, established themselves nationally. You ever hear of Big Meech?"

"Sounds like a burger sold at McDonald's."

"Not quite. Big Meech is a legend in the hip-hop community. He was the guy who started BMF. He and his brother lived large for a while. They were pretty stupid about it, you ask me. Too flashy. The best hos. The VIP table service. The best cars.

"You can't just rub it in our face like that, you know?" Pritch continued. "They were also sloppy and dumb. It ended up being one of those big RICO statute things. They got them blabbing all over the place on wires and arrested all of them, eventually. And I think they're all still in jail. The original BMF doesn't really exist anymore. As far as I know, it's been dismantled."

"So who are these guys who don't seem to like me much?"

"They're just playing around, acting like they all bad, like they're the real BMF. Everyone knows the name Black Mafia Family. Now these guys are just using the name. It's like if the real McDonald's went bankrupt and you decided to open up a fast-food joint with golden arches on it that sold hamburgers. It'd probably fool some people, but it's not the real thing."

"I have to say, it sort of felt like the real thing when they were chasing me through

Newark shooting at me."

"Well, let me ask you something: You dead yet?"

"No."

"Then, trust me, it wasn't the real thing. These guys are small-timers. They're just driving that Mercedes around, doing their best BMF imitation. The only reason we haven't shut them down is that they really haven't done anything worth shutting down. We've had bigger fish to fry."

"So why would they try to shoot the friendly local *Eagle-Examiner* reporter?"

"Aw, hell, I don't know. Maybe they didn't get their paper on time this morning. Who knows with some of these punks?"

"Does shooting at a reporter mean they've escalated into something worth frying?" I asked hopefully.

"Not when it's you," he cracked.

"Ouch?"

"Come on, I'm kidding. I'm kidding. Could you ID the driver or the shooter?"

"Nope, just the car."

"Well, that ain't gonna do much for us. But I'll put the word out with some of the guys in the unit, maybe have them put a little heat on these turkeys, get them to cool it with whatever beef they got."

"Thanks. Hey, mind answering another

question? It's about Mike Fusco. I assume you heard about that."

"Yeah. I don't know anything about it, though. And I don't really know him. He got to the Fourth after I left."

"It's not about him. It's about his gun."

"Okay, go."

Since my most recent conversation with Raul Ibanez, this question had been coalescing in my mind and was now fully formed: "The word from Captain Boswell is that Fusco killed himself with his service weapon. I got a source in the medical examiner's office that confirmed it for me, matched the serial numbers and everything. But Fusco told me the day before he was killed that his service weapon had been taken from him when he was placed on leave. So how is it possible that gun was used?"

"Well, it's possible Fusco was lying to you. His captain knew if she was placing him on leave, she'd have to take his gun. It's policy. But maybe if he bitched about it enough, she let it slide. Some cops feel naked without their weapon, even off duty. Or . . . ."

Pritch actually chuckled, but it was the kind that didn't have a lot of mirth behind it. "Or what?" I asked.

"Well, officially, all our guns are under

lock and key, tighter than Fort Knox."

"Unofficially?"

"Unofficially, we've had a problem for years with guns that were supposed to have been under lock and key showing up on the street again. I know guys who have brought in the same gun two, three times only to have it get back out."

"How is that happening?"

"We're just sloppy. Eventually, a confiscated gun gets destroyed. But the department doesn't do it right away. In the short term, the gun just gets locked up. Each precinct has a locker and there are only certain people who are supposed to have access to it, but that doesn't mean a lot. They'll hide an extra key near the locker because everyone keeps losing the main one, and before long anyone with a uniform is helping themselves."

"What about people without uniforms?" I asked. "Like, maybe, people in an overly aggressive prayer group?"

"A what?"

"Never mind. I guess I'm just asking if you thought it was possible for a civilian to have gotten his hands on Fusco's gun."

"Possible? Sure. Do this job long enough and you'll swear anything is possible," Pritch said. "But maybe if you put something in your paper about it, it'll embarrass the brass enough that they'll actually do something about it for a change."

"That sounds like a magnificent idea," I said, then asked the following question facetiously: "You want to go on the record with that, Detective Pritchard?"

He snorted. "Yeah, about as much as I want to be hanging out with you the next time that Mercedes comes around."

The tow truck and Tommy arrived within a few seconds of each other, so I ended the call with Pritch and watched as my Chevy Malibu, the car that had served me for more miles than its busted odometer knew how to count, was winched onto a flat-bed and taken away, all forlorn and dented. If this was truly its end — and I can't imagine it's very hard to total a car that doubles in value every time you fill the gas tank — it had served me well.

I said good-bye to Baldy Jones, who acknowledged me by slightly lifting his head from the form he was filling out and then immediately putting his head back down. I suspected we wouldn't be swapping cute text messages later.

"You know, if you wanted to pimp your ride, I could have found someone to do a better job than that," Tommy said as I lowered myself into his car, an import that was a bit on the small side for a strapping American male such as myself.

"Yeah, but you'd probably send me to a guy who would outfit the seats with pink slipcovers."

Tommy said something in Spanish, which is his go-to move when he wants to deliver a withering putdown that I simply cannot match.

"I accept your compliment," I said.

He snorted.

We drove for a moment in silence, giving me a chance to appreciate how nice it was riding in a car that *wasn't* being assailed by bullets.

"Your little car chase went out on BNN, you know," Tommy said.

BNN was the Breaking News Network, a company that paid people to listen to police scanners and then report the good stuff to nosy journalists like me. In the old days, BNN subscribers got broadcasts sent out on a pager; now it was an Internet site.

"Too bad they don't use names on BNN," I replied. "It would have been good for my street cred."

"Yeah, yeah. But just . . . be careful, okay? You're a newspaper reporter, remember?

We write about this sort of stuff happening to *other people.* I'm worried about you."

"Oh, I'm fine," I said, even though I really wasn't.

"You're only 'fine' because those hombres can't shoot straight. I mean, what the hell is going on?"

"I just talked to a cop source who said it's just a group of guys pretending to be the Black Mafia Family street gang."

"Whoever that is. What did you do to piss them off?

"I'm not sure, actually. I guess I should at least try to find out before they come back, huh?"

"Sounds like a good idea. Because, you know, if they start shooting at us between here and the office, I'm going to kick you out of the car and let them have you. I just got this thing paid off, and I don't want it getting all full of bullet holes."

I wished I had a ready repertoire of Spanish insults with which to counter him. Instead, I pulled up Tee Jamison's name on my phone's contact list and hit the Send button.

Tee answered the phone the way he always does, with a short, "Yeah."

"What is up, my brother?" I said, intentionally overenunciating each word.

"You know, you sound like them politicians who only come into the 'hood when it's time to hustle votes. They teach you white people to talk like that?"

"It just comes naturally," I assured him, then spent a few minutes telling him about my new propensity for having to duck bullets, thanks to my sudden association with guys masquerading as Black Mafia Family.

"So you beefin' with BMF?" he said when I was done. "You mean them guys who were hooked up with Young Jeezy?"

"And that is . . . ?"

"A rapper. For you people, that'd be like, I don't know, Neil Diamond or something."

"Well, sweet, Caroline."

"Huh?"

"Never mind. I just need to figure out what these guys are into and why they're after me."

"Oh, well, I don't really know those niggas. They sound like they a bunch of young-uns, frontin' like that. I don't know the new generation that well. But you know who would?"

"Who?"

"Uncle Bernie."

It was a good thing I wasn't drinking a Coke Zero. I would have snorted it out my nose. "Come on, he's so old I think he resold warrantied merchandise to Moses."

"I'm telling you, that dude has got feelers *everywhere.* I mean, he's getting boots from me, luggage from someone's mom. He's probably getting something from those guys, too. People in the 'hood know Uncle Bernie will give you quick cash for the right stuff. And who don't like quick cash?"

Uncle Bernie *did* mention something about knowing everyone from the *bubbas* to the *machers.* (Whoever they were.) Maybe he'd know a few bangers, too. It was worth a try.

"Good thought, thanks," I said.

"No problem," he said. "And, hey, if you see Lil J, get his autograph, will you?"

"Yeah, right after you get me Neil Diamond."

I ended the call, then told Tommy, "You mind making a little detour? It'll take us maybe twenty minutes, and you might be able to get some new Pradas out of it."

"I'd love to, but I have to be at a stupid ribbon-cutting at four o'clock. I wouldn't want to miss the North Ward councilman congratulating himself for something he actually had nothing to do with."

"All right. Then can you drop me somewhere? It's just on Irvine Turner Boulevard."

Tommy heaved a melodramatic sigh, the

kind only gay guys seem to be able to pull off with the needed gusto. "And then, what, you're going to be on the street, thumbing a ride back to the office when BMF comes back?"

"No, I'll call Ruthie, have him pick me up."

Tommy let out a groaning noise. "I don't like that kid. He's *such* a brownnoser."

"I know, I know. But he's actually not too bad once you get to know him. And I think he might be a pretty good reporter. We're going to work on a story together as soon as I can get my plate a little cleaner."

"Yeah, assuming you live that long," Tommy said, but he had already started making his way toward Irvine Turner. I gave him the cross streets, then called Ginsburg to arrange for my ride home. He didn't answer, so I sent him a text with the details of where to find me. He seemed like the kind of guy who wouldn't ignore a texted plea for help from someone he thought might help his career.

After a quick stop at an ATM machine — this story was growing expensive, but at least I would be getting good bargains — Tommy pulled up to the curb outside the anonymous cream-colored building with its one-way glassed bodega and its insides stocked with the finest warranted merchandise. I just hoped Uncle Bernie would again be chatty.

As I departed, Tommy called out, "Be safe, all right?"

"I'll be fine," I said.

"Okay," Tommy said. He seemed to want to linger or maybe say something else, but talked himself out of it. Though as he drove away, I thought I saw him shaking his head.

The alley was just as strangely clean as it was the previous time I visited it, although at least I understood why this time. Gene seemed like the type who would want things tidy. I rang the bell and was immediately greeted by the sound of Uncle Bernie's voice pouring through the speaker. "You changed your mind about the briefcase! I knew you'd change your mind."

"Yeah, that's right," I said. Why not? My current briefcase was beginning to look like it had been sat on by a few too many elephants.

"I told you he'd change his mind," Bernie said at slightly lower volume, like he was talking to someone else in the room, probably Gene. Then he returned to me: "Hang on. I'll be right there."

I stuffed my hands in my pockets and idly

glanced up at the building. It turned out the camera above the door wasn't the only one. There were also cameras high on each corner. They looked like the kind that could be controlled remotely. I guess Uncle Bernie didn't want anyone sneaking up on him. He had thousands of dollars of product that had warranties against material or manufacturing defect but not, I suspected, against theft.

The same large, taciturn black man greeted me at the door. He led me down the hallway, punched in a numeric code on the inner door, and ushered me into the merchandise warehouse, where Bernie was already waiting for me.

He was dressed in a half-buttoned Hawaiian shirt that had too many colors to possibly catalogue. His pants were pink, perhaps the only color *not* represented in the shirt. The small wisps of his barely there, chemically enhanced blond hair were slicked back into their usual position. He was wearing the same yellow-tinted glasses as last time, though I thought perhaps he had changed pinkie rings.

"How are ya, kid?" He greeted me with a handshake.

"I'm good, Uncle Bernie. How you been?"

"I'm good, I'm good," he said, then began

patting my cheek, which I pretended wasn't awkward. "Look at this kisser, heh? So young. You look good, you look good. You get a little sun since the last time I saw you? You go down south? Miami? I love Miami. We go to Florida at least once a winter. I could never live down there. I'd just be another one of those schmucks playing shuffleboard all day long. But it's nice to visit, it's nice to visit."

"Yeah, Miami is great," I confirmed. "Where's Gene?"

Bernie made a dismissive gesture. "Eh, he's upstairs, forging a receipt for the Cuisinart people. They're very picky, those Cuisinart guys. You gotta get it just right with them. After he does Cuisinart, he has to do Best Buy. Another tough one. He'll be here all night."

"Sure."

"So, briefcase, briefcase," he said, walking quickly toward what I recognized as the luggage section. "You like Coach? I got Coach. Black or brown. The brown is nice, the leather is softer. Like butter. But you young guys, I know how you are, you like the black shoes, the black belts. Maybe you like the black better, huh?"

"Actually, Uncle Bernie, I was hoping you could help me with a story I'm working on."

That stopped his white nurses' shoes in their tracks. "What, you don't want the briefcase? I got Kenneth Cole, too, if you don't like Coach."

"No, no, I'll take the briefcase. The black one is fine. I was just wondering . . . my pal Tee thought you might have heard of a gang called Black Mafia Family."

Bernie looked at me like he was mystified as to why I would care but said, "You mean those *balegoolas* who drive around in that Mercedes? Yeah, I know them. BMW makes a better car, you ask me. But, yeah, they're all right. They're a bunch of *pishers,* but they're sweet boys."

"Sweet boys? They've tried to kill me twice today."

"Eh," he said, waving it away like it never happened. "They're not so tough. You want tough? Try Fat Lou Larasso. Back in the day, he'd have someone cut out your eyeballs if you looked at him the wrong way. Those boys? Puppies. Kittens. They try their best. But I think their source dried up — sad, very sad. You need to have a good supplier in that line of work or else you're *tot.* For me? They mostly do electronics. Televisions. Vizio. Vizio was the last thing they got for me. Vizio is good. Sony is better, but Vizio is good. You want to see it? It just came in. I could give you a deal."

"Actually, I was hoping you could, I don't know, arrange for me to talk to them somehow?"

He recoiled. "What do you think I am, a *shadken*? They're business associates. This is a business I'm running here, not a dating service."

"I know, I know. I was just . . . look, they keep shooting at me, and I'd sort of like to figure out why before I catch a bullet in the ear."

"All right, all right. Hang on. You're a customer, I don't need my customers getting killed. Bad for business," he said and produced an iPhone from his pocket. Cutting-edge guy, Uncle Bernie. He held it as far out as his arm could go, muttering to himself all the while, tapped at it a few times, then brought it to his ear.

"Yeah, yeah. Don't give me that 'yo' stuff. It's Uncle Bernie."

He listened for a moment. "Yeah, the Vizio worked out nicely. You get any more, you bring 'em to me, you hear?"

Another reply. "Okay, okay. Listen, I know a goy, says you keep shooting at him."

Pause. "Yeah, tall skinny white guy. That's him."

Uncle Bernie nodded, then pulled the

phone away from his ear and put his hand over the mouthpiece. "Yep, they're shooting at you. It sounds like they're a little pissed they keep missing."

"Can you ask them why they're shooting at me? What did I do?"

Bernie returned to the phone and said, "He wants to talk." He furrowed his brow as he heard the reply, which went on for a minute or so. Finally, Bernie cut it off with "Okay, okay, I got you." He then addressed me: "It doesn't sound like they want to talk to you. Someone hired them to kill you, so they have to kill you."

"Can you ask them who they're working for?"

"He wants to know who you're working for," Bernie said into the phone, waited, then announced, "They can't tell you."

"Is it a church?" I asked.

"They said they can't tell you," Bernie objected.

"Just ask. C'mon."

Bernie gave an exasperated grunt. "Fine, fine," he said, returning to his phone. "Is it a church you're working for? . . . Okay, okay, I'm not deaf. I hear you . . . Well, that's very nice of you, I'll be sure to tell him . . . Yeah, Panasonic is good, too. The bigger the better. I don't bother with anything much under forty these days. No market for it . . . Right then, I'll see you by the end of the week."

He hung up, then turned to me. "They said they can't tell you who they're working for, but that you shouldn't worry for the rest of the day because they lost their best gun trying to kill you the last time, and they won't be able to get another one until later. See? I told you they're nice boys."

Uncle Bernie was just turning his attention back to briefcases when a chiming sound echoed throughout the warehouse. Bernie looked around, annoyed.

"Meh, what is this, Grand Central Station?" he grumbled, then shuffled over to an intercom on the wall. He pressed a button, then said, "Gene, who is it?"

I heard Gene's slightly static-garbled voice reply, "He says he's here to pick up Mr. Ross."

Bernie looked at me, "You expecting someone? What is this, your mommy coming to pick you up from baseball practice?"

Before I could reply, Gene said, "He says his name is Geoff Ginsburg."

"Ginsburg. Ginsburg?" Bernie said. "Sounds like a mensch. I probably know his grandfather. Let him in. Maybe he wants a nice pen. I got Cross, you know. Silver or gold. Very classy. I got a guy who engraves them, too. Makes a good gift."

The black guy went back through the entrance, and Bernie turned back to me. "So, the briefcase. Retails for three hundred. Uncle Bernie gives it to you for two hundred. I'm going to have to ask for cash, though. Normally, returning customer like you, I'd let you open up an account. But it sounds like you might not be around long enough to pay it off. So we're going to have to make it cash."

"Fair enough," I said, digging the bills out of my wallet just as Ruthie appeared.

Bernie was on him like twists on challah bread. "Come in, come in, my friend. Mr. Ginsburg. Fine, fine young fellow you are. A real *kluger,* this one. I bet you like to read. You look like a reader. You want a Kindle? I got the latest. Give you a good deal."

I hadn't prepared Ruthie for this, and he was looking around the warehouse with the same slack-jawed wonder I did when I first saw it.

"Geoff is an intern, which means he makes about five hundred bucks a week," I said. "I'm not sure he's in the market."

"Fine, fine," Bernie said. "When you get a raise, call me. I got some Farberware that I can tell your mother would just love."

I put myself in between Bernie and Ruthie, if only to help stop the sales pitch.

"Hey, thanks for coming to get me," I said. "I'm having a little car trouble."

"Yeah, no problem," Ruthie said. "I actually have to talk to you anyway. I got some amazing stuff on red dot. You're going to want to move it up on your schedule."

"Oh yeah?" I said. I hadn't even told Ruthie about my close encounter with a red dot gun.

"I went back and talked to those corner boys a little more. At first they were giving me a hard time, doing all that 'I ain't no snitch' stuff. Then I sorta made a deal with them . . ."

He glanced down and toed the concrete floor of the warehouse a little bit. "What?" I asked.

"Well, we got talking a little more. And it turns out they're aspiring rappers."

"Okay," I said. This was not surprising: I think roughly two out of every five young men in Newark identifies himself as an aspiring rapper, the same way two out of every five parents on a suburban travel soccer team thinks their kid is going to get a college scholarship. In each case, the chance for even a modest fulfillment of the goal is roughly the same.

"So they were saying they were having a hard time getting noticed and . . . I promised them I'd do a Good Neighbors about their group."

"A Good Neighbors? About kids who are hanging out on the corner selling drugs?"

"Well, they said that was just temporary until the stuff they have on iTunes takes off. Besides, they said they rap about positive themes — don't get your girlfriend pregnant, don't shoot anyone who doesn't deserve it, that sort of thing. I thought that'd be good enough. Besides, it was the only way I could get them to talk to me. Trust me, it was worth it."

Yes. Ruthie would end up doing fine in this business.

"Okay, so what'd they tell you?"

"Get this," he said. "The guys selling red dot guns? They're policemen."

"*What?*" I said, and not because my hearing is bad.

"They're policemen. That's why the red dot is so sought after. There's this group of cops that makes money on the side selling guns. Every gun they sell, they put a red dot on the handle. When you buy one of their guns, it comes with a promise: if you get caught with it later, they won't bust you, as long as it has their special red dot. It's like automatic amnesty. That's why the corner boys only want red dot guns. It keeps them from getting arrested."

I had certainly heard stories of cops shaking down criminals in exchange for looking the other way; or, certainly, cops who made arrests and somehow "forgot" to turn in all the cash they confiscated. It felt like we wrote that story every other year.

But cops selling guns? Arming the enemy? That was something new.

"You sure about this?" I asked. "I mean, why would these kids just tell you this? All for a Good Neighbors?"

"Well, it sounds like the cops keep driving up the price of the guns, and they're getting tired of it. It's basically extortion."

"Okay," I said. "But how do we know they're not just making it up?"

Ruthie shrugged, but I saw Bernie nodding out of the corner of my eye and turned toward him. "You know about this, don't you?" I said.

"I heard stories, yeah," Bernie said. "I don't bother with guns. They're more trouble than they're worth."

"*Cops* dealing guns?" I asked, still feeling like I couldn't quite believe it.

"What, you think it's a quilting bee out

there? It's Newark," Bernie said, jabbing his thumb in the direction of the street. "I told you some of those cops are involved in some funny business. Not many anymore. But a few."

"Like who?"

"Eh," he said, waving me away.

"No, seriously, could you ID individual cops who are involved in this thing?"

"It's none of my business, kid," Bernie said. "I don't want any trouble."

"You don't want any trouble? Young black men are slaughtering each other on a daily basis in this city, and easy access to guns is what allows them to do it. But you don't want any *trouble*?"

Uncle Bernie shook his head, like I didn't get it. "Those kids are going to do what they're going to do. They're going to get guns one way or another — if not from the cops, then from someone else. What does it matter . . ."

"It matters because these people are sworn to uphold . . ." I began to say, then stopped myself. "Never mind."

A guy who had his brother upstairs forging receipts so he could defraud consumer products companies into sending him new merchandise was not exactly worth engaging in a debate of this nature. His moral compass pointed to wherever the money was.

But this was . . . well, the word "abhorrent" came quickly to mind. I don't want to get into a debate about the Second Amendment or what it means. And hey, if you need a gun to shoot yourself some dinner — or raise a well-ordered militia to stave off attacks from the French, or whatever — I have no problem with you. What I have a problem with is a gun being owned by a seventeen-year-old kid with no impulse control and this weird idea that in order to be a "man" he needs to possess a gun and settle disputes with it.

"So these corner boys," I said, pivoting back toward Ruthie. "Will they go on the record?"

"Well, we sort of have a problem there. It's not that they're off the record. I just . . . I don't know their real names, and they wouldn't tell me."

"Yeah, we have a problem."

And that was not the only one. Even if they gave us their full Christian names, along with their dates of birth, their Social Security numbers, and their blood types, Brodie wasn't going to let us run a story like this — with such a damning accusation

— on the simple say-so of some corner drug dealers.

We needed something to substantiate it, something indisputable.

We needed to see it with our own eyes.

"Ruthie, you think your corner boys would let us watch them make a buy?"

He thought about it for a second. "Maybe," he said. "We can at least go over there and ask."

"All right. Let's go. Uncle Bernie, it's been a pleasure, as always," I said, making my way toward the door. I was starting to feel a bit dirty hanging out there anyway.

But before I could get away, Bernie grabbed my shoulder with a grip that was surprisingly strong coming from such a wrinkled old hand.

"Listen, young fella. These cops, they're not good men, you hear me?" he said. "You'd be better off leaving them alone, you ask me."

"No offense, Uncle Bernie," I replied, "but that's why I'm not asking you."

"Okay, okay," he said, releasing me. "You got to do your little crusade, that's fine. Just remember: most of the knights who went on those crusades to the Holy Land? They never made it back."

Word of Black Mafia Family's second failure reached Red Dot Enterprises quickly enough, causing discontent among the associates. Perhaps they shouldn't have contracted out that job. If they had handled it themselves — with the certainty of men who were trained in the use of guns — Carter Ross would be as dead as Mike Fusco by now.

There was a movement within the ranks to end the effort against Ross. It was not out of any sudden sense of mercy. It was just practical: now that Fusco was out of the way — and his "confession" had been happily consumed by everyone from the Newark police high command to the greater New York media — it was entirely possible life would return to normal. Killing a newspaper reporter, even one who was getting as dangerously close as Ross, was too much of a risk.

It was time to go back underground, argued some of the associates. Things had gone too far as it was. This was supposed to be about making a little money on the side, selling guns to thugs who were going to find a way to get guns anyway. That's how they had always rationalized it. If anything, many of them thought, it was a perverse kind of community policing, inasmuch as it gave them a working relationship with the criminal element — and allowed them to keep tabs on it.

The Kipps matter had been unfortunate, right from the start. Kipps had seen something he shouldn't have. Had it been some other cop, maybe they could have convinced him to shut up about it. But, no, it had to be Kipps — the one guy they could never convince to look the other way, the guy who couldn't just drop it, the guy who believed being sworn to uphold the law was more than just a way to make a decent paycheck.

Killing Kipps was the only way to ensure the mess was contained. And then once Fusco started nosing around, he had to be killed, too.

But Ross? Maybe they didn't need to get rid of him. Or at least that's what some of the associates were trying to argue when they got the worst possible news from the Black Mafia Family's botched job: the idiots had somehow dropped their gun.

And Ross had not only found it but identified it by its red dot — and started asking questions. That quickly ended any and all debate within Red Dot Enterprises on the what-to-do-about-the-reporter question.

He needed to be dealt with. And quickly.

CHAPTER 8

The parking spot Ruthie happened to choose was around the corner from Gene and Bernie's place, in plain sight of the Fourth Precinct. As we got into his car, I glanced at the building, curious as ever as to what exactly was going on inside all that brick and mortar. Staged suicides down in the locker rooms. Gun-selling cops in the squad rooms. A captain upstairs who seemed to be completely oblivious. It was a treasury of dysfunction.

"Okay, so here's how it works with these guys," Ruthie said, getting us underway. "There are usually five or six of them out there, but you don't always see all of . . . you need to get that?"

My phone had rung. I hauled it out of my pocket and saw it was Mickey the mechanic, probably calling to tell me my car had become the first in history to have a negative blue book value, because it was going to cost more to tow it to the scrap yard than it was actually worth.

"Yeah, hang on," I said, then hit that little green button and announced, "Carter Ross."

"Mr. Ross, it's Mickey," he said, with a medium-thick accent. Mickey is of Middle Eastern descent. I wasn't sure why he called himself Mickey, though I guessed it had something to do with people like me mispronouncing his given name so badly he had given up and gone with Mickey.

"Hey, Mickey. How's my hunk-a-junk doing?"

"Well, it's bad. Very bad. I talk to your insurance for you. I give them the estimate, doing it the way the insurance tell me to do it. They say it's totaled. They say they give you twenty-nine hundred for it."

"Yeah, I sort of expected that," I said, sighing.

"But I think I can still fix it for you," he said, pronouncing "fix" like "feex." Given the age and indeterminate mileage of my car, Mickey was always feexing things for me.

"What's it going to set me back?" I asked.

"It depends. You want me to cut the corners?"

Mickey was also always asking me if he

could cut the corners. It was his way of asking if he could use parts that weren't a hundred percent new and methods that didn't necessarily conform to factory standards.

"That's fine."

"Okay, I cut the corners. And you pay cash?"

This was another one of Mickey's standard questions. "Sure."

"Okay, you need new tire, new bumper. I have my body guy work on the dents, maybe touch up the paint a little. I give you new mirror. I do it for eight hundred."

I thought about it and quickly decided getting the Malibu back on its feet, as it were, made more fiscal sense than making the massive outlay of cash to buy a new used Malibu. Sure, the way Mickey was proposing making the repairs, my car wasn't going to be winning any beauty pageants. But it's not like it was exactly in the running for a tiara before.

"That sounds fine," I said, and was about ready to hang up when Mickey spoke again.

"Oh, but Mr. Ross? Your LoJack. It's not so good. It's busted up. And I can't fix it. You need special tools and I'm not authorized dealer."

"Mickey, I don't have LoJack."

"Yes, you do."

"No I don't."

"Yes, sir, you do."

"I'm quite sure I don't," I said. The guy I had bought the car from tried to sell me on a LoJack system. But I hadn't gone for it because that was the whole point of buying a used Malibu: not even the most desperate car thief would steal it.

"Mr. Ross, I find the LoJack on the back corner of your car. It's a little black box. Trust me, I know what it looks like. And your car has it."

"Mickey, you've worked on that car . . . had you ever seen a LoJack there before?"

"No, sir."

"So how did it magically . . ."

And then it dawned on me:

Someone LoJacked my car.

That's how Black Mafia Family had been able to find me the second time. It's why they weren't waiting for me outside the medical examiner's office. They didn't know where *I* was — they just knew where my car was.

It was how they found me the first time as well. Mimi Kipps hadn't set me up. My own car had done it. Did her pastor still have something to do with it? I couldn't rule it out — after all, he did show up at her house mere minutes before BMF arrived, guns blazing. But Mimi? She now appeared to be just as ignorant as I was.

"Mickey, can you please just remove it?" I said.

"Yes, Mr. Ross."

"Thanks. When will the car be finished?"

"A few days. Even cutting the corners, this one is going to take a while, Mr. Ross. It's a mess."

"I know, Mickey," I said. "Thanks. I'll be in touch."

I ended the call, and Ruthie immediately relaunched his gang tutorial. But I shushed him. I needed a moment to think. A lot of things had just started to make sense. It was like I had been spending time in an idiot box and was finally crawling out.

Because I knew: LoJack is the stolen car recovery system used by *the police.* Only cops have access to the equipment that tracks the radio signals an activated LoJack device emits.

Which meant it was the police who told Black Mafia Family where to find me; which meant it was the police who slapped that LoJack on my car, perhaps while I was inside their precinct chatting with their captain — which meant it was the police who hired BMF to kill me.

Yes, life outside the idiot box was making a lot of sense. And it would make even more if I could get Buster Hays to confirm one simple detail, something that had seemed so insignificant when he first said it. I called his desk and he picked up after one ring.

"Hays."

"Buster, it's Carter."

"You know, Ivy, I —"

"Save it, Buster. I need you to look back on your notes from the conversation you had with that IA guy."

Buster didn't reply immediately, but I could tell from the way he grunted that he was reaching for something, like a notebook. "Yeah, okay, what's up?"

"You said Kipps called the IA guy and left a message about 'seeing blotches.' Did you really mean red dots? Was he calling with something related to red dots?"

"Hang on," Buster said, then after a few seconds came back with: "Yeah, here it is. Yeah. Blotches. Dots. I guess it was dots. Red dots. Same difference. Does it matter?"

"Oh, trust me, it matters."

I got off the phone with Buster before he forced me to explain *why* it mattered. I couldn't risk telling Buster yet. He had cop sources all over the place, yes. But, without

391

knowing how widespread the gun-selling was — and how much of the Newark Police Department was involved — I didn't want Buster unwittingly tipping off someone that we were circling in.

But it was all clear now. Darius Kipps had somehow discovered red dot guns and planned to tell all. Maybe he had been part of it and finally decided to flip, figuring if he was the first to tell, he might be able to avoid jail time. Maybe he had a confidential informant who told him what was happening. Either way, he left a message with a trusted friend in Internal Affairs and planned to spill. Except before his call was returned, he was grabbed by the red dot guys, who took him somewhere, tied him to a chair, and poured bourbon down his throat until he was blackout drunk and vomiting all over himself.

Then they dragged him into the precinct, where anyone not involved would see him as just another cop on a bender, being nobly aided by his fellow officers. They guided him down to the locker room, turned on the shower, and blew his brains out — with the water nicely washing away much of the evidence that would have proven it was not a suicide.

Enter Mike Fusco, the loyal sometimes-

partner. He knew Kipps hadn't killed himself — knew it because of the drunkenness
and the bourbon. And he had decided to
dig in and get to the bottom of whatever
happened. Maybe he was just driving that
big truck of his around, leading people to
think he was on to something, maybe he
was making real headway.

Whatever it was, it had gotten him killed,
too, in yet another faked suicide. The cops
who were trying to keep their gun-selling
operation alive had been able to smuggle
his service weapon out of the precinct —
because, as Pritch said, anyone with a
uniform could get access to the precinct's
gun locker.

Then they snuck into his house and liter-
ally caught him sleeping. They forced him
to call Captain Boswell and confess to killing Kipps. They shot him, then placed the
gun in his dead hand and made him pull
the trigger, so there would be gunshot
residue. From there, they must have hoped
that no one was going to want to look too
hard at another cop suicide. And Boswell,
under pressure from her superiors to stanch
the flow of embarrassing news, played right
into their hands by taking the confession
and running with it.

There was still the issue of Fusco's affair

with Mimi. But seen in a different light —
one in which he was a victim, not a perpe-
trator — I supposed it was possible their
fling had started after Darius had been
killed. Mimi Kipps would hardly be the first
widow to turn quickly to the comfort of
another man in a time of grief. And who
was Mike Fusco to deny her? Their relationship didn't have anything to do with either
death. It was just something that I had allowed to mislead me.

So, finally, I had it mostly figured out. The
what. The when. The how. The why.

All I lacked was the who. But with young
Ruthie Ginsburg acting as my guide, perhaps his corner boys could help us fill in
that final blank.

There was a small voice in one of my ears
— one that I probably should have heeded
— that told me perhaps it was time to pull
back, return to the office, and lay it all out
for Tina and Brodie. They would immediately hand it over to the authorities (to folks
who didn't have "Newark Police Department" on their badges), then write some
big, four-thousand-word feature (a "takeout," in newspaper parlance) in a couple of
months, once all the arrests had been made.

Except that small voice was almost immediately shouted down by a more boister-

ous one that reminded me this was potentially a career story. Exposing a ring of murderous, gun-dealing cops? Pulitzer prizes had been won on less, especially in this day and age, when newspapers barely have the resources — that damn word, again? — to do real reporting.

"Sorry about that," I said. "Please continue. You said there were five or six guys?"

"Yeah. But you might not actually see all of them. I haven't quite figured out their system yet. It seems like they got one guy sitting on the stash, one guy handling the money, one guy talking to the customers, a couple guys acting as lookouts."

"Doesn't really matter, as long as they're cool with you being there."

"Yeah, they're cool," he assured me. "So how are we going to play this?"

"I don't know. I mean, they're kids, right?"

"Yeah, I guess."

"Okay, so kids are easily confused by a situation they've never encountered before. We just keep in mind we're the grown-ups in this scenario and act accordingly. Tell me a little about them."

"Well, there's a little guy everyone calls Twan. He seems to be the spokesman. Or at least he does most of the talking. But I don't think he's really in charge."

"Okay."

"There's another guy you'll see, a big guy who acts real smiley and happy. Everyone calls him Doc."

"Doc?" I said. As far as I knew, most of the world's Docs were a minimum of sixty years old, "Doc" being one of those nicknames — like "Scooter" — that seemed to be fading out of the lingua franca.

"Yeah, not sure about why he's Doc. But whatever you do, don't piss him off. I'm pretty certain he's the one who's armed at all times."

"Good to know."

We stopped at a red light, and I watched as two little boys, each gripping their mother's hand, crossed the street in front of us. They had book bags on their backs and happy little skips in their stride as they came back from school. It's funny how Newark can be both so strange — full of gun-dealing cops — and so normal at the same time.

Ruthie continued his book report: "But the guy who really matters is this tall kid they call Famous."

"Famous?"

"Yeah, Famous. I think maybe it's a rap reference, but I don't know."

I clearly wasn't going to be able to help him there. I was a little behind on my subscription to *Vibe* magazine.

"Anyhow, Famous barely says anything," Ruthie continued. "I get the feeling he's the leader, though."

"How so?"

"He just . . . watches things, like he's the king sitting on his throne. Twan will keep talking and the whole time, he's got half an eye on Famous, waiting for him to make a little motion with his head or a hand signal or I don't know what. But Famous is definitely the boss. He actually freaks me out a little bit."

"Why?"

As we pulled up to Eighteenth Avenue, I soon found out.

During my years in Newark, I have come to firmly believe that the majority of kids involved in the drug trade are guilty of little more than going along to get along. They are truly products of their environment.

I know, I know, it sounds like liberal babble — and it leaves the factor of personal responsibility out of the equation — but it also happens to be true. Put most of these kids in a nice middle-class family in Franklin Lakes, and they end up heading off to Rutgers, majoring in business administration, and working in sales for a pharmaceutical company.

Put them in Newark and they end up drug dealers. The Newark kids are not inherently any more or less evil than the Franklin Lakes kids.

The first two kids I saw as I got out of the car were perfect examples of this. One was short, muscular, and a bit on the twitchy side, though not to the extent of being diagnosable. This, I guessed, was Twan.

He was on the sidewalk alongside a big, thick kid who had to be Doc. He was about six foot three and was a couple Ring Dings above three hundred pounds. Give him to the right high school football coach and a little time in the weight room, and he would have ended up playing left guard for Wisconsin.

Famous was seated on the front steps of one of the town houses, leaning against the side railing. He was tall — probably two inches taller than Doc — and lean, with bones jutting out in more than a few places. He had skin like mahogany and eyes like a lizard, large and set wide apart. There was an attempt at a beard on his chin, though it was pretty scraggly, barely visible against his dark complexion. His arms were crossed.

And I got the feeling, right away, he was a bad dude.

He was the kid that, no matter where he grew up, would have ended up involved in some malevolent venture, taking other kids along with him. Stick him in Appalachia and he'd start a crystal meth lab. Stick him on Wall Street and he'd engage in insider trading. That's why he freaked Ruthie out: Famous was pure evil.

Still, as Uncle Bernie so pertly pointed out, this wasn't a quilting bee. And I wasn't here to ask him for advice on sashing and backing.

"Hey, what's up?" Ruthie asked Twan as he approached on the sidewalk.

"Who's he?" Twan replied, appraising me with the appropriate level of suspicion that a teenaged city kid gives a well-dressed (albeit *still* in yesterday's clothes) thirty-something-year-old white man.

"This is my boss. He's the one who needs to approve that story about you guys," Ruthie said. He could have thrown a wink in my direction, but he didn't need to. I got it.

"Oh, mos' def, mos' def," Twan said, breaking into a wide smile. I translated that to mean "most definitely."

But I wasn't going to make this all go so easily. I figured that since I had been put in the position of being The Man, I might as well play the part.

"Well, let's not get ahead of ourselves, Geoffrey," I said. "We have policies and procedures that we must follow with the strictest adherence. As you know, all candidates for an *Eagle-Examiner* Good Neighbors profile must be carefully vetted to ensure they are of the highest character and moral fiber. The committee absolutely insists on it."

There was no committee, of course. Just like there were no policies or procedures. But since I could tell Twan was only catching about half of the polysyllabic words I was using, I wasn't too worried about being called on it. I only wished I had brought a clipboard along. A white man looks that much more convincing with a clipboard.

Ruthie picked up my pile of baloney and helped me make a sandwich out of it.

"That's true," he said. "I forgot about the committee."

"There cannot be even a suggestion of turpitude."

"Right."

"I mean, remember what happened with the McNulty boy — *very* unfortunate."

Twan was watching this go back and forth and finally cut in. "Whoa, whoa. We tol' you about red dot. You ain't flagin us now?"

400

I had no idea what "flagin" was — I guess the lack of understanding of each other's vocabulary went both ways — but it sounded like something bad.

"There's no flagin of any sort going on here. Nor will any flagin be tolerated in the future," I assured him. "However, there are some minimum requirements that must be met. If we are to write about a rap group, it can't just be some boys playing around. We only write about serious musicians with legitimate futures. Tell me about this rap group of yours."

Twan launched into a long and animated description of their group — which they called Hevvy Soulz, because I guess spelling doesn't count in the hip-hop world — and how someone's cousin had gotten them some recording time in someone else's cousin's basement studio and how they had to lay it down across one of the standard prerecorded tracks, and even though it was one they never heard before, they somehow made it work.

Or at least that was my translation. I'm sure I missed some of the nuance and much of the subtlety. The only person who probably didn't miss a word — of anything — was Famous, who was watching over Twan, Ruthie, and me, never uncrossing his arms.

"And you've got a demo CD? The committee will insist on hearing a demo," I said, when Twan was done. I knew, from my previous encounters with a variety of aspiring rappers, they *all* had demo CDs, of which they were very proud and which they would supply to you whether you wanted them to or not. The backseat of my Malibu probably had three demo CDs in it, and that was just from the last two months. I had never listened to any of them, but somehow I was always reluctant to toss them until they had been there for a full season.

Twan ran to a knapsack and grabbed an unmarked CD in a clear jewel case, then handed it to me. I considered it as if my mind were a laser capable of reading the digital material recorded on it and making an instant determination as to its musical quality.

"Excellent," I said. "This will help the committee greatly. Now there's just one more thing."

"Oh, yeah," Ruthie said, as if he knew what I was about to say.

"What?" Twan said.

"All Good Neighbors candidates must demonstrate their moral fiber," I said. "But I think I have an idea as to how you can do that to the committee's satisfaction."

Twan furtively glanced back at Famous, who registered no reaction that I could see, then returned his attention to me. "Yeah?"

"Well, as I understand it, you told Geoffrey about a group of policemen who are selling guns in this neighborhood?"

"Yeah. So?"

"A Good Neighbor is the kind of person who wouldn't tolerate such behavior from a member of the law enforcement community," I said. "To help us bring these rapscallions to justice, we need to observe you making a buy."

Twan again checked in with the stoop. Famous remained impassive.

"How we gonna do that?" Twan asked.

"How does it usually work when you make a buy from them?"

"We just see them, you know, around and stuff. They doin' they thing, we doin' our thing. And then we just cool out."

"I see," I said, because that had made things so clear for me. "But what if you need a gun immediately?"

"Well, they got this number you call."

"What kind of number?"

"I don't know. You let it ring one or two times then you hang up. You don't leave no message or nothing."

"And then?"

"Someone calls you back."

"Who?"

"It don't matter."

"What do you mean it doesn't matter?"

"I'm sayin', whether you talk to one man or the other, it don't matter. They all the same."

"How many guys do they have?" I asked, because I was still trying to figure out how extensive this network was. Did it just operate out of the Fourth Precinct? Did it have tendrils reaching out to other parts of the department?

"Don't know."

"But a lot of different guys might end up calling you back?"

"Yeah."

"Okay, then what?"

"Well, you tell them where you doing your thing" — I didn't need to ask what "thing" that was — "and then they come rolling up on you. If it was, you know, real police, we'd be gone before they even stop they car. But we know it's them, so we do the, you know, the hands on the hood thing."

"Whoa, whoa," I said. "They sell you a gun right out of their patrol car?"

Twan's eyes darted quickly toward the

still-statuesque Famous, whose inaction allowed Twan to continue.

"Naw, man, they do it *in* the car."

"You actually get in the back of the car?"

"Yeah, man. Folks walking along see another nigga being shoved in the back of a car by the po-po, they ain't looking twice. You feel me? So that's where it go down."

I immediately began thinking of the photographic possibilities of that: a kid in the back of a Newark Police car, buying a gun from a cop in a uniform. Brodie might need to be hospitalized for priapism if we got a photo like that.

I pulled my phone out of my pocket for a time check. It read 4:21. The sun wouldn't set until seven or so. If I asked them to set up a buy for six, that would give me enough time to get a photographer — maybe two — in place and hidden where the cops couldn't see them, while still having enough natural light for the shooters to get decent art.

"Okay, then let's set up a buy," I said.

Twan was apparently primed to go — with Famous's tacit permission — because he pulled out his own phone and was going to dial a number before I stopped him.

"Slow down, slow down," I said. "Let's talk about this for a second. I need a little time to set this up right so we can get pictures. We'll want to hide some photographers somewhere around here, maybe even get video of this — it'd be great for the Web."

As soon as I had said the word "pictures," Famous uncrossed his arms and let them dangle at his sides. He might have even given his head a quarter shake. For him, this qualified as an outburst. And Twan heard it as clearly as if Famous had started screaming.

"What you mean, pictures?" Twan asked. "We ain't doing no pictures."

"Why not? What's the difference?"

"We just . . . we, you know, we ain't playin' with that."

Twan must have looked up in the direction of the stoop three times during his last sentence. Without Famous to tell him exactly why the pictures were objectionable, Twan was like an electric toy car whose remote control was busted: zooming around on the floor, crashing into random furniture, unsure of where to go.

Finally, Famous stood up — in a slow, unrushed manner that made it clear he wasn't going to hurry on my account. His arms remained at his side as he deliberately descended down three steps. Once on the sidewalk, he put his hands in his pockets and walked toward me but never looked at me. His head kept swiveling left and right, his wide-set eyes seemingly taking in everything except that which was directly in front of him.

He kept getting closer — much closer than he needed to be — and still never acknowledged me. It was unnerving, but I suppose that was the point. It was a game. Did he intimidate me? Yeah, a little. Was I going to show it? Not a chance. To evince fear was to lose all respect. And I had been hanging around this world long enough to know that in the hood, respect was everything.

He finally stopped when his face was perhaps twenty inches away. He was half a head taller than me, so this put my eyes roughly at the level of his scraggly chin. His gaze was fixed on some point well behind me.

"What's your deal, dawg?" he asked. His voice was raspy, almost like his vocal cords had been damaged in some way. Or like he smoked a lot of something without a filter.

I smiled. It was time to drop the Mr. White Committee Man act. Something told me it had never really worked on Famous anyway.

"Hell, Famous, I'm like you: just another

hustler trying to make my way in this world," I said. "My hustle just happens to be the newspaper."

He nodded his head without moving it — I'm not quite sure how he did it, but I'd have to learn how someday. He still wasn't looking at me.

"We do the buy, you pay for the gun?" he asked.

"Yeah."

"And we keep it?"

"I sure as hell don't want it."

This seemed to satisfy him. The pleasure was written all over his face — his cheeks actually raised one-tenth of a nanometer, which for him was like a full-blown grin.

"What you need these pictures for?" he asked

"I'm not making a collage for my scrapbook here, pal. They'd go in the newspaper. Probably big and flashy. Give your rap group a lot of publicity, that's for sure."

"And then what?"

"What do you mean?"

"Would I have to testify?"

"I don't have any control over that," I said. "I do the newspaper part. The testifying part would be up to a prosecutor, assuming there were charges brought and it went to trial."

"I ain't testifying," he said.

"You want to get rid of those red dot guys, this might be your only chance."

He stood perfectly still. After ten, maybe fifteen seconds, one of his jaw muscles flexed.

"You can do your story without the pictures, though," he said.

He had me there. "Yeah, that's probably true. As long as we see the buy go down. It's just better with the artwork."

"Not my problem," he said, pulling away. The movement was so abrupt, and it came after such an extended period of stillness that I nearly flinched.

He stopped in front of Twan and rasped, "We do the buy in an hour. Do it somewhere else, not here. And no pictures. We see any cameras, we off."

With Doc in tow, Famous glided off, all those angles and dark skin disappearing around the corner with him. He never did look me in the eye.

Now that the boss had spoken, it was left to Twan, Ruthie, and me to work out the details. The first thing we had to decide was a location. I couldn't fathom why Famous didn't want it going down on his home turf, but I guess he had his reasons.

I knew it needed to be in the neighborhood — the cops would get suspicious if we asked them to do it downtown, outside the front doors of the *Eagle-Examiner* building — but Twan wasn't offering any suggestions. The only thing I could think was that I wanted to be in a place where I could see but not be seen. Suddenly, my mind flashed up an image of the bodega in Uncle Bernie's building, the place with the one-way glass.

It was within sight of the Fourth Precinct, so the cops would be comfortable doing it there. If I had Twan and his buddies make the buy on the corner in front of the bodega, it offered a perfect vantage point to watch the buy from up-close, far closer than we'd be able to get hiding in a tree or crouching in a parked car. And if we wanted to celebrate afterward by getting a good deal on Calphalon cookware, all we had to do was go around the corner. It would be perfect.

Twan made the call to the magic number, got the return call almost immediately, and then set the details. I was going to be funding the purchase of a brand-new .22 caliber Beretta for the low, low bargain price of five hundred dollars. The buy was set for five thirty.

Ruthie and I made a quick run to a local check-cashing place, where I wrote out a check for $508.75 that allowed me to receive $500 in cash. What a deal. Then we returned to the corner boys. Famous and Doc were still gone, but a couple of new guys had replaced them.

I handed Twan the cash, then talked over the plan one more time. We swapped cell phone numbers and agreed that I would call him when we were in place. If he answered the phone by saying his name, he was in a spot where he could talk. If he answered without saying his name, I was supposed to say I had the wrong number. Either way, the call meant he knew he was free to go ahead and make the buy.

We also agreed that, afterward, we would rendezvous back at their corner, so we could inspect the gun.

"So that went great," I said, as we returned to Ruthie's car. "It's a shame about the no cameras thing. But it's possible the pictures wouldn't have shown anything anyway."

"Yeah, and we could at least take cell phone photos, right? As long as they didn't see us doing it."

"Oh, yeah, good thought." The kids and their technology. Low resolution cell phone photos through darkened windows wouldn't do us much good in the paper — I can't imagine they'd reproduce as anything more

411

than indistinguishable ink smudges — but at least we'd have some hard evidence of the malfeasance taking place in our fair city.

"So," Ruthie said, gripping the steering wheel a little tighter, "we're going to tell Tina about this now, right?"

"What are you, nuts? Why would we want to do that?"

"Well, I mean, she is the manag—"

"Ruthie, you want to be doing Good Neighbors the rest of your life? This story could be a real game-changer for you."

"I know, but what if —"

"Stop, stop, stop. Think about it. If you call Tina and tell her everything that's going on, she might just say good luck and God-speed. Orrrr . . ."

I drew out the pause a little bit, then picked up: "She also might tell us to pull back, or, worse, she might call the lawyers — who can always invent ten reasons why you should stick to covering ladies auxiliary garden club meetings. Point is, I'd rather give her the chance to tell me everything I did wrong after the fact than give her the chance to micromanage it ahead of time. It's best she not even know we're together. Trust me, the less the editors know at this stage, the better."

"Oh, o-okay," he said. He regripped the

412

steering wheel and swallowed.

"What?"

"I sort of . . . I sort of told her I was coming to pick you up."

"Ruthie!" I said sharply. "I thought you learned your lesson from the toilet water testing incident."

"I did, but . . . well, she's been texting me every ten minutes asking me where I am . . . and she's . . . I mean, she's the managing editor for local news. I can't just *not* text her back!"

"You sure can. As a matter of fact, I think this is a great time to practice."

"But I —"

"End of discussion," I said, grabbing the check-cashing receipt from where I had wedged it in his cup holder and stuffing it in my pocket. It was probably as close to documentation as I would get for this little caper. I needed to be able to expense this somehow, and I didn't think the cops were in the business of giving itemized receipts.

But the more I thought about it, they sure seemed to have the rest of the business thing down. Cops selling arrest-proof guns to thugs. From a purely economic standpoint, it was genius. Who knew the clientele — the thug marketplace, as it were — better than the cops? They had an entire police department's worth of intelligence on their potential customers. And from a certain point of view, they didn't even need it: they had been doing market research from the moment they arrived on the force.

They obviously had a good handle on the supply. I didn't know how they were getting their new guns — I would guess it was either from gun shows, which were pitifully unregulated, or from out-of-state straw buyers — but they had plentiful access to used guns. They could simply take them off other thugs or dip into the nearly endless supply of confiscated guns anytime they got low. They could even drive up demand for their product by making busts on the competitors. It was all pretty slick — until Kipps came along and somehow threatened to ruin it.

And have no doubt about it, it was a substantial threat. To say nothing of the variety of state and federal laws they were breaking by selling unlicensed guns, the officers would, at the very least, be guilty of official misconduct. And in New Jersey, that came with a mandatory minimum of a decade-long jail sentence. No former cop wants to spend ten seconds behind bars, much less ten years.

Then they killed Kipps, which meant they

could add first-degree murder charges onto that bill. If caught, they'd be spending the rest of their lives as a guest of the state. It all made the stakes high enough to justify any intervention — killing another cop, like Fusco, or killing the meddlesome newspaper reporter who kept trying to expose their crime.

Until they were all locked up — every last one of them — I was little more than a safe pick in the office Ghoul Pool.

Ruthie parked around the corner and two blocks down from the bodega, in a spot where none of our new friends would be able to see his car. We walked back up the hill, and I had a brief moment of panic as we approached the store and couldn't see any lights — had it closed at five o'clock? some of them did — but that was just because of the tinted glass. A YES, WE'RE OPEN sign stuck in the front door eased my fears, as did the sign next to it that established the hours as 6:00 A.M. to 7:00 P.M.

The bodega was called "All Brothers Market III," which might have suggested it was owned by several brothers, who also owned at least two other establishments. But Newark bodegas changed hands more often than they changed canned goods. It was entirely possibly it had gone through two or three ownership swaps, with each new owner deciding not to confuse his loyal customers by ditching the All Brothers name.

I entered to the tinkling of the little bells tied to the door. The Sikh, the same one who had been there last time, was still manning the cash register. He was probably the owner and only employee, which meant he spent thirteen hours a day, seven days a week, sitting in that lonely little bulletproof box. The bells might have been there to wake him up when a customer entered.

I went over and tapped on the plastic.

"Hi, sir, I'm sorry to bother you," I said. "We're reporters with the *Eagle-Examiner.* Do you mind if we set up in your windows for a little while so we can watch for something on the street? It's for a story we're working on. We'll be out of your hair quickly enough."

I cringed at the "hair" part because for all I knew he didn't have any under the turban. But he just shrugged at me. Maybe it was because he didn't understand why the funny guy in the tie and his tagalong friend wanted to hang out in his store. Or maybe he was just a shrugging kind of guy.

Nevertheless, I felt sufficiently empowered

to act like I had the run of the place. I surveyed the windows. One faced north, the other west. Each had a display in front of it, which meant we'd have to do a little shimmying to get access to the windows. Old magazines were the primary obstacle to the west. Chips and fried pork rinds blocked the way to the north. But beyond those impediments, the windowsills were broad enough that we would be able to stand there without disturbing any more than some dust bunnies. If we crouched, we would be out of the gaze of any curious casual shoppers who entered the store. We'd be functionally invisible.

I went outside to test the one-way glass, looking at it from a variety of different angles. It was good. I couldn't see anything beyond my own reflection.

Returning inside, Ruthie and I reviewed our battle plan. He would take the north window, while I manned the west one, which would give us a fairly full panorama of the street, including all four corners of the intersection. We would each snap a few pictures whenever the action got close, but mostly we were there to observe. We would stay low, hidden in our little sanctuaries. And we would keep our mouths shut —

because the glass was see-proof, not sound-proof.

It was 5:14. Sixteen minutes to go. I made the call.

"Yeah, it's Twan," he said.

"Hey, you guys all set to go?"

"We good. You cool?"

"Yeah. We're in the windows, but you won't be able to see us. I'm behind an impressive collection of skin magazines, and I think Ruthie is well hidden by some Andy Capp fries. We're good as gold."

"A'ight."

I ended the call, told Ruthie we were locked and loaded, then got settled into my little sanctuary, with dark glass to my left and seriously cheap particleboard — the backside of the magazine rack — to my right.

This was not the first stakeout of my career, but there was always a thrill to watching bad people do things they weren't supposed to be doing. What kept it exciting is that, for as much as you might think you knew what was going to happen, the details could surprise you every time.

And, yeah, maybe it made me feel a little bit like a badass special agent, and maybe I liked that feeling. Especially when I knew, unlike those guys, I wouldn't have to spend three straight days in a van, peeing in an empty Gatorade bottle.

We didn't have to wait long. At 5:28 VWMT (Verizon Wireless Mean Time), Famous, Doc, and Twan made their appearance, arriving on foot from the west side, Ruthie's window. Twan and Doc continued walking around to my side, whereupon they leaned against the window where I was set up. Twan rested one foot against the glass. Since I was now seated, the underside of his sneaker was practically at eye level.

I heard the bells clanging to signal that someone had entered the store. Then I saw Famous peering over me. Twan had obviously told him where he could find me, and he was checking to see that I was in place and didn't have any photographic equipment in tow. I looked up at him and nodded, but he said nothing — he wasn't exactly the kind of guy who was going to stop and inquire how my mother was doing. I heard the sound of his footsteps go over to the other window, where I assume he performed a similar inspection on Ruthie.

Famous went over to the Sikh in the box and said, "Get me some blackies."

"Blackies" were Black & Milds, a brand of cigar popular enough in the hood that their white plastic filters were a familiar sight wherever fine urban litter could be found. After making his purchase, Famous went back out on the street, the bells chiming as he departed. He unwrapped his cigars, casually tossing the cellophane wrapper on the street, then extracted one and lit it. After taking one puff, he peeled off to the right, in the direction of Ruthie's window. I didn't know if Ruthie could still see him, but he was out of my line of sight. All I had to look at was the tread of Twan's sneaker.

Then, no more than ninety seconds after Famous sparked his lighter, a Newark squad car came through the intersection and rolled to a stop in front of the fire hydrant on the corner outside the bodega. I felt a rush of nerves and excitement and, mostly, curiosity: Who were these guys, anyhow?

I expected the cops to leap out and toss Twan and Doc on the hood — to put on a good show, like Twan said they liked to do. But two cops exited their car in no particular hurry.

They were African American, medium height, fairly undistinguished in appearance. One had a mustache. The one without the mustache was darker skinned. I tried to press the image of their faces in my brain in case I needed to identify them from head shots. They were not yet close enough that I could see their name badges.

They moseyed over to Twan and began idly chatting, keeping their distance. It was like they were at a large family reunion, greeting some distant cousins. They weren't *too* excited to see them, but they also didn't mind stopping to gab for a while.

I was absorbed in trying to pick up any small piece of their conversation, concentrating so intensely on a futile attempt to read their lips that I only barely noticed when the bells on the front door of the bodega clanged again. Then I was jolted by the sound of a commanding, somewhat-familiar voice on the other side of the magazine rack, pointed down in my direction.

"Excuse me, sir, you're loitering," it said.

I looked up to see six-feet-eight-inches' worth of Officer Hightower looming above me with a menacing sneer, pointing his gun at my face.

The call came in like all the others did. One, two rings — long enough to get it on the phone as a missed call — then a hang up.

The associates at Red Dot Enterprises, who were all sworn police officers working out of Newark's Fourth Precinct, took turns manning the cell phone, almost like it was a pager in a medical practice. It wasn't terribly onerous: there were ten associates altogether, so someone was always working anyway. Plus, there weren't too many calls. Their business was based more on chance encounters than prearranged ones. The thug set wasn't much for scheduling.

So when the second call came in from the same number, the officer testily called it back, starting the conversation with, "What's up, Twan? I'm kind of busy here."

"This ain't Twan," replied a hoarse voice. "It's Famous."

"Yeah, fine, what's up," the cop huffed. He

knew Famous, or whatever he was calling himself now. His real name was Raynard Jenkins. He fancied himself a real tough guy, with his stone-cold stares and crossed arms. He was like hundreds of other corner boys, with a juvenile record far longer than anyone with that short a life should have. He was unlike most of the corner boys in that he had managed not to get arrested during his first eighteen months as an adult. He was smart that way. He was also smart enough to turn situations like this one — a couple of his boys striking up a relationship with a couple of overly trusting newspaper reporters — to his own advantage.

"Y'all got some people who don't like you much," Famous said.

"We probably got a lot of people who don't like us," the cop replied, annoyed. "What's your point?"

"What if I served up two of them for you?"

"Depends who you're talking about."

"Some newspaper reporters. Couple of crackers."

Famous had come up with this plan while he had been listening to his boys arrange this deal and was pleased with himself for it. It was the perfect double-cross. Especially since it would allow him to get payment out of both sides.

Little did Famous know just how pleased the cop would be to hear it, that as soon as he said those words — "newspaper reporters" — he had the officer's attention. All the associates at Red Dot Enterprises knew full well about Carter Ross and the problem he presented.

"How are you going to serve them up?"

" 'Cause I know where they're gonna be."

"And where's that?"

"Depends," Famous rasped. "What's it worth to you?"

"It's worth me not sticking a PR-24 up your ass the next time I see you out on that corner, Raynard, that's what it's worth to me."

"I ain't playin' like that, Officer," Famous said. "Have a nice day."

"Wait, wait," the cop said. "Talk to me. What do you want? You want a gun? I got some nines and some twenty-twos. Just came in. Brand-new."

"Nah, man, I don't want that kid stuff. I want me a Dirty Harry gun, a big ol' forty-pounder. Something with some punch to it."

"Fine, we can do that. It won't be new, but I can get something out of the locker for you."

"Yeah. And the next time me or one of my boys gets jammed up, we friends, right?"

"Yeah, nothing too big, but I think we can handle that."

424

They made the arrangements, agreeing that when the cops saw Famous walk out of the store and light a cigar, it meant the deal was on.

And just like that, Carter Ross had been sold out. For a used gun and a get-out-of-jail-free card.

CHAPTER 9

What had felt like a sanctuary — my little perch, wedged between solid objects and out of sight — was now my personal mousetrap. I was too hunched down to even think about vaulting over the magazine rack or trying to run. And I suppose that menacing hunk of black composite in Officer Hightower's right hand made it all something of a moot point anyway.

With his nongun hand, he grasped the upper right corner of the magazine rack and swept it haphazardly out of the way until it ended up leaning at a forty-five degree angle against the bread display. He walked into what had been my box and grabbed a fistful of shirt and tie. His hand was roughly the size of an octopus, and he used it to pull me to my feet with a quick, effortless yank.

"Lace your fingers behind your head, sir. You are under arrest," he snarled.

I turned to look at the Sikh in the box, to

begin protesting the injustice that was about to transpire in his store. But the Sikh wasn't visible. Bulletproof glass or no, he had probably ducked down the moment he saw that gun come out. He was a shrugger, after all. He didn't want to be involved.

Hightower dragged me, stumbling, into the aisle, trained the gun at me, and repeated, "Fingers behind your head, sir, nice and slow."

Since I didn't have much choice, I complied with the order. "Two steps forward," he ordered, and I did it.

Just as Hightower went to walk behind me, I saw his nameplate for the first time: LeRioux.

Officer LeRioux. Maybe in Louisiana that wouldn't be a terribly unusual last name. But up here, there was only one other LeRioux I could think of having met.

"LeRioux," I said. "I feel like I've seen that name on a few billboards around here."

"Yeah, I heard you met my dad," Hightower said and began handcuffing me roughly, slamming metal against bone with vicious delight.

His dad. Of course. They were both unusually tall, and now that I knew about the connection, I could see they bore some resemblance. It had just been hard to see because one was a uniformed cop and the other was a pastor in two-thousand-dollar suits.

But it made sense. Pastor Al had started his noisy, blustery call for an independent investigation, then had suddenly backed off — probably right around the time his son came crawling around, explaining to dear old dad that maybe some stones were better left unturned.

From there, the elder LeRioux had been acting more like a father protecting his guilty son and less like a pastor aiding his grief-stricken parishioner. That was the real reason he had instructed Mimi Kipps to avoid me. He knew she would just help me stir the pot, and he didn't want that. Even when he showed up at her house moments before the BMF wannabes came cruising by, that was likely because Hightower — having used LoJack to tip off BMF as to my whereabouts — had told Dad that perhaps it was best to remove Mimi from the scene of the crime.

By the time I had all that figured out, Hightower had finished fastening the cuffs behind my back. I looked across the store and saw Ruthie was getting the same treatment, only his arresting officer was another familiar figure — Baldy Jones.

"You get that report written on my car yet, Officer Bryson Jones?" I called out. "What about that gun with the red dot on it? You put it in the evidence locker yet, or did you just sell that to some thug on your way back to the station?"

Hightower thumped the butt of his palm into the back of my head hard enough I thought my skull was going to separate from my spinal column. "Shut up!" he yelled.

"Oh my goodness, what have we here," Baldy called out, holding up a freezer-size Ziploc bag filled with a white substance. "It looks like this gentleman had a big ol' bag of heroin. I bet he's going to go away for a long time, selling this much heroin."

"That's not —" Ruthie started, but I couldn't hear the rest of it because Hightower was yelling in my ear.

"Not as long as this guy," he bellowed. "Look at all the rock I found on him."

Without bothering to look, I could guess that Hightower had magically found crack cocaine on me. Because, yeah, I always like to carry a few hundred grams on me. Gets me through the day when I need a little pick-me-up.

"Crack and heroin. Looks like these punks had a major distribution network set up," Baldy shot back. "Good thing we got them off the streets."

Baldy shoved Ruthie out the door. Hightower and I soon followed. I was slowly overcoming the shock of having my perfect hiding spot discovered and was reaching the obvious conclusion: the corner boys had flipped on us. I had even paid them five hundred dollars to do it. And that was on top of whatever they were getting out of the cops.

As if to confirm this fact, I heard the grating, raspy sound of Famous laughing at me as I was herded out on the sidewalk.

"See you later, Mr. Newspaper Hustler," he said, the Black & Mild dangling from the side of his mouth. "Have fun with the five-o."

Blocking him out, I did a scan of the sidewalk and nearby area, hoping to see a bystander gawking at me. A grandma. A workingman. A schoolkid. There had to be someone normal passing by at this time of the day, someone who might just listen when I screamed that I was a newspaper reporter being wrongly imprisoned by corrupt cops; someone who would act when I hollered for them to call Tina Thompson, the state police, the attorney general, or some combination of the three.

But there was no one in sight. The Fourth

Precinct building was maybe forty yards away. And having been shoved off the sidewalk and onto the street, I could see that was where I was being led.

It was around this time I felt a real panic setting in. I was stuck in this netherworld where the cops and the crooks were indistinguishable. And there wasn't anyone who was going to save me from them. The pit of my stomach was dropping quickly out of my body. I was, not to put too fine a point on it, screwed.

Up until that moment, I had been walking on my own across the street, albeit prodded by Hightower, who had a bruise-inducing grip on my right arm. No more. It was time to put up at least a token effort at resistance, if only so someone coming along realized the funny-looking white guy was being taken against his will.

I yanked my right arm, planted my right heel in the asphalt, and tried to make a break for it, pushing off as forcefully as I could. I didn't know how far I could make it, running with handcuffs on, but I at least had to try.

It turns out the answer was: not very far. My bucking and squirming did exactly no good. Hightower, with his octopus hand, never relinquished his grip. One of the other

officers, the one with the mustache, antici-
pated my move, which he had probably seen
a hundred times before, and took the opportunity to knee me in the groin.

He didn't get me square in the kiddy-
maker, but he got close enough that I felt a
momentary lurch of nausea and doubled
over. The mustachioed officer grabbed my
left arm, and with Hightower still on my
right, they dragged me up the front steps of
the precinct — just like the cab driver, John
Smith, on that long-ago hot summer night.

I could still hear Famous's raspy laughter
as the doors closed behind me.

Inside the precinct, the first thing I saw was
the desk sergeant, a different one from the
other day. I didn't know if he was involved
with the red dot scheme or not, but I was
growing desperate. If nothing else, I didn't
want to go quietly.

"I'm a reporter with the *Eagle-Examiner,*"
I said in a high, panicked voice. "These officers are involved in a major gun-selling
operation that I'm about to expose and now
they've taken me —"

"Would you shut up, you freakin' hop-
head?" Hightower outshouted me while giving me another thunk on the head, this time
on the side. "You want us to add slander to

432

all those CDS charges against you?"

The desk sergeant didn't even look up. I guess he was accustomed to loud, crazy, half-coherent people being dragged past him, shouting their various conspiracy theories and claiming police brutality. I might not have even been the first one that shift. All he did was nonchalantly buzz us in.

I inhaled and was about to start shouting again — this time with a little more diaphragm behind it — but Hightower seemed to anticipate it. In a low, deadly serious voice he said, "If you don't shut the hell up, I will crack your skull like an eggshell and scramble whatever I find inside. Yeah, I'll end up on administrative leave for a month. But you'll end up eating through a tube for the rest of your life. You get me?"

For emphasis, he took his nightstick and placed it about four inches from my forehead. I quickly took stock of my situation and realized that in my current state — I was the handcuffed hostage of a gang of killer cops — a concussion wouldn't do anything to help matters. So I took this as an opportunity to keep my thoughts to myself and retreat into a period of personal reflection.

Ruthie, who was still on his feet, wasn't

trying anything daring either. And so, together, we were shunted down a hallway, then through some heavy double doors into what appeared to be a holding cell area. The fourth cop, the one who was neither dragging me nor shoving Ruthie, opened up one of the cells and in we went.

"Face the wall," Hightower ordered, and we did. Didn't seem like much point in resisting now.

I felt hands going for my pockets and was soon relieved of their contents: cell phone, keys, wallet, notepad, pen. Then the hands ran roughly up and down my legs, arms, and chest.

"Aren't you at least gonna kiss me before you cop a feel, Officer?" I asked.

Hightower answered with another palm to the base of the skull that, to me, sounded like all the low keys on the piano had been hit at once. I thought that was going to be the worst of it, then out of the corner of my eye I saw him remove his nightstick from his belt, wind up, and take a swing at the back of my right leg.

The next thing I knew I was on the floor, my leg having momentarily lost the will to hold me up. For the first few seconds, I wasn't feeling any pain — just disorientation — and then a piercing ache rushed up from my knee.

"Fffaaa!" I shouted. I'm not sure what language "fffaaa" is, but I'm sure it's an expression of pain in some primal proto-language.

Hightower kneeled one leg on top of my chest, then rested his baton on my nose, grinding it into the cartilage for good measure.

"You keep your mouth shut, princess," he said. "You got that? You keep it shut or this is going to get a whole lot worse."

"Hey, get off him!" Ruthie shouted.

"You want it next?" Baldy Jones said. I heard something impact Ruthie's midsection and most of the air rush out of him.

I whipped my head to the side, to get Hightower's stick out of my face. He roughly brought himself back to standing, using my sternum as a trampoline. Hightower wasn't the thickest guy, but he had to weigh two forty, easily. I felt like I was lying in the middle of the street on road-paving day.

As he walked away from me, he gave my right knee a sideswipe with his boot. It wasn't a full-on toe kick and didn't have too much momentum behind it, but it still sent another shock wave up my leg. I twisted into a fetal position, if only to get my throbbing knee some protection.

At that moment, rolled up in a ball on the floor, I decided it was time to stop being brave. And cute. What little satisfaction it was bringing me just wasn't worth the agony. I heard Ruthie moaning and saw he was doubled over, leaning against a bench for support. I suspected he was reaching the same conclusion.

"Ordinarily, I'd remove the cuffs right now," Hightower said. "But not for a couple of dangerous drug dealers like you."

Then, as abruptly as they had arrived in our lives, the four officers left.

I took a moment's worth of stock in our situation. We were alone and trapped in a windowless dungeon. No one knew where we were, and we had no way of communicating our whereabouts or predicament. Our captors were police officers who could presumably use their perverse version of the law to keep us here for quite some time, assuming they didn't kill us first. And my leg felt like it had glass shards inside it.

In short, we were in a bad way.

"You okay?" Ruthie said, panting and still leaning against the bench.

"No," I replied, because honesty is the best policy.

I was about to ask him how he was doing,

but before I could, he staggered over to the small metal toilet in the corner of the cell and vomited. Twice. That seemed to answer the question.

He spit a few times, then eventually straightened partway up and lurched over to the bench. He sat down with his head between his knees. I was still in my baby ball, but at least the throbbing in my knee wasn't getting any worse for the moment. It helped that no one was hitting it anymore.

"So what happens now?" he asked, spitting again.

"I don't know. Probably nothing good."

"You got any brilliant ideas for getting us out of here?"

"Nothing that comes to mind."

"I guess asking for a phone call the next time they come back is out of the question?"

"I wouldn't recommend it," I said.

"What are they going to do to us?"

I didn't answer him. I didn't want to. We eased into something like a respite, neither of us saying anything, each of us nursing our hurts.

How long we stayed like that, I couldn't accurately say.

At least an hour passed. Or maybe more like two or three. I was a little disoriented from the beating, and it's not like we could look outside and see the sun setting. Our only illumination came from the dim fluorescent lights in the hallway outside the cell.

I wasn't going to tell Ruthie this, but I had no doubt our captors intended to kill us. We knew too much, and they knew we knew it. Famous would have told them. And besides, they had already been trying to get rid of me before I got tangled up with the corner boys. I was a double-marked man.

The only reason they hadn't gotten around to it yet was that they hadn't worked out the best way to do it. They seemed to be big fans of the staged suicide — maybe they'd make us hang ourselves by our shoestrings in the cell? — or perhaps they would get more creative, realizing folks would start getting suspicious about all those supposedly morose people at the Fourth Precinct.

Maybe we were going to meet some kind of unfortunate "accident." Or perhaps they were going to put bullets in our heads and devise some ingenious way to get rid of our bodies so they'd never be found. Cops would probably have a pretty good idea how to do that. Would we be weighted down and tossed out somewhere off Sandy Hook? Buried in some defunct landfill? Stashed in an airtight barrel in someone's attic?

I tried to stop thinking about it. I pondered, instead, what was going on in the outside world. Had Tina Thompson put out an all-points bulletin for us? Probably not. If she even noticed we were both gone, she would have chalked it up to my usual wanderlust. I was not particularly good about keeping in touch. Plus, I had already filed a story for the day. If she didn't need me for copy, I wouldn't necessarily be foremost in her thoughts.

At some point, the adrenaline drained away, the shock dissipated, the exhaustion caught up to me, and I think I drifted off. Actually, I know I did, because I started having one of my classic anxiety dreams, one where it's ten minutes to deadline and I realize I've forgotten to do any reporting on a story I have to write.

It must not have been a very deep sleep, though, because I was stuck in the usual spot in the dream — the part where I'm trying to figure out *why* I haven't done any reporting — when I heard those big double doors opening. I jolted wide-awake and scrambled to my feet, my knee swollen but holding my weight. I wanted to be alert and prepared for whatever came at us, ready to exploit any small opening, for however unlikely it was there would be one.

My eyes were aimed somewhere high above the six-foot mark, expecting to see Hightower. Instead, it was Captain Boswell. An angel couldn't have looked any better than that short black woman with her shelf-like butt. Sure, she had probably been told I was in here for dealing crack cocaine, but she had to know that was a sham.

"Captain Boswell, oh thank God," I said. "I know this is going to sound like crazy talk, but —"

"Shh . . . keep it down," she said. "I'm not supposed to be here."

"What do you —"

"Shh!" she hissed more fiercely. "Listen to me and listen carefully, because there's not much time. LeRioux and Jones are coming back. They're going to move you to an interrogation room, and they're probably going to kill you."

"So, wait, you know about the red dot guns?"

"Yes," she said quickly.

"So . . . I'm sorry, you're the captain here. Why don't you just blow it out of the water? Report it to the higher-ups downtown? Throw LeRioux and Jones in —"

"It's not that simple," she said, her face pressed close to the bars so she could keep her volume down and still be heard. "I have a son."

"I don't understand," I said.

"I've only been here six months, remember? This had been going on for years under the nose of my predecessor. I don't know if he was blind or stupid, but I don't think he ever knew about it. I'm pretty sure no one downtown knows about it, either. These red dot guys have been very careful. I only learned about it myself recently, but I was sort of clumsy in how I went about things in the early stages. They figured out that I was onto them and they . . . they . . ."

She turned away for a moment, and I could see only half of her face as she scrunched it in an effort to stay composed. "They threatened to hurt my son," she said when she turned back. "Not just hurt him. Mutilate him."

"I still don't understand. You could have him put in protective custody, and —"

"And what?" she demanded with quiet ferocity. "Wait for three years until the thing goes to trial and just hope that no one protecting him slips up between now and then? No way. Look, I've always loved being a cop, and I hate what these guys are doing to the department's reputation. Ever since I heard about this thing I've been trying to figure out how to defuse it and keep it quiet. But at the end of the day, this is just my job, okay? My son is my life. I've got three years left until I've put in my twenty, and then we can move to Oklahoma or Kansas or someplace where I can raise him in one piece, and Newark and everything that happened here can become a distant memory."

"Okay, okay, I get it," I said. "Look, I appreciate your situation, but that doesn't have any bearing on us. Why don't you just march us out of here and we'll —"

"I can't," she interrupted.

"Why the hell not?"

"Because I still don't know who's involved and who isn't," she said. "I know several of them must have killed Mike Fusco. I never believed that phone call he made to me, even if I had to go along with it for that stupid press conference. I know several of them killed Darius Kipps, too. But I don't know who. And I don't know how many of them there are. If one of them sees me taking you out of here, it's all over."

"So where does that leave us?" I asked.

"Like I said, they're moving you to the interrogation room," she said. "I overheard some talk that made it sound like they're going to stage a scene that makes it look like you smuggled weapons in here. They're going to kill you and call it self-defense."

"Oh, lovely."

"Okay, so I'm trying to help you. Turn around and stick your arms through the bars so I can do something about those handcuffs," she ordered. Ruthie and I complied. As Captain Boswell started going to work with a key, she said, "I'm not taking these off. I'm just unlocking them. LeRioux and Jones have to think they're still on, okay?"

"Got it."

"There's a door at the end of the corridor near the interrogation rooms," she continued. "It's an emergency exit. LeRioux and Jones aren't going to be worried about it because it's always locked. But I've disabled the lock. When you get to the interrogation room, either LeRioux or Jones is going to have to take out his keys and open the door. The lock is always fussy and takes a second to jimmy open. That's your chance. You make a break for it and run like hell for that emergency door."

"And then what?"

"Keep running," she said, having finished unlocking both sets of handcuffs.

"And what if they catch us?" I asked as she turned to leave.

Her last instruction going back through

the double doors was unequivocal: "Make sure they don't."

Ruthie and I began discussing the merits of this new plan and quickly agreed it was the worst we had ever heard. We also agreed the only thing it was better than was nothing at all, which had been our plan before.

"When we get out the door, I'll run left, you run right," I said. "Hopefully, they'll only catch one of us."

Ruthie nodded. Any further discussion was squelched when the double doors swung open and Officers LeRioux and Jones — Hightower and Baldy — came stalking through them.

"Hey, guys," I started, "why don't we —"

"How many times I got to tell you to shut the hell up?" Hightower growled. "You say one more word I'm busting up that other knee. And this time I'll go for the front of the knee, not the back."

Baldy Jones slid open the door to the cells. Ruthie and I stood there, frozen, uncertain, a couple of scrawny newspaper reporters well out of their weight class.

"All right, come on out, ladies," Hightower said. "We're going to take a little walk up to the interrogation room, ask you a few questions about all that dope we took off you. Let's go, let's go."

At least he didn't noticed that our cuffs were unlocked. Ruthie eased out of the cell first, and I limped out after him. As we walked toward the interrogation room, I kept telling myself there was no way they would get away with this. No one would believe that Ruthie and I had smuggled weapons into a police station or would know how to use them even if we had. What were they going to do, put metal shivs in our dead hands and claim we tried to stab them? Give themselves superficial wounds to make it look more convincing? It was absurd.

But to a certain extent, it didn't matter. Sure, there would be an investigation into our deaths — the paper would put up a hell of a stink — but as long as the cops stuck to their stories, what would there be to contradict them? Ruthie and I would go down in history as a bizarre cautionary tale: a pair of dope-dealing newspaper reporters who got killed by the cops.

"Keep walking," Baldy said, as we passed through the double door and were led upstairs and down a hallway. We took a left turn down another hallway. I could see the emergency exit at the end of it. My heart started pounding and, strangely, I felt the

445

urge to urinate. I guess there's something to the old saying, after all, about being nervous enough to pee your pants.

I limped a few more steps down the hallway until Hightower said, "Stop here."

We had reached the interrogation room. I casually positioned myself so that neither cop was between me and the emergency exit and saw Ruthie do the same. The exit was perhaps thirty feet away, a distance I could cover in, what, a few seconds? Would that be fast enough?

Baldy Jones started going for his keys. Hightower was resting his hand on his gun, an ominous development. Was that just a reflex for him, or was he expecting trouble? Was the gun strapped in or was it loose? Could he draw it during those two seconds I was running down the hall?

Ruthie and I agreed that the moment the key touched the door, we would both make a break for it. I bent my legs to prepare for our mad dash down the hallway and glanced over at Ruthie, who returned my gaze with eyes that had doubled in size.

Then the lights went out.

This being an interior hallway — in a building where the windows had been bricked over decades ago — we were plunged into immediate and total darkness.

There was not a shred of ambient light. Not even the pinprick of a single LED. It was like being in a mineshaft.

Hightower swore and Baldy uttered a panicked, "What the . . . ?"

I heard the creaking of leather, like a gun being removed from a holster, and I dropped to the floor. If Hightower started firing in the dark, I wanted to be as small a target as possible. I began desperately crawling in the direction of the emergency exit — how long would it take to get there on my hands and knees? — when I heard a lot of shouting and slamming coming from the front of the building. No, maybe it was the back. Or maybe it was just all over. It was hard to tell.

I had traveled perhaps eight feet when I bumped into the far wall, which I used as a guide to keep going. Then the emergency door light kicked on, casting an orange-yellow hue on the hallway. I could see over my shoulder that Baldy Jones had grabbed Ruthie. The shouting and slamming was getting closer.

Hightower had been groping in the dark for me, never realizing I had gone low. But even with the dimness of the emergency lights, he couldn't miss me crawling along the floor. And sure enough, from the way his body turned, I could tell he had locked onto me. As he swept his gun in a smooth arc in my direction, I tried to get my legs back underneath me to scramble away — at least it would give him a more difficult shot — though I was having trouble getting my bad leg to respond with the necessary urgency.

Then a flash blinded me and smoke filled my lungs. The world went yellow and gray and burnt-smelling. I closed my eyes and my mouth and tried to stop inhaling, too. But I had been breathing too hard. I couldn't help but take gulps of air, even though I knew it was bad.

I was immediately consumed by what had to be the worst allergy attack in human history. Some combination of tears, sweat, and snot began pouring out of every opening on my face. Then, as if there wasn't enough moisture in the mix, the building's sprinkler system went off. I kept gasping for air that just wasn't there. All the oxygen had left the planet, replaced by poison gas and spraying water.

It was pure misery, but even in all the confusion, I knew it was still preferable to being shot. At some point, my brain finally grasped the idea that someone had tossed tear gas, a flash-bang grenade, or something similarly loud, bright, and smoky into the hallway. I didn't know whether this was a mission of mercy or just a different kind of offensive from a yet-unknown enemy, but I was struggling too hard to survive to make that much sense out of it.

I kept trying to get my eyes to unscrew, but every time I did there was just more stinging and, besides, even when I could force them to open more than a slit, I couldn't see much. Between the tears and the sprinkler, it was like being underwater.

I felt someone — no, make that *two* some-ones — grab me by the armpits and the crotch. Out of instinct, I thrashed against it, but the action was fairly futile. The pepper spray or mustard gas or whatever the hell it was had taken the fight out of me. As I allowed myself to be carried along, I could only hope that one, it wasn't Hightower and Baldy Jones doing the dragging, and two, the officers had been just as incapacitated by the smoke as I was.

Soon I was outside the building, not that I was sure how it happened. Through my watery eyes I could finally see that I had been seized by a pair of guys in gas masks that made them look like some kind of bug-eyed aliens. They carried me in the direc-tion of two more bug-eyed guys, who each grabbed a side of my upper half and then dragged me to a spot of empty sidewalk, where they laid me facedown.

I was beyond resistance at this point — that gas packed an indescribable punch — and I actually relaxed as I felt my hands and legs being fastened by strips of plastic. After a lifetime of never once being hand-cuffed, it had now happened to me twice in one day. Suddenly I knew what it was like to be a character in *Fifty Shades of Grey*.

Then I was left alone. I tilted my head to the right and finally began to gain focus on the surreal scene unfolding around me. There were several handfuls of other people — some of them cops, others dressed as civilians — arrayed on the street and side-walk around me, also facedown. I spied Ruthie, lying a few bodies away from me. Otherwise, none of them looked especially familiar.

Beyond all the prone figures was a small army of men in gas masks and dark com-mando gear. Their job was to accept victims from the smoky building. The commandos seemed to be intent on getting everyone out. They would leave the sorting of who was who — and who was on what team — to some later time.

I was starting to feel like I had been saved

but still couldn't figure out who my savior had been, how they knew where I was, or what had tipped them off to the idea that there was someone in need of saving.

Then, in the distance, I saw a man in a dark blue windbreaker with ATF in yellow letters. Then another. Then a guy with an ATF hat. Okay, so they were employees of the Bureau of Alcohol, Tobacco, Firearms and Explosives. I could imagine they were folks who wouldn't take kindly to a group of cops selling guns to thugs. That might just be their kind of case.

Did they already know about red dot? Had they been keeping an eye on the precinct and then moved in when they realized something was amiss about Ruthie and me being dragged into the building?

At that point, I couldn't guess how it had all come down. I just knew I was safe.

I was so happy I didn't mind when, seconds later, another wave of nausea slammed me and I vomited all over the sidewalk.

The next two hours or so were something of a muddle. I spent the first part of it lying contentedly on the sidewalk, enjoying the Newark night air, which had never tasted so sweet and clean. The action and commotion continued around me, but it now felt more like a pleasant distraction.

Slowly, the number of people being led from the gassy building diminished. There were perhaps thirty of us by the time it was done, all suffering a variety of unpleasant symptoms from whatever version of bug spray they had used.

After a while, I was unbound and led into a large tent that had been hastily erected as a kind of mobile command center. I was asked for identification but, of course, didn't have any — my wallet was still stewing in the stink somewhere inside the Fourth Precinct. But when I told them I was Carter Ross, *Eagle-Examiner* investigative reporter, they seemed to accept it without question, almost like they knew they were going to find me inside somewhere.

There was just as much chaos inside the tent as outside. At one point, I overheard a guy in a suit telling a woman in a windbreaker that Captain Boswell had started spouting names and details just as soon as she had been able to get her nose to stop running. I didn't know whether she'd get sanctioned for her inaction — the failure to report a crime has rather dire consequences for those in law enforcement — but if she was able to substantiate the threats made against her son, I was hoping the ATF would cut her a break. I doubted she'd be allowed to continue as precinct captain, but maybe she'd find a soft landing somewhere else until she got her twenty in.

As for the other cops, there would be no mercy. And it was only time until one of them — or, perhaps, all of them — started informing on one another. Cops will talk endlessly about the blue wall and brotherhood and solidarity and all that lovely stuff. But when lawful push came to legal shove, I'm sure they knew when they were defeated. They were going to do whatever they could to save their own hides. It was only a question of who would take the hardest fall. I was hoping for Hightower, the brutal bastard. I was also hoping his old man might be in on it, just for good measure.

I thought I'd have to wait my turn to be interviewed or interrogated, and given the number of people they had fished out of the building — and how low a priority I would be — I figured it might be a while.

Instead, the guy in the suit eventually came around, looked perplexed to see me there, then asked for, of all things, my phone number. After I gave it to him, he told me I'd be contacted in a few days and my cooperation would be greatly appreciated. In the meantime, I was free to go home.

Actually, that's not quite accurate. It's more like they were kicking me out. When I tried to ask a few questions — the journalistic instinct dies hard — I got a friendly smile and a hardy no comment. Then I got an escort to the perimeter that had been set up for the operation.

As I approached the barricade, I understood why: on the other side, there was a hungry horde of content providers the size of which you'd be unlikely to see anywhere except for perhaps Super Bowl media day. When I passed through the checkpoint, a good portion of them mobbed me.

Unfortunately for them, the *Eagle-Examiner* has rules about its reporters giving interviews (basically, we're not allowed unless we have permission). So I held my tongue. From their questions, they seemed to think the raid had something to do with terrorism, because they have been trained to think *every* unexplained occurrence in the New York/New Jersey area has to do with terrorism. Eventually, when they realized they were only going to get two words out of me — "no" and "comment" — they left me alone. The gauntlet around me dissipated and waited for other fresh meat to emerge from the scene.

The only one who remained was Buster Hays. I never thought I would admit this, but I was actually happy to see the man.

"Blotches. Red dots. I think I understand why it matters now," he said, allowing a knowing grin.

"I guess I shouldn't be surprised, but how did you figure it out already? Everyone else around here seems to think Osama bin Laden got reincarnated and was cooped up in there."

"You see a guy in a suit in there? Seemed to be running the show?"

"Yeah."

"Let's just say he owed me a favor or two," Buster said, the grin growing a little wider. "Hey, before I forget, that girl from the library has called me four times since I've been out here. She wants to know if you're okay."

I smiled. I could get used to Kira worrying about me. For whatever happened between Tina and me — that would need to be sorted out — Kira and I seemed to have some kind of future.

"Oh," he continued. "And Tina Thompson told me as soon as I laid eyeballs on you, I was supposed to tell you to give her a call."

"Yeah, I might have to borrow your phone,

mine is still in there," I said, gesturing toward the battered-but-still-standing Fourth Precinct.

"Sure," he said. "But it's going to cost you a Good Neighbors."

I drew breath to start my protest, then he grinned and handed me his phone.

Tina, naturally, wanted me to file a story immediately. In the coming days and weeks, there would be a lot more of the same. The thrilling first-person narrative. The hard-hitting follows. The put-all-the-pieces-together takeout. Ruthie and I were kept busy.

So was the justice system. It eventually came out that poor Darius Kipps, working late that Saturday night, had seen Hightower unloading guns from his trunk after a trip down south to purchase a load from a prearranged straw buyer. Kipps immediately confronted Hightower about what he had seen. Hightower had tried to bribe him, threaten him, whatever he could do to ensure Kipps's silence. But Kipps, ever the good cop, wouldn't back down. He called Internal Affairs and left a message that night. By the next night, he was dead.

In the end, there were charges filed against eight officers, all of whom had been active participants in the conspiracy, all of whom would wind up with multiple life sentences — and only because there is no death penalty in New Jersey. We tried taking another run at Pastor Al, but with his church still behind him in what he characterized as a smear campaign by the Great Satan newspaper, he found a way to survive the scandal. Guys like him always do. Darius Kipps and Mike Fusco were buried with full honors. Mimi had to put back together the pieces of her life, although at least she'd be doing it with the aid of widow's benefits and a life insurance policy.

All that was to come. But at that point, standing outside the Fourth Precinct, I needed to figure out how to get back to the newsroom — and then, eventually, to my empty home and lonely cat — without the aid of my car, which was still in the custody of Mickey the mechanic. I was starting to look around for someone to give me a ride when, of all people, Gene and Uncle Bernie shuffled up to me.

"I told you they were bad men, but did you listen? Noooo, of course not," Bernie said, doing a dismissive shooing wave. "You had to be Clint Eastwood, huh? You're lucky Gene had that Best Buy receipt to do. Otherwise, we might have gone home and you'd be kaput."

"That's Yiddish for —" Gene started

"Yeah, yeah, I don't need the translation this time. Thanks, Gene," I said. "So, wait, *you guys* are the one who called this in?"

"I was doing the receipt," Gene said. "Bernie was watching the camera and —"

"Tut, tut, tut, he doesn't need all the details," Bernie interrupted. "Geez, Gene, someone asks you for directions and you pave a damn road for them."

"But," I stammered, "but how do you guys know ATF agents?"

"How many times do I have to tell you, kid: in this business, you gotta know *everyone,*" Bernie said.

"I don't know what to . . . I mean, thank you."

I reached my hand out and clapped Bernie's shoulder. "You're lucky you had the Ginsburg boy with you," he said. "If it's just you, a goy? Well, maybe I call, maybe I don't. But nobody messes with a member of the tribe on my watch."

"We would have called anyway," Gene assured me.

"Anyhow, enough of that," Bernie said, then fixed me with a look of genuine concern. "You chilly? You look chilly, scuffling around without a coat on. You'll catch the death of you from cold. Lucky for you, I got coats. I got in a London Fog the other day — just your size, too. Forty-two long, am I right? What do you say? London Fog makes a good coat, you know, and Uncle Bernie gives you only the best. The best, I tell you."

ACKNOWLEDGMENTS

I am forever mystified by authors who whine. They whine about how hard it is to write a book, about how hard it is to sell a book, about their publishers, their publicists, their critics, their manicurists, their dog trainers, and everyone else who apparently thwarts them in this world.

Not me. I have a great life. The best. I get to write books for a living and I love it unabashedly. (Maybe it helps that I don't have a dog and don't get manicures.)

But I am constantly aware that I wouldn't have that life were it not for the support of many hard-working people.

That starts with my terrific editor, Kelley Ragland; her undaunted assistant, Elizabeth Lacks; and everyone else at St. Martin's Press/Minotaur Books, including — but not limited to — Hector DeJean, Jeanne-Marie Hudson, Kymberlee Giacoppe, Matt Baldacci, and Talia Sherer. Thanks also to Andy

461

Martin, Matthew Shear, and Sally Richardson. I'm proud to be one of your authors and am deeply grateful for all your efforts on my behalf.

I'm also fortunate to have the kind and thoughtful counsel of Dan Conaway of Writers House, who is a big part of the reason I don't have anything to whine about.

And I can't tell you how happy I am to have the energy and passion of my publicist/secret weapon, Becky Kraemer, back with me after a brief hiatus. I missed you, Becky. Don't have any more kids, okay?

Thanks are also due:

To all the library scientists who keep pushing my books, including Bess Haile of the Essex Public Library and her friends-group president, Hannah Overton (I will always be your Knight in Shining Armor).

To bookstore owners like Marilyn Thiele of Moonstone Mystery Books, who succeeds in this difficult modern bookselling environment the old-fashioned way: by offering first-rate customer service and great books.

To Tony Cicatiello, James Lum, Jorge Motoshige, Leslie Jennings, and all people who offer aid and comfort to me while I'm on tour.

To Lucinda Surber and Stan Ulrich, Toby

and Bill Gottfried, Janet Rudolph and everyone else at Left Coast Crime who went along with this crazy idea to make me their 2014 Toastmaster.

To Lindsy Gardner, for all her help. (I'm going to stop there, mostly to keep her patrons guessing.)

To Miss Teresa, Miss Denise, Keshia, Zabrina, and everyone else at my local Hardees who make my favorite writing haunt — yes, I really write at a Hardees — feel like a second home.

To Kieran O'Brien Kern, who first suggested that an absinthe-sucking librarian could make a great character; to Janie, Allan, Zach, and Lexi Links, who know all about the inspiration for Uncle Bernie; and to all the other readers out there. Like I said, I have the best job in the world, but I am mindful that I'll get fired if I can't keep you entertained. So it's my fervent hope you enjoy reading this stuff as much as I do writing it.

And, most important, to my family. I mentioned my parents, Marilyn and Bob, in the dedication, and I would say that means they've gotten enough ink for one book, except I know I can never thank them enough for all their sacrifices. I'm also grateful to my brother, Greg, who will be my first phone call if I ever get arrested; my in-laws, Joan and Allan Blakely, without whom so much would not be possible; and to my son and daughter, who brighten my daily existence with their joy and wonder.

Last, I need to thank the one person who, more than anyone else, enables this dream life of mine. I love you, Melissa. I know there are times when we feel like we can't keep up. But the fact is, as long as we have each other, we'll always be well ahead.

ABOUT THE AUTHOR

Brad Parks is the first author to win both the Shamus Award and the Nero Award for Best American Mystery for his debut novel, *Faces of the Gone.* A former reporter for *The Washington Post* and *The [Newark] Star-Ledger,* he lives in Virginia, and this is his fourth novel.

The employees of Thorndike Press hope you have enjoyed this Large Print book. All our Thorndike, Wheeler, and Kennebec Large Print titles are designed for easy reading, and all our books are made to last. Other Thorndike Press Large Print books are available at your library, through selected bookstores, or directly from us.

For information about titles, please call:
  (800) 223-1244

or visit our Web site at:
  http://gale.cengage.com/thorndike

To share your comments, please write:
  Publisher
  Thorndike Press
  10 Water St., Suite 310
  Waterville, ME 04901